NO LONGER PROPERTY OF
SEATTLE PUBLIC LIBRARY
JUN 3 2017

# THE

# CALEDONIAN

# GAMBIT

D0964264

JUN 3 2017

# THE CALEDONIAN GAMBIT

A NOVEL

## DAN MOREN

TALOS

Copyright © 2017 by Dan Moren

All rights reserved. No part of this book may be reproduced in any manner without the express written consent of the publisher, except in the case of brief excerpts in critical reviews or articles. All inquiries should be addressed to Talos Press, 307 West 36th Street, 11th Floor, New York, NY 10018.

Talos Press books may be purchased in bulk at special discounts for sales promotion, corporate gifts, fund-raising, or educational purposes. Special editions can also be created to specifications. For details, contact the Special Sales Department, Talos Press, 307 West 36th Street, 11th Floor, New York, NY 10018 or info@skyhorsepublishing.com.

Talos® and Talos Press® are registered trademarks of Skyhorse Publishing, Inc.®, a Delaware corporation.

Visit our website at www.talospress.com.

10 9 8 7 6 5 4 3 2 1

Library of Congress Cataloging-in-Publication Data is available on file.

Cover illustration by Sebastien Hue
Cover design by Rain Saukas

Print ISBN: 978-1-940456-84-3
Ebook ISBN 978-1-940456-85-0

Printed in the United States of America

To my mom and dad, who never took a book away from me.

# PROLOGUE

Elijah Brody was being attacked by butterflies.

To be fair, they were only targeting his stomach, but they were angry and fluttering around in a malevolent way that he wouldn't previously have associated with butterflies.

His digestion gurgled, and he patted at his midsection through the thick synthetic fibers of his flight suit. Pre-mission jitters. Perfectly normal. *How would you know?* he chided himself. *You've never been on a real one before.*

"*Venture* is in system." The calm, collected tones of the ISC *Venture's* flight controller filtered through his headset. "Green Squadron, you are clear to launch." There was a slight pause and when the woman continued, Eli could tell she was smiling. "Good hunting."

Eli triggered the explosive bolts connecting his fighter to the *Venture*. A sound like muted firecrackers reverberated through the hull, and the fighter began to drift slowly out of the bay.

*Eight . . . nine . . . ten.* Safely clear of the *Venture*, Eli punched the ignition.

The whole ship shook as the engine roared to life. He grinned, and the breath that escaped his lungs felt like it had been stored up for hours—days, even. The engagement seemed a foregone conclusion: in his mind, he was already back aboard the *Venture*, the mission accomplished and Green Squadron toasting each other with their ration of the victory champagne.

All around him, Eli saw the flares from his squadronmates' engines. Green dots representing their fighters sprinkled across his heads-up display. He found the blip marked as Green Six and increased throttle to form up on Larabie's wing, then toggled to his wingman channel.

"All right, Chris?"

"Yeah. You want to see something incredible, Brody? Take a look at your six."

Eli raised an eyebrow. Flipping his main display to the rear camera feed, he saw the immense bulk of the *Venture* stretch away behind him. But as it drifted slightly to port, the gate came into view and he gave a low whistle.

"Damn," said Larabie quietly. "I never get tired of that view."

Hanging in space like a giant baleful eye, the hexagonal metal structure stretched a mile across. In its gaping maw spun a blue whirlpool, almost hypnotic in its undulations: the wormhole from which the *Venture* had recently emerged.

"Hell of a thing," said Larabie, a tinge of awe still in his voice. "You know they're self-sustaining, right? We did a case study on them back when I was in engineering school."

"Huh. I didn't think they *had* inter-system spaceflight that long ago."

"Hilarious. Just let me know when *you* come up with an idea half as brilliant as using the wormhole's own gravimetric energy as a power source."

"That actually works?" Eli wished he could rub his temples through his helmet. "Sounds like a goddamn Moebius strip."

Larabie snorted. "Don't overtax your poor brain, Brody. Good news is it works in our favor—there's so much juice in those suckers that once they switch them on, they're pretty much impossible to turn off again."

"Good," said Eli, "because I slammed a door on my finger once and it's not an experience I'd like to have reproduced on a galactic scale."

"Green Squadron, this is *Venture* control." The transmission crackled with static. "Be advised we have inbound bogeys. LRS read two squadrons coming in fast—profile suggests heavy bombers and interceptors." Red blips appeared on Eli's HUD as the *Venture*'s long-range sensors fed in locations for the enemy ships.

"That was fast," muttered someone over the squadron-wide comm channel.

"Two full squadrons sure doesn't seem like the usual welcoming committee." Maggie O'Hara was Green Three and the squadron's intel expert. "And they shouldn't have been able to ID us until we were in system."

"They've got their own intel sources," Larabie pointed out.

"Let's just hope they aren't better than ours," quipped Green Five, Jun Kwok.

"Green Squadron, shape it up," said Captain Lila Randall, the squadron leader. "Tag your targets and prepare to engage. We need to secure the gate area before the rest of the fleet comes through the wormhole. Six, Seven, you're on point."

"Roger that," said Larabie. "Setting an intercept course."

"Copy," said Eli, turning the ship's nose toward the foremost red blips on his display. The whine of the engines pitched up, inertia pushing him back against his seat. He toggled back to his wingman channel.

"These guys do seem awfully prepared."

"Yeah," said Larabie, "but all the preparation in the world isn't going to give these poor bastards enough of a leg up when the rest of the fleet comes through the gate." He paused, and Eli could picture his wingman shaking his shaggy head. "They're outnumbered and outgunned, and if they *have* ID'd us, then they know it. I'm not sure why they haven't just surrendered."

*Because nobody likes to just roll over and die.*

"The entire Fifth Fleet for one relatively isolated world." Eli increased the magnification of his HUD until he could see the globe of mottled blue, green, and white. "Seems like overkill to me."

"The Imperium's making a point, kid. Sabaea was in talks to join the Commonwealth, and the Illyrican Empire's not about to let that slide."

*No, they're sure as hell not.* Eli shifted uncomfortably, feeling the seat squeak underneath him. His homeworld, Caledonia, had been a free planet before the Imperium had invaded. "Is that really the only option?"

"They don't exactly need our approv—"

A warning tone blared, and the ship's computer overrode Eli's magnification to show that one of the inbound enemy fighters, now highlighted in a red box, was trying to acquire a missile lock.

"Intercept!" he yelled. He wrestled with the flight stick, trying to slip the lock while lining up his own shot.

The reticle on his display flickered green and Eli squeezed the trigger, sending magnetically-propelled slugs peppering out of the fighter's nose-mounted tubes. The tracer rounds phosphoresced yellow-green against the black of space, but his own inertia sent them arcing to port. He twitched the stick back to starboard, finger still on the trigger.

The enemy fighter was close enough now that it was visible with the naked eye, juking left and right in an attempt to avoid fire and keep its lock. Two of Eli's rounds clipped its engines; fuel leaked into space, floating in droplets. A second burst hit the engines, and Eli saw one of the tracer rounds pierce the fuel tank.

That was all it took. The ship fireballed, the explosion spectacularly silent against the dark backdrop.

"Lead, this is Six," said Larabie. "Chalk up a kill for Seven."

"Virgin no more," whooped Kwok. "That means the beer's on you, right?"

Eli winced, the afterimage of the explosion still dazzling his vision. First kill. He should be proud, not feel like he'd just done a belly-flop from thirty thousand feet. *This is what you trained for, Brody.*

"Simmer down," said Captain Randall. "Good work, Seven, but there's plenty more to go around. Green Squadron, you are free to engage."

The squadron broke as it closed with the enemy ships, and suddenly the whole area was a mess of dots on Eli's display. In a blur, he found himself going head-to-head with a second fighter; he swung around, trying to get on its tail. But the other pilot was good: they cut their throttle to let Eli overshoot them, and his guns caught only empty space. Yanking on the stick, Eli flipped his ship over, putting the other ship effectively upside down—but still square in his sights. *Gotcha.*

"Lead, Six." Larabie's measured tones broke Eli's concentration. He swore as his shot went wide of the mark.

"This is Lead," said Captain Randall over the comms. "Go, Six."

"Something odd: Those capital ships in Sabaea's defensive screen aren't engaging."

"They're just holding them in reserve," Rafi Kantor, the squad's second in command, broke in. "No point exposing them to fire until there's something bigger than fighters for them to target."

"Maybe," said Larabie. "But there's something . . . I don't know. Not right."

"Getting paranoid, Six?" needled Kwok.

"Knock it off, Kwok," said O'Hara.

Randall's voice cut through the chatter. "Six, keep an eye on the cap ships, but they're not high priority. We'll worry about them after we take care of the fighters. Speaking of which."

The enemy squadron had regrouped and was coming around for a second pass. Eli brought his fighter up on Larabie's port wing and tagged his target on the shared display. One by one, the red blips turned gray as the rest of the squadron did the same.

"Here we go," said Randall. "Break on my mark."

Anticipating Randall's order, Eli's hand gripped the throttle.

"All ships, this is *Venture* control." Panic colored the normally even-keeled tones of the flight controller. "Something's happening at the gate. Repeat, there appears to be activity at the gat—"

A bright white flash blinded Eli, and the transmission from the *Venture* dissolved into a screeching mess. The high-pitched noise dug into Eli's sinuses and he scrambled to dial down the volume on his headset. Bits of incoherent babble from the rest of the squadron punched through the interference.

". . . god . . ."

"The gate . . ."

". . . squadron . . . beam . . . channel . . ."

". . . on your six . . ."

A giant hand suddenly picked up Eli's ship and shook it like a child's toy, sending it careening end-over-end. Alarms of three or four different flavors blared in his ears, and Eli had to squeeze his eyes tightly shut as the dizzying streaks of stars through his canopy threatened to evict the butterflies and everything else in his stomach. *Don't throw up in your helmet, don't throw up in your helmet* . . . His teeth rattled so hard he thought he might have swallowed a couple. Fighting against the pressure that wanted to keep him pinned against his seat, he reached out with a jittery hand and cut the throttle.

Then it was over and his ship began to drift, propelled only by its own momentum. He let one eye slide open, then the other.

The heads-up display flickered and wavered in front of him; he banged his hand against his helmet but only succeeded in making his head ache further. With a growl, he set the computer to reboot, which also took the cameras and thruster control offline. He craned his neck to try and peer out the canopy, but flightsuits weren't exactly built for mobility. *We missed something. Did a bomber get through to the* Venture?

The computer whirred back online. Eli stomped on the attitude thruster controls and yanked hard on the stick, pointing the ship's nose back toward the *Venture*. It left his back exposed to any oncoming fighters, but the flagship was a higher priority right now. *Whatever hit it must have been big . . .*

*Holy shit.*

The *Venture* was still there, but the rear half of the ship was drifting *away* from the front half, as though the same hand that had flung Eli's fighter had simply snapped the mile-long carrier in half like a dead branch. Plumes of gas vented into space and sparks of electricity played about jagged edges.

But that wasn't what took Eli's breath away.

The gate was gone.

"Seven, this is Six on tightbeam. You copy?" Larabie's voice, loud and clear, cut through the static.

Eli switched his comms over. "What the hell happened?"

"They blew the gate, Eli. They blew the *fucking* gate." The usually unflappable Larabie sounded throaty with shock. "They must have rigged it to go after we came through. I—I—that's *insane*."

Eli swallowed, a lump rising in his own throat as he watched the faint sparkle of gate debris spiraling away like a miniature galaxy.

"The wormhole just collapsed," said Larabie, still in disbelief. "The gravity differential, it—I saw it tear the *Venture* in *half*. I've never seen anything . . ." His voice caught. "Oh, god. The fleet."

The rest of the fleet had been waiting in the wormhole for the *Venture's* all-clear. Standard operating procedure.

Larabie was almost inaudible, though Eli couldn't tell whether it was the transmission or the man himself. "They're trapped in the wormhole. All of them."

All those people—friends, classmates, thousands Eli had never even met. Trapped. In the wormhole.

Eli swallowed again. "They can just go back, right? Back to the Badr sector, where they went in?"

"No, they can't. You can't keep just one end of a wormhole stable. It's like a rubber band: let go and it snaps."

"What if . . . what if we rebuild the gate?"

There was a short, bitter laugh from Larabie. "It'd take years. Best-case scenario, they've been spat out halfway across the galaxy. Worst . . ." He trailed off. "Either way, they're gone, Eli."

A sudden squawk came over the comm channels, and an unfamiliar voice rang in Eli's ears.

"Illyrican ships, this is Admiral Vogel of the Sabaean Planetary Defense Forces. You are outnumbered and outgunned. Kill your engines, power down your weapons, and we'll accept your surrender."

*Outnumbered and outgunned.* Eli choked back a hysterical laugh. *That was* our *line.*

"Repeat, this is Admiral Vogel of the Sabaean Planetary—"

"Fuck *you*," cut in Kwok's voice.

Eli watched in horror as the pilot matched actions to words, throttling to maximum and careening at the enemy fighters, guns blazing away. Her screams echoed down the comm channel.

"You motherfucking murde—"

A missile streaked out from under one of the enemy bombers, hitting Kwok's ship head on. Eli's heart leapt into his throat as the fighter became a ball of expanding, briefly burning fragments.

"No!" He wasn't sure who yelled—it could have been him, for all he knew—but it was the last thing he heard before the hiss of broad-spectrum jamming descended.

Green Squadron scattered, picking up the nearest enemy ships. Eli threw his own throttle wide open and rocketed toward a group of fighters.

He saw the same bomber launch another missile in his direction, but he spun toward the fragments of Kwok's ship, putting the cloud of remains between himself and the projectile. The missile veered off, detonating harmlessly in the debris field.

Coming around at the enemy squadron, he loosed two of his own missiles, sending them directly into the heart of the formation.

One shot through the gaps between the fighters; the other hit dead on, turning one ship into a hail of shrapnel that shredded through two of the others. Eli punched through what was left of the formation, guns clearing the way by eliminating yet another fighter. Before fully comprehending what he was doing, he found himself barreling toward the capital ships that still hung in the distance like an oncoming storm.

*Let's see how you like it when the fight's brought to you, you smug bastards.*

Eli glanced at the weapon status on his heads-up; the missile-ready indicator burned a steady green. From this far away, the big cruisers would have plenty of time to shoot down anything he fired; his only chance was to get as close as possible before launching. He pointed his nose at the nearest capital ship.

The bigger ships clearly hadn't expected to engage with fighters this soon—even just one of them. That surprise gave Eli the precious few seconds he needed to close the gap.

An electronic warning shriek ripped at his eardrums as the cruiser let loose a barrage in his direction, trying to get a bead on his ship. Smoothly rolling his fighter to starboard, Eli arced away from the fire, then wove back toward the cruiser. Just another few seconds and he'd be inside the perimeter of its defensive fire. His thumb hovered above the missile launch button.

Abruptly, the communications jamming disappeared.

"Illyrican fighter, this is the Sabaean cruiser *Dogs of War*. Cut your engines *now* or we will fire for effect."

That first salvo hadn't been a near miss; it had been a warning shot. In Eli's stomach, the butterflies returned with reinforcements, but he batted them away as he once again saw Kwok's ship disintegrating. His jaw clenched.

Their mistake. They should have taken him out when they had the chance—now he was too close. His targeting reticle was still locked on the cruiser's bridge as the enormous ship filled his canopy; he fancied he even caught sight of one or two crewmembers at viewports, pointing at him, mouths agape.

His finger lingered above the missile trigger. He could do it—he could decapitate the cruiser.

Steeling himself, he toggled his comm and took a deep breath. For all he knew, these could be his last words. Better make them good ones.

"You can all go to hell, you sons of—"

# CHAPTER ONE

The toilet gleamed. It sparkled. It shined. In fact, the man known as Kyle Rankin thought as he rocked back on his heels, he would go so far as to say that no other toilet in the known universe had *ever* been quite so clean as the one that sat before him now.

*You know, when my sixth-grade teacher told me to shape up or my future would be in the toilet, I'm not sure even* she *thought it'd be literally.*

But it definitely looked as good as the day it was installed. He supposed he could take pride in *that* if he ever ran into Ms. Fitzhugh.

He maneuvered himself up from the crouch, sucking a breath in through his teeth as his knees protested. Eight-hour cleaning shifts, it turned out, were murder on the joints. He felt like he had the knees of a seventy-two-year-old—which meant somewhere out there was a seventy-two-year-old with the knees of a twenty-seven-year-old. Some day he'd find that guy and have a few words.

The bathroom door creaked—he grimaced and reminded himself to lubricate the hinges—and a voice echoed off the tiles.

"Rankin? You in here?"

*Oh, good. Farrell. This day just keeps getting better. Maybe if I don't say anything he'll—*

"I can't tell you how happy I am never to have to do latrine duty again." A Cheshire-cat grin was plastered across the blond man's face as he leaned against the sink counter. His crisp, immaculately pressed uniform was code-perfect, except for the unfastened collar at the top, open just far enough to show a hint of chest.

Kyle jammed his mop into the auto-wringer and watched with satisfaction as it squeezed out every last drop of water. He probably shouldn't be picturing Farrell's head while doing that, but hey, it was a free planet.

"What do you want, Farrell? Or did you come here just to enjoy my misery?"

Farrell laughed, but it was a little too forced, like someone had once told him they liked his laugh and he'd spent the last ten years trying to achieve that perfect guffaw again. "No, my son, I'm not here for the company—we have business to conduct."

Kyle's jaw clenched. *The bloody gate.*

"The first ship is due through the gate in a few minutes. It wouldn't do for us to be lurking in the johnny when we should be getting ready to pay out. We need to be down in the Ops Center with everybody else."

Suddenly, cleaning the rest of the toilets didn't seem like such a bad idea. "You handle it," Kyle said, shaking his head. "You don't need me there."

"Oh, come now," said Farrell, waving a hand expansively, "we're *partners*. And aren't you the least bit curious?"

*Because curiosity never got anybody killed.* "Honestly? No. What's it matter to me? I'm not going anywhere long as there are toilets to be scrubbed."

"It's been five *years*, Rankin." Wide-eyed, Farrell shook his head. "Jesus. Five years of our lives stuck in this ice-hell. All because some idiots thought it was a good idea to blow up our wormhole gate."

Acid roiled in Kyle's stomach. "The planet *was* being invaded at the time," he pointed out.

Farrell snorted. "We could have taken the Illyricans even without destroying the gate."

"Well if *you'd* been up there, sure."

"Hey, not my fault I was still in the academy. I could have flown rings around any of those Illyrican flight jockeys."

*Or, more likely, you'd be an expanding pile of space dust right about now.* If the entire Illyrican fleet had made it through the gate, they would have outnumbered the paltry Sabaean Defense Forces about five to one.

"I tell you, I am not going to be sorry to see the ass end of this place," Farrell said, talking right over Kyle's thoughts. "I am *done* with the fucking tundra. I mean, on a *nice* day the winds are gusting up to 50 kilometers per hour. You have any idea what kind of nightmare it is to land a jump jet in that kind of shitstorm?"

Kyle's stomach did a sympathetic barrel roll. "I'd rather not think about it."

Farrell, though, was on a different sort of roll. "They ought to have put this goddamn place in mothballs a long time ago."

"Come on, you know the brass keeps Davidson Base around so they have somewhere to dump the people they're pissed at."

Farrell's smug expression faltered, but it wasn't enough to permanently dent his enthusiasm. "Maybe for Antony, but not me. The minute the gate is open, I'm out of here. They're going to need trained pilots by the boatload—the military, transport lines, private contractors; they'll be fighting it out over someone with *my* qualifications."

Kyle did his best to turn a snort into a cough, but Farrell was too wrapped up in his rich fantasy life to even notice.

"It's too bad you can't come with me," Farrell continued, laying a comradely arm around Kyle's shoulder. "We're a good team. Think of all the trouble we could get into out there." He waved a handy slowly in front of them at a vista only he could see. "Of course, I'd need a reason to bring you along." His face lit up suddenly. "You could be my butler! People still have those, right?"

"If I go to Ops with you, will you leave me out of your grandiose plans?"

"Absolutely," said Farrell, drawing an "x" across the place where science had not proven he had a heart. "First drink's on me."

"Great." Kyle leaned his mop against the stall door with only slightly less reticence than most soldiers leaving their sweethearts to go off to war.

Five minutes later, after wending their way through the base's labyrinth of mostly similar-looking corridors, Farrell pushed open the door to the Operations Center. A raucous cheer of his name greeted him, and he waved and smiled like he was on camera, acknowledging his adoring public with a slight bow.

No such reception met Kyle. Few would recognize him without a mop in his hand and, even then, most wouldn't be able to come up with his name without consulting the tag on his chest.

"Told you it was a party," said Farrell, slapping Kyle on the back. "Even Antony's still up." He nodded at a glass-walled cubicle overlooking the Ops Center's concentric rings.

Tall and spare, with close-cropped silver hair, Colonel Indira Antony cut an imposing figure, even in her everyday uniform. The colonel's eyes met Kyle's, and she tilted her head in a casual nod.

Kyle returned the nod, ignoring a searching glance from Farrell.

"You never did tell me how you managed to get so buddy-buddy with the Old Wolf," Farrell said, nudging him with an elbow.

Kyle's shrug was noncommittal. "Even a colonel's wastebasket doesn't empty itself."

Despite the late hour, the base's personnel were surprisingly cheery—even those who were nominally on the graveyard shift. Kyle suspected that the bottles of booze being freely passed around were to thank for that. Normally, anyone on duty would have been on their way to the brig before they could take a single sip. But given the celebratory mood, Antony seemed to be turning a blind eye to the proceedings. Kyle thought he even spotted a tumbler on the colonel's desk.

A drink appeared in his hand, courtesy of Farrell. The pilot grinned and clinked it with his own plastic cup. "To our return to the galaxy," he said. "To clear skies and new horizons. And," he added, under his breath, "last but not least: to getting the hell out of here."

*Some of us, anyway.* Kyle raised his glass. "Cheers."

The Sabaeans threw a decent party, at least. But it wasn't quite enough to make Kyle forget that they were the architects of their current predicament. Confronted by an overwhelming invasion force, they'd taken the one tack that their enemy hadn't expected—because it was absolutely, brain-bendingly, antifreeze-drinking crazy: the Sabaeans had blown up their own wormhole gate, and with it their only connection to the rest of the galaxy.

Still in transit through the wormhole, the majority of the Illyrican fleet—dozens of ships, thousands of people—had vanished in an instant. They'd been carved right out of the fabric of the universe, their last remaining echo a hollow pit in Kyle's stomach.

Raucous laughter echoed from one corner of the room. Farrell had found a refill and was now leaning on a nearby console, leering down at one of the recent arrivals—a communications lieutenant by the name of Polakov. In the two weeks she'd been here, Farrell had dedicated himself to getting into her uniform, but her expression suggested he'd have better luck going topside, building a snowman, and propositioning it instead.

Someone jostled Kyle, splashing his shirt with alcohol. He glanced over his shoulder, but the offending party was already gone. Sighing, he cast around for something to dry his shirt, but somebody had evidently forgotten to lay out any napkins. *Typical military efficiency.*

His gaze caught upon Antony, leaning over the balcony railing in front of her office. The colonel was staring at the large holographic display that floated overhead, showing the solar system. A large green circle—Sabaea—stood at the center. Not far off hung a smaller blue dot: the reconstructed gate. A few green blips around the planet sketched the Sabaean fleet, loosely arrayed in a defensive formation. The last time something had come through the gate, it had been an invasion fleet. The Sabaean Defense Forces weren't taking any chances. *Let's hope they have a different strategy this time.*

Antony's eyes caught Kyle's; smiling slightly, she tilted her head in his direction. Kyle looked around, but none of the other partygoers seemed inclined to risk conversation with a lowly maintenance tech, so up the stairs he went.

Still leaning on the railing, Antony glanced over at Kyle as he reached the top, then nodded to the holographic display. "So, who's your money on, Mr. Rankin?"

*Shit.* Kyle summoned the blandest expression he could manage. "Ma'am?"

The colonel fixed him with a knowing look. "Your little pool with Mr. Farrell? On who's going to be the first to come through the gate?"

Kyle suppressed a grimace. He'd kind of hoped they'd flown under the radar. "Odds favor a trade ship from the Bayern Corporation," he admitted. "Though a surprising number of people seem pretty convinced that an Illyrican ghost fleet is going to pop out and take their revenge." He tried to summon a laugh, but it lacked conviction.

Antony snorted. "Well, if they've figured out how to survive in a wormhole for five years, then maybe they deserve to win next time."

*But nobody survives in a wormhole,* Kyle thought. *Despite all those "wormhole survival training" drills they run.* It was like falling through the ice—and then having the ice freeze over you. Kyle shivered, the hair on the back of his neck standing on end.

"If there'd been any other way . . ." Antony murmured, glancing over at him.

It was Kyle's turn to snort. "Well, until some brainiac figures out a way to travel between star systems *without* using a wormhole gate, I'd say it's a pretty effective tactic." Figuring out how to prop open the naturally occurring wormholes that humanity had stumbled across had been hard enough; anything beyond that had so far proven elusive.

Antony shook her head. "Doesn't make it right."

*No, it doesn't. But it's done. Time to move on.*

They stood in silence for a moment, both watching the carousing below.

"So," said Kyle, scratching a temple. "I guess you'll want me to return the personnel's money, ma'am?"

"That won't be necessary. As long as it's all in good fun." She raised her eyebrows. "It *is* in good fun. Isn't it, Mr. Rankin?"

"Yes, ma'am."

"Good," said Antony. "I'd hate to have to confiscate Lieutenant Farrell's cut."

Kyle grinned, some of the tension finally ebbing away, and raised his own nearly empty glass. "You have a favorite, then, ma'am?"

"That depends on what kind of odds you're offering."

"Well," said Kyle, his face scrunching up in thought, "the Illyricans—the non-ghost ones, anyways—are on the board at 9 to 2, with the Commonwealth a little bit ahead at 4 to 1. Bayern is definitely the favorite, at 2 to 1—and nobody's really expecting the Hanif to come near the place."

"Thorough. I'm impressed. You considering a new line of work as a bookie?"

"Beats cleaning bathrooms."

Antony ran her thumb around the glass's rim. "About that," she said, looking up at Kyle. "This is going to change a lot of things." She nodded at the screen again.

"Why?" said Kyle. "Are we finally getting that new auto-mop I've had my eye on?"

"Not exactly what I meant. Just that, with your situation being what it is—"

"Colonel!" came a voice from the floor, as if on cue. Polakov, the communications officer, was looking up at them, one hand on her headset.

"Yes, lieutenant?"

"Message from gate control, ma'am. Something's coming through."

The entire room trickled into silence as their eyes swiveled to the display overhead, staring at the blue dot of the gate. Kyle's breath caught; beside him he could hear the colonel's doing the very same. It wasn't hard to imagine the entire population of Sabaea holding their breath at this very moment, staring at the same image with equal feelings of hope and fear.

A yellow dot blinked into existence next to the blue one.

There were a couple of scattered cheers, but the crowd quickly went quiet again, the bigger question still unanswered.

"Incoming transmission from the ship, wide spectrum," said Polakov.

"On speakers, lieutenant."

A filtered voice blared through the room, caught mid-sentence. "—to the Sabaean monarchy. We welcome you back to the galactic community, and hope to usher in a new age of prosperity and cooperation between our two cultures."

"Get on with it," muttered Kyle.

"Repeat: this is the frigate *Indefatigable*, bringing greetings of the Commonwealth of Independent Worlds to the Sabaean monarchy."

A murmur of surprise rippled through the room. There were more than a few people on Sabaea who believed that the Commonwealth should have come to their aid during the invasion; most, though, didn't seem to blame them for not wanting to put themselves in harm's way. *Either way, they probably won't get a hero's welcome.*

"Four to one, was it?" said Antony. "Not bad, considering that five years ago the Illyrican Empire had them more or less painted into a corner."

"Yeah, well, the Illyricans have one less fleet than they used to." It came out more flip then he'd intended.

Antony grimaced. "It's never wise to speak ill of the dead, Mr. Rankin. You never know when it might come back to haunt you."

Kyle swallowed. "Yes, ma'am."

"As you were," said Antony, waving her glass at the party. "Enjoy the revelry. Eat, drink, be merry, all that."

*For tomorrow we . . . what exactly?* Drawing himself up, Kyle turned toward the stairs.

"Kyle?"

He glanced over his shoulder, and saw that Antony's expression had thawed slightly. The colonel nodded down at the Ops Center. "I know you don't exactly feel like you fit in down there, but everybody's Sabaean today."

With a nod, Kyle excused himself and returned to the party, already well underway. Somebody—Farrell again, he thought—shoved a mug of what smelled like 120-proof motor oil into his hand, and knocked their own cup against it before disappearing back into the crowd.

Kyle stared at the drink. There were some things that not even liquor could wash away, despite his best efforts.

A blonde head snapped up in the middle of the crowd. Kyle raised his eyebrows as he recognized Lieutenant Polakov, trying to flag down Antony. After a moment, she gave up, peeling off her headset and taking to the stairs, two at a time.

Kyle watched as she tapped the colonel on the shoulder. Polakov said something to her, and Antony frowned. The colonel's eyes searched the crowd, suddenly locking onto him. Holding his gaze, Antony's lips thinned and she jerked her head at Kyle, summoning him again toward the platform he'd just left.

*Uh oh.*

Discarding the untouched mug of liquor on top of a convenient console, Kyle reluctantly climbed the steps back up to the colonel's station, passing Polakov on her way back down. She eyed him as if seeing him for the first time.

As Kyle reached the top, the colonel motioned him into her office proper. The din cut off abruptly as Antony closed the door.

"Ma'am?"

"Mr. Rankin. Sorry to interrupt your celebrations so soon, but there's been an interesting development." She inclined her head toward her own private screen, which was currently mirroring the display that hung in the Ops Center. On it, the Commonwealth ship—now marked green for friendly—was closing the distance between the blue dot of the gate and the larger green dot of Sabaea. "You have friends in the Commonwealth?"

Kyle frowned blankly. "Uh. No, ma'am. Can't say as I've ever even been in Commonwealth space."

"Peculiar," mused Antony, staring at the dot. "Very peculiar."

"Colonel?"

"After the initial greeting was acknowledged by the Crown, the *Indefatigable* sent a second message over a secure channel to the Ministry of Defense.

"Seems the Commonwealth's looking for someone. Someone they believe to be on Sabaea." Antony crossed her arms. "The Crown was only too happy to confirm his existence, and the *Indefatigable* is sending down an envoy to talk to him as we speak."

"Uh . . ." It was the best he could come up with on short notice.

Antony turned, fixing him with a curious look. "The person they're looking for is an Illyrican flight lieutenant by the name of Elijah Brody."

Kyle's stomach poured into his nice, comfy boots.

The colonel's head tilted to one side. "Why, I do believe that's *you*, Mr. Rankin."

# CHAPTER TWO

This whole trip was a waste of time.

That was Simon Kovalic's opinion, anyway. He'd looked into Elijah Brody a few weeks ago, when the name had first cropped up in his research, but all the data on him had pointed to one inescapable conclusion: Brody had been dead for almost five years.

Then, two days ago, a Sabaean fast courier had jumped through that planet's formerly defunct wormhole gate, and all hell had broken loose in the upper echelons of the Commonwealth's intelligence apparatus. The general had insisted they follow up on the lead—no matter how slim it might be.

Because if Elijah Brody *was* alive, they couldn't risk anybody else finding out first.

As the shuttle made a bumpy approach, Kovalic peered out of the small window by his seat. Not that there was much to see up here on the tundra: Even if it had been daytime, the swirling snows would have obscured most of the ground below. At this time of night, it was just a big dark mass. He leaned back and closed his eyes, trying to ride the waves of turbulence without falling asleep; not easy, especially when his last shut-eye had been over twenty-four hours ago.

Despite his strenuous objections that his talents would be best utilized elsewhere—any place other than digging up what was, best case, a corpse and, worst case, rumor and hearsay—the general had decided they would go to Sabaea themselves, and that Kovalic would personally fly down to the surface. Because if you wanted something done right, you did it yourself or, in this case, had your most trusted subordinate do it.

He glanced down at the tablet on his lap, skimming the dossier he'd drawn up. Five years ago, Brody had been assigned, fresh out of the academy, to the Illyrican Fifth Fleet—which had promptly been dispatched to invade Sabaea. And then he'd disappeared, along with the rest of the fleet and any ability to contact or reach Sabaea. All that had remained was an inactive wormhole gate, floating in space like the eye of a dead god. Kovalic had seen it once or twice, and he didn't mind admitting that it creeped him the hell out.

Brody's name had appeared on the list of "missing, presumed dead" that the Illyricans had broadcast on their state-sponsored communication network, and that had been all she wrote for Elijah Brody. And, for that matter, the independent world of Sabaea.

Until now.

A thump marked the shuttle's contact with the ground. It was supposed to be a landing pad, but from what Kovalic could see in the pre-dawn, it was indistinguishable from a snowbank. Flakes whirled past the viewport, occasionally sticking to the transparent aluminum for a moment before melting away into drops of water.

The Sabaeans had scrambled when the Commonwealth had transmitted the request about Brody, eventually responding with instructions to land at this facility near the planet's northern pole, but without providing further detail. He got the feeling nobody had thought about Elijah Brody in a long time.

He shook his head, trying to wrap his mind around this mission. He'd set foot on plenty of worlds in his lifetime, but this was hardly his average op: here he was, the first person to step onto the Sabaean surface in five years. A world that should, by all rights, never have been heard from again. A world of ghosts.

Kovalic sighed and pinched the bridge of his nose. The wormhole lag and lack of sleep must be hitting him if he was starting to get maudlin. The sooner he wrapped up this fool's errand, the faster he could get back to the ship and grab some rack time.

He unbuckled and worked his way forward. Besides the pilot, he had the shuttle to himself; this mission was more or less unsanctioned—as the general's operations tended to be—so the fewer people that knew their true purpose here the better. The hatch opened with a hiss, and Kovalic trod out into the snow. It crunched underneath his boots, his footprints all too quickly subsumed beneath the endless onslaught of flakes as the wind bit at his cheeks.

Two soldiers met him at an unassuming metal structure that looked barely a step above a temporary survival hut, though at least it had the decency to boast a heavy security door. Both of his escorts wore large, puffy parkas, their faces shadowed behind fur-lined hoods. Kovalic cast an envious look at the outfits and tried not to shiver.

Fortunately, the two soldiers had pity on his insufficient garb and quickly swiped open the door, ushering him into a short hallway that was, if not warm, at least icicle-free.

From there, it was an elevator trip down—way down—into what was apparently the base proper. Once they were in the lift, the two soldiers peeled off their hoods and unwrapped their scarves: one was a surprisingly young man, red acne spots spattered across a greasy forehead; the other was a somewhat older woman, who stood ramrod straight, eyes front.

"So you're the welcoming committee, huh?" said Kovalic, briskly rubbing his hands together before raising them to his mouth and blowing on them.

"Yes, sir," the woman said, her eyes flicking to his face only for a moment before returning to the apparently much more interesting elevator door. The kid didn't say a word, though the frightened expression that crossed his face made Kovalic wonder if maybe the military had not been his original career path.

"Well, sure is a nice place you got here," he said, offering a smile. "Though if you could have arranged for some better weather, I'd have appreciated it."

Neither responded. The kid looked like he was about to pass out.

So this was the vaunted military that had taken out an entire Illyrican battle fleet. Granted, it was a victory you'd find filed under *pyrrhic* in most textbooks, so maybe this *was* the best the Sabaean Defense Forces had to offer. With a sigh, Kovalic lapsed back into silence. His spirits and hope of finding anything useful fell along with the elevator's descent.

The lift ground to a halt, the door sliding open with a loud clang. His escort led him into another gray-tiled corridor that, had he not felt the motion of the elevator, he would have concluded was the same one from above, though it did feel merely chilly rather than blisteringly cold. Neither of the soldiers gave any more concession to the heat than unzipping their parkas.

What followed was a short trip through a maze of corridors that seemed more like utility tunnels than the hallways of a military base, wallpapered as they were with snaking conduits, pipes, and bundles of cables. They arrived at a door marked OPERATIONS, where Kovalic was carefully chivvied through a room of control panels and screens. A handful of officers sat amid the detritus of what had clearly been some sort of celebration, but they perked up as Kovalic was paraded through, eyeing him like he was some sort of exotic animal. He was glad to be out of uniform—an obvious Commonwealth military officer would only have raised awkward questions.

At the top of a short flight of stairs, he was deposited in front of a frosted glass door; the two soldiers took up spots flanking it.

Apparently the tour ended here. Kovalic glanced around, then rapped on the glass and, at the muted acknowledgement from beyond, let himself in.

Two people sat across a desk from one another, nearly as dissimilar as the soldiers who'd escorted him there. Behind the desk was an older woman, lean and sharp-featured with short, steel gray hair. The colonel's insignia on the immaculately pressed collar took Kovalic by surprise—there was something in the woman's bearing that he'd pegged as a general's confidence.

A man was slouched in the chair opposite, as if trying to blend in with the upholstery. His brown hair was long and unkempt, and he sported a scruffy beard that would have been more appropriate to a recluse. He shifted slightly in the chair, glancing in curiosity at Kovalic, and in that moment Kovalic's breath caught in his throat.

It was the eyes that did it—even bloodshot, they'd lost none of the blue from the picture that Kovalic had been staring at for the last two days. Mentally, Kovalic took five years off the man, trimmed his hair back to regulation length, and shaved off the beard.

Elijah goddamned Brody.

Maybe this trip wasn't going to be a complete waste after all.

The woman rose and extended a hand. "Colonel Indira Antony."

"A pleasure, colonel." Kovalic shook the hand absently, his eyes still on Brody. After spending much of his trip studying the man's file, seeing him in the flesh was a bit like meeting a celebrity, albeit one whose best days were probably behind him.

Antony gestured to a second, empty chair across from her desk, next to Brody. "Please, have a seat, Mister . . . ?"

"Fielding," Kovalic said, forcing himself to meet Antony's gaze and dusting off his most diplomatic expression.

It was a new alias—they didn't get reused, for security reasons—but it came out without so much as a hitch. If there was one thing he'd gotten good at over the last ten years, it was lying about his name. Which probably wasn't something he should be proud about, but, well, that could have described any number of skills he'd built up in a decade of intel work. He settled into the chair, then cleared his throat. "Thank you for accommodating this impromptu visit, colonel. I know this must be a lot to take in."

Antony gave a faint smile. "We've been waiting to rejoin the human race for five years now. I like to think we've prepared a bit in that time."

"Well, we're certainly glad to have you back. The blow you dealt to the Illyrican military was," Kovalic paused, head cocked to one side, searching for the right word, ". . . substantial."

Brody shifted again at that, his eyes blankly fixed somewhere that was decidedly not Kovalic. For her part, Antony's expression held like she was posing for a photograph.

So, that was apparently a touchy subject.

Again clearing his throat, Kovalic launched into the carefully worded speech that the general had drilled into him for what seemed like the bulk of their twelve-hour trip. "As we speak, diplomatic representatives of the Commonwealth are engaging in high-level talks with your government to join our coalition. Sabaea would be a welcome addition and we could provide you with considerable assistance in rebuilding your planet."

"I'll take your word for it," said Antony, eyebrows raised. "But that's all well above my pay grade."

Kovalic just barely avoided letting out a sigh of relief and relaxed into his chair. Antony was clearly not the type to be impressed by ten-dollar words. Just as well: Kovalic preferred the dime-store variety himself. "You and me both, colonel. Personally, I'm fine letting the diplomatic muckety-mucks upstairs work out all the fine print. I'm just here for Lieutenant Brody."

Out of the corner of his eye, Kovalic saw Brody stiffen. Neither Kovalic's nor Antony's gaze turned to him, their eyes still locked on each other.

"I see," said Antony. Her fingers, long and narrow as those of a concert pianist, rippled across the surface of the desk. "Could you perhaps enlighten us as to *why* the Commonwealth is so interested in Mr. Brody?"

Kovalic sucked a breath in through his teeth. "I can't. Hell, I can't even say 'I wish I could.'" He smiled, apologetically. "You know the deal, colonel."

Antony's forehead creased. Orders were orders, and you didn't make colonel without a healthy dose of respect for them—then again, you also didn't end up in an icebox like this unless you'd made the shit list of some very important people.

"Look," said Kovalic, leaning forward, "soldier to soldier, what I *can* tell you is that a lot happened while you guys have been out of commission. You dealt the Illyricans a serious blow five years ago—twenty percent of their naval strength destroyed in a single engagement is nothing to sneeze at." He shook his head. "But they're hardly on the ropes. We're just trying to make sure the battlefield stays level, for all of us: the Commonwealth *and* the independent worlds that have been trying to stay out of it. And at this very moment, that—hard as it may be to believe—requires Lieutenant Brody's help."

"It's not 'Lieutenant.'" It took Kovalic a moment to realize that it was Brody who'd spoken. If his voice wasn't the most confident Kovalic had ever heard, neither was it the piteous squeak that one might have expected from watching his body language. Narrowing his eyes, Kovalic took another, closer look at the man he'd come here to find.

Brody had unfolded slightly from the chair, his legs improbably lanky for a man who'd once had to squeeze into a fighter cockpit. His expression was guarded, but the eyes, despite the bleary redness, still had a certain spark in them.

"I'm sorry?" said Kovalic, tilting his head.

"It's not 'Lieutenant' Brody," he said, his eyes meeting Kovalic's for the first time. "I resigned my commission in the Illyrican Navy as part of an agreement with the Sabaean government."

Kovalic blinked, then nodded carefully. "I see. Mr. Brody, then."

Brody shrugged. "That's what it used to say on my tax forms."

"Well," said Antony, leaning back in her chair and folding her hands, "given that it seems likely we're about to be allies, I see little harm in you talking to Mr. Brody." She gestured in the younger man's direction.

Kovalic's brow furrowed. "I think you misunderstood me, colonel. This isn't just a matter of debriefing—I'm taking Mr. Brody with me."

The shockwave from that pronouncement rippled through both of them, though Kovalic had a hard time telling who seemed more bothered by it: Brody's eyes had widened, more startled than angry, while Antony had sat forward again, clearly marshaling for a fight.

"Mr. Fielding," Antony said; her voice was all honey and diplomacy on the outside, but there was no mistaking the reinforced steel beneath, "I appreciate that you have your orders, but Mr. Brody's situation here on Sabaea is a complicated one. You have to realize that I can't just let you whisk him away for your admittedly vague purposes."

"All due respect, colonel, but you don't have a choice."

A mere tap would have shattered Antony's expression. "I don't respond well to threats, Mr. Fielding."

The gentle chime of a communicator echoed in the silence, accompanied by a light winking on Antony's desk. The colonel ignored it, holding Kovalic's gaze.

"That's going to be your boss," said Kovalic, nodding to the desk. "And I know that because she's been talking to *my* boss. And my boss can be very, very persuasive." The general always got what he wanted, one way or another. Pushing back his chair, Kovalic rose. "I'll be outside when you're through." He tried to shrug off the twinge of regret. Antony seemed decent enough, but that was beside the point: right now, she was just in his way.

It couldn't have taken more than a couple minutes for the colonel to finish her conversation, but with Kovalic's only company the two taciturn guards at Antony's door it seemed like an hour. He'd taken the opportunity to browse some of the files that the general had just uploaded, including some of the data on what had happened to Brody after the invasion.

At the click of the door latch, the comm disappeared into Kovalic's pocket and he pushed himself off the wall he'd been leaning against. The two guards straightened up as Antony and Brody walked through.

"Good luck, Mr. B—," the colonel's voice caught, "Mr. Rankin." Her eyes crinkled, and for a moment her expression softened. "Take care of yourself."

"You too, ma'am," said Brody, a smile tugging at one corner of his mouth. "Make sure Farrell stays on the straight and narrow."

"I'm not sure I have the depths of patience required for that endeavor," Antony said with a sigh. "Give me a moment with Mr. Fielding, will you?"

Brody eyed the two of them, unable to excise the faintest hint of suspicion from his eyes, but in the end he nodded. As he took up a spot outside the office, he turned suddenly and clicked his heels together, offering Antony a surprisingly sharp salute—albeit an Illyrican one, elbow crooked and palm facing out.

A smile crossed Antony's face and she returned the salute in the more abbreviated Sabaean style.

The pleasant expression dropped from her face as she ushered Kovalic back into her office and closed the door. One on one with a senior officer was never Kovalic's idea of a Friday night out; the full brunt of Antony's attention descended upon him and he felt himself unconsciously adopting a parade rest. She lowered herself into her chair.

"You're a military man, Mr. Fielding," said Antony, eyes narrowed, "so I think we can speak plainly with one another."

Kovalic resisted the urge to swallow. "Yes, ma'am."

"If anything happens to Eli Brody—if he nicks himself shaving, if he stubs his toe, if he doesn't so much as get two sugars in his goddamned coffee—I will hold you personally responsible. And then you and I will have a problem. Is that clear?"

"Yes, ma'am," Kovalic repeated. It came automatically; there was no other possible reply.

Antony relaxed slightly. "Good," she said, nodding as if to punctuate the point. "I may not know you, Mr. Fielding, but I know your kind. Special forces, I should think? Before your current career in," she waved a hand, "whichever branch of the Commonwealth's intelligence services you report to."

He could have dissembled, could have given the polite but noncommittal denial that they both would have known to be a lie, but what would be the point? Kovalic kept his expression bland, but he acknowledged the assessment with a tilt of the head.

Antony pursed her lips. "Too many of your sort are more concerned with the big picture than with the . . . smaller details." Her eyes flicked to the door. "That young man has been through a lot already. Too damn much, at his age." The unnerving gaze returned to Kovalic. "See that he comes through the other side of this no worse than he went in."

Some long dormant instinct prodded Kovalic to full attention, though he stopped just short of offering his own salute, instead substituting a curt, professional nod. "Yes, ma'am." The address might have been a formality before, but this time he gave it the weight he deserved. Looking out for their personnel was the foremost responsibility of a commanding officer; Kovalic could get behind that. "For what it's worth, we're not in this to destroy lives."

Antony tilted her head to one side, casting a regretful look at Kovalic. "We always like to believe that, Mr. Fielding." She waved a hand at him and turned her attention to a display on the desk.

Kovalic let himself out. Once the door clicked shut behind him, he drew a deep breath and slowly exhaled. Over the last twenty years of service he'd been commended, chewed out, and dismissed out of hand by superior officers—but rarely in the same two-minute conversation.

There was a snort from nearby. "Yeah, the Old Wolf can have that effect on people." Brody was leaning against the wall, arms crossed. "You need a minute?"

Kovalic shot him an irritated look, but didn't reply, instead jerking his head in a "follow me" motion. There was no sign of the detail who had escorted him in; evidently they had better things to do than see him out.

"Jesus," said Brody. "Where's the fire?"

Kovalic stopped and turned around. "No, no, take your time, Mr. Brody. I love dropping onto arctic tundra before dawn on no sleep—it's a hobby of mine. You want a cup of coffee? Can I whip up a couple of eggs for you?"

Brody raised his hands. "Sorry I asked."

Kovalic brought his best drill sergeant's stare to bear and allowed himself an inward smile as the man swallowed. Without another word, he spun on his heel and continued walking. Brody's tentative footsteps followed. Some training was so deeply ingrained that it never really left you.

The two of them tromped down the stairs into the Ops Center, ignoring the curious glances of the few personnel still on duty—Kovalic trusted

Antony would tell them that they'd seen and heard nothing. The longer the exact details of Eli Brody's fate were in question, the better.

Once out in the corridor, Brody started to turn to the left, but Kovalic grasped his arm. "Where do you think you're going?"

Brody frowned, jerking a thumb over his shoulder. "My room, to get my stuff."

"Really?" said Kovalic, crossing his arms. "Name one thing you own that I can't have replaced in twenty-four hours."

"But, my . . ." He trailed off as he apparently performed an inventory and came up short. ". . . comb?"

Kovalic eyed the bird's nest on top of Brody's head. "Lot of sentimental value, huh?" Firmly, Kovalic shifted his grip on Brody's elbow and, not ungently, guided him back in the opposite direction.

"Okay," muttered Brody, freeing his arm. "No need to get physical."

Kovalic rolled his eyes and continued down the hallway. Finding the way out wasn't hard; he retraced his steps to the lift he'd ridden down, where he punched the control to summon the elevator. The machinery began grinding away, the screech of metal on metal even more horrific in the cold. Kovalic rubbed his hands together, studying the man across from him.

His height had been in the file, but he was still taller than Kovalic had expected—the younger man had a couple of inches on him, though his somewhat gangly build made it seem like more. His nose had gone reddish, though Kovalic wasn't sure whether from the cold or the alcohol he could smell on the man's breath. Or both.

"Pretty sweet gig," he commented.

"What?"

"Most guys help invade a planet, they get free room and board compliments of a military prison, but you . . ." Kovalic glanced around, nodding appreciatively. "You lucked out."

"Oh, yes, *so* lucky. Cleaning latrines in the middle of an arctic wasteland. You know, most people never get to fulfill their dreams."

"Prison's worse. Trust me." A cramped room with a bare cot and concrete block walls arose in his memory. It had been damp and cold all the time, though not perhaps as cold as here. His teeth ground together and he consciously pried them apart.

An objection had started to form on Brody's lips, but it died as he made eye contact with Kovalic.

"Yeah, okay," he said finally. "I was only in one for a little while. Right after the battle."

"So, how'd you swing this?"

The kid avoided his gaze. "Antony was the warden. She went to bat for me, convinced the government to furlough me as a maintenance tech. Argued that with the planet in isolation, they might as well have an extra hand somewhere instead of just an extra mouth. Ended up as a two-for-one deal, turns out." There was a touch of belligerence at the end there, and just the slightest curl of a fist.

So they'd sent the kid someplace he couldn't get in trouble—and for good measure, they condemned Antony here for sticking up for him. Say a lot of things for the military, but they weren't generally known for the touchy-feelies.

"I've been looking at your file," said Kovalic. No need to tell Brody he'd committed almost the entire thing to memory. "Not a lot of folks from Caledonia itching to join the Illyrican military after, you know, being crushed under their boot heel during the war." Earth's two major colonies, Caledonia and Centauri, had fallen to the Imperium shortly after the homeworld had.

"Just because I flew for them doesn't mean I subscribed to their politics."

"So if it wasn't out of a sense of patriotism and duty, then why? No offense, but you don't strike me as much of a soldier."

Brody's cheeks reddened to match his nose, and his tone turned almost defensive. "I'm not." His jaw clenched. "Look, I went to fly ships, and because it got me off that dirtball. I didn't ask to be in a war."

"I always worry more about the ones who do." A certain eighteen-year-old private with delusions of grandeur came to mind. Much like Brody, that kid had learned about reality the hard way. But he was still walking and talking, and that counted for something.

They were interrupted by a chime signaling the elevator's arrival; the doors slid open and Kovalic stepped in, Brody trailing after.

"What about you?" said Brody, when the doors closed. "I suppose joining the Commonwealth military isn't so surprising for someone from Earth."

Kovalic's eyes flicked to him in surprise, quickly masked. "What makes you think I'm from Earth?" he said evenly, trying to suppress a grimace. Antony getting a read on him he could understand, but *this* kid? Maybe he was losing his touch.

"Caledonia's just a wormhole jump away from Earth, so I've met my fair share of folks from the old world. Most never do manage to shake that accent—though, you ask me, that's partially on purpose." Brody shrugged, eyes rolling up. "Earthers always like to remind you where they're from."

Kovalic scratched his chin. To be honest, he'd never thought of himself as having an accent. Everybody *else* had accents. "Can I offer you a piece of advice, Brody?"

"Sure."

"Talk less."

He wasn't entirely sure, but he thought the hand Brody raised to cough into might have been covering a smile. Disheveled as the kid might look, it was pretty clear that *he* still thought he was clever.

The elevator let them out into a hallway with a patina of frost, which they followed to a large, heavily shielded security door. Kovalic punched the release button on the wall beside it, and with a heaving groan, the door's servos kicked in and it began to slide open. A gust of icy cold wind swirled through cracks, whipping a wispy tail of rapidly disintegrating snowflakes.

"Uh, I'm not really dressed for the occasion." Brody plucked at the relatively thin sleeves of his work uniform.

"Don't worry, we won't be out there long. Our ride's waiting."

Kovalic turned up the collar of his jacket and slipped out through the still-widening crack in the door. He heard a deep breath from Brody as the underdressed man plunged out after him.

Snow and wind enveloped them—the few flakes that Kovalic had seen upon their arrival had apparently grown into something just short of a blizzard. Ice particles nicked at his face, melting even as they made contact with his skin. His nose started running.

At a noise from behind him, he turned to see Brody doubled over in a fit of coughing. Kovalic had figured the man would have adjusted somewhat to the cold after having been stuck here for almost five years, but apparently he hadn't spent a lot of time outside of the "comfortable" environs of the base.

Kovalic thumped the younger man on the back until Brody put his hands up, warding him off.

"Invigorating, isn't it?" Kovalic shouted.

Brody just stared at him.

With a grin, Kovalic tugged him further onto the tundra. A thrumming permeated the air, and powerful lights cut through the darkness, refracting off the whirling flakes. The snow began blowing at them in even greater gusts.

"There's our ride!" Kovalic hollered over the sound of the engines, pointing to the shuttle.

The ship's thrusters were powering up, melting deep gouges in the snow around them, and its repulsors blew the flakes out from beneath, surrounding the vessel in its own little protective circle.

A hatch on the side of the ship slid open and a makeshift staircase unfolded, beckoning them into the blackness inside.

Brody's eyes darted, panicked, between Kovalic and the shuttle. He yelled something over the noise, which Kovalic managed to interpret, after a moment, as "You want me to get on *that*?"

He gave Brody a curious look. "Obviously. How else did you think we were getting out of here?"

Brody's face had turned as white as the snow surrounding them, and his expression reminded Kovalic of the young, pimply soldier who had escorted him into the base: pure, stark, untempered fear.

Brody wiped his hands against his trousers. "I—I—I *can't*."

Kovalic blinked. "Why the hell not?"

The bloodshot eyes flicked away from him. "I'm afraid of flying!"

Kovalic stared at him, dumbfounded. He'd read Brody's personnel record front to back, and if there was one thing that every instructor and commanding officer had agreed on—besides his smartass-verging-on-insubordinate attitude—it was that Eli Brody was an ace pilot, the best many of them had ever seen. The man was born to fly.

Shaking his head, Kovalic closed the distance between them and put a hand on the other man's shoulder.

"Brody."

"Yes?" He looked up, hopeful.

*"Get on the goddamned ship."*

# CHAPTER THREE

In the list of experiences that Eli Brody hoped to recall on his deathbed—many, many years from now—the flight up from Sabaea's surface would rank very near the bottom. His stomach churned and roiled from the moment he set foot on the shuttle's entry ramp, and it kicked into overdrive as soon as they lifted off.

It had been four years since the last time he'd been on a ship, back when he was first transferred to Davidson Base. He'd thought that maybe the nausea and shaking would have passed with time, but if anything they seemed to have gotten even worse.

The very fact of the illness offended him; he'd been flying since he was a kid. He'd sat on his Aunt Brigid's lap during her short haul trips between the Caledonian mines and Raleigh City. He'd logged hundreds of hours in every simulator he could get his hands on. At the academy, he'd put in more time in training ships then almost any other two members of his graduating class combined.

And in all that time he'd never had so much as a hint of space-sickness. Not a flutter, not a twinge, not even a burp.

Then came the Battle of Sabaea.

"Who the hell is flying this thing?" he muttered, raising his head from between his knees. "Didn't anybody ever tell them that piloting and amphetamines don't mix?"

The ship juked and shook as it ascended, every little jolt making Eli's stomach lurch, dance, and twirl in time. Fielding, seated next to him, watched his distress in wry amusement—just one step short of full-blown sadism from Eli's point of view.

Gripping the armrests so hard he worried he might wrench them off the seat, Eli lolled his head to one side and favored Fielding with a sickly look. "Enjoying yourself?"

"What can I say?" Fielding gave him a death's-head grin. "The pilot who can't stand flying? I'm a sucker for irony."

*He won't be laughing when I throw up on those nice boots of his*, thought Eli with a grim pang of satisfaction.

If the ascent was bad, the docking maneuver was worse. *Like two beached whales mating*, his flight instructor had once described the process, and this pilot seemed determined to wring every ounce of truth from that quip. The ships flopped and bucked against each other, flailing around until sheer persistence finally paid off.

When the clank of the docking collar's seal reverberated through the hull, Eli offered up a silent prayer of thanks to whatever almighty power had seen fit to spare his life. He reached for the seat-belt release, but it slipped out of his shaking fingers. His second attempt was no better, and even a deep breath did little to banish the tremors.

"So," said Kovalic. "You realize you're going to have to do that all over again on the way down, right?"

Eli opened his mouth to fire off a choice rejoinder, but his stomach spasmed and heaved for the final time, and he scrambled free of his restraints just in time to dash for the head.

●

Cleaned up and newly minted—by virtue of a swig of mouthwash—Eli stepped onto the deck of the CMS *Indefatigable*.

"Kind of a stupid name, isn't it?" offered up Eli as he followed Fielding down the narrow gunmetal corridors. The size of the ship, coupled with the fact that it maintained its own gravity, had helped trick his brain into thinking he was on solid ground—at least temporarily.

Fielding quirked an eyebrow. "It means 'tireless.'"

"I know what it means, but it's a pain in the ass to *say*. In-dee-fat-eeg-a-bull. The military always gives their ships these overblown names, as if to convince people that they're totally invulnerable. And you know what? They *aren't*. I've seen bigger ships than this blown into itty-bitty pieces."

"What do you suggest?

"I don't know. Honesty, I guess?" He smiled. "There was this old corvette at the academy used for training exercises: the ISC *Dauntless*. Its crew called it the *Dentless* because of the sheer number of engagements it survived. But the academy used it as bait in ambush scenarios during live-fire combat exercises, so we called it the *Deathtrap*."

To Eli's surprise, the other man laughed. The pair reached a T-intersection, and Fielding nodded to the right.

"When I was a private," Fielding said suddenly, "we had a drill sergeant that would yell and scream his head off at us for not running fast enough, not doing enough push-ups, or generally being lazy no-good maggots. But it was the damnedest thing: when he got up close to yell at you, his breath always smelled like lavender." He shook his head. "We used to call him Sergeant Lilac—not to his face, of course; we were lazy no-good maggots, but we weren't stupid." His eyes had gone unfocused. "I hadn't thought of him in years," he muttered.

"Was that on Earth?"

Fielding's expression shifted into neutral. "Yeah," he said. "A long time ago."

They didn't exchange a word for the rest of the walk. Eventually, Fielding came to a stop before a nondescript door; its placard bore no name, only an identification number: 3-174. He rapped on the metal with his bare knuckles and, at a response from within, slid the door open.

The room itself wasn't much more distinctive than its door, but shipboard cabins never offered much in the way of personalization. This one had been fashioned into an office, though that didn't mean much more than the addition of a small metal desk topped with a computer terminal. The normal stark blue-white light was softened by a warmer yellow glow from a decidedly non-standard-issue desk lamp.

Behind the desk sat the room's only notable feature. The man was in his seventies by Eli's estimation, mostly bald save for a thin fringe of white hair around his head that matched a pointed white mustache and neatly trimmed Vandyke, making him look like a bleached devil caricature. Like Fielding, he wore military-style clothes: a long-sleeved high-collared black shirt that, as with Fielding's jacket, was devoid of any sign of rank or affiliation.

He set down a stylus and leaned back in his chair as Fielding and Eli entered. Brilliant blue eyes stood out against skin the color of tarnished bronze; they settled on Eli, seemingly taking him in at a glance.

"You must be Lieutenant Brody," the man said. Something about his voice conveyed not just assuredness, but also an undertone of culture and learning that went far beyond the military. His slight accent rang a bell in Eli's memory, but he couldn't quite place it. Whatever it was, it had been a long time since he'd heard it.

"Just Brody," said Eli, shifting restlessly from one foot to the other. Something about the man's manner made him feel ill-at-ease, as though he had stumbled into an interrogation.

"Please, have a seat."

The chair wasn't comfortable, nor did Eli think it was meant to be; it was standard military issue, fit for everything from the officer's mess hall to a prisoner's cell. He squirmed as the cold metal leached out his body heat.

"I trust your trip up was satisfactory?"

Eli bit back a sarcastic comment about the bumpy ride. Fielding might take a ribbing, but something about this guy suggested he wasn't the right person to crack wise to. "Uh. Yeah, sure."

"Good, good. Can I get you anything? A cup of coffee? Some . . ." He glanced at his wrist, frowning. "Breakfast? Dear me, it *is* early, isn't it?"

Eli's stomach roiled audibly at the thought of food. He suppressed a burp that left his mouth tasting like acid. "Uh, I think I'll pass, thanks."

"Down to business, then. Mr. Fielding probably hasn't told you why you're here."

"Not so much," said Eli with a sideways glance at Fielding. "The guy's a riddle wrapped in an enigma coated in a hard candy shell."

*Well, so much for avoiding the wisecracks.*

The old man's lips flickered in a brief smile. He didn't say anything for a moment, just smoothed his neat, pointed beard between his thumb and forefinger and stared at Eli with those unnerving blue eyes.

At a touch from the old man, a holographic screen shimmered to life over the desk. He cleared his throat and read. "Brody, Elijah Hamish. Age 27. Born in Glenfin, Caledonia, to Connor and Molly Brody. One brother, Eamon Brody, and one sister, Meghann Brody. Graduate of the

Imperial Naval Academy. Assigned to the Fifth Fleet as a Flight Lieutenant in the 42nd Fighter Wing, Green Squadron, aboard the ISC *Venture*. Missing in action, presumed dead." He looked up, meeting Eli's eyes. "Does that about sum it up?"

*The collected works of Eli Brody—a paragraph.* "More or less," he said. "You left out the part about my dashing good looks."

"I'll make an addendum," said the old man dryly, dismissing the screen.

"So," said Eli, looking back and forth from the old man's inscrutable face to Fielding's impassive one. "For sale: one washed-up fighter pilot. Who's buying?"

Neither man cracked so much as a smile.

After a moment, the old man leaned back and steepled his fingers. "I think you can be of great help to us, Mr. Brody. In fact, there's a task at hand for which you are, I might say, uniquely suited."

Eli's eyebrows arched upward. He couldn't imagine anything he was "uniquely suited" for these days. *Unless you want some toilets polished to a shine.*

The old man nodded to Fielding, who was leaning against the wall. He pushed himself upright at the gesture and cleared his throat. "The Illyrican Empire is in the process of creating a new weapon, one that we believe has the potential to drastically change the balance of power in the galaxy. And they're building it on your homeworld of Caledonia."

Eli blinked. "You're kidding, right?" He glanced over to the old man, but there was not a batted eyelash between them. "He's kidding, right? Am I on some sort of hidden camera?"

"We're not in the habit of pulling people's legs, Mr. Brody."

"I should hope not," Eli said, "because if you *were*, you'd have come up with a story that doesn't sound like you lifted it from a third-rate action vid."

"You've been out of it for a while," Fielding said, "so you may not be aware of the changes to the galacti-political scene. With the destruction of the Fifth Fleet, the Illyricans lost their invasion capability, so they regrouped and fortified around the planets they already occupy: Earth and its colonies, including Centauri and Caledonia."

Eli's stomach burbled again, and this time it wasn't just from the memory of the shuttle trip.

"The war's gone cold," said Fielding. "The Commonwealth and the Imperium are staring each other down from across the galaxy, and that's fine—for now. But this weapon, whatever it is, could give the Illyricans a leg up. Sure, the Sabaean invasion didn't go well, but there's no guarantee they won't try again, somewhere else. It's just a matter of time."

"If the Illyricans get this project working then any chance of détente will evaporate," the old man added, his expression hardening. "I can say that with some assurance."

"Spare me the propaganda," said Eli, throwing up his hands. "I get it. You don't want the Illyricans to have a new toy that you can't fight." He leaned forward. "Just cut the crap and tell me why *I'm* here."

Fielding hesitated, glancing at the old man, who nodded. "We had an asset on Caledonia feeding us information about the Illyricans' project, but we've lost contact." Fielding grimaced. "We think that he may have been compromised."

"Okay," said Eli, "so all this guy told you is that the Illyricans are building some big scary gun on my homeworld. Sounds bad. But I'm still not sure what this has to do with me."

The old man blinked owlishly. "I should think it'd be obvious, Mr. Brody. As a Caledonian native and a former Illyrican officer, you have the advantage of being intimately familiar with several facets of this situation. We'd like to put you on the ground to help us gather further intelligence about the project."

Eli had once heard that on Earth there were snakes that could unhinge their jaws and swallow an entire egg whole, and for the first time he thought he understood how they felt. He snapped his teeth together with an almost painful click, just avoiding biting his tongue.

"Me? I'm not a spy. I don't know the first thing about sneaking around and stabbing people in the back—whatever it is you guys do. I'm a janitor; I just clean up other people's messes."

The old man smiled. "You might say we're in the same business."

"Jesus, do you guys buy crazy in bulk around here?"

Fielding snorted. "No, but we do get a hell of a discount."

"Counterintuitive as it may sound," the old man said, shooting a mildly disapproving glance at his subordinate, "your lack of expertise actually makes you ideal for this assignment. And Mr. Fielding and his team will be with you every step of the way. Besides, you'll be going home."

"Some people would kill for that chance," Fielding said quietly.

*Home*, thought Eli glumly. *They say there's no place like it.* "Yeah, well, check your records. I *left* Caledonia first chance I got, and if you ask me, five years cut off from the rest of the galaxy wasn't nearly long enough."

Cocking his head to one side, the old man eyed him like he might a bug under a magnifying glass. "Oh, your reticence is well . . . documented." A gnarled finger tapped a button on the desk and once again the holographic screen flickered into view, this time facing Eli.

A face appeared on it, all too familiar with its red curls and green eyes and, as the message began to play, a cold hand clutched at Eli's heart. Not only did he know the face, but he knew the words by heart—he'd played it over and over . . . but that had been in a different life.

"Hey, big brother. It's me." Even now, reaching out over the gulf of five years, the tone of her voice still wrenched at Eli. Meghann sounded weary, defeated; the dark circles under her eyes, apparent even in the grainy compression of the video message, did nothing to diminish his concern. "Eamon doesn't know I'm using the transmitter, but I needed to talk to you. I *need* to talk to you. I know you're busy with everything, but I really . . ." she drew a deep breath.

"I think you should come home. Please, come home." She froze in place as the recording ended.

"That was dated a week before you shipped out for Sabaea, but there's no record of a reply." The old man's eyes were ice. "It takes a lot of something—anger, hate, fear—to not respond to a plea like that."

Eli stared into the empty space where the screen had been. *Meghann.* Just her name was enough to send his brain into a tailspin. He gritted his teeth. "I don't know who the hell you are, but I *do* know that you're a goddamned bastard. What gives you the right to go through my personal correspondence? My *life?*"

"Needs must, Mr. Brody. This is bigger than her or you."

"So, what?" said Eli, bitterness creeping into his voice. "I'm supposed to fold into a crying heap and do whatever you tell me to? Because of a five-year-old message?"

A smirk that Eli would have dearly loved to wipe off the old man's face twitched at the corner of his mouth. "Apparently not," he said. "But I thought you might appreciate the chance to . . . make amends, let us say, for the sins of your past." He leaned forward, fixing that cold-fish stare on Eli. "Your sister is still on Caledonia. You didn't go home five years ago when she asked, but help us now and you can make good on that. The Commonwealth will ensure that you're able to provide for her—if you help us."

Eli didn't say anything for a moment, considering the entire situation, viewing it from every possible angle. But each new turn yielded another dead end.

"You should have just left me there," he muttered finally. "I was *fine* until you guys came along and started digging up ancient history." He'd buried all those memories and feelings deep—deeper than Davidson Base underneath that frozen tundra. "Just send me back down." Even as the words came out of his mouth, he knew he didn't believe them.

The two men exchanged a glance. "That's not possible," said Fielding, shaking his head. "Now that Sabaea's gate is open again, the Illyricans are bound to start nosing around sooner or later. And if they found out that you were still alive? Well, for one thing that deal you made with the Sabaean government isn't going to look very good, is it?"

The aching feeling had only expanded, and he worried that if it got any larger it would turn inside out and consume him whole. The deal with the Sabaeans was going to look even worse when the entire truth came out.

"Not to mention," the old man added, "the information that we've disclosed so far is all highly classified, which I'm afraid makes you a security risk. If you're not going to work with us, then I will have no choice but to put you in protective custody."

Eli snorted. "We've had the carrot, now have the stick?"

The old man gave a beatific smile that wouldn't have looked out of place in a saint's portrait. "Not at all, Mr. Brody. I'm very confident that the situation won't come to that."

*I bet you are.* "Okay, let's say for argument's sake that I take your lunatic offer. What makes you so sure I won't run the first time I hit the ground?"

The old man exchanged a glance with Fielding. "Where, precisely, would you *go*?"

Eli stared bleakly at the desk in front of him. If he ran, he'd be looking over his shoulder for the rest of his life. Which, caught between two superpowers who were *both* gunning for him, probably wouldn't be very long.

And there was the matter of Meghann. Whatever else the old man was selling, he was right about her: Eli had screwed up big time. Not responding the first time had made him a bad brother, but turning down a chance to make things right might make him irredeemable as a person.

"Fine," he said, letting out a breath. "You win."

"Perhaps not the most *ringing* endorsement I've ever heard," said the old man. "But it'll have to do." He glanced at Fielding. "Inform the bridge that we'll be departing immediately." The soldier nodded and stepped out of the office, closing the door behind him.

"So I guess we're in a hurry."

"Our information is somewhat limited," the old man said, and if his tone wasn't exactly apologetic, there was something of regret in it. "All we've been able to dredge up is that *something* is happening three days from now. We assume that's when the project will be operational, but I'm afraid we don't even know that for sure."

"Jesus," said Eli, rolling his eyes. "And I'm the best plan you could come up with? What kind of fly-by-night operation are you guys running here?"

"Bureaucracy." The man raised his hands helplessly. "What can you do?"

"Seriously, though, you've got Mr. Scarypants out there, and probably a dozen more like him. Why not just air drop in a platoon?"

The old man laughed. "I'm afraid you've quite overestimated the resources at my disposal, Mr. Brody. That being said, I was prepared to deploy Captain Fielding and his team had Sabaea not taken this rather opportune moment to emerge from its isolation." He shook his head. "But they don't know the ground on Caledonia—not like you do. You're still our best chance." It was delivered smoothly enough, but Eli had enough experience to tell when something was being kept from him. Then again, in this guy's line of work, he probably had enough secrets to fill a fighter hangar.

"This thing the Illyricans are working on has you spooked, huh?" Eli said finally. "What the hell does it do?"

The old man leaned forward. "Honestly?" An almost wistful smile played on his lips as he shook his head. "We have no idea. But if you'd

seen the things the Imperium has in development in its weapons division
. . ." He trailed off, shaking his head. "Any one of them would be bad for
the innocent people of this galaxy—many of them would be devastating."
His eyes hardened. "You saw the Sabaean invasion firsthand, Mr. Brody.
We can't let that happen again. I know the Illyricans: they'll steamroll
right over the Commonwealth and the last of the independent systems.
Emperor Alaric's current advisors are not known for moderation. If they
believe they have an advantage, whatever equilibrium we've established
in the last five years will simply vanish, and the galaxy will once again be
thrust into open war.

"But not if I have anything to say about it."

The waves of intensity emanated so strongly from the old man that Eli
found himself unconsciously leaning backwards, away from him, ready
to curl up like a pill bug. He swallowed, his throat dry, and was only
saved from formulating a response when Fielding slipped back through
the door.

"We're underway, sir. Time to the wormhole gate is about an hour."
Beneath them, Eli could feel the telltale rumble of the ship's engines spinning up, as though catching a snippet of conversation in a language he
thought he'd long since forgotten.

"Thank you, captain."

"You give him his marching orders yet?" Fielding jutted his chin at Eli.

"I was about to," said the old man, turning his attention on Eli. "Your
assignment is this: We'd like you to try and make contact with our missing
asset and obtain any further information he might have. That's it." The
old man spread his hands. "See? Simple."

*Simple as a spacewalk: just close your eyes and put one foot in front of
the other.* He'd never quite gotten that expression until now. Sure, it was
simple—but it got you exactly nowhere.

"I wouldn't even know where to start. I may be from Caledonia, but
don't think they're going to welcome me back with open arms after I ran
off to join the 'Illyrican oppressors.' If your asset's a local, he probably
won't even give me the time of day." *Or throw a glass of water on me if I'm
on fire.*

"Oh, I think he'll talk to you," said the old man. He touched a control
on his desk and once more, a holographic screen appeared between them.

And, once again, the face it showed was as familiar to Eli as his own; it even looked similar, except with a pair of striking green eyes and bright red hair.

"Close your mouth," advised Fielding, "or flies'll get in."

Eli's head whipped up, eyes locking with the old man's blue gaze. "Is this a goddamn joke?"

"It's not a joke, Mr. Brody. Our missing asset is your brother, Eamon."

# CHAPTER FOUR

The sizzle of meat frying on a grill mingled with the hubbub of the crowd as Kovalic stepped into Parliament Square Market. Clustered around the low-slung concrete building at the center of the plaza, itself at the heart of Caledonia's capital of Raleigh City, were a patchwork quilt of stalls: farmers boasting of the freshness of their produce, artisans hawking their handcrafted goods, and every manner of food that could be baked, aged, or even served raw was on order. Kovalic's stomach would have rumbled if it weren't still unsettled from the time adjustment.

There'd been places like this on Earth when he was growing up. His dad, a baker, would set up a stall every weekend at the farmer's market, on occasion enlisting his son's help. During breaks the two would wander around the market, where his father would show him how to pick the ripest tomatoes and freshest cheese. But this was like looking in a pitted, slightly warped mirror: the cadence of speech, the smells, the colors were all just *slightly* off. A pang of nostalgia nicked him, a knife finding a chink in his armor.

He shook it off. Now wasn't the time. He was on the job, and professionals didn't have heartstrings to pluck.

Capitalizing on the milling crowds, brightly dressed street performers roved the square, juggling or doing magic tricks in exchange for a few marks, and the strains of at least four totally different—and largely incompatible—music styles assailed Kovalic's ears from each corner of the square.

In short, the market was the perfect place for a covert meeting: Little chance of eavesdropping, plenty of people in which to lose yourself and, of course, great shopping opportunities.

Kovalic was fingering a bolt of homespun cloth when the other man strolled over. Though he stood four inches shorter than Kovalic's own modest height, Tapper was built like a traffic bollard—you wouldn't want to drive into either of them. They made folks tough as riveted armor plating where he came from.

Despite the two decades he had on Kovalic, nobody would mistake the clean-cut gray-haired Tapper for an officer. Something about the way he carried himself: quick, efficient, with an air of potential brutality. Long after he'd someday retired—the very idea of which Kovalic had trouble wrapping his head around—people would still be addressing him as "sergeant."

"How was your trip?" asked Kovalic, letting the cloth slip through his fingers. The fabric was rough, but there was still something luxurious about the *idea* of handmade cloth in a day when everything that he wore was a machine-produced synthetic. Offering a smile to the vendor, he fell into step with the sergeant.

"Not bad," said Tapper, yawning, "although the in-flight entertainment was on the fritz. And you know what I noticed? Nobody likes to talk to strangers anymore. Disappointing, I say."

"I know how much you enjoy the art of conversation. No problem with immigration, then?" He let the din of the crowd wash over them.

"None at all."

"And our friend?" As much as Kovalic would have preferred to keep close tabs on Eli Brody, it had seemed safer to send his team on a separate shuttle flight. Brody's entry needed to be as bulletproof and aboveboard as possible— any red flags and the customs and immigration officers might just decide to run his biometrics against the Imperium's databases. Good as Brody's forged papers were, there was no easy way to change one's fingerprints or retina pattern. If the supposedly dead Elijah Brody turned up alive on Caledonia, you could bet the Imperium would have a lot of questions for him.

"He arrives in about half an hour, on the 15:40 from Jericho Station," said Tapper. Caledonia's day was close enough to the same length as Earth's that they'd stuck to the standard 24-hour clock, which was one less adjustment for Kovalic and his team to make. "Three has the eyeball."

"Excellent," said Kovalic, as the pair strolled down the path. They slowed to a stop in a no-man's-land between several booths, and Kovalic looked around to make sure they weren't in any danger of being overheard.

It didn't take much to see that Tapper was unhappy. The older man's arms were crossed over his chest and his face wore the expression he usually reserved for someone trying to make him eat broccoli: dubious and stubborn.

"What's on your mind?"

Tapper gave his head one short, sharp shake. "I don't like this, boss. Eamon Brody wasn't *our* asset, so why are *we* the ones down here looking for him?"

Kovalic sighed. "Because when Eamon's handler, James Wallace, stopped reporting in about a month ago, our colleagues at the Commonwealth Intelligence Directorate declined to look into the matter and instead swept the whole operation under the rug." He'd worked with a lot of intelligence agencies over the years—military and civilian, foreign and domestic—and none of them were known for being particularly altruistic. Still, this seemed unnecessarily callous.

Callous . . . or extremely suspect.

Tapper seemed to agree; if anything, the scowl on his face only darkened. "CID cut Wallace loose? On the ground? With no backup?" His voice had lowered to a dangerous growl. "What lame-ass excuse did they give for that?"

"You know how broadly the general likes to interpret his authority for 'oversight.' You think he bothered asking them?" The relationship between the Commonwealth's main intelligence agency and the general's small task force was frosty in a way that made the Sabaean tundra look temperate. But the general had the ear of the people that mattered, and in the end he tended to get his way. And if he didn't, well, he had a habit of going ahead and doing it anyway.

Tapper relented slightly, belligerence fading into his usual background grumpiness. "Fair point."

"Plus," Kovalic added, casting a quick look around, "this is all tied up with that mysterious Illyrican project. Eamon Brody was feeding the intel, Wallace was relaying it back to CID."

"Seems kind of a big thing for CID to drop like a hot potato."

"It does, doesn't it?" said Kovalic, raising his eyebrows significantly. "The general wants to know what the Illyricans are up to—and he wants to know yesterday. Something's going down two days from now; we just have no idea what."

"Under the gun, as usual." Tapper rolled his eyes.

"That's about the size of it. Based on the limited intel the general had, I'd say we've got about 36 hours to run Eamon Brody to ground . . . and maybe less than that." Above them, the sun had already started on its long descent toward the horizon.

"What happens if we don't?"

"Well, as the general would have it, the Illyrican Empire will roll over the Commonwealth, darkness will swallow the land, and we'll all be forced to live under the rule of an aging autocratic dictator whose policies are increasingly informed by a coterie of counselors with their own selfish interests at heart."

"Ah," said Tapper. "Must be Thursday, then."

"Also, we might be out of a job."

"Well *that* would be a damn shame. So what's our move?"

"Eli Brody will be looking for his brother. *We* need to find out what happened to Jim Wallace." He nodded to Tapper. "You know him, right?"

"Sure," said Tapper. Sometimes it seemed like he knew—or at least had drank with—almost everyone in the service. "I know ol' Grim Wallace. We spent some time raiding supply ships in the asteroid belt during his stint in covert; that was on Earth, after the occupation. Heard he mustered out, went civvy. Good man." His face took on a wistful expression. "And I will say this: the man could *cook*. We once intercepted a freighter full of provisions; I don't know how he pulled it off, but Grim made a braised lamb shank so tender it brought a tear to the eye." He shook his head slowly. "Haven't had a meal that good since."

"Family?"

"Ex-wife, I think." Tapper scratched his head. "No kids that I remember. Wasn't much of a guy for personal relationships. All business."

A familiar enough refrain. Personal relationships tended to be the first casualty of a career in covert operations, something to which Kovalic could attest personally.

"Any reason Wallace might go dark?" Kovalic asked.

A thoughtful expression crossed the sergeant's face. "If he thought the mission was going to be compromised, sure. But he's not a rookie; he's not going to panic for no reason."

"No . . . sympathies?" It wasn't common, but it did happen—Kovalic had arranged a couple of defections himself, including at least one that could rightfully be called "high profile." You never knew exactly what people were really thinking all the way down on the inside.

Tapper made a face. "Please. If Grim tried to defect, he'd have himself shot on sight."

"I had to ask."

"I know, boss." Tapper glanced at his wrist. "Look, Three asked for a break in about an hour; I said I'd spell him while he grabbed some food."

Kovalic nodded, then abruptly pulled out a round plastic Illyrican cash chit and a pen out of his pocket and scribbled something onto it. "See that this gets to Brody." He handed it to Tapper.

"Sure thing, boss. What about you?"

"I'm going to follow the only other lead we've got. We know that at least some of Wallace's reports found their way home." The general had worked every angle he could to try and find copies, but CID had been remarkably thorough. One of the general's sympathetic sources inside the agency had gotten them the termination order for the op, but everything else was gone. Secrecy was nothing new for spies, but there was a not so fine line between compartmentalization and cover-up.

"Right. Otherwise we wouldn't even be on this lovely vacation," Tapper said with a snort.

"I'm guessing they were sent via diplomatic courier. Which means Wallace had to have contact with someone through official channels."

"And that means the CID station in the Commonwealth embassy."

"I'm going to be honest," said Kovalic, breath whistling out from between his teeth. "I'd *really* hoped that we were going to be able to avoid letting CID know we were here."

Tapper hesitated. "You do know who the current head of station is, right?"

"Yeah," said Kovalic glumly.

"You could just save yourself the time and have *me* stonewall you."

Drumming his fingers against his thigh, Kovalic grimaced. "Well," he said finally. "I guess I'm just going to have to appeal to his better nature."

"Yeah?" said Tapper. "Try not to break any bones."

•

The deputy consul's office wasn't quite nice enough to make Kovalic reconsider a career behind a desk, but it was pretty close.

Perhaps fifteen minutes had elapsed, during which Kovalic had helped himself to a drink from the well-stocked liquor cabinet and put his boots up on the coffee table, when the room's owner, a reedy man with a pair of spectacles perched on his nose, pushed his way in. Under one arm he had tucked a briefcase, while the crook of his other overflowed with file folders. He peered down at the top one.

"Now, Mister . . . Fielding," he said, reading the name off the sheet. "I hear you're having an issue with your papers. What seems to be the prob . . ." His voice dissipated as he looked up at the man before him.

"*You.*" He spat the diphthong.

"You look overworked, Walter," said Kovalic. "Sit down and have a drink."

Drawing himself up, Walter Danzig stalked to his desk and dropped the multitude of files on top of it in a heap. He scowled at the top folder, as if it were the source of all his troubles, then turned his attention to his visitor.

"'Fielding,' is it?" said Danzig, pushing his glasses back up on his thin nose. "As I recall, the last time we met it was 'Defoe.' Working your way through literary history?"

Kovalic shrugged and swirled the liquor in his glass.

Shuffling files with a violence that he clearly wished he could apply to his unwanted guest, Danzig frowned. "What do you want?"

Kovalic glanced around, then circled his right forefinger in the air, a questioning look on his face.

"Oh, I assure you it's quite safe," snapped Danzig. "This office is swept daily by CID counter-intelligence."

Frankly, Kovalic would have felt better if the room had been checked for listening devices by someone he trusted more—the catering staff, perhaps—but he nodded. "I suppose it'll have to do."

Danzig sat down primly in his office chair and pulled it to his desk while unsuccessfully trying to hide his annoyance. "I presume you're here on official business, and this isn't just a social visit."

"I wasn't aware that we had a social relationship."

Danzig leveled an icy glare in his direction. "After what happened on Haran, I ought to have you tossed out of here on your ear—or deported!"

"For what it's worth, I am sorry about that particular . . . incident, but I was just doing my job. Seems you managed to land on your feet." He glanced around the room, taking in the furnishings and decorations.

"Anyway," Kovalic continued, "we both know it would take twenty hours for your fastest courier to make the round trip to Terra Nova for confirmation of my orders. Help me out and I'll be gone in less than that."

Danzig snorted. "Fantastic. Maybe after whatever you have in mind this time, I can end up with a transfer to the embassy on Sevastapol. I hear the temperature gets above freezing at least a couple times a year."

Kovalic ignored the dig. "I'm looking for an operative by the name of Andrews." They'd gotten Wallace's work name from the termination order for the op; at least it had given them a place to start.

The change of tack made Danzig blink, but he nodded. "Yes," he said shortly. "I know of him."

Kovalic eyed him, waiting, then cleared his throat. "And?"

Danzig crossed his arms. "I'm not prepared to disclose any further information without actual written orders."

Kovalic sighed in exasperation. "I don't *have* written orders, Walter. And I know that *you* know that, so let's not play this game. These are heightened circumstances."

"Oh, it's always 'heightened circumstances' or 'matters of galactic security' with you lot," said Danzig, his fingers forming twitching quotes around the phrases. "But you don't stick around to see the consequences of your actions. That's left for *us* to clean up."

Kovalic stared at him for a moment, then got to his feet and crossed to the desk. Danzig flinched as he reached over and plucked an object off the desk: a heavy paperweight in the shape of a silver orb with a flat bottom. Hefting it, Kovalic tossed it up and down a few times.

"Well, let's put it another way," said Kovalic. "You *don't* help me out, you won't have to worry about 'heightened circumstances' or 'matters of galactic security' or even 'being employed.' In fact, in all likelihood, unless you help me out, this whole building and everyone in it is likely to be rendered unimportant."

"What the hell is that supposed to mean?" said Danzig, his voice pitching up an octave. "Are you threatening me?"

Kovalic sighed and snagged the paperweight in midair, only to place it gingerly back on the desk. "Wouldn't dream of it. I'm just saying that we're looking down the barrel of what some in our line of work call a 'fundamental destabilization event.' You might be more familiar with its colloquial name: a shitstorm. It's heading toward us at full speed, and it's going to uproot anything standing in its way, including you and me. Got it?"

Danzig's fingers beat out a nervous rhythm on his thigh; Kovalic could almost hear the gears turning. "This is most irregular," the station chief said. "*Most* irregular." He sighed, and seemed to come to a decision that he could live with. "Fine. What do you want to know about Andrews?"

Clasping his hands behinds his back, Kovalic inclined his head. "Whatever you've got."

"It isn't much, I'm afraid. He came into the office a few months back with an op authorization. Strictly hush-hush, something about developing a local asset. Beyond that, he passed me a report every so often to send back in the diplomatic pouch."

"Did you read those reports?"

Danzig eyed Kovalic sharply. "Of course not. They were above my clearance level," he bridled. "If you examine the document receipts, you'll find the cryptographic seals quite intact."

Kovalic gave a tight smile. He was sure the files would still be sealed, had they not been wiped with the rest of the records. Inconvenient though Danzig's rule-abiding nature was, he couldn't claim it wasn't predictable. "When was the last time you received a communique from Andrews?"

At that question, Danzig frowned in thought. "His reports were often irregularly spaced, but they usually came every couple of weeks. I'm not sure when the last one was." He stood and crossed to an attractive lacquered armoire in the corner and swung open the door, revealing a military-grade safe, secured with a retinal scan and keypad.

Opening the safe with the requisite scan and code, the station chief pulled out a notebook. Kovalic wandered toward the cabinet, surveying it with professional interest. A LaoChe 5000, unless he missed his guess—tough to crack, almost impossible to do so quietly. He'd seriously toyed with the idea of sidestepping Danzig altogether, which would have given him immense joy, but it was just as well he hadn't: they definitely hadn't packed the equipment needed to break that sucker open.

"Does anybody else have authorization to open this safe?"

"Only in the event that something happens to me," said Danzig, closing the door to shield the contents from Kovalic inquisitive gaze. "There's a dual-person override that requires both my assistant, Lawson, and the resident head of CID counter-intelligence to be present in order to open it. Any failed attempt results in the immediate destruction of the safe's contents by micro-charge." He squinted. "You'll find we follow protocol to a 'T' here, Mr. Fielding. We work inside the system, not *around* it."

Kovalic swallowed a laugh. "I'd expect no less."

Danzig traced his finger down the page. "My last logged contact with Andrews was four weeks ago." He shook his head. "But a week or so after that I was notified that the op had been terminated."

That fit with the information the general had given them. "On whose authority?"

"Some mid-level operations officer." Danzig glanced down at the journal. "The codes checked out."

"And Andrews? Was there any note about what happened to him?"

"Not specifically. I assume he made his way off-world. My involvement ended with the termination."

Kovalic paced the length of the room, then turned back toward Danzig. "And nothing about any of this struck you as suspicious, or strange?"

Danzig blinked. "I don't know what you're asking, Mr. Fielding."

Of course he didn't. That would require thinking outside the box in which Danzig had sealed himself no less securely than his safe. "Was there *anything* odd about Andrews's op or the termination?"

"Not that I noticed," said Danzig, frowning. "Everything seemed to be by the book."

Kovalic leaned against the windowsill in contemplation. "It would be," he muttered.

Danzig's patience had clearly worn threadbare. "What the hell is all this about?"

"I wish I knew," Kovalic admitted. "Did you have any contact information for Andrews? A way to reach him?"

"Most of his communication was via dead drop, but emergency proto-col dictates that there be some sort of backup, in case something were to happen." Licking a finger, he reluctantly paged through the ledger. "Looks like he was renting a place over on Kelvin Boulevard."

He picked up a small square notepad and jotted down the address, then peeled off the top sheet and handed it to Kovalic. "Anything *else* I can help you with?" he asked, his voice tight.

Kovalic glanced at the note, then folded it up and slipped it into a pocket. He leaned forward, staring out the window. The sun was nearly at the horizon now, the encroaching darkness escorted by a fleet of incoming clouds streaked with the reds and pinks of sunset.

"I don't suppose you happened to keep a copy of any of Andrews's reports?"

"Certainly not. The instructions stipulated no trail. All physical and electronic copies were destroyed after transmission."

"Great," said Kovalic. "Everybody actually followed instructions for once." He sighed. "Well, as long I'm here, maybe you could give me a quick overview of the situation on the ground." He dropped into the chair on Danzig's side of the desk. The leather squeaked as he leaned back.

The gritting of Danzig's teeth was almost audible. "Quiet, mostly. We're far enough into Illyrican-controlled space that we're largely insulated from external politics."

"What kind of presence does the Illyrican military have on-world?"

"Modest. They've got a base, Westenfeldt, outside the capital city, but it's mainly used as a spaceport for shuttling Illyrican personnel up to the orbital shipyards, or for intersystem travel." Danzig pushed his glasses up on the bridge of his nose.

"Nothing out of the ordinary, though?"

"Nothing legitimate. The Caledonians are more than happy to sound off on all the nasty things they *think* the Illyricans are doing. This month alone I've heard about mind control drugs in the drinking water, a secret military base on one of Caledonia's moons, and satellites that seek out and erase pornography."

Kovalic grunted. The usual—or, well, unusual, he supposed—conspir-acy theories. "There's always something. And, as I recall, there's no love lost between the locals and the Illyricans. Even some sort of homegrown group, right?"

"Ah," said Danzig. "The Black Watch." Leaning over the desk, he tapped a few commands into his terminal; a holographic screen popped up, oriented toward Kovalic. "It's a self-styled resistance movement, based out of Raleigh City. Estimated membership of a couple hundred, though most of those are casual, drawn from a street gang called the Tartans. The core group of the Watch is only about twenty-five people, led by a man called De Valera."

Kovalic had come across the name in some file or other. "He's been at this for a while, hasn't he?"

Danzig nodded. "From what we can tell, he started the group himself twenty years ago, shortly after the occupation began, and we believe he's continued running it to this day."

"You 'believe?'"

A slight flush crossed Danzig's face. "We actually don't know much about him."

"Vitals?"

"No."

"A picture?"

"Not as such."

Kovalic drummed his fingers on the table. A ghost, then. Staying hidden for that long wasn't impossible, but it sure as hell wasn't easy. "What *do* you have on him, then?"

Danzig keyed something into his terminal and pages of text spooled across the display. "Angry tirades, mostly, posted on various networks over the last two decades, all of them insisting that Caledonia must rise up and free itself from Illyrican tyranny by any means necessary—though, as you can see, it appears force is preferred."

The text was replaced by a series of images, each showing the remains of what had clearly been buildings, but whose twisted, charred metal now resembled abstract sculpture more than architecture. "The Watch's chief modus operandi consists of attacks on Illyrican military and occasionally government targets, mainly bombings using crude but effective improvised devices.

"Under De Valera, the Black Watch have killed nearly three hundred people over the last twenty years, more than a few of them Caledonian 'sympathizers' who happened to work at those facilities."

"Christ," murmured Kovalic, shaking his head. He knew several career soldiers and operatives who didn't have that high a body count put together. A ghost *and* a butcher. Not a good combination. "How the hell has Eyes not nailed this guy?" He'd seen enough of the Imperial Intelligence Service's work up close and personal to have a grudging respect for his counterparts on the other side . . . on a purely professional level, of course.

Danzig removed his glasses and wiped them with a cloth. "I wouldn't be surprised if IIS finds itself . . . hampered in that regard. The Black Watch claims it takes its mandate from the populace and, despite the number of Caledonians killed in their attacks, the locals still aren't particularly willing to turn on them. De Valera may be a monster, but he's *their* monster, and he can be quite the charmer when it comes to patriotic rhetoric. If you'd like, I can provide you with copies of his manifestos and statements of responsibility."

Kovalic just shook his head, trying to ignore the roiling of his stomach. "Thanks. I think I'll pass—I've heard enough justifications of this particular brand of bullshit."

Dismissing the screen, Danzig tilted his head to one side. "And here I'd have thought you'd be a fan of taking the fight to the Illyricans."

"I don't object to the Black Watch's motives," said Kovalic, his chest tightening. If he hadn't joined the military, chances were he'd have been doing something pretty similar back on Earth right now, though he hoped with somewhat more restraint. "I object to their methods. Killing innocent bystanders—your own people—and brushing it off as 'collateral damage' doesn't really inspire my admiration. This De Valera asshole sounds like a real piece of work."

"Well," said Danzig. "It seems we agree on *something*, at least."

"I'll try not to get all mushy about it."

Danzig cleared his throat and looked back down at the stacks of files on his desk. "If there's nothing else . . ."

"There is *one* more thing," said Kovalic, leaning forward in his chair. "As long as we're on the subject of security, do you have an ID on your opposite number in IIS?"

Danzig's eyebrows arched. "Why do you ask?"

Kovalic shrugged. "No offense to your professional," he paused to glance around the room significantly, "*capacity*, but the Illyricans have been here longer, and the situation with the Black Watch means they need to have their ears to the ground." And, he didn't add aloud, *even if they can't catch this De Valera bastard, they still probably have more on him than we do—not that that would be hard, apparently.* The trick was getting them to share nicely.

Danzig grimaced, but once again leaned over and punched in the request at his terminal. The holographic screen above the desk shimmered and displayed a dossier.

"His name's Shankar—Major Jagat Shankar, Imperial Intelligence Service, Section D." The picture showed a man with a broad, jowly face, a nut-brown complexion, and a neat white mustache and goatee that were much too small for his generous countenance. "Ranking IIS officer in Raleigh City for about five years; prior to that, he was in counter-intelligence on Earth."

Danzing skimmed through the record, summarizing as he went. "He's an effective, if not particularly exacting officer, and a man of routine. Commutes into the office at almost the same time every day, takes lunch at the same time, leaves at the same time. Follows the same route every day. On Fridays, he stops for a drink at a local establishment—a pint of Bowman's stout, just the one—and then goes home. He's married with three children, the oldest of whom is at university back on Earth." Danzig shrugged. "CID doesn't have him expressly marked as a threat."

Kovalic eyed the picture and just barely contained the urge to snort at Danzig's assessment. "Oh, he's a threat all right. You just haven't gotten close enough to make him react. Every good intelligence officer—especially a highly-ranked one—knows that the opposite side's keeping tabs on them." Danzig colored under Kovalic's sideways glance, but the operative steamed forward before the other man could get in a word edgewise. "Routines make surveillance teams comfortable, but more than that, they make them *sloppy*. You never know how the bear will react until you actually poke it with a stick." He pressed a few keys on Danzig's terminal and had a secure copy of the dossier sent to his comm.

Down to work, then. Cracking his knuckles, Kovalic leaned forward to peer at the screen. He glanced up at Danzig, hovering nearby. "Sorry, I need to file a quick report. Classified, of course," he added apologetically.

"If you could just give me the room for a minute?" He smiled. "Wouldn't want to break protocol."

Danzig's expression froze on his face, lips pressed together in a thin line. Without another word, he spun on his heel and marched stiffly from his own office.

When the door closed behind him, Kovalic leaned back in his chair and allowed himself a brief, quiet chuckle before opening up a new message to the general.

# CHAPTER FIVE

From space, Caledonia was a subtle patchwork of different shades of brown, from the almost gray of its ore-laden mountains to the rust brown, dried blood color of its scrublands. But the dark blue-green of its seas broke the monotony, lending just enough color to turn it into something more than a clod of dirt: an entire world.

Granted, Eli hadn't spent much time looking at his homeworld from space on this trip—he'd been too busy concentrating on staying calm, despite the cold sweat trickling down the side of his head. It hadn't been made any easier by the throbbing headache and persistent dry mouth that were his reward for having sobered up. His hands, white-knuckled, had barely let up off the armrests for the entire eight-hour ride from Jericho Station. *Pretty sure my cramps have cramps.*

So he couldn't conceal his relief when the commercial transport finally set down at the Raleigh City Spaceport, bouncing slightly as its landing struts flexed under the pressure. The engines whirred to a stop, leaving only a brief respite of silence before the passengers started unbuckling and wrestling their luggage out of the overhead storage compartments.

Everyone except for Eli. He took a deep breath as the lights came back on and ran a shaky hand through his hair, recently cropped short by a Commonwealth military barber. He was still getting used to the bristly feeling, like petting a cat the wrong way.

"First time?" asked the man who'd been seated beside him, a portly older gentleman. His bushy eyebrows wriggled like fuzzy caterpillars.

"It's, uh, been a while."

The man nodded knowingly. "You coming or going?"

Eli thought about it. "Neither, really. Well, both I guess."

"Complicated, huh?"

"Yeah, you might say that."

As the passengers filed off, Eli slung his military duffle—on loan from the Commonwealth's stores—over his shoulder and traipsed out after them. His current clothes had been borrowed from the quartermaster on the *Indefatigable* as well: a casual jacket, shirt, and trousers.

At least he'd gotten to keep his boots. They'd lasted from his days in the Illyrican Navy all the way through five years of captivity on Sabaea, and he wasn't about to give them up now. If the Sabaeans had had their way, the boots would have been tossed on the nearest rubbish heap—just in case they'd contained a secret weapon or been molded from a highly explosive resin—but Eli had decided to put up a fuss. Not for any sinister reason, but because they were comfortable and he'd figured the Sabaeans wouldn't have much interest in keeping him comfortable. *Small victories.*

Stepping onto the jetway, he glanced through one of the small portholes that looked out onto the tarmac. For a moment he was fifteen again, peering through the chain-link fences around the spaceport on a blistering summer day, smelling the fuel and baking asphalt while feeling in his chest the rumble of transports and freighters arriving or taking off. The only ships at Raleigh City Spaceport were civilian; Westenfeldt, the main Illyrican military base for the region, was thirty kilometers west and its perimeter was highly defended. If he'd gotten as far as the fence there, he probably would have been disintegrated.

Since the duffle bag was all he had, and all it contained were a few more sets of clothes, he walked straight to the immigration control station.

"Good day, sir," the young woman behind the desk said as he approached. "May I see your identification card, please?"

Eli was unreasonably proud that his hand didn't tremble when he handed the papers over. Much as he'd worried about getting through security, it seemed easy enough after the flight itself. He put on a smile, hoping it didn't look too sickly.

The woman scanned the ID card and inspected her monitor, glancing briefly at Eli's face for confirmation. He kept the idiot grin fixed in place. *I'm Marcus Wellington. I'm Marcus Wellington. I'm Marcus Wellington.*

"Welcome home, Mr. Wellington," she said brightly, handing his card back. Holding his breath, he kept smiling as she continued. "I hope you find everything just as you left it."

*Wish I could say the same.* He nodded to her and trucked his gear through the checkpoint.

At the bottom of the ramp, the automatic doors of the terminal slid aside, and the heat rolled over him in a thick, heavy wave. During the day, Caledonia's capital region was sweltering nearly year round—not something he'd missed, despite his frigid time at Davidson Station. With a sigh, he looked around the barren arrivals terminal.

*So, here I am . . . Now what?*

The air whooshed out of Eli like somebody had let go of a balloon. He'd been running at full steam since the shuttle had picked him and Fielding up from Sabaea twenty-four hours earlier. Between the stomach-churning flight and the lack of any alcohol it had all been a bit hazy, but the heat and the dirt had dragged him back to reality. And in that reality, he wasn't entirely sure what he was supposed to do next.

Not that he'd expected to find a guy in a suit holding a sign with his name on it. During Fielding's curt briefing on the *Indefatigable*, he'd only said that he or someone on his team would make contact once Eli was on-world, but neither a time nor a place had been specified. The briefing had also been short on leads to locate Eamon; that, as the operative had reminded Eli, was why he was here after all.

*Only where the hell am I supposed to start?* What information the Commonwealth had on his brother could only charitably be called "thin." They'd tried all the usual planetary databases, but even the vaunted efficiency of the Imperium had done little to improve the spotty nature of Caledonian bureaucracy. People frequently slipped through the cracks of the system, whether by accident or by design, and while there had been records of Eamon's birth and meager public school attendance, the system lost track of him after his juvenile arrests.

As for Meghann, the Commonwealth operatives had promised that Eli would get a chance to see her as soon as he'd located his brother. Fielding and his boss were holding all the cards on this one, which didn't make the pit in Eli's stomach any smaller. In his head, he could still hear the message they'd played back, her pleas for him to come home.

*Home.* He'd been avoiding thinking about it, largely because he'd sworn that he would never go back to that damn shoebox of an apartment. He fancied he could still hear the echo of the door slamming behind him from the last time he'd walked out, his father's voice—scratched and hoarse from years of work in the mines—shouting that Eli would never cross the threshold as long as Connor Brody drew breath. *Well, that much held true.*

His mother and Meghann had been the only ones to say goodbye; he could still remember his sister clinging tightly to him, trying not to cry. His mother had slipped him a sandwich she'd made him for the trip: ham and cheese, his favorite.

But all of that had paled beside Eamon's reaction. At least his father had said *something.* By that point Eamon had been spending a lot more time with the guys his own age; they worked in the mines by day, then at night it was off across town to get up to who knew what mischief. His rhetoric had gotten increasingly fiery as well, constantly harping on about the "unlawful occupation" of their world and "oppression of the masses." Eli had been surprised his brother had managed not to spit every time he'd mentioned the Illyricans.

So when Eli had told him he was going to the academy, he'd expected an outburst. A rant. Perhaps even a knock-down, drag-out fight. He'd braced himself for the worst. But in the end Eamon hadn't said a word—just looked right through him, like he didn't even know him, then turned around and walked away. When he thought about it, Eli realized that he couldn't even remember the last words his brother had said to him.

Eli shook his head, feeling a weight descend in his stomach. He was going to have to go home; it was the only lead he had.

And even that wasn't particularly solid. His parents had died while he was at the academy—a skimmer accident—and in one of her subsequent messages Meghann had told him that Eamon wanted to find the two of them a new place to live. Eli assumed his brother had followed through on that at some point during the last five years. Still, somebody from the old neighborhood might remember Eamon or know where he lived. With any luck, Eli and, hopefully, Meghann, would be off this dirtball in no time.

Hoisting his bag, he joined the queue climbing aboard the transpo bus to the city.

It was about a twenty-minute trip from the spaceport into Raleigh City proper. The dirt-caked windows of the transpo bus didn't offer a very good view. Some might laugh and say that there wasn't much to see anyway, but Eli disagreed: dirt-covered though they might be, he'd always felt the hills and scrublands of Caledonia had held a kind of austere, desolate beauty. At least, the parts that had remained unspoiled by people's attempts to strip mine them for every bit of their worth. He'd been born on Caledonia's rocky plains and they remained the most wide open space he'd ever lived; after all those years of cramped quarters on spaceships and military bases he could feel the tug of freedom stronger than ever. It was the same wide openness that had drawn him to spaceflight—but without the whole, you know, gut-wrenching fear.

The transpo bus's speed began to decrease as they hit the city's outer limits. The yellowish light that filtered through the windows started to flicker into shadows as they passed between taller, manmade structures. Everything closed in around them and that feeling of openness was replaced once again by pressure pushing in from every side.

Eli held onto the cool metal bar atop the seat in front of him as the bus bounced through the cramped city streets. After another few minutes, the vehicle shuddered to a stop and an automated voice announced that they had arrived at the city transit hub. Eli retrieved his bag and stepped down into the terminal.

It was late afternoon in Raleigh City, about four o'clock. The sun—or what you could see of it through the haze—was sinking on the horizon, and over the next couple hours the streets would bustle with those on their way home from work. For now, though, the city was eerily quiet.

Eli's eyes were drawn upward to the glowing names and logos of the most prominent Illyrican and Caledonian firms splashed across their high-rises: Thane Systems, Forth Technologies, the Imperial Bank and Trust, Galway Corporation. The skyline had changed shape, acquired a few new buildings, like an old friend with a new haircut. He ran his fingers through his own hair again, much as he could given its shortness, and gave a rueful snort. *We've all changed, I guess.*

Craning his neck even further skyward, Eli caught the familiar brightly glowing points in the sky, even in the late afternoon light: not stars, but the orbital ship-building facilities that drove so much of Caledonia's life and work. Since the occupation, Caledonia had become the primary ship construction and refitting outpost for the Illyrican military, though it still produced many of the galaxy's commercial ships as well.

In spite of himself, he found a smile crossing his face. Stars had been hard to come by once the Brody family had moved to the city. So the planet's two moons—erratic Aran, whose orbit regularly took it far from Caledonia, and the closer, larger Skye—and those shipyards had made up the constellations of his youth. *My old friends.* At least some things didn't change.

The jostle of the crowd in front of the terminal knocked this thought from his mind. Shaking his head, he skirted the taxi stand; he might have been away for almost a decade, but that didn't change the fact that the city's autocabs were for tourists and suckers. He could take a crosstown bus from here, then swap to the line that would take him home, but the rising tide of nostalgia made the idea of walking surprisingly appealing.

The soles of his boots rasped like sandpaper over the sidewalks as he navigated the streets of Raleigh City. Everything, even the tall buildings, looked smaller than he remembered. Not physically—Eli was pretty sure he'd been done growing by the time he'd shipped off to the academy—but the reality of the place was dwarfed by his memory, in which it had all seemed much more imposing. It had the disturbing effect of making everything that had happened in the past decade seem like a dream. Had he ever really left? Joined the Illyrican military? Been stuck at an arctic installation on a remote planet for five long years?

And then, as he waited to cross a boulevard, he caught a whiff of the city's distinctive smell and his eyes widened. *Well* that *hasn't changed.* A heady bouquet of engine exhaust from the ground-skimmers and transpo buses mixed with the sharp sea air and just a hint of stale beer. He could remember asking his dad about that last one when he'd been a little kid, but Connor Brody hadn't been a man for answering questions, simple or otherwise. It wasn't until his own first trip to a bar at the age of sixteen that he'd put two and two together and gotten thoroughly drunk. *Threw up in the middle of the street, too, as I recall.* It hadn't been the last time for either of those.

He slowed as he reached a large plaza, arranged around a square park. Someone had spent considerable time and resources cultivating a carefully manicured patch of greenery, in contrast with the general brown of Caledonian grass. Little question who, either: In the midst of the park stood a bronze statue about two stories high, dressed in a classical style with robes draped artfully over his body, one hand outstretched as though issuing a blessing and the other clutching a scroll. The face was chiseled, both literally and figuratively, with sharp, stern features and blank, unseeing eyes.

Eli came to a stop and let the duffle bag slide from his grip to the ground. *Bloody Alaric. It wasn't enough the old bastard took over our home—he wanted us to love him for it.* Emperor Alaric II of the Illyrican Empire had been middle-aged when he'd begun his conquest, and that was roughly the age at which the statue depicted him. That had been over twenty years ago, though, and the conqueror in the meantime had grown old and, if the persistent rumors were to be believed, infirm.

There were streamers hanging from the bottom of the monument, and as he looked around he could see other banners that had been affixed to lamp posts and strung across streets: crimson and gold, the colors of the Illyrican Empire. The traditional decorations of the highest of Illyrican-imposed holidays—the Emperor's Birthday. *That time of year already, huh?*

He'd lost all track of time while on Sabaea, but a quick glance at the comm Fielding had given him showed that the Emperor's Birthday was in fact just a couple of days away. Looking around, he tried to picture the square thronging full of people getting drunk, followed by a riot or two—the locals weren't big fans of pomp and circumstance, especially when it was a reminder of their continued subjugation. *If there's anything Caledonians enjoy, it's a good riot. Practically a national tradition.*

This particular statue of Alaric—and there were many scattered about the planet, because "humility'" was not in the emperor's vocabulary—was an especially popular target for abuse. Though the Caledonian Public Works department had removed the frequent and colorful vandalism almost as fast as it appeared, Eli wondered what the Illyricans would have said if they'd known that more than one morning had found a civil servant cleaning off insults that she herself had scrawled there the night before. *Probably something along the lines of "put your back into it."*

Then again, maybe the Imperium had caught on. Eli's grin faded. The statue was freshly polished and gleaming brighter than ever; any trace of spray-on graffiti eradicated. There were still spots where people had actually carved things into the metal—"crims go home" and "occupy this"—but even they were faded and buffed to the point of illegibility. Actually, he and Eamon had once taken their dad's pocket knife to this very statue, producing a rather respectable if crude illustration of male genit—

"Oi, mister."

Eli looked over his shoulder to find a grizzled but hopeful-looking old man dressed in tattered clothes and holding out his hand.

"Spare a mark for a veteran of the Occupation War?" The man rubbed his filthy thumb and index finger together.

Eli jammed his hands in his pockets, searching for some of the currency Fielding had given him on the *Indefatigable*. Producing a handful of the plastic chits that the Illyricans used as cash, he flipped through the various denominations, trying to ignore the hawkish eyes of the man before him.

"Here you go." A pair of five-mark chits rattled into the old man's hand.

"Bless you, sir. Bless you." The old man clasped his dirt-stained hands around Eli's. His grin showcased a full and surprisingly white set of teeth. "You're a good man, sir. A good man."

"Er, thanks."

"Too many youngsters got no respect for their elders these days," said the man, still pumping Eli's hand. "I fought the crims at Kinsale, you know."

"Oh, really?" He dimly recalled the battle from a history class—like so many of them, a slaughter by the Illyricans. "Well, uh, thanks. Keep up the good work." *Keep up the good work?* "I've gotta go."

"Course you do, sir. Course you do." He relinquished Eli's hand at last. "You have a good day, now." With another grin, he strolled off down the street, whistling a jaunty tune to himself.

Eli shook his head, then suddenly noticed that though he'd given the man two fives, he was somehow still holding a twenty-mark piece. About to call after the old man, he flipped the disc over and his mouth snapped shut. In neat black letters around the edge of the obverse were the words "295 W. Highland; 1900H. -F"

He looked around for the panhandler, but the man had vanished into the bustling rush hour crowds that had begun to surround the square.

*Cloak and dagger*, Eli thought, rolling his eyes. Why not just send him a comm message?

His heart thumped slowly. Maybe Fielding thought the comm was bugged? Or maybe he thought Eli was being followed? After all, if the Commonwealth had found him, surely the Illyricans could as well. Trying to look casual, Eli surveyed the area, scanning the crowd for familiar faces. Had he passed one of those women at the terminal? Was that the man he'd sat next to on the shuttle?

The world spun slowly and Eli leaned back against the statue and took a deep breath. *Don't get carried away.* Fielding was a spy; all this subterfuge probably came second nature to him. No reason to think that the Illyricans knew anything. As far as the Imperium was concerned, Elijah Brody was dead and the only person who had showed up on Caledonia was the perfectly innocent Marcus Wellington.

With that note of sanity injected, Eli rubbed a hand against the stubble on his chin and hefted his bag once again. Fielding wanted to meet in less than three hours; by that point, he'd better be well on his way to finding Eamon. Home or not, this was going to be the last trip he made to Caledonia; that he swore.

Fortunately, Caledonia's traditionally inefficient public transit authority hadn't developed a burning need for self-improvement in the last nine years. The same bus routes that he'd taken as a kid were still in operation, and a half-hour ride through the winding streets of Raleigh City deposited him on the outskirts of the planet's capital.

Upham had been designed by the colony's civil engineers to be a pleasant, tree-lined residential district of Raleigh City, but as so often seemed to happen, the place had fallen into disrepair and neither the local government nor the Illyricans seem to have been interested in spending the money to improve it.

The few street lights that were still operating flickered to life as the last vestiges of sunlight faded into evening. Eli shouldered his duffle bag and stepped through the forbidding concrete pillars that marked the entrance to Block 17—the One-Seven, as it was called by its residents. The knot that had settled into his stomach since he'd arrived on-world was accruing mass in a decidedly black hole-ish fashion.

If anything, the One-Seven looked even worse than it had when Eli had lived there. Broken bottles and discarded food packets littered the ground, and the few plants and saplings that had once lined the walkway into the block proper had been uprooted and removed, leaving only dry patches of dirt. There wasn't even any brown grass here, just concrete and metal.

High above rose the towers, a few lit windows shining against the dark background. Each block had four residential units, twenty-two stories tall, and each story contained a dozen apartments of various sizes. In theory, the towers had been designed for a thousand-some residents each—in reality, they'd housed at least twice that. Families of six or ten were regularly packed into apartments meant for two or three. Pay from the mining companies had always been low, and it had gotten even worse when the Imperium had nationalized the industry, citing matters of "Imperial security."

As he rounded the corner of the 17-East tower toward his own childhood home of 17-North, Eli was struck by how much brighter and more open the block seemed, even in the twilight. Nothing like the claustrophobic environment of his childhood where he'd felt constantly hemmed in on every side. The wind whipped at him, raising tears in his eyes.

It took him a minute to realize exactly why the block felt so much more open, why the sky in front of him seemed a far vaster expanse than the one he'd known as a kid.

The enormous 17-North residential block, his childhood home and his best chance at finding Eamon, was gone.

# CHAPTER SIX

**K**ovalic strode with purpose down the street, hands jammed in his pockets, eyes front. Raleigh City's late afternoon crowd brushed past him, most on their way home from work, all ignoring the single man threading his way upstream.

He'd spent an hour after leaving the Commonwealth Embassy strolling around the city, getting his bearings and reviewing the matter at hand. Danzig hadn't quite been the font of useful information that he'd hoped but, despite that, the bureaucrat had been more helpful than he had expected. What he wouldn't give for a copy of just *one* of Jim Wallace's reports: putting together a puzzle was infinitely easier when you had the picture on the front of the box.

As he reached the next intersection, he glanced up at the address on the illuminated street sign then took a sharp right onto Kelvin Boulevard. The busy thoroughfare divided the less well-to-do neighborhood known as the Flats from the more affluent Highgate area. Strange to think that the difference of a dozen yards represented a median income change of roughly four or five hundred percent, but that was exactly the case. Then again, the rich and the poor had always lived within spitting distance, even on Earth—it was just a matter of how much heed they paid each other.

Another few blocks and Kovalic reached the address Danzig had given him. Unsurprisingly, it was on the seedier side of the street, in a tenement house that had clearly never seen better days, jammed between a place that offered payday loans and a hole-in-the-wall eatery that could only have passed health codes by the good graces of a guardian angel or straight-up bribery. Strangely enough, that didn't make the smell of cooking sausage wafting from the doorway any less appealing, though the tubby man in the greasy, sweat-stained shirt who was standing at the door effectively curbed Kovalic's appetite.

Climbing the crumbling steps up to the door of Wallace's building, Kovalic let himself in. The foyer, no less dingy than the outside, narrowed toward the building's rear while a set of threadbare, carpeted stairs rose to the second floor. A vacant front desk to his left said that this wasn't the kind of place where people wanted their movements accounted for by an automated kiosk. Here, it was face-to-face interaction, probably handled in cash.

As if summoned by the thought, a weedy, thin-faced elderly woman appeared behind the counter. Though she tottered like she might fall over, her green eyes sharply sized up Kovalic—his dress, his bearing, his clean-cut appearance—and hung a price tag on him.

"Two 'undred marks a week, love." Her voice creaked like an old door, and Kovalic couldn't help but think of the tales his father had told him of the witch Baba Yaga and her chicken-legged house.

He resisted glancing around for a mortar and a pestle and instead donned his best dealing-with-people face. "Actually, I'm looking for a friend of mine who's staying here."

The woman didn't reply, just sat and watched him expectantly. Kovalic fancied he could hear her mentally tallying the money she was losing by him standing there.

"A Mr. Andrews?"

"Never 'eard of 'im," said the woman automatically, but her eyes darted involuntarily toward the stairs.

Kovalic produced a twenty-mark chit from his pocket and casually slid it onto the counter, one finger pinning it in place. The woman eyed it and shrugged.

"We 'ave a lot of folks in and out," she wheedled. "I can't be expected to remember 'em all."

With a raised eyebrow, Kovalic placed a second chit down next to the first. The woman eyed them hungrily.

"Andrews, you say?" She gave the appearance of racking her memory, and then her face cracked into a broad grin of yellowed and missing teeth. "Oh, yes, Mr. Andrews. Big gentleman; 'andsome, too. Lovely man. Paid tree months in advance, 'e did. Room 207."

With a nod and a smile, Kovalic slid the chits over the counter. "Thanks for your help, ma'am."

The woman waved her hands and the credit chits vanished into her safekeeping—never to be seen again, Kovalic trusted. He crossed to the stairs and already had his foot on the first step when the woman called out to him.

"I'm not sure 'e's *in*, love. 'Aven't seen 'im in a while."

"That's all right," said Kovalic over his shoulder. "I can wait."

The stairs, as befit their advanced age, protested as he climbed to the second floor. At the top, hallways stretched off to the left and right with no sign indicating which rooms lay in which direction. Kovalic tried the left hand corridor first, working his way down the hall while checking the room numbers. That turned out to be a dead end, terminating in what, upon inspection, appeared to be a shared bathroom. This wasn't exactly the kind of place that prided itself on its facilities, he supposed. He reversed course to check the other direction.

Room 207 proved to be halfway down the other corridor. The door looked like all of the others: wooden, thin, with an old-fashioned mechanical lock. It showed no sign of having been forced—no splintered wood, no undue scratches other than what looked like claw marks probably left by a stray cat. He knocked quietly.

There was no response from within, so he crouched down and studied the knob. Wallace was a pro—he would have left something to prevent his room from being tampered with. He scanned the door's seams and peered at the lock, but turned up nothing.

Reaching into his jacket pocket, Kovalic slid out the thin folder that contained his lock picks and pulled out the torsion wrench and one of the long rake picks. Most operatives didn't bother to learn lock picking these days; the vast majority of locks one encountered were electronic, not mechanical, and for those that weren't, many favored the speed and simplicity of a pick gun. There was just no appreciation for history or the lost arts in his line of work. For him, though, there was something about the careful work of picking a lock that he found surprisingly calming.

The lock on Andrews's door was cheap, yielding up its secrets in under a minute. Kovalic smiled as he heard it click open, carefully replacing his picks into his pocket. Next he removed a small telescoping mirror with a light attached. This he ran under the edge of the door, looking for any of the telltale signs of a tripwire or other trigger.

Nothing.

He frowned. The only thing more worrisome than finding a trap was *not* finding a trap. Getting to his feet, Kovalic slowly pushed the door open with his foot and surveyed the room. The curtains were drawn, leaving the entire apartment cast in a twilight dimness. Kovalic waited at the doorway until his eyes adjusted. There was a small foyer before the main room, but his view inside was obscured by the angle of the entryway wall.

He checked again, scanning the room for anything Wallace might have left to keep himself apprised of visitors—could be as simple as a piece of gum on the floor—but still came up with nothing. Which meant either there really was nothing there or that Wallace was a lot better at hiding things than Kovalic was at finding them.

There wasn't a lot of choice in the matter, so Kovalic took the risk and stepped inside, closing the door behind him. No klaxon sounded, there was no telltale click of a grenade trap being armed—nothing. Somehow that was the opposite of reassuring.

He walked slowly down the short entryway, pausing as he reached the end of the wall that blocked the view of the room at large, then peered around the corner.

The room wasn't huge; it extended maybe another fifteen feet in that direction. In one corner, against the back wall, was a single bed, rumpled from use. Between Kovalic and the bed was a small kitchen table flanked by a countertop and simple kitchenette; against the opposite wall was a cheap, rickety desk and equally suspect bureau. There was no en-suite bathroom that he could see but there had been that shared one at the other end of the hall.

Other than that, the room was more or less empty. Operatives tended to lead a spartan existence, especially when they were in the field, and Wallace appeared to have been no exception.

Kovalic walked over to the desk, then used the end of his telescoping mirror to jimmy the drawer open. Empty. The bureau was a little more rewarding: piles of shirts, trousers, socks, underwear—all clean, but not folded or neatly put away. In fact, they gave the distinct impression of having been rifled through. Frowning, Kovalic poked at the piles, swishing them around with the end of his mirror. If somebody *had* gone through them, then it looked like anything interesting had been removed.

Upon closer investigation, the same went for the rumpled bed. From the way it sat off kilter on its wooden platform, the mattress had clearly been pulled up, its underside examined. Kovalic turned back to the room at large, letting his eyes drift across it—no sign of a struggle. Between that and the lack of countermeasures he didn't like his conclusions.

Someone had already turned over Wallace's apartment. They'd clearly been looking for something, so Wallace hadn't told them where to find it, whatever it was. The real question, to Kovalic's mind, was whether or not they'd located it all the same. Kind of an existential query, unfortunately: the only way to know would be to find it himself. Which was going to be tricky, since he didn't know what he was looking for.

Sighing, Kovalic started at one end of the apartment and did a full sweep. He checked the undersides of every drawer, the space behind the drawers, and behind and underneath the bureau itself. He checked every inch of the desk, the metal chair that sat next to it—including unscrewing the feet—and behind the room's lone painting, a grotesque mass-produced landscape that looked like something out of an impressionist's nightmare. He pulled up the bed again, producing a knife and slicing through the mattress to check the inside; he felt a little bad about that, but it was a cheap mattress, and he *had* already handed over forty marks.

None of the cupboards in the kitchen escaped his attention either, but they yielded only cooking ingredients like olive oil and vinegar, a variety of dried herbs and spices, and a half bulb of garlic.

The microwave oven was empty and the small refrigerator had a couple bottles of juice, a small container of milk that Kovalic uncapped to smell and subsequently wished he hadn't, and a few containers of fruit and produce that were also well past their prime. The ice cube bin in the freezer had congealed into a single solid mass and the stack of frozen dinners had developed a thin layer of frost.

There were two trash bins—one in the kitchen, which a quick survey suggested held only some food refuse, and one tucked under the desk that provided the first interesting find: a discarded package for a small, off-the-shelf data chip. But there was no terminal or comm—or the remainders thereof—in evidence; so either Wallace had taken his device with him or whoever had turned over the place had taken it. In which case, they might have the data chip, too.

Leaning against the wall, Kovalic surveyed the room with a frown. Taking a deep breath, he let his eyes slide closed, then mentally flipped back through everything he'd seen and heard—in the apartment, about Wallace, about this mission.

The vaguely unsettled feeling in his stomach told him he'd missed something. No scientist had ever been able to pin down exactly why the gut had developed as some sort of intuitive radar, and really, Kovalic thought, wasn't that the point? Some things defied rational, scientific explanation.

He opened his eyes. The place had a kitchen. That was unusual; most boarding houses of this type would probably make do with a hot plate or assume that people would eat out.

Wallace, though, had been a cook of some repute, at least according to Tapper. He'd have specifically picked a room with a kitchenette so he could cook meals himself; the ingredients in the cupboard bore that out.

His gaze fell upon the refrigerator, and he tensed. Pushing himself off the wall, he quickly crossed to the appliance and pulled open the freezer door. Instant dinners were probably better today than they were a hundred years ago, but they still didn't compare to a home-cooked meal.

Pulling out the four frosted boxes, he put them down on the table and inspected each one. Two were frozen pizzas, the third a frozen Indian meal, and the last a traditional Chinese dish. All appeared to still be sealed—except one of the pizzas, where the flap wasn't quite flush. He produced a pocket knife and flipped it open, then deftly sliced under the box flap, folding it back. Tape, not glue, was holding it in place.

Upending the box, a slab of pizza slid out and hit the table, but nothing else. Kovalic frowned, then held the box up to peer inside. At the far end, again affixed with a square of tape, was a tiny data chip. Grinning, he reached inside and pulled it out, turning it over in his hand. A little bit of frost had collected on the outside, which he brushed off, but these things were rated for storage well below freezing, so as long as he let it warm up a bit before plugging it in, any data on it should be intact.

Slipping the chip into his pocket, he replaced the pizza in the box and resealed it, then returned the frozen meals to a stack in the freezer, leaving the taped side to the rear. If whoever had tossed the place hadn't found the chip the first time, they might be back. No use giving away too much.

He gave a last glance around the apartment just in case another ingenious hiding place presented itself, then exited the way he'd come in, carefully locking the door. It might be locking the barn door after the horses had bolted, but any extra time he could buy to prevent these people from knowing someone else was interested in Wallace was a bonus.

Turning back toward the stairs, he was just in time to see a man reach the top and look down the hallway at him. Average height, he wore a thigh-length ratty brown coat and a hat. His dark eyes locked on Kovalic, and he started, slowly but deliberately, in his direction.

Kovalic swore under his breath but kept a neutral expression on his face as he continued toward the stairway. There wasn't a good alternative; any way out of here was going to mean going past this guy, whoever he was.

When they were about ten feet apart, the man slowed, and gave Kovalic a nod. "Excuse me, sir. Do you live here?"

"Nope," said Kovalic, coming to a stop himself. "Just visiting."

"Can I ask who?"

Kovalic raised an eyebrow. "And you are?"

The man reached into an inside pocket and Kovalic tried to ignore the automatic impulse to rush him; the longer he could keep his "'average citizen" cover, the better. But instead of a gun the man produced a black wallet, which he flipped open to display a badge and ID card.

"Special Agent Messner, Caledonian Security Agency."

Whatever Kovalic been expecting, that wasn't it. CalSec was planetwide law enforcement—the feds. Less corrupt than local cops, to be sure, but one hundred percent more cooperation with the Illyricans.

He blinked as Messner returned the badge to his pocket and leaned casually against the wall, sizing up Kovalic.

"So, can you tell me who you were visiting?"

"A friend."

The expression on Messner's face was a decided flavor of skeptical. "Their name?"

"Rogers."

Messner frowned; that clearly hadn't been the answer he'd expected or wanted. Then again, that was probably going to be the first in a long line of disappointments for Agent Messner today. The cop's hand drifted to his hip, hitching in his belt.

"The landlady said somebody matching your description asked after a resident—a Mr. Andrews?"

Kovalic smiled apologetically. "Afraid it wasn't me. I guess I've just got one of those descriptions."

Eyes narrowed, Messner was about to say something when a woman with a long black ponytail reached the top of the stairs.

"Messner?"

The agent glanced over his shoulder. "Down here, Liang. I got—"

Agent Messner's day went from bad to worse as Kovalic swept into motion. He'd closed the distance between them while the cop was still looking back at, presumably, his partner; Messner saw the alarm on her face and started to turn, but he was still unbalanced, leaning against the wall.

Using that to his advantage, Kovalic hooked his foot inside Messner's legs and yanked them out from under him. The man slid down the wall, his head bouncing off the plaster. It wasn't the first time he'd had to assault a law enforcement officer, and it probably wouldn't be the last, but Kovalic always felt a little bit guilty; after all, they were just doing their job.

But he was doing his.

With a shout, the woman came charging in, reaching for a sidearm holstered in the small of her back.

He couldn't reach her fast enough to stop her from drawing her weapon, and once she had it out somebody was a lot more likely to get hurt. That somebody probably being him. Getting shot had definitely not been on his agenda when he'd woken up this morning.

Her arm had to swing wide to clear the weapon from its holster, increasing the amount of time before she could bring it to bear on him. Closing with her, Kovalic plowed his shoulder into her sternum, grabbing her weapon arm and flipping her onto her back where she landed with a thump and a groan. He bent her wrist back until she released the pistol then ejected the clip, racked the slide to dump the chambered round, and tossed the whole mix of weapon and ammunition down the hall.

The woman—Liang, Messner had called her—was looking up at him, coughing, her eyes slightly unfocused.

"Nothing personal," he murmured. He backed down the hall toward the stairs and risked a glance into the entryway. The old woman was peering over her desk up the stairs; catching sight of him, fear struck her eyes and she pulled her head back.

Kovalic's foot had just grazed the top stair when he saw the front door open. Of course they had brought backup, and the noise would have gotten their attention. Not particularly relishing the idea of bulling his way through another set of gun-wielding agents, Kovalic crossed the front door off his list of escape routes.

Looking up, he caught sight of a sign pointing its way toward the shared bathroom he'd noticed earlier. Without pausing to think, he made a run for it—even as Liang finally managed to yell for help.

Pushing his way into the restroom, he put his back against the door. The room had a few stalls for toilets and showers on one side and a line of sinks set below a long mirror on the other. One frosted glass window was cracked open to let out the steam. He yanked it open and peered out. He was only on the second floor, so it was the work of a moment to slip out the window, dangle from the ledge, and then drop the last ten feet to the pavement.

Affecting his best casual air, he walked out of the alley like he'd had every reason in the world to be there, and then turned to stroll past the front of the tenement.

A groundcar was parked directly in front of the building. It was empty, but Kovalic had seen plenty of unmarked cars in his day, and this one oozed ineffectual subtlety.

The door to the tenement was swinging closed as he passed, and Kovalic just caught a glimpse of someone running up the stairs. Without changing his pace or sparing a second look, he crossed the street and made for the nearest crowd.

On the upside, he hadn't gotten shot. On the downside, CalSec was looking at Wallace, and now they knew someone else was interested too— and they'd seen his face. He patted his pocket to reassure himself that the data chip was still there. Wallace had obviously decided to hide it for a reason; hopefully whatever it contained had been worth the risk.

●

"So?" Tapper asked.

It was an hour later and Kovalic had regrouped with the sergeant in another of Raleigh City's many squares, this one dominated by a tall, stone cathedral that looked like it might give some of Earth's finest churches a run for their money.

"Hell of a thing," said Kovalic, craning his neck up at the crown-shaped steeple overhead. Eight stone buttresses combined to support an even taller spire atop them.

"Mixture of Gothic and Renaissance architecture," Tapper mused. "Unless I miss my guess, it's modeled after the St. Giles Cathedral in Edinburgh, back on Earth."

Kovalic raised an eyebrow.

"What?" said Tapper, shrugging. "Man's gotta have a hobby."

"Well, it seems to fit the neighborhood, anyway," said Kovalic. He gestured to Tapper and the two of them started slowly circling the stone edifice. Whoever had commissioned the structure had thoughtfully laid in some gardens, though like the rest of Caledonia's greenery they'd turned mostly brown. Kovalic ducked under a low-hanging skeletal branch. "What'd you find out?"

"I did a quick check of the hospitals and the morgues—or at least, pushed it as far as I could with a somewhat vague local reporter cover. Upshot was no stiffs that matched Wallace's description. Ran back through the local crime logs, too; nothing there either. If Wallace *is* dead, the authorities don't have his body yet."

"I can't say that makes me feel that much better," said Kovalic grimly.

"Any luck at the apartment?"

Kovalic produced the data chip from his pocket and handed it over to Tapper. The sergeant turned it over in gnarled hands then returned it to Kovalic. "Anything on it?"

"Good question. I plugged it into my comm, but it's been secured with fingerprint authentication. I thought maybe I'd ask Three to run it through some decryption filters."

Tapper hesitated. "I'm not sure how much luck you'll have with that. CID mandates the use of one-time pads for all its field communication. And if the key's biometric, we're not going to get it open without Wallace's fingerprint. We could try to bypass it, though—any chance of lifting a print from his apartment?"

"Yeah, I think that ship has sailed," Kovalic said, returning the chip to his pocket. "I had a little run-in with Caledonian Security, who are apparently sitting on Wallace's apartment."

Tapper's eyebrows went up. "The feds? That's weird. What the hell's their angle?"

Kovalic shook his head. "I didn't stop to ask. I assumed Eyes was using them to keep tabs on the place without tipping their own hand."

"Which would be a great theory—if the Imperial Intelligence Service was the kind of outfit that liked delegating."

"It's not exactly their style," Kovalic admitted.

Tapper chuckled. "No, they're not exactly the helpful sort." He ran his hand along the tops of some dry evergreen bushes. "A parallel investigation, maybe?"

"Maybe, but how'd they get onto Wallace in the first place?"

"Good question."

"Yeah, I was really hoping you'd have an answer to go with it."

Tapper snorted. "Sorry to disappoint, boss. So, now what?"

Hands in his pockets, Kovalic looked up at the steeple again, the late afternoon sun shining through the openings in the crown—the light of God descending upon it, he supposed the faithful might say. He smiled slightly, remembering his mother's daily veneration of the saints' icons sprinkled about their house.

"Well, those CalSec agents have got me curious, I must say. And I think I know just the man to talk to. Though," he paused, looking again at the sinking sun, "it may have to wait until the morning."

"And our friend?"

"Three's got the eyeball again. Last contact from him said they were bound for the northern edge of the city, the Upham district. We'll regroup with them at the safe house in a couple hours."

"Sounds like a plan," said Tapper. There was a rumbling from his midsection and he patted it apologetically. "In the meantime, how about we get something to eat?"

# CHAPTER SEVEN

The transpo bus back to the city center was almost empty, which conveniently meshed with Eli's unsociable mood. A little digging around the few remaining inhabitants of Block 17—most of whom had shied away from Eli as though he'd either had some sort of disease or was going door-to-door with religious pamphlets—had revealed that 17-North had been demolished a couple years ago as part of an attempt to reclaim the land for more productive uses, as well as to reduce the crime and violence that seemed to hover around the area like a cloud of flies. The rest of the residential towers had been slated to follow, but the initiative had run out of both money and fervor.

Only a few families were left in the block, many of them squatters. None remembered a red-haired man of about Eli's height and build or recognized the name Eamon Brody.

*Dead end.* He shouldn't be this disappointed, given that it was only the first attempt he'd made but, as he'd realized while staring up at the vacant space where his home had been, he had no idea where to go next. Surely, somewhere, *someone* must know what had happened to Eamon and Meghann. He'd racked his brain for memories of old friends, distant family, even past girlfriends. But most of the Brodys' extended family was dead or had moved off-world; their friends had been the people they'd known from the block. At school, they'd kept largely to themselves—though there had been that girl who had followed Eamon around like a puppy for some time. He searched vainly for the name, but couldn't bring it to mind: Laurie? Ruthie? Blonde girl, very thin, very smart. *Yeah, that and a five-mark chit will get you a bus ride.*

Images continued flipping past his mind's eye: snatches of faces he dimly remembered, places his brother had dragged him in their teenage years. He'd gone along, despite his uneasiness, because Eamon had been there—because, once upon a very long time ago, he'd trusted his brother implicitly.

That had lasted right up until Eli had begged off going to one of the "protests"—really, nothing more than a thinly-veiled riot held by the gang Eamon had fallen in with, the Tartans. He'd told Eamon he wanted to stay home with Meghann but, in truth, he'd been scared shitless—of getting hurt, of being arrested, of worse.

"Fine," Eamon had sneered. "Go home and play."

His ears had flushed red, as they always did when he was embarrassed, and he'd stalked off with the jeers of the older boys still ringing in the air. Two days later a police officer had appeared at the Brody's door hauling a bruised and defiant Eamon along with him; Eli's mother had burst into tears at his appearance but the cop had been reassuring if not exactly comforting. Eamon had been sent to his room, but Eli had taken the opportunity to lurk around the corner from the living room, overhearing every word.

"He got himself bruised up this time, ma'am, but next time . . ." The police officer let out a breath, worrying at the hat in his hands. "Well, it's going to be a whole lot worse if there *is* a next time."

Eamon, for his part, hadn't been particularly apologetic, even after their father, sooty and sweaty from a long day, had gotten home. The two of them had gone at it in the room that Eamon and Eli shared, so Eli had retreated into Meghann's room where the two of them had crawled under the bed and shared stories of far-off worlds and heroic spacemen.

Eli had no doubt his father would have dearly liked to give his older son a good thumping, but Eamon had already started to grow into his not inconsiderable adult frame, and what he lacked in the calloused hands of experience he more than made up for in sheer youth and vigor.

But starting then, there had been a motivation in Eamon—a fire behind his fury. It wasn't about crime or random acts of violence, it was about something far more damning: ideology.

A chime sounded, breaking Eli's reverie. "Highland and Fifth," announced the androgynous synthetic voice. The stop would let him off a short walk from the address that Fielding's man had given him. So, he could go and report in to Fielding that he'd found . . . exactly nothing. And no luck finding Eamon meant that he was that much further from seeing his sister.

Eli sighed. Something told him Fielding wasn't going to be impressed by his having thrown up his hands at the first sign of an obstacle. He pressed the palms of his hands against his eyes. *A drink would hit the spot right about now.*

A drink.

Neurons, long since rusted from disuse, fired suddenly, reigniting memories that had likewise been submerged for almost a decade. A smoky room. The taste of whisky. The loud clamor of thick Caledonian accents all around him as he followed Eamon up to the bar.

And more than a few tartan-patterned armbands, scarves, and even the odd kilt or two among the crowd.

The bus picked up speed again and he suddenly realized that he had missed his stop. No big deal, really—he could always get off at the next one.

*Or not.* Just a few stops farther and he could transfer to a bus that would take him down to Leith, Raleigh City's port district. Not the best place to be wandering around at night, perhaps, though the muggers and other petty criminals didn't really venture down to those parts— which was just as well, since the police didn't walk that particular beat either.

Instead it was patrolled by roving packs of young folks wearing those same plaid armbands and rebuffing the unwise few who ventured into their territory with threat and intimidation—and, occasionally, with far less gentle means.

Safe passage could, of course, be assured with the right greetings. And lucky for Eli, those words were never changed. They were handed down from generation to generation, because once you were in the Tartans, you were *always* in the Tartans.

●

"Oi," said a sharp voice in the darkness. It associated itself with a shadow that slid away from the larger and equally murky mass of a nearby building and strode in Eli's direction.

With a gulp, Eli forced down the acid that was rising in his stomach. What if they'd changed the password? A little voice in his head reminded him that they *never* changed the password, but that first voice didn't exactly seem too interested in the finer points of logic. What if they'd made an exception after he'd left and joined the Illyricans?

"*Fàilte, a charaid. Dè nì mì dhut?*" said the voice.

Eli cleared his throat and let the familiar, alien-sounding words roll off his tongue, just as they had in his youth. He hoped his pronunciation wasn't too rusty.

"*Mas olc am fitheach, chan fheàrr a chomann.*"

While he knew more or less what the words meant, he didn't really speak the language—though there were those on Caledonia who did. Like even the most casual of gang members, Eli had simply memorized the few turns of phrase and ritual expressions that all in the Tartans were expected to know so that they could keep up the pretense of holding on to their deep cultural heritage. It was a sham, mostly, but it was an important sham, especially for those that really believed in it.

To Eli's relief, the shadow didn't hesitate and the traditional response came at once.

"*Is binn guth an t-eòin far na rugadh e.* You are welcome, *a bhràthair.*"

Eli nodded in the direction of the shadow, which had once again slipped away to glom onto the building that it had presumably been leaning against. A loud whistle from the shadow—*incoming, all clear*—was echoed in turn by a fainter whistle of acknowledgement from down the block.

Jamming his hands in his pockets, Eli walked down the street and tried to control his nerves. At least the night air, which was a bit on the chilly side, gave him a reasonable excuse to shiver.

As if darkness and cold weren't enough, a fog was coming in off the water, sketching the few street lights that dotted the area in impressionist blurs. Despite that, it was easy enough for Eli to find his way to the Pig and Thistle—even after ten years, he thought he could probably still do the route blindfolded.

If there were other Tartans tracking his progress, he caught no sign of them. But as long as the old rules were in play, he wouldn't expect any problems—he'd been cleared by the sentry, so there ought to be no further challenges.

The Pig and Thistle itself stood on the very edge of the water, the two only separated by about twenty paces of pavement. The harbor was still pretty deep here—deep enough to lose a body in—and cold enough that most people left to tread water in it would give up their secrets easily enough.

Exclusive and dangerous though its clientele was, the pub looked almost quaint and touristy from the outside. A wooden plank hung above the door, painted simply with the establishment's two namesakes: a pink cartoonish pig squealing in a field full of the prickly purple flowers. Warm, bright lights gleamed through the steamy window panes, giving off a diffuse, almost homey glow.

Eli walked toward the bar then froze as he saw the two burly men standing at the door, hands clasped in front of them. He'd never known there to be security at the pub's door before—what would you need them for, anyway? It was a neighborhood bar, not a trendy nightclub with a line around the block. That same worrywart part of him suggested that maybe he should just keep on walking, but the rational side counter-argued that he didn't have much of a choice. Besides, the passphrase had worked. Things couldn't have changed *that* much.

Squaring his shoulders, he walked straight up to the door, nodding off-handedly at the guards and reached for the handle.

A meaty hand slowly but firmly reached out and seized his wrist with a grip that would have left fingerprints pressed into an iron bar.

"Evening," said the hand's owner, the beefy gentleman to Eli's right. "Can we help you?" Eli frowned at the accent, which was neither the dockhand-influenced cadence of Leith nor the Upham towers brogue. It was something else, more . . . sophisticated. Downtown Central, maybe?

"Uh, hi," said Eli, his voice cracking only slightly. *"Mas olc am—"*

The man cut him off. "None of that malarkey, pal."

"Easy there," said the second man, who spoke, to Eli's relief, in the familiar tones of born-and-bred Upham.

Over the years, Eli had lost a lot of his native accent, in part from being surrounded by peers whose own speech veered more toward the flat, inexpressive Illyrican Standard. But he'd mostly dropped it by choice while at the academy when he'd desperately wanted to cut his ties with his homeworld and be taken seriously by his comrades and commanders alike.

Now he found himself slipping it on for size, just like the comfortable, broken-in boots on his feet.

"Just here for a drink, lads," he said as cheerfully as he could manage, lending a subtle roll to the R's, stretching the "uh" of "just" into more of an "oo," and stressing the short "a" of "lads" for the whole package. "You wouldn't begrudge a brother a nip on a cold night, would you?"

The grip slackened on his hand, if not releasing it entirely, but Eli could see the other man relax. "Let him through, Tsui. He won't be any trouble."

With that, Eli's hand was free. He shook it out and grinned, teeth clenched, to show no hard feelings, even though he was pretty sure that the cops could have identified the man from the fingerprints pressed into his arm.

The second man reached over and pulled the door open for him; the raucous noise of the crowd spilled into the quiet dockside evening. Eli gave a friendly nod and walked into the pub.

Nothing had changed.

Eli felt reasonably certain that the planetary health and safety codes had been updated since he'd left home, but if so, then the Pig and Thistle had ignored them all. That didn't exactly surprise him—MacKenzie, the bar's owner, might be a loudmouth and a braggart, but he knew how to throw some weight around. Years ago he'd gotten the government to declare the Pig and Thistle a historical landmark, according it all sort of legal protections and, more importantly, allowing him to avoid keeping up with pesky rules and regulations. Which explained not only how the Pig and Thistle could serve alcohol late into the wee hours, when the rest of Raleigh City's bars had long since closed up shop, but also how it was pretty much the only public establishment on the planet that still allowed people to smoke. Eli's lungs made their protest known with a fit of coughing.

The clientele, however, had changed quite a bit. There were a lot of younger faces—or just plain young faces, to Eli's mind. Some of the older folks had clearly passed on. Old man Kitano's stool was vacant, he noted with a pang of regret. The ancient fellow had been a fixture at the bar for Eli's entire youth, right up until he'd left for the academy. Nobody seemed to know where he'd come from or exactly what his connection with the Tartans was—it was rumored he'd been a hitman back in the colonization days—but he'd sat in the same corner seat every night for years, drinking pint after pint and barely saying two words strung together.

The face behind the bar was unfamiliar too—or at least, Eli thought it was until the man smiled broadly, and Eli recognized the gap-toothed grin of MacKenzie's oldest son, William. About Eli's age, he'd lost his two front teeth in a brawl with the rival Campbell boys—a fight that he'd won, despite the bat to the face that had left him dentally impaired. He'd grown up and filled out, going from gangly youth to broad-shouldered man, but now that Eli knew what to look for he could see the trace of the broken nose and the scar near the right eyebrow left by the same encounter.

Suddenly, it was like he'd never left.

He found himself wondering how different he must look after ten years away and whether anyone would even recognize him. Eamon would, he was sure of that, but he didn't feel as certain about the rest of his acquaintances. Nor was he sure that was a bad thing, given the circumstances under which he'd left.

That train of thought was abruptly derailed as Eli felt himself collide with another, smaller figure. He put up a hand automatically to steady himself and felt it make contact with a decidedly non-masculine body part. His cheeks flushed red as he looked down to find a short woman staring at his hand, a somewhat flummoxed look on her face.

"Christ," he said, snatching his hand back as though he'd pulled out a hot pan without an oven mitt. "I'm sorry," he managed. "It was an—"

"Accident?" said the woman, her eyebrows arched. She straightened her shirt—a nice, green top that did flattering things to her . . . Eli hastily brought his eyes back up to her face. Her face was rounded and freckled, framed by red curls that verged on copper.

"Yes," said Eli, groping for words this time instead of anatomy. "My mind was, er, elsewhere."

"How flattering," said the woman dryly.

Eli scratched his head, at a loss. "Look," he said hastily, "let me buy you a drink."

"Funny," said the woman, "most blokes go in the other order."

Eli offered a weak grin. "It's been a while since my last visit to the Pig and Thistle, but I'm pretty sure that if you accidentally cop a feel, you're obligated to apologize to the lady in some way. You don't even have to drink it with me," he added, watching the protest form on her lips.

The woman's expression turned grudgingly accepting. "Fair enough," she said. "But don't expect this to work every time."

"Wouldn't dream of it," promised Eli, his hands raised in defense.

They fought their way through the press of the crowd, Eli only taking one inadvertent elbow to the ribs and narrowly dodging a slosh of beer. He eyed the woman sidelong; she reminded him a bit of Maggie O'Hara, his former squadron mate—Maggie with the light red hair, as they'd called her back at the academy. The thought awoke a subtle leaden thud in his heartbeat: like so many of his other classmates, she'd died at the Battle of Sabaea. He hadn't thought of her in years. And if the freshness of her death was not what it had once been, it was still present, like the echo of a bad toothache.

Eli waved for the bartender's attention, mentally running over the details of his story for when William MacKenzie inevitably recognized him: he'd served five years in the Illyrican Navy, had been stationed at the Illyrican colony on Archangelsk. A boring five years in homeworld defense, never even a shot at real combat. Sabaea? No, he'd never even been near the place, much less involved in the invasion. His term had ended just recently and he'd decided to come home and mend fences with his brother. By the way, he hadn't seen Eamon lately, had he?

William ambled over, his gap-toothed smile broad. "Gwen, love," he rumbled at the woman. "The usual?"

"Aye," said the woman.

"Make that two," said Eli, holding up a pair of fingers. "On me." The bartender's eyes didn't even venture near Eli's face, but he nodded and strolled off. Eli stared after him, puzzled. Then again, William had never been the most observant of boys, he reflected. If he had been, maybe he would have seen that bat coming.

The red-haired girl—Gwen, it seemed—leaned against the bar. "Not that I want to encourage conversation with deviants, but I haven't seen you around here before." Her brown eyes looked neutral, but there was a faint narrowing at their edges.

"It's been a while. I used to spend a lot of time here when I was younger."

"Oh? So where have you been, then?"

Eli bit his tongue. Giving his Illyrican history as an explanation for finding Eamon was one thing, but telling a cute girl—the first cute girl, his quickening pulse reminded him, who'd spoken an entire sentence to him in the past five years, give or take—that it wasn't so long ago he'd been wearing a crimson uniform was a quick way to end a conversation.

"Away . . . off-world. I've been traveling."

"Really?" Her wariness gave way to genuine curiosity. "Anywhere interesting?"

*Yes, I lived in a closet at an arctic station on a world cut off from the rest of civilization for five years. Great sightseeing, little bit chilly in the winter.* He hedged his bets. "I was doing some work on Archangelsk, mainly."

"Ah. Nice place?"

"Not really."

William chose that moment to return, setting down two shot glasses of pale gold liquid. "Here you go, dearie," he said to Gwen. "Two Saltyres."

"Thanks, Will," said Gwen. Eli mumbled his own thanks in addition, fumbling through the pile of chits in his pocket. He tossed a twenty-mark piece on the bar, which William palmed before slipping away again.

"So, I take it this is your first time home in a while?"

"Nine years."

Gwen whistled, impressed, and raised her glass. "Welcome home then. *Slàinte.*"

The burning of the spirit cascading down his throat brought tears to his eyes, and not just because it was one step shy of moonshine. It was pungent and flavorful and tasted not a little bit like the vaguely metallic dust that was everywhere on the planet. For nine years, Eli had not missed a single thing from his homeworld: the heat, the dirt, the violence, the anger.

But he'd missed this.

Somehow the master distillers of Saltyre's had perfectly captured the spirit of Eli's homeworld and everything that went into its founding, its subsequent occupation, and the ensuing resistance. It brought back memories of watching his first baseball game with his father, who had always kept a flask of Saltyre's in his pocket; of his first brawl with the Tartans; even of the first time he had gotten laid. Which, truth be told, he owed largely to a bottle of ten-year-old Saltyre's he'd nicked from his dad's private stash.

It was a lot for one liquor to hold, and he savored the taste.

When he opened his eyes—he hadn't even realized they'd been closed—he found Gwen staring at him, her expression amused. "You look like you needed that."

"Aye," he said with feeling, turning the shot glass over in his hands. He smiled to himself.

With a grin, Gwen hopped up on her tippy toes and flagged down William, waving two fingers that he acknowledged with an off-hand nod. She turned back toward Eli, her smile finally turning authentic.

"So what brings you back to the old dirtball . . ." she trailed off and laughed. "I don't even know your name."

"It's Eli."

"Eli," she said, nodding. "I'm Gwen, in case you missed that loudmouth MacKenzie."

"Pleasure to meet you, Gwen." He felt more relaxed already. This wasn't so hard, talking to women. He'd known how to do it once upon a time, and it was probably like riding a bike, right? The turn of phrase sent him down other avenues far more risqué.

"Ahem?" said Gwen, giving him a nudge.

Eli coughed hurriedly, hoping she hadn't noticed the somewhat glassy-eyed expression on his face. That'd been the Saltyre's talking, anyway.

"Uh, I'm sorry. I forgot what we were talking about."

Gwen gave him a knowing look that dripped at the edges. "Why you came back?"

"Oh, right. Actually, I'm looking for someone."

"Yeah?" Her eyebrows went up. "Someone from your past, eh? Old flame? Long lost love?" She grinned.

"Nothing quite so poetic."

"They got a name?"

Eli turned the question over in his head. If William MacKenzie's greeting was any indication, Gwen was a regular in the Pig and Thistle. Which meant that if Eamon still frequented the bar, there was a good chance that they'd crossed paths—or that she'd at least know his name and how to find him. Couldn't hurt to try, could it?

"His name's Brody. Eamon Brody. You know him?"

Maybe it was Eli's imagination, but he thought Gwen's expression went fixed for a second, as though she'd been insulted but didn't want to show it. William returned, bearing their drinks, and by the time Eli looked over at her again, she looked perfectly normal. *Better than normal. Perfect.*

"Eamon Brody," she murmured. "Certainly sounds familiar." She picked up both the drinks off the bar, letting them swing in her hands for a moment; it looked like she was a bit drunker than Eli had thought. With a sudden frown, she put the drinks down. The one closest to Eli sloshed heavily and about half the drink ended up on the bar.

"Oh, for heaven's sake," she snapped at herself. "I'm sorry. Hold on, I'll have William top it up." She raised her hand toward the bartender.

"That's okay," said Eli. "Probably more than enough for me anyway."

"No, no," said Gwen, spreading a hand on her chest, where Eli found his attention once again avoidably drawn. "It's the least I can do."

"Uh huh."

The gap-toothed bartender reappeared, and Gwen quickly explained what had happened, taking the man's hand in her own and pleading for sympathy. He looked over at Eli, who found his breath catch as the man frowned—had he recognized Eli at last? Finally, he patted Gwen's hand. "I'll take care of it, lass. Don't fret. Back in a flash."

Gwen looked over at Eli again and smiled, but there was something slightly off about it, like it was painted on.

"Don't worry about it," Eli protested again. "I should probably be going anyway."

"Oh, no," said Gwen, leaning forward to take his hand between hers. "Not on account of my clumsiness, please." Her hand was warm on his and her fingers traced his veins, raising the hairs in a sensation he hadn't felt in a long time. He couldn't even summon the words to respond to her, distracted as he was by her touch.

True to his word, William was back a moment later setting down another full shot glass for Eli. The bartender carefully straightened the napkin on which it was set and nodded to Eli and Gwen, who gave him a warm smile in return.

The red-haired woman raised her glass. "To friends, old and new."

Eli lifted his own and echoed her words. "Old and new." He threw the shot back and swallowed. The familiar taste was still there, but this time it was overshadowed by something much heavier: a bitter, syrupy taste that reminded him of the cough medicine his mother used to make him take.

"*Augh,*" he spat, turning the glass over with a frown and wiping his lips with the back of his hand. "That's gone off, I think. Must be a rotten cask?"

Gwen frowned. "Well, that's no good."

"No, not good at all," said Eli, trying to get the foul taste out of his mouth. "Think we can get that one on the house?" The syrupy flavor lingered on his tongue and the sensation made his eyes water. He rubbed at the corners of them.

Gwen sighed, shaking her head and eyeing the bottom of her empty shot glass. She placed it delicately on the table. "You know, it's a shame."

"What is?" said Eli off-handedly, still rubbing at his eyes. His vision wouldn't clear and he felt his movements getting sluggish. *Two drinks? I must be more out of practice than I thou—*

He stiffened suddenly and his mouth went dry. *Shit, shit, shit.* Too late, he levered himself off the bar stool, feeling his knees wobble beneath him. He looked over at Gwen, who was regarding him with a mixture of pity and regret, and then back at his empty glass.

"I was just beginning to like you," said Gwen.

Eli took a deep breath, but everything seemed cloudy and hot. He pulled at the collar of his shirt and stumbled away from the bar. The crowd suddenly seemed to clear in front of him, but he staggered through it like he was lost in the fog off the harbor.

"Should be going," he slurred to nobody in particular. He felt hands firmly seize both of his elbows, and the next step he took met only air. There was a sensation of being lifted up gently, borne on a stretcher made of clouds. A bright light shone in his eyes; it was the last thing he remembered.

# CHAPTER EIGHT

"So on a scale of one to complete blithering idiot, where are we putting this kid?"

Kovalic gave Tapper a sidelong glance. The older man had never been one to mince words. Perks of being an old codger, he supposed. For his own part, he couldn't come up with any response better than a noncommittal grunt as the two of them wound through the darkened streets of Raleigh City.

"He's new at this. Give him time."

"Come on, you don't have to be a wormhole physicist to figure out an address written on the back of a credit chit."

The first message from Three, that Eli Brody had failed to get off at the bus stop for the safe house, had come in about twenty minutes ago. Since then, the third member of their team had been keeping close tabs on Brody, who apparently had decided that a nighttime stroll in the capital's port district might do him a world of good.

"You think he's going to ground?" Tapper asked, giving voice to the thoughts that Kovalic himself was trying to ignore.

Kovalic grimaced. "I don't think so." As the general had pointed out, there was no place for Brody to run. No place that kept him out of the way of both the Commonwealth *and* the Illyricans, anyway. Besides, he had to know that Kovalic would find him.

And even though Brody hadn't been thrilled to help them, Kovalic didn't think he was the type of person to go back on his word. Besides, there was still his sister, and from what he could tell Brody genuinely did want to see her again.

His side twinged at that thought; the general had maintained that omitting elements of the truth was not the same as lying, but it still didn't sit right with Kovalic. Not that he hadn't lied plenty in his life—you might call it a core competency of his current occupation—but there was a difference between deception as part of the job and lying to get someone on your side. He'd argued to the general that they should tell Brody everything about his sister, but he'd been overruled.

Kovalic sighed. Splitting hairs, wasn't he? They'd needed Brody's help, and his sister had been the easiest way to get it. No use getting all conscientious about it now.

His comm buzzed and he answered it. The calm, collected voice of Three, otherwise known as Lieutenant Aaron Page, filtered into his ear; he looped in Tapper's comm.

"There's some sort of sentry set up here." Page spoke in a quiet tone that hopefully wouldn't draw too much attention to a man strolling down the street by himself. "Looks like a sign-countersign, but I wasn't close enough to make it out."

Tapper gave Kovalic a look of mock horror and covered his own mic. "You mean there's something the boy wonder *can't* do? This day's proving full of surprises."

Kovalic hushed him. "What's your twenty, Three?"

"Found a vantage, and I've got eyes on. Looks like he's heading to a . . . bar."

"Can you get a read on it?"

"Not from here. I'll send you my location—maybe you can cross reference it against the city grid."

Kovalic and Tapper's comms pinged in unison as the positioning tag showed up. He jutted his chin at Tapper, who nodded and started looking up the address.

"Orders?"

"Give him a nice long leash. We don't want to spook him. Two and I are inbound." He glanced at Tapper, who looked up from his comm and flashed him five fingers three times in quick succession. "ETA fifteen minutes."

"Copy that. See you then." Page clicked off.

Kovalic scratched his chin. Brody had made a beeline for this place, whatever it was, and he'd known how to get past the security that Page had decided to avoid. There was the chance, as Tapper had suggested, that the kid was trying to shake them, but something about it just didn't seem right.

Nor did he think Brody was simply thirsty. Though the kid had smelled like alcohol back on Sabaea—and, to be honest, it hadn't seemed like an isolated event—there were any number of places along Brody's route that would have served the man a drink *and* wouldn't have required knowing some sort of passphrase.

That left a third possibility: Brody was doing exactly what he was supposed to be doing, following a lead. In which case, it was their job to support him . . . and make sure he didn't get himself killed in the process.

"What'd you find?"

Tapper was reading something on his comm. "Looks like the only place in that vicinity that matches the description is a watering hole called The Pig and Thistle."

"Public records?"

"Gimme a second, gimme a second." He cursed, stabbing at the device with his finger. "I hate these bleeding things. I thought we brought Three along to handle the paperwork."

Kovalic suppressed a smile. Page might have been far faster when it came to digging up intel, but he was also far less entertaining to watch.

"Okay, here. Liquor license issued for a Liam MacKenzie, but that was a while back. Looks like his son may be the current proprietor."

An old friend of one of the brothers Brody, perhaps? Or something more? The sentry was the key, and it definitely wasn't the kind of thing the Illyricans went in for. No, it sounded more like . . . a gang?

"Do me a favor and run that location through the police logs. See if anything pops."

Tapper rattled off a muted string of invective once again, as he pretty much did whenever he tried to finagle any technological device more complicated than an explosive charge. "Yeah, okay, there's something here. Looks like the usual number of drunk-and-disorderlies for your average establishment of this type. Couple of brawls." He sucked in a breath and

raised his eyebrows. "Ooh, unlawful political rally. Doesn't look like anybody was charged, but there was some definite anti-Imperium shit going
down."

Danzig had said something about a street gang connected to the Black
Watch—the Tartans. That could explain the sentry. And from what they'd
seen of Eamon Brody's record, the man had not been a shrinking violet
when it came to politically inspired violence. So maybe the kid was on
the right track.

Didn't mean he wasn't about to get himself into a world of trouble.
Kovalic quickened his pace and Tapper fell into step with him.

"So . . . closer to the 'blithering idiot' end of the spectrum, then?"

Kovalic grimaced. "For all of our sakes, let's hope not."

●

Eli's head hurt. His mouth tasted like he'd been licking a rug and everything smelled like stale dampness. He moaned, but it came out muffled; it
felt like somebody had tightly wrapped a towel around his head.

Upon second appraisal, this appeared to be because somebody *had*
wrapped a towel around his head. Not a nice fluffy, freshly-laundered,
smelling-of-spring towel either. More like an oh-crap-the-dog-threw-up-
on-the-carpet-again towel. And here he'd been pretty sure that they didn't
allow dogs in the bar. So where exactly had they gotten the towel? And
more importantly: what kind of dog was it? Maybe he could figure it out
by taste.

That was a decision he immediately regretted.

This prompted an unfortunate cycle of events that involved Eli trying to
spit out the towel, only to find that sucking in the air to do so ended up
with the towel back into his mouth. And yet, his fuzzy brain kept trying
anyway, convinced that somehow he'd get the best of the situation.

After three or four rounds of this particularly engaging game, he discovered that he wasn't alone in the room. There appeared to be three
or four other people around based on the sounds of conversation. The
towel muffled his hearing, but they talked over each other enough for
him to distinguish different tones. At least one of them was a woman, he

thought. Or perhaps a young man. Or maybe a man who'd just sucked the helium out of a balloon to disguise his voice. Clever.

It was at that point he realized that his line of cogent thought had made a break for it. He chalked part of it up to the whisky he'd had at the bar and then, after some careful, focused consideration, blamed the rest of it on whatever the hell that woman had put into his drink.

He'd never been drugged before—definitely not by a woman. Part of him thought maybe he ought to be flattered by the attention, but the part of his brain that was quite reasonably panicking over the situation poured cold water on that.

The voices ceased overlapping—arguing?—long enough for him to make out the woman's voice saying something. ". . . any more part of this."

"Tough," said a man, "you brought him in."

Eli's slowly returning faculties were coherent enough to piece together that these were the people who'd grabbed him and not, say, fellow tied-up towel-draped abductees.

A moment later he wished he hadn't thought of being tied up, since the sudden realization that he *was* indeed bound to something—a hard chair, from the testimony of his numb rear end—had made his nose start to itch rather furiously. To be fair, he would have noticed it earlier had he any feeling in his hands or feet.

The panic started to rise in his chest like vomit—or maybe that was vomit—and he quickly tried to push it back down. Panic wasn't going to help him and throwing up on the towel, gross as it already was, was an equally unappealing option. He tried to reassure himself: *Fielding and the others are supposed to have my back. They'll track me down.*

The thought of Fielding made him breathe easier. The man was clearly a pro at this sort of thing. All Eli had to do was hold on until Fielding charged in, guns blazing, and rescued him.

Only he hadn't told Fielding where he was going. He'd skipped the meet and followed his own brilliant intuition down to the Pig and Thistle. Which meant the Commonwealth team had no idea where he was at this exact moment.

The bile started rising in his throat again. *This isn't helping.*

He had to stay calm. *Fielding. What would Fielding do?* As a game, it was far more entertaining than spit-the-disgusting-towel-out-of-your-mouth.

That was job one, actually: get them to take the bloody thing off his head. He cleared his throat loudly, which didn't seem to get any reaction from the voices, who had returned to arguing. He tried for the polite approach.

"Uh, excuse me?" Unfortunately, it came out rather muffled and ended with the towel back in his mouth. Frustrated, he took as deep a breath as the towel would allow him and went for volume.

"OI!"

The argument ceased and Eli had a very distinct feeling of several pairs of eyes swiveling toward him, which quickly bled into a self-conscious feeling of helplessness. "Uh, can somebody take this goddamn thing off?"

There was a murmured discussion from the voices and some movement next to him, followed by blessed fresh air as someone whisked the towel off his head. He blinked rapidly, as he found himself squinting into an array of bright lights that someone had pointed in his direction. It also had the added effect of obscuring the other people in the room, who were shielded by the glare.

*Well, I guess they're not going to make it easy for me.* He had to conclude that his abductors were part of the Tartans, since he'd been drugged in a bar known to be affiliated with them and in plain sight of a hundred people or so. Didn't really seem likely that the authorities would have gone that route.

Eli wrinkled his nose. The person who had removed the towel was standing behind him now, out of his view. Then again, he didn't need his eyes for that, since the scent that wafted down toward him was plenty familiar.

"You know, you didn't have to drug me to get me back to your place, sweetheart. Although, this *is* a bit kinky for my tastes."

The red-haired girl from the Pig and Thistle, Gwen, slid into his field of view, her arms crossed over her chest. She was dressed the same as she had been at the bar, leading Eli to surmise that he hadn't been out for too long. They must have hit him with something concentrated to drop him that fast. Maybe his body was already filtering it out.

*And that was the wrong metabolic process to start thinking of.* Now his nose itched and he had to take a piss too . . . all of which was difficult to do while tied to a chair. He eyed the woman, who was watching him with a guarded expression.

"I don't suppose you'd give my nose a scratch?" he asked hopefully.

"You said you were looking for Eamon Brody," said Gwen, ignoring his request.

Eli blinked and a memory rose to his mind: something about her had changed when he'd mentioned Eamon. Like she'd known him. Or of him, at least. Given his circumstances, it seemed like maybe they weren't on the best of terms.

"Yesssss?" he said slowly.

"What do you know about him?"

Eli shrugged—or he tried to anyway, coming dangerously close to tipping his chair over. "Well, actually, quite a bit. Let's see. His favorite color's blue, he's got a birthmark on his back that kind of looks like a duck if you squint . . ." he was rambling, he realized, but he found that he just couldn't stop; it was like someone had pulled a string. *What the hell did she dose me with?* "He couldn't hit a baseball if his life depended on it, and once when he was a kid he gave himself a concussion when he tried to steal—"

He was still talking when the woman backhanded him across the face. It wasn't a light slap, either, like the kind you might give to somebody who seemed a little bit out of it. This was a full-on shut-the-hell-up-or-you'll-get-worse-when-your-father-comes-home slap. Then again, he'd had worse—it was more the shock of her hitting him that made him decide to stop talking than anything else.

"You've done your homework, clearly," said Gwen, biting her lip as she massaged her left knuckles. Eli took a small amount of pleasure from the fact that his face had bruised her hand, but with the initial shock fading the throbbing in his cheek suggested that he'd still gotten the raw end of the deal. "Let's try a different tack. Why are you here?"

"I assume that's not a philosophical question—okay, okay!" He cut off as the woman raised her hand again. "I'm trying to find him. I haven't seen him in nine years, I just wanted to catch up."

One of the figures behind the lights, whom Eli had forgotten all about during the woman's ministrations, coughed loudly. Gwen looked up, shading her eyes, and walked over toward the source of the noise. There was a quiet murmuring from the other figure and the woman nodded, then walked back to Eli.

Hands on her hips, Gwen fixed him with a stony glare. "Perhaps you'd like to tell us why you're using a fake name, Eli—or is it Marcus?"

Eli blinked a couple of times, then frowned. *Marcus?* It took him a minute to place the name. Right, Marcus Wellington: the ID he'd used to get on planet. He swallowed.

"Uh, I can explain that." *I think.* His mind raced. He *could* explain it, of course, but not in a way that didn't blow his cover. *Think, Brody. Think.* Well, the truth was always a good alternative, especially when people thought it was a lie anyway. In that case:

"All right, all right. You got me," he said with a weak smile. "I was in the Illyrican military. Served five years at Archangelsk."

"I *told* you he was a goddamn crim," growled a coarse voice from behind the lights. It was accompanied by a broad, muscled figure who stepped forward into the pool of lights. Another hand snaked out and grabbed his shoulder, but he shook it off.

A bare-knuckled bruiser of a man, his face had a lengthy scar that ran the length of one side, cutting through the bristly stubble that spoke of several days of not shaving. His eyes were a liquid brown that on any other face might have been considered warm—on his, they verged on molten. "I say we kill the son of a bitch and be done with it."

*Kill?* Eli's throat went drier than the Caledonian outback. Maybe he'd overplayed it just a *wee* bit.

To Eli's surprise, Gwen stepped in between them. "Back off," she snapped. "We're not killing *anybody* until we figure out what he's doing here."

That ought to have been a relief to Eli's ears, but for some reason he found his mind kept circling back to the "until" part like a seagull wheeling around its next prospective meal.

The big guy tensed. "You're telling *me* what to do? Who put you in charge, lass?"

Gwen closed the distance between her and the scarred man and poked a finger firmly in his chest, which looked a bit like a climber picking a fight with a mountain. "You said it yourself—*I* brought him in. Now, back the hell off."

The sound that issued from the man wouldn't have been out of place coming from a rabid dog and, for a second, Eli was worried the man was going to bulldoze his way past Gwen and try to throttle him anyway. But the woman didn't give an inch of ground and, after a moment of impasse, he threw up his hands and stalked back behind the lights. Eli heard the sound of something heavy being kicked over.

Gwen turned back to Eli, nodding to herself. There was something else in her eyes, a brief flicker that he thought might have been relief, but it disappeared in a flash.

"So what are you doing here?" she said, circling slowly around him. "The crims send you in as some sort of spy, just because you're from here?" The way she pronounced the last two words it was clear she disagreed with the sentiment; to her, he might be Caledonian, but he'd never be "from here."

She passed out of view behind his head. Eli stared straight ahead, aware that craning his neck to see her would make him look desperate, not to mention being more than uncomfortable in his current predicament.

"I wasn't aware it was a crime for a guy to come home."

She snorted at that. "Depends. Why'd you leave the Illyricans?"

Eli let out a breath. "Honestly?"

"No, I want you to lie to me."

Eli cracked a grin despite himself. "I can do that too, if you like."

"So I've seen."

His smile faded. *Don't play it too smug, or they'll never buy it.* "I was tired of the life," he admitted. "Following orders every day, training to kill. It was boring . . . and terrifying all at the same time. I never really wanted to be a soldier."

"You shoulda thought of that before joinin' the crims," she snapped back, her voice harsh as her accent got thicker. "That's what they do."

To that, Eli had no response. He sat quietly, his appendages numb, the rest of his muscles tight against the restraints that held him to the chair.

"This is a waste of time," came the scarred man's voice from behind the lights. "I still say we kill him and dump the body."

"Those aren't our orders," said another man's voice, this one with what Eli could only describe as more cultured overtones than the first. "The boss said anybody looking for Eamon Brody was to be brought in, questioned, and held."

*What is it with all this talk of* killing *people?* Eli's racing brain had finally slowed to a modest blur, and with it had come an uncomfortable leaden feeling in the pit of his stomach. This didn't make sense: the Tartans didn't kill people—they beat the crap out of them and left them bleeding in the street.

Come to think of it, they also weren't in the habit of tying people to chairs and interrogating them. It was all a bit paranoid and, frankly, not quite heavy-handed enough for a street gang.

*That's because they're not a street gang.* His stomach did loop-de-loops as the pieces started to come together in his head. *Oh, shit. These guys aren't just Tartans . . . they're the fucking* Black Watch. He swallowed: De Valera's crew.

Eli was as familiar with the group as any Caledonian, and certainly enough to know how considerate they were to those they viewed as Illyrican sympathizers: namely, not very considerate.

De Valera and the Black Watch had acquired an air of taboo when Eli had been young; his parents had spoken of them only in hushed tones when they thought the children were asleep. But Eli and Eamon had lain awake in their small apartment, listening to them argue about the justness of De Valera's cause. Connor Brody had, unsurprisingly, been a full-throated backer of armed revolt no matter the cost, though Eli suspected he himself would never have had the courage to raise a weapon. Molly Brody, never one for violence, had called De Valera a murderer and a thug. He suspected his wasn't the only family into which the Black Watch had driven a wedge.

"Well, we can't leave him here," put in another voice which, unless Eli totally missed his guess, belonged to a second woman.

*Where's here?* Eli thought suddenly. It had barely occurred to him to check out his surroundings; he could picture Fielding—wherever the hell he was, goddamn him—shaking his head in disappointment. There wasn't much to see beyond the bright lights shining in his eyes, but if he rolled his head back slightly he got the impression of a tall ceiling with iron rafters beneath a corrugated metal roof. Between that and the short amount of time he thought he'd been out of commission, he guessed that they'd taken him to one of the warehouses in the port district.

The icy cold finger of reality traced a line down the back of his neck. It seemed unlikely they'd just trundled him out the front door, in case they thought he had backup. But from what Eli remembered of the bar, there was only the one door in and out. Which meant they had some other way to move him unseen.

*A tunnel. Must be a tunnel connecting the bar with the warehouse.* It made sense: the Black Watch probably shipped a lot of illicit goods in and out of the port—weapons, at the very least—and this would be a good place to store them. The Pig and Thistle provided a solid and, in its own way, reputable cover.

The voices were still arguing over Eli's fate, which meant that they missed his next three or four polite attempts at getting their attention. He cleared his throat and drew a deep breath, then let it out in his best drill sergeant voice.

"Ex*cuse* me."

The chatter stopped as suddenly as if he'd pressed pause.

"What?" growled the bruiser, stepping again into the light.

"I think this has all been a terrible misunderstanding," Eli said, donning his most charming smile. "If you just want to throw me out on the street, I promise not to go to the cops or the Illyricans, and we can all forget this ever happened. I won't even tell them about this place or anything. Not that I know anything. Because I don't." He tried to conceal a gulp with a smile.

There was silence at that pronouncement. Somewhere in the distance Eli heard the creak of a door swinging open, followed by footsteps slapping against the concrete floor. If the others noticed, they gave no sign.

"What kind of idiots do you take us for?" said the scarred man.

*Brutal, nasty, violent idiots?* Tempting as it would have been to say out loud, Eli could see the man's hands already clenched into fists. Despite the warm-up slaps earlier, he wasn't sure that he was ready to move on to the next round.

The footsteps Eli had heard a moment ago had gotten louder as they approached, then suddenly ceased as they neared the production on the main stage.

Gwen, who had been largely silent, suddenly stepped in front of him again. She bent over until her face was on a level with Eli's, hands on the tops of her thighs like she was talking to a small child.

"I tell you what," she said, her breath floating into his face in a hot cloud. He could still smell the vestiges of whisky on it. "You give us something, we'll give you something."

"A bullet in the head?" He couldn't imagine De Valera being particularly understanding of an Illyrican soldier, the ex- part notwithstanding.

An unpleasant laugh issued from the scarred man. *Great, at least I've succeeded in amusing him.*

Gwen's eyes darted to Scarface, and then back to Eli. "Just give me *something*," she said, and Eli thought a note of worry had crept into her voice. He frowned as he met her gaze. If he hadn't known better, he'd say there was genuine concern there, like she didn't actually want her compatriots to hurt him. But maybe it was just wishful thinking.

"Sure. What do you want?"

She eyed him for a moment before speaking. "Tell me your name. Your real name. Is it Marcus Wellington?"

"His real name is Elijah." A new voice chimed in, a familiar one that Eli had never thought he'd be this relieved to hear again. "Elijah Brody. And, for better or worse, this idiot is my little brother."

*Eamon.*

Eli grinned up at Gwen, who was staring at him in wide-eyed surprise, colored with just the barest tinge of guilt, like a kid who'd been caught with her hand in the cookie jar.

"Oh," said Eli brightly. "Didn't I mention that?"

# CHAPTER NINE

**"Y**ou son of a bitch," said Eamon when the door closed behind them. "You're *alive*."

It was ten minutes later and he'd led Eli off the warehouse floor and into a small office. It was a cramped room with a metal desk and two chairs, one of them facing a small, antiquated terminal. Papers covered every available surface: invoices, pay stubs, purchase orders. Hanging on the wall was an old-fashioned flip calendar on which a number of dates had been circled in red pen. Unusual, but not unheard of: if the business here was anything like what Eli suspected, having a paper-based trail was probably less traceable, a benefit to those who moved goods in and out.

Having been cut loose from his aluminum chair perch, Eli was massaging his wrists where the plastic restraints had cut into them and left his skin red and raw. He eyed his brother, who was shaking his head, not yet come to terms with the ghost in front of him.

The picture that Eli had seen in the Commonwealth's dossier had been out of date, but it didn't really matter: he would have known that face no matter what. Five years his senior, Eamon had inherited their father's looks, right down to the bright red hair. That color had softened with age, fading from the fiery mane of his youth toward a burnished copper. He'd grown a beard, too: a full red one that, even trimmed short as it was, covered his cheeks and chin. The green eyes flanking the broad nose were also pure Connor Brody, whereas Eli's own blue ones stemmed firmly from their mother's side. But more than anything, it was the subtle twist of the mouth that made him think of their father, a slight jag that Eli had always associated with unpredictable violence.

So when Eamon stepped toward him, Eli found himself involuntarily bracing for a slug. But, to his shock, his brother enfolded him in a bear hug, squeezing him to the point that he thought his shoulder might pop out of its socket. When he finally released Eli, Eamon held him out at arm's length, his eyes sweeping up and down as if they could take in the last nine years in a glance. "Christ," he said, his voice grating and rough, "I can't believe it."

"Hey," said Eli awkwardly.

"We thought you were dead." To Eli's continuing surprise, he thought he saw his brother's eyes glistening. *Must be a trick of the light.* "Meghann and I. When we heard about Sabaea, about the Illyrican fleet—which wasn't until, god, a week or two later—Meg looked you up in the rolls they posted on the net. 'Brody, Elijah, Flight Lieutenant; 42nd Fighter Wing, ISC *Venture* carrier strike group, Fifth Fleet: missing in action.'" He rattled it off as quickly as Eli could have recited his name, rank, and serial number. "She would have cried for weeks if she'd had any tears left in her."

A pang of guilt jolted through Eli like somebody had punched him in the gut. Meghann had been just fourteen when he left for the academy, a bright-eyed, red-haired, energetic girl with a smile for everyone she met. In his head, the last message, the one the old man had played, echoed back at him.

*I think you should come home.*

"Any other time, I would have been thrilled to hear the crims had gotten a swift kick to the bollocks," Eamon went on, shaking his head again. "But not at that cost."

Eli blinked; he didn't think he'd ever heard Eamon say a single thing about the Imperium that wasn't scornful, if not out-and-out violent. The red hair hadn't been the only thing Eamon had gotten from their father— his legendary temper had come with it. As a kid it had been employed to keep his younger siblings protected from their father's choleric bouts. As he'd grown older, that anger had turned outward, to the people that had invaded their planet. His brother had been about twelve when the Illyricans had arrived and, with the pubescent hormones intensifying his already established restlessness, the gangs had been a natural outlet.

"I saw about the gate to Sabaea reopening," his brother continued, walking over to an ancient-looking coffee maker that sat by the door. "It was all over the news—could hardly hear about anything else all day." He waved a paper cup toward Eli, who nodded in response. Eamon poured two cups of black sludge that looked as though it had been sitting on the burner for at least a couple of weeks, then handed one to Eli. He took it gratefully, letting the steam waft into his nose.

"But I never in a million years imagined you'd turn up back here. You were stuck there the whole time?" A note of something else—suspicion, maybe—had crept into Eamon's voice.

"Pretty much," said Eli, staring down into the cup.

"Pretty much," Eamon echoed. "Gwennie said you ditched the crims." His head cocked to one side, eyes watching Eli. "That true?"

He gave a careful nod. "Yeah, I did. Thought you'd be ecstatic about that?"

Eamon gave a deep snort. "Not unless you did it while you were traveling in your time machine."

"Sorry," said Eli. "It's in the shop."

He thought that might get a laugh out of his brother, even if only a bitter one, but the elder Brody just rubbed a hand across his face. "Sweet mother of mercy, Lije. What the hell are you *doing* here?"

Eli winced at the nickname. His family had called him "Lije"—no one else had. "I came home."

"Nine years gone by and you stroll into the Pig and Thistle like a tourist and start dropping my name?"

"Well, I didn't know how else to bloody *find* you," said Eli, heat rising in his face. "You don't have a comm number that I know of, mom and dad are dead, they *bulldozed* the One-Seven. Where the hell else was I supposed to go? For all that I'm supposed to be dead, you're the one who's practically a ghost."

Eamon crossed his arms over his chest, his expression neutral. "You could say I value my privacy these days." He softened. "You're a lucky bastard, you know that? Those guys would have sliced you up and fed you to whatever's swimming around the harbor at this time of night."

"And what the hell is up with *that*?" said Eli, waving his arms in exasperation. "Armed guards at the door of the Pig and Thistle? Thugs dragging me into a warehouse just for asking after you? Who the hell are these people? Your drinking buddies? Your ragtag band of misfits?"

"Just colleagues."

"Colleagues I wouldn't want to meet down a dark alley. The *Black Watch*, Eam? Really?"

Eamon's eyes narrowed. "What do you know about it?"

"Enough to know they're bad news. That they *kill* people. The attack on the Illyrican trade delegation when we were kids? The Bloody Hundred? De Valera? Everybody knows he's a maniac, even if they're too scared to say it. And you're, what, *working* for him?" Eli shook his head. "Christ, Eamon. What the hell happened?"

Eamon's expression was hard. "You've been gone a long time, Lije. Things have changed."

"No kidding." His wrists still ached and he rubbed at the raw flesh. *But I'm not sure if it was too long or not long enough.*

The older Brody shifted and leaned back against the desk, coffee seemingly forgotten in one hand. "Spill, Lije."

"What?"

Eamon rolled his eyes. "You're telling me it's a coincidence that less than three days after Sabaea miraculously returns to the galactic fold you just show up, out of the blue, in the Pig and Thistle? From what I heard, the Illyricans are only now looking to see if anybody from the invasion fleet is still alive." His green eyes narrowed. "But you're *here* already. No muss, no fuss." He shook his head. "I don't believe in coincidences. Someone's pulling your strings, Lije. The question is 'who?'"

Eli fought the ire rising in his chest. It wasn't so much *what* his brother was saying, but as always there was something so damn infuriating about the *way* he said it. Eamon's question, however, seemed to be of a rhetorical bent.

"The Illyricans would surely love to see me hanging by my thumbs." The coffee cup crumpled slightly in Eamon's hand. "Did IIS ask you to do them a favor and track down your troublesome brother? After all, no love lost between us, is there? Did they even offer you anything, or did you just do it out of the goodness of your heart? Or maybe it was patriotic love for emperor and empire?" With each question, his expression turned grimmer until Eli fancied he could hear the grinding of his older brother's teeth from across the room.

"Whoa, whoa, whoa," said Eli, raising his hands, palms out. "It wasn't the Illyricans. Geez, who do you think I am?"

"Once a crim . . ."

*Yeah, heard that one before.* "Well, I'm not anymore."

"So?" said Eamon, eyes hard. "Who?"

"It was your buddies in the Commonwealth, you moron. They got me off Sabaea and asked me to help track you down. They said you might be in danger."

"From who?" Eamon gave a bitter laugh. "I'm a wanted man, Lije. They're going to have to be more specific."

"I don't know exactly," said Eli, shaking his head. "The Illyricans, I guess."

Eamon snorted. "The day I need the Commonwealth's help to stay one step ahead of the crims is the day they'll be picking out my coffin."

"Look, they told me you were doing some work for them, feeding them information on some Illyrican secret project. It's got 'em all hot and bothered."

Eamon sighed, pushing himself off the desk. The coffee cup looked rather the worse for wear; the elder Brody glanced down at it in distaste, then tossed it into a nearby garbage can with a sloshing sound. He wiped his hands on his trousers. "What do they want?"

Eli let out a breath he didn't realize he'd been holding. "Just a meet. They want whatever information you've got that they don't. That's it."

A skeptical snort issued from Eamon's direction. "That's rarely 'it.' Everybody's got an agenda." His gaze returned to Eli, once again taking on an air of thoughtful appraisal. "Speaking of which, what do *you* get out of this whole arrangement?"

"Besides not having to spend the rest of my days as a mandatory guest of one government or another?"

Eamon didn't blink.

He sighed. "Meghann. They said they'd make sure I was able to take care of her."

A stillness hung in the air between them, like the moment before a thunderstorm unleashed a driving torrent of rain. Eli tugged at his collar, which suddenly seemed too tight.

"Meghann?" repeated Eamon. His voice had gone quiet—dangerously so—but it wasn't hard to see something simmering below the surface.

"Yeah."

"Our sister is not a *bargaining chip*, Lije," he growled, stepping toward him. "What the *fuck* makes you think you have the right to make deals about her future?"

Something in Eli's chest stretched, then snapped, and he pushed off the wall toward Eamon. "I'm her brother too, Eam. It's my job to take care of her, just as much as it is yours."

"And you *left*."

The anger sloughed off his brother like a shockwave, and Eli instinctively took a step back, only barely avoiding cowering beneath the holy wrath that Eamon had summoned. Under a darkened brow that reminded Eli uncomfortably of their father, he fixed his younger brother with a cold stare.

"Don't fuck around, Lije. She grieved for you, you hear me? There wasn't a body to bury, but that didn't stop her from mourning—not least because there was no one else to do it. Everybody left her: mom, dad, Aunt Brigid, Uncle Kieran, *you*. Everyone left her, except for *me*." His expression had turned fierce, eyes glinting. "So you stay the hell away from her. Take whatever deal the Commonwealth is giving you for finding your errant brother and get the hell off Caledonia."

"Fine," Eli bit off. *You righteous asshole*, he didn't add.

Eamon nodded sharply and huffed out a breath. "Okay. Long as we got that settled, I'll go to your goddamn meeting—but I don't want you there. This is between me and the Commonwealth. Your part is *done*." He picked up a pad of paper from the desk and scribbled something on it, then ripped off the top sheet with a swift motion that looked like he'd have preferred it to be Eli's arm.

Eli took it gingerly, as though it might burst into flames, and glanced down: Café Écossian, 9 a.m. The address below was in Raleigh City's upscale Highgate district, the polar opposite of Leith and Upham. The kind of place you went when you had money to burn.

Crossing his arms, Eamon nodded again. "So, Lije, I guess this is it." Something around his eyes softened ever so slightly; Eli didn't think he'd have noticed it on anybody else. "Look. I'm glad you're okay, but this," he said, waving his hands at the office around them, but encompassing something larger, "this isn't for you. It was never your world." He shook his head. "Find something else. Somewhere else."

An empty feeling plucked at Eli's stomach. Maybe there was truth to the old saying: You couldn't go home again. Especially when there wasn't anywhere left to call home. Suddenly, cleaning out the toilets on Davidson Station didn't seem so bad.

*No*, part of his brain reminded him, *it was pretty bad.*

"Yeah," he said at last. "Okay."

"Good. Now, I'm afraid I'm going to have to ask you to let my friends out there blindfold you and take you out of here. It's better for all of us if you don't know exactly where you are. All right?"

Instinctively, Eli prepared to object, then closed his mouth when he realized he had little to gain from it. If he didn't agree then all it meant was they'd do it the hard way, and that man with the scarred face had seemed a little too eager at the prospect of violence.

"Well, I guess I don't have much of a choice, huh? Otherwise you'll just have to pry my eyes out?" he said, trying to inject a note of levity into the conversation.

Eamon just nodded. "It's one option."

"Right. Uh, I think I'll go with the blindfold."

# CHAPTER TEN

**K**ovalic was getting impatient. Strike that: he'd passed impatient about half an hour ago on the express train to Anxious City. The ceaseless drumming of his fingers on his thigh would have been enough of a clue for anybody, but in case that wasn't sufficient he kept pulling his comm out of his pocket, flipping it open, and then closing it again, like a parent whose kid was out past curfew.

"That's it," he said finally. "We're going in."

"'Bout bleeding time," said Tapper, slapping his hands together. "I scrounged up a couple sluggers—they're kind of on the vintage side, but they checked out all right. Also, found a pair of concussion grenades for cheap. Good chance at least one of them's a dud, but doesn't hurt to carry just in case. Oh, and a spring-loaded composite blade."

Kovalic shook his head. The sergeant's knack for somehow acquiring a mélange of dangerous and deadly weaponry within twenty-four hours of landing on a planet—any planet—never ceased to amaze him. There seemed to be something about the man that black marketeers responded to, though he wasn't sure if it was respect or just plain old intimidation.

"Anything on the non-lethal side?"

"Well the conkers aren't going to kill anybody if they actually work."

"I was looking for something a little more . . . subtle?"

"Subtlety is Three's department, cap."

"Speaking of which." Kovalic flipped the comm open again and called Page. The lieutenant opened the line, but didn't say anything.

"We're going to take a stroll," said Kovalic. "Eyes sharp, let me know if you spot anything."

"Got it," murmured Page.

Kovalic rang off as Tapper dug into his rucksack full of armaments. They'd taken up a spot a few blocks from where Page was keeping watch, just in case the man needed backup. Skimming Tapper's offerings, Kovalic took the blade but decided against the pistol. With a shrug, Tapper loaded a cartridge into one of the guns and checked it.

The two slipped out of the alley into the narrow, winding streets of Leith, lit only by foggy pools of light from the faux-antique street lamps. This late at night, the only other people walking were either trouble or looking for it.

"Weird place," muttered Tapper.

"Yeah, why's that?"

"All this . . . pretense." Tapper waved his hands at the buildings and streetlights. "Designing the things to look like Earth five hundred years ago, like it was some sort of golden age." He shook his head. "I'm as much a fan of revivalist architecture as the next fellow, but it's just not practical."

"I don't think practicality is necessarily what they had in mind." But Tapper was right: there was an almost theme-park feeling to this part of Raleigh City, as though the streets were lined with facades fronting empty houses. Eerie.

Shaking off a slight feeling of unease, Kovalic made for the turn he'd identified earlier. He'd taken advantage of their holding pattern to pull up maps of the area and plan their approach. A block or so down from their position they found the narrow entrance to Deadman's Close and turned inside, their steps echoing from the vaulted stone ceiling overhead. Tight quarters with a chokepoint at either end; that made it a good place for an ambush. He was fairly confident he and Tapper could handle your average street thugs, but they did have the disadvantage of not knowing the terrain.

The fears proved unfounded as they exited the tunnel back into the night and started down a long, winding staircase. The condensation from the fog had made the steps treacherous and the lack of a real railing meant the only option was to go slowly and brace yourself against the opposite wall. Instead of an ambush, Kovalic supposed you could just wait for people to start down the stairs and then chuck rocks at them until they fell. Just as effective, really, and certainly looked a lot more like an accident than a knife in the gut.

To Kovalic's relief, they made it without incident. At the bottom of the stairs, Kovalic consulted his mental map and turned left, then right. The water of Leith Harbor came into view: a dark, empty mass ahead of them. A few ships bobbed in the fog, red and green lights blinking; they bounced up and down like a drunken Christmas tree.

The same sense that had kept him alive this long gave him a nudge before his dark-adjusted eyes even saw the figure emerge from the deeper shadows. He felt Tapper tense beside him and casually put a hand on the sergeant's forearm.

The figure was small and wiry, and strolled over to them as though it were the most natural thing in the world. In the darkness, Kovalic had a hard time appraising the threat the shadow might pose. Even if it were armed, it didn't seem prepared for a fight—which might merely mean that it felt confident in its backup or that it was very dangerous indeed.

"*Fàilte*," a man's voice said.

"*Fàilte*," Kovalic echoed back, wrapping his mouth around the unfamiliar word.

The man seemed to be waiting for something else.

"Nice night we're having, huh?" said Kovalic cheerfully.

He saw the figure stiffen and shift his weight but, before the man could act or move, Tapper had slipped forward and punched him in the stomach. The air went out of him in a single *poof* and he doubled over. That turned out to be a particularly bad idea, since it presented ample opportunity for Tapper to bring an elbow down on the back of the man's neck. The figure went down like a sack of potatoes. Tapper brushed his hands off and straightened his coat.

"Something tells me that he wasn't the only one," murmured Kovalic.

"Well, maybe if you'd let Three bring that night-vision gear he loves so much we could know for sure. But what's done is done."

Kovalic looked down at the dark shape crumpled at their feet and sighed. "We can't just leave him out in the middle of the street. Grab an arm."

The sergeant complied and the two of them dragged the man back over to near where they thought he'd come from. Kovalic rifled his pockets quickly, finding only a wallet with a handful of marks and a comm unit. Skimming the unit's memory yielded a handful of calls to unnamed numbers; Kovalic dumped them into his own comm but didn't hold out much hope—this guy was just a foot soldier after all.

Tapper gave the figure a nudge with his toe and it yielded a slight groan. He'd be okay once he woke up; they'd be okay, too, just as long as they were long gone by that point—Kovalic doubted the sentry had been able to make them out in the dim light. But they didn't have time to take out each and every gang member between here and the bar.

"I think we're going to need a distraction," he said slowly. "How's your belligerent drunk?"

Tapper tilted his head to one side. "Are you talkin' to *me*?" he half-slurred, half-growled.

Kovalic raised an eyebrow. "A bit much, but it'll probably do. Weapons." He beckoned with a hand.

With a sigh, Tapper reluctantly pulled out the pair of concussion grenades from his pockets, the pistol from the back of his waistband, a backup pistol from a holster on his right ankle, and a six-inch combat knife from his left boot. The last he slapped into Kovalic's open hand with a sigh. "Christ, buy a guy dinner before you get him down to his skivvies. What if they jump me?"

"It's not you I'm worried about," said Kovalic with a roll of his eyes as he returned the gear to Tapper's rucksack and shouldered it himself. "I'd rather do this without a body count. If you're not back in an hour, Three and I are going to come looking for you."

"Roger, boss."

"All yours then." Kovalic gave him a slight bow and gestured toward the street at large.

Tapper rolled his shoulders, then made a good show of stumbling out into the street. Throwing his head back, he yelled loudly enough that his voice—now tinged with the rough, slurred tones of the intoxicated—reverberated off the flanking buildings. "Olly oxen free!"

Kovalic shook his head and then, sticking to the shadows, slipped off the main drag and onto one of the many side streets. As long as he kept out of sight and away from whatever ruckus Tapper was causing, he ought to be able to make his way to the Pig and Thistle largely undisturbed.

The side streets weren't nearly as well-lit as the main road—and that was saying something. The few street lamps that dotted the area were flickering or giving off only a dim orange light that illuminated little more than their immediate surroundings. Kovalic let his eyes adjust to the dark, but even so could barely make out anything more than the blocky shapes of the buildings. Not that there was much else to discern at this time of night; the streets seemed to be largely empty.

As he prepared to round a corner, something made the back of his neck itch—he'd seen nothing and heard nothing, but he'd learned to trust that feeling. Pressing himself against the side of the building, he edged to the corner and gave the barest of peeks around. Nothing presented itself to his field of vision and he was about to chalk it up to a false positive when the hint migrated from his subconscious to the forefront of his mind: the smell of cigarette smoke. His mind automatically cataloged it; it wasn't one of the popular commercial brands, and the faint hint of the burning paper suggested that it had been rolled by hand.

A glowing orange ember burned briefly in the shadows of a building that was about halfway down the street he'd been about to turn down; it faded just as quickly. Another sentry. One who, had Kovalic continued blithely along his path, would have clearly seen him silhouetted in even the faint light from the street lamp. And, unfortunately, the sentry was positioned right smack dab between Kovalic and his destination.

What he wouldn't have given for one of CID's electrical disruptors—those things could knock out a street light from a hundred yards away. Unfortunately, they also weighed several pounds, which made them somewhat impractical to pack on a whim.

Glancing around, he took stock of his situation: the intersection formed a T, and he'd been about to swing a 90-degree left turn. Thanks to an unlikely cluster of streetlights, crossing the junction was out. He briefly considered breaking one of the streetlights with a loose brick or rock, but that seemed likely to attract more attention than he wanted.

As he took in the scene, he chanced to look upward and caught sight of a stone arch that overhung part of the street, connecting two buildings on opposite sides of the street. It was an odd architectural choice and one for which Kovalic figured he could thank the Caledonian forebears' fascination with this particular branch of Earth architecture. Still, he wouldn't look a gift arch in the mouth, as it were.

Sadly, the same city planners had failed to leave him a convenient fire escape to climb up. But the virtue of this architectural style was that it had plenty of nooks and crannies to use as footholds. It had been a while since he'd last free climbed, but luckily the buildings in this part of town were only a few stories high. It took him about seven minutes, at the fastest safe pace he could manage, to climb to the top, followed by another two minutes of quietly leaping from rooftop to close-set rooftop until he made it to the archway.

Here, at least, providence smiled upon him. The top of the arch was wide enough to walk across, as long as he didn't topple over in one direction or the other. Placing heel to toe, he held his arms outstretched and slowly made his way across.

He'd made it to about the halfway point when the sharp voice of a woman rang out from below him.

"Oi!"

Kovalic froze, his heart pounding. As far as places to get caught went, he was hard pressed to think of a single one that could be worse. Explaining what he was doing tiptoeing his way across rooftops at this hour, in this particular part of town, was not likely to be met with a jovial laugh and a slap on the back. He tensed, poising himself to sprint the rest of the way across.

"What're ye doin' here, Duffy?" came a second voice. It wasn't a loud voice, but thanks to the acoustics of the buildings it echoed up to Kovalic just fine. Kovalic risked a look down, then wished he hadn't as his vision spun into a merry carousel. Looking up, he fixed his eyes on a stable point—the end of the bridge. Despite the ill-advised look, it had been enough to establish that the second voice probably belonged to the sentry whose cigarette he'd seen.

"Some nutter's hammered out of his mind. He's trawling up and down the waterfront, lookin' for a punch-up. Shouting something about being the toughest bloke this side of Jericho Station."

Kovalic stifled a chuckle, which, fortunately enough, probably would have been masked by the sentry's own laugh.

"Is he now? Well, give 'im one for me, would ye?"

"What, you don't want to come and try it yourself?"

"And have De Valera sic his pitbull Brody on me for abandoning my post? Ye'd have to be a sight more cracked than that feller out there to want those blood-soaked bastards on your case."

Kovalic blinked at the mention of the names. There were such interesting things to be learned when people didn't know you were listening. He shifted his position slightly to get a better vantage on the conversation, but his foot slid over a patch of crumbling masonry; a chunk about the size of his fist arced off the bridge and plummeted toward the ground below, nearly taking Kovalic with it. Instead he followed his instinct and dropped flat, clinging onto the arch for dear life.

The stone hit the ground not far from where the two gang members stood talking, and Kovalic heard a startled exclamation. He hugged the bridge, trying to remain as still as possible.

"Bloody hell," the woman was saying. "Where'd that come from?"

"All these old buildings are falling apart."

Kovalic risked peeking over the edge, where he could see the two of them squinting up toward him. Fortunately, the darkness seemed to shroud him from their gaze.

"Probably just a rat or a stray cat," said the woman. "There's plenty of them about at night."

"Rats," said the other, with a decided note of distaste. "All this science and technology and whatnot, ye'd think we'd have gotten rid of rats by now."

"Ah," said the woman, "but then what would the cats chase?" There was the sound of a friendly shoulder clap. "Well, I'm back at it, but you go on keepin' the night safe from those little critters."

"Fuck off," said the sentry, in a cheerful enough tone. "I'll hold ye to a drink at the Pig later."

"Count on it."

Footsteps marked the woman's departure, and Kovalic let out a sigh of relief. After a moment to be sure that the sentry wasn't still looking in his direction, he bellycrawled his way across the rest of the bridge. He'd never been so happy to set foot on a stable surface, even if it was a rooftop. Fortunately, this building did have a fire escape that he clambered down as quietly as he could, dropping the last half story to the alley below.

Crossing back downwind of the sentry, he ended up on the main drag again.

The light coming from the Pig and Thistle was visible from a block away, along with the low hum of activity that surrounded the place. Kovalic could see a handful of folks outside, most of them laughing and talking, but there were a pair of gentlemen standing guard outside the pub. These guys were bigger than the sentry Tapper had taken down—they looked more like professional muscle. Was the gang outsourcing its security? That seemed odd.

The small knot of people outside didn't look alarmed by his being here; having gotten this far, it seemed he was considered harmless until proven otherwise. Not particularly smart, but these were gang members, not soldiers. At least the two men standing guard had the decency to eye Kovalic suspiciously as he walked toward the bar's entrance—then again, it was probably the same look they were paid to give everyone.

They never got a chance to follow through on that suspicion, however, as the door to the Pig and Thistle slammed open and two similarly large gentlemen—one, Kovalic's trained eye noticed, with a large scar down the side of his face—manhandled a smaller fellow out the door. Without fanfare, they pitched the man out into the street where he reeled forward and toppled into Kovalic.

Instinctively, Kovalic caught the man, a split-second later regretting the move, since it left him without a free hand. Looking down, he found himself, to some surprise, meeting the eyes of a dazed and somewhat bruised Eli Brody.

Brody, unfortunately, didn't have the benefit of Kovalic's long history in covert operations, nor was he helped by his current disoriented state. Kovalic watched as the other man's eyes widened and his mouth opened. "Fiel—" he started to say.

"Roll with the punches" was the cardinal rule of any good operative, and not just in combat situations. You never knew exactly what curveballs life was going to throw your way, so all you could do was trust and hone your instincts. With no other options at hand, Kovalic took the advice at its most literal.

"Fucking hell," he growled. "Watch where the *fuck* you're going."

He saw Brody's expression turn from bewilderment to confusion, though it didn't have long to live on the man's face as the curse was followed up with a punch that was close cousin to the one Tapper had given the Tartan sentry. Brody, softened by whatever abuse he'd endured earlier, crumpled, giving Kovalic just enough time to bend over and whisper in his ear.

"Stay down," he hissed, then shoved Brody backward as realistically as he could manage without putting his full strength into it. Brody stumbled and hit the ground, unmoving, though whether from Kovalic's instructions or just the natural effects of being punched it was impossible to say.

"Looks like your friend can't hold his liquor," Kovalic jeered, wiping his hands. "Get him sobered up before you send him out into the streets, why don't you?"

With a laugh Kovalic continued on his way around the corner. The moment he was out of sight he already had his comm out of his pocket and was calling Page.

"That was quite a show," the lieutenant answered without any preamble.

"Gave 'em the best tickets in the house. Make sure our friend gets home safely, all right? Two ought to have cleared things out a bit for you. I'm heading back."

"On my way." Page clicked off.

Kovalic stowed the comm. He'd have to take the long way round back to the rendezvous to swing wide of any festivities Tapper might be having, so he and Page would probably pass like ships in the night. Not that Kovalic was particularly worried about the lieutenant; if he could run the gauntlet himself, there was no reason to think that Page wouldn't slip through it like sand through a sieve.

It took him about twenty minutes to get back to the rendezvous point and he was more than a little surprised to find Tapper already there, leaning against a wall. The sergeant's clothes were a bit torn around the seams and his face had acquired a coating of grime, peppered with a few fresh scrapes, but otherwise he didn't look much the worse for wear.

"Soooo," said Kovalic, raising an eyebrow, "how'd it go?"

"Oh, you know," said Tapper. "It was all just one big misunderstanding." He brushed at a spot on his jacket. "They send their regards. Did you find Brody?"

"Yeah, Three is seeing to him. Actually, I'd say he looks considerably worse than you do."

Tapper shrugged. "We aren't all blessed with my natural good looks."

With a sigh, Kovalic leaned against the wall, next to Tapper. He'd have cracked a beer if they'd brought one. "That whole thing was a little too close for my comfort. So far tonight I've been accosted by a gang, almost fallen off a building, and nearly had my cover blown by an amateur."

"Well, look on the bright side."

"Remind me, please: which one's the bright side?"

"Despite Brody's best efforts, he's not dead."

"Yeah," said Kovalic. "Something tells me he'll have another shot at it."

# CHAPTER ELEVEN

Eli was pretty certain he didn't deserve the massive hangover he'd ended up saddled with. For one thing, he'd had all of two drinks, albeit one of them dosed with some sort of particularly powerful sedative. So, yes, logically he could explain *why* his head felt as though someone were very *sloooowly* running it over with a truck. But he still didn't think he deserved it.

They'd let him sleep for a few hours before he'd been rudely awakened by Fielding pulling back the drapes and letting Caledonia's bright, early morning sun douse the room in liquid gold—which sounded a lot more pleasant than it had actually been. Eli, for his part, had never thought of sunlight as particularly malicious, but maybe he'd just never gotten on its bad side before.

If nothing else, the debriefing that had followed his rousting was considerably more pleasant than the one he'd endured at the hands of his brother's "colleagues" the night before. Fielding had raised his eyebrows at the news that he'd found Eamon, exchanging a glance with the rest of his team, and had asked calmly but persistently for any details on where Eli had been taken. Eli, naturally, had pointed out that he had been drugged on the way in and blindfolded on the way out, neither of which made for quality intelligence-gathering.

"Look," he said finally. "I got him to agree to your damn meeting. Isn't that what you wanted?"

Fielding seemed somewhat less ecstatic at his accomplishment than Eli had hoped. The other two men maintained a steady, careful neutral expression, but that told Eli as much as he needed to know.

"That's not it, is it?" he sighed. *Damn it. I would have enjoyed throwing that in Eamon's face.*

"It's an important part," said Fielding. "But no, it's not everything." He eyed the shorter and older of the two men, who had been introduced as "Two," and who Eli had recognized belatedly as the same "veteran" who had passed him Fielding's message the previous afternoon. Of the two, he had the worse poker face by far, and right now he wasn't holding anything better than a high card.

"I dunno, boss," he said, shifting his weight from foot to foot. "Seems a little too . . . easy."

"Easy?" snapped Eli. "Sorry, I didn't see *you* in there, blindfolded and strapped to a chair."

The man gave a deep, ripping snort. "Quit being such a baby."

Fielding gave him a warning glance, but it seemed to more or less rebound off Two, who simply jammed his hands back in his pockets and shrugged. The operative turned his attention back to Eli.

"Given your experience, your brother seems somewhat more . . . well connected than we'd thought."

*The Black Watch.* "Yeah, that was news to me, too." *Though perhaps not really surprising, given his trajectory when I last saw him.*

"The Illyricans have this Black Watch group earmarked as terrorists. And given the hired muscle we saw outside the Pig and Thistle, they're not just your friendly neighborhood radicals." Fielding's eyes narrowed. "What exactly is your brother's role in the group?"

*Good question.* "Search me. He got mixed up with the Tartans when we were kids, but it's not like we've been exchanging letters the last few years."

Fielding sighed, then seemed to abandon the line of questioning. "All right, then. Where and when's the meet?"

And there it was, plain and simple. Eli had been thinking it over in the spare time that he'd had between being tossed out of the Pig and Thistle and being questioned by Fielding, and he'd come to one inescapable conclusion: He was short on leverage.

*Now or never.*

"About that," he began.

"Oh, lord," said Two, his eyes rolling up. "There's always something."

Eli ignored him. "I need something in exchange."

Fielding raised his eyebrows. "You want to renegotiate our deal? Now?" His head tilted to one side. "I don't think you understand how this works."

"I'm not renegotiating. I just want what I was promised in the first place—part of it, anyway. I want to go see my sister." *Sorry, Eamon. She's my blood, too. You don't get the only say in this.*

The sigh that issued from Fielding could only be described as long-suffering, and the man pinched the bridge of his nose between thumb and forefinger. "After the meet."

Eli shook his head. "No. Eamon said he doesn't want me there. As far as he's concerned—hell, as far as *I'm* concerned—our deal is done. Let's call it a fair trade: an address for an address." Besides, Eamon being busy with Fielding meant it was the one safe time for Eli to see Meghann. And then maybe the two of them could get off-world before their brother was any the wiser.

"Listen, you little prick," Two started, but Fielding waved his hand, cutting him short.

"You're putting me in a bind here, Brody. This meeting doesn't pan out, then I don't have much left in the way of intelligence."

Eli shrugged. "I'm not sure what else I'm supposed to tell you. I did the job you guys dragged me here to do."

Five o'clock stubble rasped against Fielding's nails like an emery board. "How about that warehouse? The one where they took you."

"The one where I woke up drugged and blindfolded? Oh, sure, let me just get you the address out of my contacts here." He held Fielding's gaze.

"Anything you can give us would be helpful."

"The best I can offer is that it's somewhere within a few minutes of the Pig and Thistle. Probably connected by a tunnel, from what I can tell."

"There are two dozen warehouses that could fit that description," the tall, thin man called Three said, his eyes rapidly flicking back and forth in the process of mental calculations.

"Come on, Brody," said Fielding. "You're an observant guy. I've seen it firsthand. There must be *something* else you noticed."

"Oh, sure: I noticed there were four industrial-strength lighting rigs pointed in my face."

"What about the people?" Fielding persisted. "You said there were others."

With a sigh, Eli cast his memory back. "Four or five. Plus Eamon. At least two women among them, but I think the rest were men. The only one I ever got a clear look at was the girl from the bar—Gwen."

"A redhead named Gwen," muttered Two. "Well, that narrows it down. Might as well say 'find somebody on this goddamned planet that enjoys the taste of alcohol.'"

Fielding ignored his comrade, still staring at Eli. "Let's try a little exercise," he suggested. "Close your eyes."

Eli fixed him with a suspicious look. "I'd rather not."

"Brody."

"Okay, okay!" With a last skeptical look, Eli exhaled and let his eyes slide closed. It wasn't quite black when he did so, he noticed; the bright sunlight from the room, not yet obscured by the afternoon haze, still leaked in through the edges.

Fielding's voice slid in and wrapped around him, reminding him uncomfortably of the way his captors had questioned him. Deprivation of sensory cues could be an effective tactic in interrogation, he recalled from some class he'd taken at the academy; it helped throw the target off balance.

"I want you to picture your experience last night. Remember what it felt like, what it sounded like, even what it *smelled* like. Put yourself back there, and then talk us through it . . . slowly."

"Really? We're playing imagin—"

"Just do it, Brody." There was a pause as Fielding cut himself off, the sound of an indrawn breath. "Trust me."

"Okay, fine." And with a breath of his own, he launched into a description of last night's activities, starting with his awakening tied to a chair with a towel around his head. He ran through as much of the conversation as he could remember, which was less specifics than the general gist of what Gwen and her friends had wanted to know: who he was, why he was there, why he was looking for Eamon Brody. The more he talked, the more he found himself remembering by sheer association, whether it be Gwen's scent or the feeling of sweat trickling down his brow. Once he'd picked up steam, Fielding remained quiet during the recitation until Eamon's appearance.

"And then?" he interrupted gently.

"Eamon had them untie me, and we went up to an office overlooking the warehouse floor. I couldn't see the rest of the floor," he said quickly, anticipating Fielding's question. "My eyes weren't adjusted to the darkness."

"What did you see in the office?"

"It was kind of a mess, like a real office. There was a coffee machine—foul stuff, that—and stacks of papers everywhere." Somehow he felt Fielding tensing; the air had changed in the room. This was what they were looking for.

"Could you make out anything on the papers? A name? An address?"

Eli shut his eyes tighter, trying to make out something, but his memory was blurry. There had been invoices and pay orders on the table opposite him, but they had been upside down and he was having trouble deciphering what he was seeing. But there was something above that, too: something on the wall?

"A calendar," he said suddenly, as it resolved in his memory. "There was a calendar on the wall, with a bunch of dates circled in red; every couple weeks or so. And . . . there was a name on it. Mc . . . Mac? One of those."

There was a snort in the room that Eli would have wagered came from Two. "Yes, I know," said Eli crossly. "Imagine! But it's got a letter after it. A "D"—probably a MacDougal or a MacDonald? And there's more words after it, but I can only really remember the sense—some sort of generic company name. Shipping Incorporated? Transit Company? Something like that."

"Anything else?"

Eli shook his head; nothing else had rattled loose. "Eamon and I talked. Personal stuff, mostly."

"You can open your eyes."

The bright sunlight made Eli blink and his eyes water. Fielding was sitting across from him, hands folded, elbows resting on his knees. He looked, well, if not impressed, then at least appreciative.

"Well, that's something. Thanks."

"No problem. You guys sure know how to have a good time." He cleared his throat. "So what about our deal?"

Had there been a clock on the wall, Eli was sure he could have felt the breeze from the seconds ticking by as Fielding considered his request. Two had taken the opportunity to lean back and examine his fingernails with extreme interest. Three stared off into the distance, as though he were consulting some internal database.

"What," said Eli, breaking the silence. "You think I'm going to run off? Like the old man said, where am I gonna go?" He gestured around the room. "All the identification papers I have came from you guys. Tracking me down would barely qualify as a walk in the park."

"It's for your own safety as well," said Fielding.

"From who?" said Eli, rolling his eyes. "Besides you guys, almost nobody in the galaxy knows I'm still alive."

"Your brother knows, for one. And from the evidence we've got so far, it's pretty clear that he's highly placed in the Black Watch."

"If they wanted to kill me, they'd have done it last night. They wouldn't have let me go just to track me down again. Besides, he's my *brother*."

Fielding looked far from convinced, but Eli could tell he saw the logic in his argument.

"Come on, Fielding. I took you as a man of your word and I followed through on my part of the deal. Now it's your turn to deliver."

Maybe he was going out on a limb, but something about Fielding—the way he'd talked to Antony back on Sabaea, even the few conversations they'd had—told Eli that the man had a code. And the great thing about a code was that you could use it to your advantage.

"Fine." Fielding gestured to the other man, the lanky one who hadn't said much. "But Three will go with you to ensure your safety." Eli considered objecting to that, but as he'd already played his hole card there wasn't a snowball's chance of foregoing an escort. And, truth be told, part of him relaxed a little bit at the thought of the tall, quiet man watching his back.

"All right," said Eli. "Say hi to Eamon for me." He paused. "On second thought, don't."

●

The mismatched pair boarded the southbound maglev train for Galway less than an hour later, with stops in Rye, Donan, Oban, and Berwick— the town in which Fielding told Eli he'd find his sister. They packed light: Eli had brought nothing more than his Marcus Wellington identification papers, the comm that Fielding had given him, and his hangover—he assumed Three, on the other hand, had enough weaponry to blow up the train and confront any other threat that might arise.

They traveled separately. Having made contact with the Black Watch, there was a chance that someone was keeping tabs on Eli, so they each bought their tickets from the automated kiosk. Though they were in the same car, Three had taken a seat several rows away, where he sat calmly reading the morning news on the train's complimentary display screens; just another daily commuter.

Having gotten an early start, thanks to Fielding's bedside interrogation at the crack of dawn, they arrived in Berwick just around 9:30.

The town was not remotely what Eli had expected. Most of the settlements in the south were little more than mining outposts, there to maintain the corporate interests and accommodate the workers, overseers, and their families. They were intensely practical, lacking any sort of frill or luxury.

At Berwick, the coast jutted inland to form a small protected harbor; the town was situated atop a rocky cliffside. It was small, little more than a village, and summoned to mind words like "quaint" and "picturesque," which Eli had never before associated with his homeworld. Most astounding of all, there was actual greenery in Berwick, thanks in no small part, he determined by looking it up on his comm, to the efforts of a nearby de-salinization plant that helped turn the ocean water into life-giving irrigation for plants, trees, and grass.

The train depot itself set the mood for the town. A low, one-story building with a rounded, gabled roof, it looked as though it had been transplanted from a historical Earth novel and plopped down on this planet, light years away from its home. And yet it was of a piece with the rest of Berwick. Pleasant, paved streets ran through wooded neighborhoods; over the treetops Eli could see tiled roofs, even a steeple or two.

*It's like walking into another bloody world*, Eli thought, shaking his head. One that hadn't seen the occupation, the resistance, even the economic depression of the mining settlements. An isolated pocket, immune to the ravages of time and tide.

It gave him the creeps.

As he left the depot, Eli pulled out his comm and punched in the waypoint Fielding had given him: 712 Nicholson Street. Map directions popped up on the screen, guiding him through each turn. As he looked up again, he realized he'd lost sight of Three; his first instinct was to crane his head and look for the tall skinny man, but he caught himself just in time. *If someone is watching, that'd be a bit obvious.*

The arrows on the map led him on a merry chase through the small, winding streets of Berwick, showing him veranda-fronted houses—some with turrets, towers, and even stained glass windows—all bathed in shade from the tall trees overhead. Eli tried to keep from gawping at the surroundings, but it was all so unreal that he couldn't help himself.

After fifteen minutes of walking, the comm made its polite chime to alert him that he'd reached his destination. The charming white clapboard house at 712 Nicholson Street was similar to many of the structures he'd passed, with a wide porch that encircled it like a battlement. On the porch sat a number of rocking chairs, including one long wooden bench swing. A blue-green Caledonian flag—not the hawk crest of the Illyrican Empire, Eli noticed—snapped in the breeze.

It wasn't until the voice came through the screen door that Eli realized he was being watched. There was no question of its origins, either; the accent was distinctly Caledonian, and not the rough-and-tumble tones of Eli's own upbringing, but the romanticized rural lilt that you saw in colonization-era vids, where the parts had regularly been played by actors from Scotland and Ireland back on Earth. Somehow it had fed back into actual Caledonian society; life imitating art and all that.

"Can I help you, lad?" It was a woman's voice with a timbre that brooked no argument. If Eli had had a cap, he would have doffed it and wrung it nervously in his hands. As it was, he put on the most ingratiating smile he could summon and stepped toward the cliché of a white-picket gate.

The screen door swung open, squeaking on its hinges just as you'd expect such a screen door to squeak. Holding it open with one hand, a woman stood in the doorway, eyeing Eli with a weighty gaze. The broad features of her face, combined with the heavy coating of freckles and the pronounced auburn tint of her hair—wrapped up in a bun at the back of her head—testified to the many and varied heritages of the planet's founders. A flowered apron covered her from neck to knee, above a plain white blouse and a pair of sensible trousers.

"Morning, ma'am. I, uh—I'm looking for my sister."

Her gaze fixed him as solidly as though he were nailed into place, but there was something of recognition in it. "So you'll be the other one, then. Elijah, is it?"

"Uh, yeah, that's me," said Eli, blinking. "I'm afraid you have me at a disadvantage."

"A feeling which, I take it, you're not unused to," she said with an appraising look.

Eli hesitated, caught flat-footed by the pointed remark. "Er."

Her expression softened. "Now there's a look you'd never see on your brother's face, the cocksure bastard." The epithet was laced with an almost motherly affection. She shook her head. "There's no mistaking that face on you. Three peas in a pod, you are. Well, don't just stand there gawking all day." She turned sideways, displaying the not insubstantial bulk of her figure, and held the door open, inviting him in. Eli fumbled with the gate and let himself in, climbing the creaky wooden stairs to the porch.

Close up, the woman was no less daunting. As with her voice, there was something solid about her; it implied a steadfast resolve that not only knew more than you did, but more than pretty much anybody else you knew.

"Um," he said, finally managing to get a syllable in edgewise, a hesitant and unremarkable one though it was. "And you are?"

"I'm Sui. Sui Munroe. I look after your sister," she said while ushering him through the door and into the house.

The inside of the building was no less anachronistic than its exterior. A carved wooden balustrade swept up to the second floor from the front hallway, accompanying the lushly carpeted stairway. A glass chandelier-style light fixture hung overhead, though it was off in the daylight hours. There were paintings on the wall—some of them originals, some of them prints of more famous works—and an embarrassment of knickknacks that was far more than Eli could ever remember seeing in one place. It was altogether more *stuff* than he was accustomed to, given the places he'd lived for the last decade.

The academy had been sparse on personal possessions; during most of his time there he'd shared a bunkroom with around seven other class-mates. Then there'd been his all-too-brief stint on the *Venture* where, again, he'd had no space to himself. Then to a military prison on Sabaea, which didn't bear much remembering, and then to his janitor's closet on Davidson Base. Even his brief accommodations on the *Indefatigable* had been stripped to the bare essentials. Confronted by the assortment of decorations and material goods arrayed in the hallway, he felt a dizzy-ing sense of claustrophobia, coupled with a sensation of profound waste. *Pretty much all I've had for the last nine years are the boots on my feet.*

He caught his hostess watching him and flashed her a quick smile. "Sorry, it's not quite what I expected, I guess. This is probably the most extravagant place a Brody's ever lived."

Her forehead wrinkled slightly, but if Sui was offended by the comment she didn't show it. "Well, we like to maintain a comfortable, welcoming environment for our girls."

*Girls?*

"So," said Eli, looking around slowly, "this isn't all for Meghann?"

Sui let out an abbreviated laugh that sounded more like a bird chirping. "Dear me, no. We have around fifteen girls here at any one time. Some are only passing through—others, like your sister, are with us for longer."

Eli frowned. "I see." He looked at the woman, and then smiled awk-wardly and scratched at his head. "Well, okay, I don't really. I guess you probably know I've been away for a while."

"So I've heard. Well, you're here now, and that's what's important, right?" Still, there was a tone in her voice that made Eli feel as though she weren't convinced—something hanging in the air. *I'm missing something. Damn it, Eamon. What'd you conveniently forget to tell me?*

"Can I . . . see Meghann?"

Sui hesitated, glancing up at the stairs behind her. "I'll just go up and let her know you're here. Would you mind waiting through there?" She nodded her head toward a pair of varnished sliding wooden doors. "I'll just be a moment."

"Of course." Feeling no less confused, he watched as she climbed slowly up the stairs. Then he slid one of the doors open and stepped into the room.

Like the entryway, the room was awash in a collection of ephemera. There were framed photos on many shelves, along with a few older-looking pieces: an antique metal lantern, what looked like a centuries-old navigation device, and a large framed map that appeared to show the main continent of Caledonia, rendered in a faux-antique fashion. Light shone in through a pair of large windows draped in gauzy white curtains, and the furniture—a love-seat, armchair, and sofa—were of overstuffed red plush, almost the crimson of an Illyrican soldier's uniform.

The room was also occupied.

"Some things never change," said Eamon from the armchair. "Tell you to do one thing and you'll do the exact goddamn opposite. It'd be hilarious if it weren't so predictable."

Eli's breath caught in his chest. "Eamon? What the hell are you doing here? You're supposed to be going to the meet."

The older Brody raised an eyebrow, a move that set Eli on edge, so closely did it match his own habit. The urge to wipe the expression off his brother's face was powerful. "And you're not supposed to be here at all."

*Son of a bitch.* "So what is this, then? Interrogation, part two?" A thought occurred to him and he gritted his teeth. "Jesus, is Meghann even here? Or was this all just some bizarre ruse to get me out here?"

"Don't worry, she's here." Eamon's brow darkened. "She's hardly been anywhere else for the last five years. But that's not really the point." He got to his feet and wandered over toward the window. Standing next to the edge of the frame, he glanced outside, twitching the curtain to keep himself shadowed. "I see your babysitter came with you. You must be pretty important to the Commonwealth."

"The only reason I'm of any use to them was to find *you*. I told you: I help them, they help me."

His brother sucked in air through his teeth, adopting an air of mock regret. "Sounds tempting, but I'm afraid I'll have to pass on your little blind date."

"I don't get it." Eli's brow furrowed. "You already gave them a bunch of information. Why back out now?"

Eamon examined his fingernails. "I do business with a lot of people I'd rather avoid."

Eli stared at him. "Christ, you're still the same contrary son of a bitch, aren't you? I had my life *upended* by these bastards trying to find you, and you're not even going to spare ten minutes for them? You're going to that goddamned meeting, Eamon."

"And what, you think you're going to make me? You and your babysitter?"

"Well, I don't see any of *your* 'colleagues' from last night." He gestured around the room. "They don't exactly have your back here."

"At least I can trust them," he shot back. "They didn't take off and join the people who brutalized our planet."

Eli felt his teeth grind together. "Oh, spare me the politics. That was never my fight—you just dragged me along like a puppy on a leash."

"This is *our* planet we're talking about." Eamon's hands clenched into fists. "It's all of our fights."

"Yeah, right. I see not much has changed here."

"What's that supposed to mean?"

"For chrissake, Eamon—it's been *nine years* and you're still in the exact same place you were when I left. How's that fight going, huh? Get rid of the Illyricans yet?"

"Fuck off."

The room felt like it was suffused with flammable gas just waiting for a spark. Eli hadn't come to fight, but the more he thought about it the more he had trouble remembering why exactly he *had* come back to Caledonia in the first place. He'd thought Eamon was in trouble, and part of him had wanted to help his brother; but having found him, he'd started to wonder if that had been such a great idea. All he wanted to do now was get his sister and get the hell out of here. His deal with Fielding was looking more tantalizing by the minute: he and Meghann could be sitting on a sandy beach on one of the Commonwealth worlds, getting a tan and drinking something fruity and highly alcoholic.

Anywhere but here.

"You know what you missed, being gone for all that time?" said Eamon suddenly, his eyes burning. "I'll show you." And without further preamble, he strode across the room, seized Eli by the arm, and dragged him toward the front hallway.

"It's time you learned, little brother, that actions have consequences."

# CHAPTER TWELVE

Eamon dragged Eli all the way out of the parlor and into the foyer, his grip still fastened securely around his younger brother's wrist. They made it all the way to the base of the stairs before Eli wrenched away, rubbing at his wrist. "Bloody hell," he snapped, shoving at Eamon. "You don't have to take my arm off."

"You're lucky it was just your arm," he said in a low growl.

"Otherwise, what? You going to hit me?"

"Keep it up and I just might, wise-ass."

"*Boys.*" It was a voice with whip-crack authority. Eli winced from a phantom pinch on his ear, the maneuver that his mother had fallen back on when all else had failed. It had been surprisingly effective.

Sui Munroe had appeared and stood with her hands on her hips, somehow looking down on them despite the fact that she was a head shorter than either of the brothers.

"If either of you says so much as *one more word* at anything above an inside voice, I will have your behind out of here so fast that your eyes will still be watching it go. *Are we clear?*"

Eli's gaze had dropped sheepishly to his shoes; he nodded. "Yes, ma'am."

"Yes, Sui," said Eamon, biting at his lip. If his jaw was clenched any tighter, it would have been wired shut.

"Good," she said, dropping her hands from her hips. Her face softened. "Now, let me take you upstairs." Wiping her hands on the apron at her waist, she bustled past the two and began climbing.

The carpet that ran the length of the stairs was thick and lush. Eli ran his hand up the smooth wood of the bannister, marveling again at the sheer amount of apparent extravagance. He shook his head and glanced over at his brother.

"What is this place, anyway?" Eli murmured. His eyes darted to Sui's back cautiously.

Eamon shot him a glare. "Some place no one can find her—or at least it *was*."

"So, what? You squirreled her away so that your many and varied enemies wouldn't be able to use her as leverage on you? Nice."

Eamon paused mid-step. "You don't have a clue what you're talking about, so why don't you shut the fuck up." He resumed trudging up the stairs.

Eli's mouth set in a firm line, his brow darkening. *Sure, whatever you say.* Eamon had always been bossy—as the eldest it had been his prerogative and, with their parents both working all day, he'd been in charge of the two younger Brodys by default. But it had been nine years since Eli had taken orders from anybody not wearing a uniform, and the idea rankled like an itchy sweater.

They hung a left at the top of the stairs, walking down a lengthy hallway that was no less well-decorated than the rest of the house. As on the stairs, their footsteps made nary a sound in the rug, though Caledonia's dry air made it a perfect breeding ground for static electricity.

The doors they passed all wore brass numbers once shiny, now tarnished with age. Twenty-nine, twenty-seven, twenty-five; they stopped at twenty-three. Sui knocked, rapping twice in quick succession, but it appeared to be little more than a formality as she went ahead and opened the door anyway.

Bright light streamed through a south-facing window and white cotton curtains flapped in the ocean breeze. The room was predominantly white: whitewashed walls, white sheets on the neatly-made bed, white painted dresser and bed frame. It was crisp and homey, reminding Eli of the one summer their parents had taken them on vacation to a small cottage on the continent's east coast. It had smelled like salt water and sand, and Eli swore he caught a whiff of the exact same scent, transporting him back to that place more effectively than any wormhole.

In the center of the room, ensconced in a white rocking chair, sat a young woman with long red hair, dressed in a pale, red-checked gingham dress. A wool shawl was draped about her shoulders to fend off the slight chill from the outside air; she rocked back and forth idly, her gaze fixed on some point out the window, which overlooked the cliffs above the sea.

Even after the nine years that had seen his sister grow from a girl into a woman, there was no question of Eli not recognizing her. Like her brothers, Meghann had a face that was balanced on the knife's edge between the broad, plain visage of Connor Brody and the sharp features of Molly Brody née McKay. Likewise, her hair, all waves and almost-curls, was neither quite the fiery red of her older brother's locks nor the more subdued brown of Eli's own, but a mix of the two: auburn strands flecked with the highlights of a sunset.

Her eyes, though, were the same green as Eamon's and their father's. But as Eli looked closer, it became apparent that there was something not quite right about them: they were unfocused, distant—as though staring at something that nobody else could see.

Ms. Munroe smiled at her and bustled over to the rocking chair. "She's having a good morning, aren't you, love? She slept well, ate her breakfast, and no fussing." Plumping the pillow behind Meghann's back and smoothing down her hair, the older woman seemed to be perfectly capable of carrying on both sides of a conversation by herself. "And we've got a special treat for you today—*two* visitors. I know! You must be quite the special girl to get the attention of these two handsome gentlemen."

The longer the conversation continued, the more Eli realized that Meghann wasn't expected to respond. A faint tickle from the outside breeze raised the hairs on his arms, even underneath his long-sleeved shirt, and sent his skin crawling. It took him a long time to summon the courage to speak and, when he did, it was in a low whisper meant for Eamon alone.

"What happened?"

Eamon's face was carved from stone. "Not here." He tried on a series of grimaces, finally finding one that looked at least marginally happy. Plastering that one on his face, he went over to sit down on the wooden chair next to the rocker. "Good morning, kiddo," he said, taking her hand in his own. "How's my favorite girl?"

Sui Munroe tidied up a few things, then took up a spot next to Eli. "This *is* a good morning for her," she said softly. "Sometimes she gets upset and angry, won't touch a bite of her food. Once she threw a tray across the room." She nodded at a dent on the wall that had been inexpertly plastered over. "She scared Sally—that's my niece, she helps out around the place—half to death."

"I . . ." Eli started, and then realized he had no idea what he was going to say. What *could* he say? "I didn't know," he finally said, wincing at the pathetic inadequacy of the sentiment. "Excuse me." He took a step backward and retreated into the hall where he leaned his back against the wood-paneled wall and drew a shaky lungful of air.

The door creaked open and closed and a hand squeezed his shoulder. He looked up into the sympathetic face of Sui Munroe.

"I'm sorry, lad. I thought your brother had told you."

Eli snorted, though it became more a sniffle about halfway through. "The things he hasn't told me over the years, well, let's just say that they could fill a bulk freighter."

"Well, that's family for you, isn't it? I talk to my sister Rae every week, and what does she neglect to tell me but that she's gone into the hospital for surgery. A minor operation, sure, but she could have said, right?"

Eli rubbed at his face with his palms. "It's not all his fault. I was . . . away for a long time." He paused, then looked up. "What happened to her?"

The woman sighed, fingers pinching at the fabric of her flowered apron. "Young women come to us for all manner of reasons. Some just need a little time to get back on their feet. Others have more . . . complicated problems. As for your sister, I think perhaps that's a story best left for your brother to tell. You're her family; I'm just here to look after her." A faraway almost-smile crossed her face, but it was tinged with a faint air of sadness.

*She's personally invested*, he realized. *Someone close to her was in a place like this.* He nodded slowly in return. "I understand. For what it's worth, thanks."

"For what?"

"For looking after my sister."

"It's my job." There was an almost reproachful edge to her voice.

"To feed her and put a roof over her head, maybe," said Eli. He leaned over and kissed her cheek. "But not to care. That's all you."

Ms. Munroe blushed and swatted at him. "You're a charmer, aren't you? Just like your brother."

Eli's spirits fell at the comparison, then dropped further at the realization that he had to go back into Meghann's room. As though about to plunge underwater, he took another deep breath, opened the door, and dove in.

They were sitting together, a picture-perfect tableau in the white morning light: Meghann in the rocker and Eamon holding her small pale hand between his own. His brother looked up, brow furrowing, as Eli returned. Eli put his hands up, miming surrender, then closed the door behind him.

Eamon was talking in a low voice to Meghann; he raised a finger toward Eli, asking him to wait a second. Eli took the opportunity to wander around the rest of the room. There was a wooden dresser, whitewashed like the rest of the furniture, on top of which lay a lace-edged cloth that held a hairbrush, a few modest pieces of jewelry, and one framed photograph. It was the photo that caught his eye—not least of which because he was in it.

In fact, the whole Brody clan was there: a ten-year-old Eamon, grinning furiously at the camera, his face freckled from the sun; a more suspicious-looking Eli, at five, squinting at the light while clutching his older brother's hand; and Meghann, just around a year old, held in their mother's arms, while Connor Brody stood with his arm around her.

*The happy family.*

Not that things had been perfect then—it would have been a whitewashing job as thorough as that of the room's furniture to pretend otherwise—but they had been *better*. He wanted to tell the five-year-old Eli to enjoy it while he could, but even now he could recall how few and far between those moments had been. All three of them had been forced to grow up fast.

"I brought somebody with me," he heard Eamon say suddenly and became aware that his brother was looking at him. "An old face." He beckoned to Eli slowly.

The younger Brody placed the picture back on the dresser and walked over to his two siblings. He could see Meghann shrink away, clutching Eamon's hand tighter, as he approached.

"She doesn't like new people," Eamon said quietly, meeting Eli's eyes. "Be gentle."

Eli shot him a glare and crouched next to her. "Hey, sweetheart. It's me. It's Eli."

Meghann's shoulders hunched and her eyes stayed fixed on the window in front of her.

"It's all right." Eamon spoke softly from her other side. "He's not going to hurt you."

"Of course I'm not going to hurt her," Eli said, more sharply than he'd intended. Meghann winced at the tone and clung tighter to Eamon. "Sorry. Sorry. Meggy, it's Lije." If anything, she only shrunk into a tighter ball at his pleading tone. Her grip on Eamon's hand was white-knuckled.

*She doesn't know me. She doesn't know me at all.*

"Okay," he said slowly. "Okay." His gaze shifted to Eamon. "Maybe it'd be better if I waited outside?"

His brother glanced down at Meghann's hand, still tightly clasping his own, and gave Eli a curt nod. As Eli retreated, Eamon continued making soothing noises to Meghann, stroking her hand until she began to uncoil.

Eli stood by the doorway, out of his sister's line of sight, and watched silently. He drew a quiet breath to stave off the unpleasant feeling that somebody had poked a finger into his heart and was wriggling it around experimentally, trying to see how he'd react. *How can she not know me?*

*"I think you should come home. Please. Come home."* That was the last message he'd received from her, five years ago, only a year or so after the news came that their parents had died in a traffic accident in Raleigh City. Even then he hadn't come home, hadn't gone to the funeral, didn't—he realized now—even know where they were buried.

With a last squeeze of her hand, Eamon gently untangled himself from his spot at Meghann's side. Her hand fell, listlessly, back to the arm of her rocking chair and there was a faint noise like a whimper, but she didn't move—just kept rocking in her chair, back and forth, back and forth.

"Come on," said Eamon quietly, steering Eli out the door.

He stared blankly as he let Eamon usher him, eyes focused on his boots and the ornate rug beneath them.

Eamon shut the door firmly behind them, letting out a pent-up sigh that had probably been building since Eli had landed on-world. His heavy hand descended on Eli's shoulder in an unusual display of brotherly affection.

"Sorry to spring this on you, Lije."

Eli shrugged the hand off. "Yeah. Well, it's not like you couldn't have told me at some point. There's such a thing as interstellar couriers."

"Hey, I thought you were dead for the last five years."

"Come to terms with your grief, then, have you?"

Eamon scowled. "I'm glad you're alive. But I'm not going to pretend that I haven't had my own life here for the last nine years—and I'm not going to disrupt it."

"*That* much is clear."

His brother's face flushed as he drew in a breath for a sharp retort, but something seemed to stop him, deflate him. He raised his hands slowly. "Look, I don't want to fight. Especially not here."

"Yeah." Eli glanced sidelong at Meghann's door. He didn't want to look at it straight on—its reality was incontrovertible at that angle. "Eam, what the fuck happened?"

A hand passed across the trimmed beard on Eamon's jaw and his eyes unfocused. "It's a long story."

"Best get started then."

The green eyes snapped back to Eli like a fleet jumping in from a gate. "Come downstairs. We'll talk."

Back in the anachronistic parlor, Eamon produced a flask and, unscrewing the top, took a deep belt from it. He passed it to Eli, who was in the process of raising it to his own lips when a memory jolted up through his fingers. He stared at the battered silver container, turning it over in his hands to reveal the engraved letters on the front: CWB.

"Dad's flask."

"There wasn't much left after they died," Eamon said. "By the end, they'd sold most of it, just so they could live. All that was left were some pictures, mom's fiddle, and that."

Eli snorted. "So in the end, it was about as important to him as mom's music was to her, huh? That seems about right. I hope you had that put on his grave: 'Connor Brody: loving husband, father, drunkard.'" He raised the flask in salute to Eamon, then tipped it to his lips. The familiar taste of

Saltyre's filled his mouth, this time untainted by the unpleasant bitterness of sedatives.

He passed the flask silently back to his brother, who screwed the cap back on and stowed it in his jacket.

"They're buried out by Glenfin," Eamon said quietly. "Not far from the homestead. I figured that's where they'd want to be."

"By the house that was repossessed when the mining interests were nationalized? Oh, yeah, I'm sure that's a memory they want to be reminded of *constantly* in the next life."

"I was thinking about the good times."

"Sorry. Forgotten most of those."

"I know you're angry—"

"Angry?" Maybe it was the whisky, but Eli felt his cheeks burning. "*Angry?* I'm bloody *furious*, Eamon!" He was on his feet though he didn't remember getting up. "My parents are dead, my sister's in some sort of *catatonic* state, and my fucking *brother* is mixed up with kidnappers and thugs." His voice was too loud even in his own ears, but like an animal that had leapt in front of the groundcar at just the wrong moment he saw no way of swerving to avoid it. "And nobody thought to tell me a fucking *thing!*" His chest heaved as he realized that he'd run out of words.

"Are you finished?" asked Eamon mildly.

"I'm just getting *started*, you fucking selfish bastard."

Eamon's mouth snapped shut, and the hairs on the back of Eli's neck stood to attention. There's an inherent sense of propriety, of politeness, of where the lines are drawn in any given conversation and, more importantly, when you've just taken a flying long jump across one of them.

*That*, Eli realized, *was the red button.*

"*I'm* selfish? Sit down and shut up, you worthless, good for nothing piece of *shite*. Let me tell you a thing or two about selfishness. *Selfishness* would be running away to side with the very people who brutally invaded your home. *Selfishness* would be leaving behind a brother, a sister, and parents who were just scraping by and could have used the extra income. *Selfishness*, my fucking idiot brother, would be not returning your sister's message when she asked you desperately to come home.

"You want to know what happened to Meghann? I'll tell you. After you left, she decided she needed to help mom and dad out. She was *fif-*

*teen*, Lije, but she lied and said she was eighteen. Got a job working in a pub down by the military spaceport, serving drinks and fending off the advances of fucking crim flyboys. Mom and dad, they didn't know—but I knew. Tried to talk her out of it, too, but she reasoned that she was safe enough. And why? Because they were Illyrican soldiers, just like her big brother. That was enough for her.

"She got wise after a year or so, realized the punters would tip better if she teased 'em a little bit, so she'd flirt and smile and think nothing of it. Didn't take it any further than that, though—until she met Padaria."

Eamon spat the name out, his expression darkening like a storm cloud drifting in front of the sun, jaw clenched with pure, raw fury.

"Lieutenant Karim Padaria. Illyrican-born nobility, the very picture of an officer and a gentleman. Except he wasn't much of either in the end. They shipped him out here because he'd gotten into too much trouble back on Illyrica, drinking and whoring it up. So his father, the bloody fucking Minister of Information, pulls some strings and, instead of getting dishonorably discharged, Padaria's given a commission on a tip-top secret project out here. Of course, it's more title than actual job, so instead of doing his officering he's planetside in the bar every weekend.

"And he takes a shine to our little sister."

Eamon trailed off and Eli noticed for the first time his brother's hands were trembling. Reaching into his coat, Eamon pulled out the flask again and took another slug. He wiped his mouth on the back of his hand and paced to the window and back again. Eli heard him take a deep breath and let it out slowly.

"So what happens next? Connect the fucking dots, little brother. Padaria's handsome and charming, even if he is a rotter underneath. And Meghann—she's just shy of eighteen at this point, barely more than a girl—she falls for him. Hard. He's bad news, Padaria, which I begin to figure out when Meghann starts stumbling in at all hours. At first, it's just drink, but it doesn't take long before he's getting her on the harder stuff. Dope. Stims. Hop. Sometimes all three. More often than not, she isn't coming home at all, and when she does, she's high as a fiend."

Eamon paused, cracked his knuckles meaningfully. "I figure it's gotta end, but Meg, she doesn't want to listen to me. She's in *love* with this bastard and I'm just prejudiced because he's Illyrican and I'm still angry at *you* for leaving to join 'em. So I do what I feel a good brother should: I round up a few of the boys and we go to have a *talk* with young Master Padaria."

He sighed and sat down heavily in the chair. "I'll admit, probably not my finest decision. It's late when Padaria and his buddies come out of the bar, and it goes from talk to brawl in about thirty seconds flat. Lucky Jim, he takes a bottle to the side of his head. Someone gets a knife into Padaria, who goes down, but that's about when the military cops show up. Most of the boys scattered in time, but I'm trying to help Jim rabbit and they nab the both of us.

"Next day, we hear Padaria's dead. The blade hit an artery and he bled out on the way to surgery. Won't say I shed a tear, but like I said, his old man's a muckety-muck back on Illyrica, so they're looking for someone to put up in front of a wall. Only trouble is, nobody's taking credit for stabbing the blighter, and the boys aren't about to talk to the crims, 'specially with me and Jim still in lockup.

"So they charge us with inciting a riot. Lucky Jim, unfortunately, ain't the fastest car in the garage. Turns out he's been tied to half a dozen jobs, including ones with 'known terrorist involvement.' That hits the press and it goes from bar brawl to political incident. Me, though, I fade away next to Lucky, because nobody's breathed a word of my beef with Padaria, so everything's pinned on Jim. I don't feel good about that, 'course, but it is what it is."

Eamon scratched his head and Eli thought he caught a note of uneasiness. It may have been years since he'd last seen his brother, but some expressions never changed—Eamon was embarrassed about that.

"By that time, though, I'd met some good lads in lockup—folks with ties to the higher rungs of the Black Watch's ladder. They'd sussed out the full story somehow, talking with people on the outside, and they were . . . well, they were impressed. They told me to stay quiet and, sure enough, a week into the thing, I get sprung on account of insufficient evidence.

"Lucky Jim? Turns out he wasn't so lucky. Death penalty's off the table since they can't prove he put the point to Padaria, but he's still got terrorist written all over him, so they ship him off to the Belt for hard labor—life sentence. Died there not long after." Eamon shook his head. "My bloody fault."

Silence fell on the room and Eli noticed that the light outside had moved firmly into the late morning.

"Anyway, I went underground when I got out, but I had to see Meghann first. She'd had a hard time of it, coming off the hop. It's a nasty thing when it's got its claws in you, and shortly thereafter there was the accident, so it was just . . . me and her. I helped as much as I could, but I had to keep my head down by that point—keep out of sight of the Illyricans—just in case they decided to dredge up my record. I started doing more jobs for the Black Watch, and they looked out for me and for Meghann. The old man, De Valera, he was good to me, made sure we wanted for nothing—said he'd been keeping an eye on me. I thought maybe we were out of the woods."

He stared at the floor, face in his hands. "Then we found out Meghann was pregnant."

Eli's breath caught. *Pregnant?* "Padaria?"

"Padaria. Of course, he was stone cold by that point and Meghann still wasn't herself. But, after talking with the doctors, we went ahead and told her anyway; I guess we thought it might give her something to live for.

"A week later, she relapsed. Dosed herself with enough hop to take down a horse."

Eamon kneaded his palms into the tops of his thighs. His gaze was still fixed somewhere in the middle distance, not looking at Eli or his surroundings. "She lost the baby. We were lucky it didn't kill her. But she wasn't the same after that. The doctors, they tried meds, they tried therapy, but she didn't respond. Something about the combination of mental trauma with the residual effects of the drugs, it—it fried her.

"I looked around for a place, and old Mrs. Kimball recommended this one. Meghann's been here five years now. Sui does a good job looking after her and Meghann's . . . well, she's happy. Reasonably so, anyway. And De Valera, he insisted that the Black Watch pay for it all.

"There you go," said Eamon, finally meeting Eli's gaze. The green of his eyes shone emerald hard. "That's what happened to our sister. That's why she stopped writing. That's why I joined the Black Watch. And that's why I'm having a slight bit of trouble accepting that my own flesh and blood wore the same uniform as the man who ruined her life."

He paused. "But, my flesh and blood you are. And that still means something."

Eli's hand was frozen over his mouth, his eyes still wide from taking in the entire story. He opened his mouth to say something from between his fingers, but the words died on his lips more surely than in a vacuum. An urge swelled in him, to do something, anything—sob, punch the wall, scream—but it was sucked out of him just as quickly by the realization that it would be like railing at absent gods. It was years too late to make a difference, even if he had any means to do so.

*Means.* That was what he'd come here to do, right? Take care of Meghann.

"I can help." He looked up at the dubious expression on his brother's face. "I told you, the Commonwealth said they'd help me take care of Meghann."

"And what, take her away from her home? From me?"

"This isn't about you *or* me. It's about *her.* Look, come with me and meet this Fielding guy. All they want to do is talk to you, get some information. That can't be too much to ask. We can get Meghann the best treatment in the galaxy." His breath caught, but he barreled through the next part anyway. "You could come too—we could be a family again."

Eamon eyed him for a moment, then slowly shook his head. "I'm sorry, Lije, no."

"I can help her," He leaned forward and met his brother's eyes. *"Please."*

There might have been a waver of doubt on Eamon's face, or it might have just been a trick of the light. "Wheels are in motion, Lije. There're bigger things afoot here."

"Great," said Eli, throwing up his hands. "So I'm supposed to just go back to Fielding and shrug my shoulders when he tells me you didn't show up at the meet?"

"Actually, you're not going back to your new friends. I've got too much at stake here; I can't have your Commonwealth pals trudging through the rose garden. So until this is all over, you're staying somewhere nice and safe." He shifted to one side and his jacket fell open on the black butt of a pistol. "I insist."

# CHAPTER THIRTEEN

A bus deposited Kovalic and Tapper into the hot, dusty Caledonian afternoon, but in a world decidedly unlike the one where they'd spent most of their trip to date.

Strolling down High Street, they passed ornate brownstone buildings with their just-so trees and carefully groomed greenery—perhaps the most ostentatious way to display one's wealth on this dusty rock of a world. The lampposts in this district had been bedecked with crimson and gold, and celebratory Illyrican flags and banners had been hung from many a window.

Although it had its share of residences, the area was primarily a high-end shopping district, and there were plenty of fashionably dressed women and men toting bags up and down the street, stopping every once in a while to peer into windows. Their workman-like dress made Tapper and Kovalic stand out, but not enough to garner the attention of those that passed—unless it was an upturned nose or a stifled titter.

They found the Cafe Écossian easily enough and arrived early—fifteen minutes before the scheduled meeting. They stopped at a nearby shop window, as if having a discussion about the merits of one of the baubles it displayed.

"What's the plan?" asked Tapper in a low voice.

"Wide search," said Kovalic. "If there's anybody there, they'll be in place by now, and they'll make us easily in a close pattern. I want to be outside their bubble if possible." He frowned as he eyed the café: Their dress was going to stand out even more on the approach. Wardrobe was all a matter of context—they'd dressed to be inconspicuous in most environments, but in a setting as rarefied as this one their very inconspicuousness made them stand out: horses in a paddock of zebras. He wished Page was here;

blending into pretty much any crowd was the man's gift, and even Tapper would grudgingly concede that the younger man was his superior in matters of surveillance if nothing else.

A distraction might have worked, but he didn't want to draw any more attention than he had to. No, subtlety was the order of the day.

He turned around to face the street, arms crossed, and looked for inspiration. There was a man walking a dog, but there were some lines Kovalic wouldn't cross, even for work, and pet theft was near the top of the list. A well-dressed young woman was traipsing down the street, twirling her finger in her hair while chatting away on her comm, but her other arm was linked with a young man who was craning his neck at a display showing last night's ballgame while lugging a pair of pink shopping bags. He smirked at that and turned to see a middle-aged woman, kneeling and tying the shoes of a toddler. From there, his glance jumped to an older woman, probably in her sixties or seventies, exiting a store, her arms laden down with bags full of purchases. And then on to a tweed-garbed older man with a pipe protruding from under a bushy white mustache.

His eyes jumped suddenly back to the old woman.

"Take the wide arc." Kovalic pressed his comm's earbud into one ear. "I've got an idea."

Without waiting to hear Tapper's assent, Kovalic hustled across the street toward the older woman, who was struggling to manage both her parcels and the shop door. Sliding in next to her, Kovalic took the other side of the door and held it wide.

"Allow me, ma'am," he said, lowering his voice to its lowest register— he'd always thought that people, especially women, trusted deep, strong voices more—and straightening to his full height. He gave her his best boy-scout smile.

The woman peered over her packages at him, and Kovalic saw the lines crinkle around her eyes. "Why, thank you, young man."

Kovalic inclined his head. "My pleasure." He hesitated—just enough to make it look like he was acting on the spur of the moment. "Those look heavy. Could I offer you a hand with them?"

Pleasant surprise flooded her face, but Kovalic could see the automatic rejection coming. He needed a sweetener. "I couldn't possibly—" she began.

"It's no bother at all," he said, keeping the smile in place. "I'm just waiting for my wife and," he dropped his voice to a mock conspiratorial tone, "if I know her, she'll be in there for a while. I was just going to head over to the café for a drink." He nodded in the direction of the Écossian. "But my mother always told me never to abandon a lady in need."

He kept his tone light and cheery and his face open and friendly throughout. He'd thrown in "wife" and "mother" as safe words—after all, what older woman wouldn't trust a polite, married man who still took his mother's advice to heart?

The rejection had been wiped clean, as if with an eraser. "Well, I suppose it wouldn't hurt. My driver's on the way, but I am a bit nippish, now that you come to mention it."

"Say no more." He began to gently relieve her of her burden which, he noted with surprise, was quite a bit heavier than he'd thought she'd be capable of handling. The pile of packages removed, he got a clearer picture of her for the first time. She'd been a looker in her youth, he could tell, but even with all the advancements in science and medicine nobody had yet managed to crack the secret of not growing old. Still, some did it more gracefully than others: the curls around her head had gone snow white, untempered by any of the more common coloring techniques. She'd embraced her age rather than trying to conceal it.

"At least allow me to buy your drink, Mister . . . ?"

"Malory," he said, the fake name rolling off his tongue. "Tom Malory."

"Mr. Malory," she said, taking his arm. "Thank you very much for your gallantry."

"Not a problem, ma'am. Just happy to be of help."

"Please, you must call me Elsie—everybody does."

From there to the café, Kovalic made a great show of paying attention to all of Elsie's conversation, from laughing at the antics of her grandchildren to murmuring appreciatively at her comments on the political situation. In return, he told her he was a mid-level executive at the Thane Corporation, in charge of real estate development in Raleigh City's less prosperous districts, a cover that was both boring enough not to have her delve into the details but sympathetic enough that it let her exclaim over the poor plight of the working class and discuss her own charitable activities.

Behind that, though, Kovalic was carefully scanning the faces of everybody they passed, looking for any sign that someone was out of place or taking an unusual interest in the café. Nobody they encountered on the way rang even the slightest alarm bells—he felt pretty confident that had there been any eyeballs on the Écossian, he would have spotted them.

They had no trouble getting a table for two at the café, where Kovalic ordered a coffee and the old woman went wild and ordered a scone with jam, confiding with a smile that her personal trainer would have her hung out to dry if he ever found out. Kovalic chuckled at the joke and took in the café.

Nothing. He spared a glance for an ornate clock with wrought iron hands hanging over the counter. Right on time for the meet with Eamon Brody, but no sign of him. The back of his neck had begun to tingle and, despite the reassuring smell of coffee, his stomach was on high alert. Beneath the table, he slipped his comm out of his pocket and thumbed the button that would connect him with Tapper.

"Hey, boss," said the sergeant's voice in his earbud, even as Kovalic smiled at Elsie and took a sip of his coffee. "No sign of Eamon Brody or, for that matter, any of his crew."

Had something happened to Eamon on the way? Kovalic's mind cataloged the possibilities: traffic, car accident, sudden illness—there were plenty of rational reasons why the man might not have shown up.

But his gut was telling him that they were all rubbish. Eamon Brody might not have been a pro, but given the way he'd handled his brother he clearly had some connections and perhaps even some formal training. When you had a meet, you planned for contingencies. You left early to scout the place ahead of time, you drove carefully because you were hyperaware of your surroundings, and well, you didn't get sick. To Kovalic's mind that left just two possibilities: either someone had stopped Eamon Brody from coming or he had decided not to.

He was so deep in his own thoughts—the rest of his brain regulating the nodding and smiling at appropriate moments—that it wasn't until about ten seconds after Elsie's comment that it actually reached the part of his mind responsible for processing speech. He ran it back in his head, parsing the various components and identifying why he'd flagged it in the first place—something in there was significant.

"What was that?"

"Oh, I was just saying that Richard and I might try to get out of town tomorrow—it's going to be such a circus."

Her expression turned quizzical at the sight of his blank stare. "The Emperor's Birthday? It'll be a madhouse, what with all the celebrations and security. The locals, you know, they don't much care for it," she said in a tone somewhere between sympathy and eye-rolling.

"Of course, of course," Kovalic said. "I get so wrapped up with work, you know—sometimes I forget what day of the week it is." He laughed at his own expense even as his brain wormhole-jumped across the galaxy. Tomorrow, the same date that had been in their admittedly sparse intelligence, was also the Emperor's Birthday, the biggest holiday in the Illyrican Empire. He'd seen all the decorations around town but had barely given them a second thought. But it signified something: a piece of the puzzle they'd been sent here to assemble.

"Poor dear," Elsie clucked, patting his hand. "That wife of yours—Natalie, was it?—she must have her hands full with you."

"She makes do," said Kovalic, then glanced toward the front of the establishment. "Well, look at the time. Speaking of the missus, she'll be looking for me, to be sure, and if she finds out I've been carrying another woman's packages, well, let's just say I'll be the one with my hands full." He winked at her, and started reaching inside of his jacket.

"No, no, I insist!" Elsie protested, setting her purse on the table. "It's on me."

"Very gracious, ma'am. Thank you."

"Thank *you*, Mr. Malory. I do so like to see that chivalry isn't dead."

"Not dead, ma'am, just on sabbatical. Thanks again—for everything." He leaned down and gave her a peck on the cheek, then strolled out of the café and back toward the shops. There'd been no sign of Eamon Brody, that was true, but he hadn't exactly walked out empty-handed.

●

He found Tapper loitering near a shop that sold high-end men's clothes, looking generally puzzled. "I just don't understand fashion," he muttered, eyes sweeping up and down an audacious taupe suit with flared collars. "Hideous."

"Hideous *and* expensive," Kovalic confirmed with a glance at the tag. Certainly out of his price range—even with hazard pay.

"So, no sign of our friend then?"

Kovalic gave a short, sharp shake of his head. "Not a whisper." Acid ate at the lining of his stomach and he pulled his comm from his pocket.

"That as bad as I think it is?"

"It's not *good*." Kovalic punched in Page's number and waited as it rang. The lieutenant answered on the second ring. "Yep?"

"You have eyes on Eli Brody?"

"Not presently. He's gone into—"

"Get there. Now."

"Sir." There was a sound of rustling from the other end of the line as Page moved into action.

Kovalic shifted the comm away from his mouth. "Something's not adding up," he said to Tapper. "We're missing something. Wallace's disappearance. Eamon Brody and the Black Watch. This fairy tale, or whatever it is, about an Illyrican superweapon. It's all connected somehow."

"What do you want to do about it?"

A shout, more surprised than alarmed, came from the other end of the line, and distantly Kovalic could hear Page's voice, placating but firm. Further movement, and then a quiet, controlled huffing of breath, as of someone taking a flight of stairs.

"You got him?" said Kovalic into the comm.

"Hold," grunted Page. A door slammed. "Negative, sir. I appear to have lost the target." A tinge of some emotion—embarrassment, anger, regret—colored the voice of the normally impassive lieutenant.

"Shit."

Tapper's eyebrows raised in question and Kovalic shook his head, then covered the mouthpiece. "We lost Eli."

"Knew letting the kid go was a mistake," muttered the sergeant.

Kovalic rolled his eyes, but raised the comm again. "See if you can run him to ground, lieutenant. Call me when you've got something."

"Yes, sir. Sorry, sir."

Kovalic rang off. "Okay." He took a deep breath. "*Now*, it's bad."

"All right," said Tapper. "Square one. What's our play?"

Pressing the comm to his forehead as though it could somehow impart wisdom directly into his brain, Kovalic squeezed his eyes closed and tried to marshal the information they had into some sort of usable order. Despite all evidence to the contrary, he didn't think Eli Brody had gone down to Berwick with the intent of taking off. But if he *had* gone to ground, then Kovalic had a pretty good idea of who was involved—and that, at least, gave them their next step.

Kovalic opened his eyes. "We need to find that warehouse where they took Brody last night."

Tapper snorted. "Easier said than done. We're going to have to comb through a whole lot of warehouses to find the right one."

"*We* would," said Kovalic slowly, "but I think I know someone who might be able to narrow the field for us. And maybe we can kill two birds with one well-placed stone."

●

Every morning, Major Jagat Shankar stopped to buy a cup of coffee and a pastry from the same small corner café. The coffee was black, the pastry a Caledonian variation on a chocolate croissant—heavy on the chocolate. As he sipped the coffee and nibbled at the pastry, he scanned through the morning headlines on his handheld comm, marking any that merited further investigation. Nobody ever joined him at his table—by this point, the café proprietor knew his order and would bring it without asking. And, given that Shankar's position as the chief Illyrican spy on Caledonia was, if not known outright then at least heavily rumored, the whole thing was, needless to say, on the house.

So it would be hard to say who was more shocked, Shankar or the café manager, when Kovalic—carrying his own cup of coffee, pastry, and comm—plopped himself into the seat across from Shankar, not two minutes after he had begun his morning ritual.

Kovalic gave a low whistle as he read something on his device. "Fifteen to seven!" he exclaimed, shaking his head in disappointment. "The Griffins got shelled last night. Looks like that trade for O'Neill didn't pay off for them, huh?"

To his credit, Shankar's initial surprise lasted only a moment. Unfortunately for him, however, that moment was just long enough for Kovalic to prod him under the table with something very much like the business end of a gun.

Shankar leaned his bulk backwards—he was a big man, there were no three ways about it—and clasped his hands on top of his paunch.

Kovalic offered a friendly smile. "Isn't this the part where you indignantly exclaim 'Don't you know who I am?'"

Shankar gave a shrug which rolled down from his incongruously narrow shoulders through the rest of his body, like a waterfall pouring down a mountainside. "I presume you know who I am. Why else would you choose to accost me in this particular manner?"

"With a brain like that," said Kovalic, tapping his temple with his free hand, "I can see why the Illyricans are lucky to have you."

Beady, deep-set brown eyes flicked Kovalic up and down, scanning him from top to bottom. "So, unless I miss my guess, you are Mr. Danzig's mysterious visitor."

If he'd been trying to shock Kovalic, Shankar had shot wide of the mark: As Kovalic had told Danzig, station heads were always surveilled—it was just the way the game was played.

The hand that was above the table opened and closed in modest acknowledgement. "I'd say he sends his regards, but he doesn't know I'm here."

Shankar raised a white eyebrow. "And what brings you here, mister . . . ?"

"You can call me Fielding. And I've got a business proposition."

"Very well. As long as we are conducting *business*, I suppose you realize that your window of opportunity here is fairly limited. When I don't show up for work in—" he paused to glance at the clock ticking away on the café's wall, "—fifteen minutes or so, alarms will be raised."

"Ah, so we've moved on to the part where you offer to forget all about this if I let you go?"

Shankar chuckled, his stomach heaving up and down in almost hypnotic undulations. "Dear me, no. Right now, your options have merely been reduced to whether you rot in prison or are simply shot on sight."

Kovalic grinned. "Believe it or not, those are my favorite options. But I wouldn't worry about that—your building won't notice your absence for a little while yet; they're busy dealing with an unscheduled fire alarm." He gave Shankar a sympathetic look. "I know: it's a little cliché, but if it makes you feel any better, there *is* an actual fire." He raised a hand, thumb and forefinger slightly apart. "A small one."

The big man pursed his lips but didn't seem discomfited by the news. His head bent toward Kovalic in a nod. "I suppose the least I can do is indulge you—though, really, must you hold that weapon on me? It's a bit *theatrical*."

With a shrug, Kovalic pulled his hand out from under the table and placed its contents—a bottle of peach soda with a long narrow neck—down on the table. "I hope I didn't shake it up too much. This carbonated stuff can get a bit explosive."

The big man leaned back and laughed. "Well played. Commonwealth intelligence agents are always so . . . resourceful."

Kovalic didn't take the bait, letting the remark sail past him. "But before you get any ideas, I should let you know that one of my colleagues is outside the café and is armed with considerably more than a fizzy drink. So I advise you to choose your actions carefully."

"Fair enough. To business, then. What is it you want, Mr. Fielding?"

"Information—your stock in trade, I believe."

Shankar's head cocked to the side. "You must know I wouldn't give you anything of a sensitive nature. Whatever kind of example would that make me for my own subordinates?"

Kovalic leaned back, crossing his arms. "Well, what I'm looking for is more in the vein of local color. Think of yourself as an exceptionally well-informed tour guide."

The noise that emerged from Shankar's mouth sounded a bit like a small pocket of pressurized gas escaping; Kovalic took it as a sign of interest and continued.

"I'm interested in the Black Watch."

Surprise gave way to a scowl on Shankar's face. "Not that I imagine my advice means much to you, but just in case it carries any weight—professional to professional—I would strongly suggest you avoid associating yourself with this organization. Not only can they not be trusted, but they are the worst sort of terrorists."

"Oh?"

"They cloak themselves in patriotic rhetoric, claiming to be 'freedom fighters.' But all they seem to care about is violence. You have heard, I take it, of the Bloody Hundred?"

Kovalic frowned. "Vaguely."

Shankar folded his hands. "This was, oh, seven years ago. One of our cruisers, the ISC *Trident*, was being retrofitted at the Caledonian Shipyards, so the Black Watch smuggled up a bomb." He shook his head. "Not only did it destroy the *Trident*, but it killed twenty-five Illyrican servicemen—along with seventy-three civilian contractors. Both Illyrican *and* Caledonian."

He leaned forward, the tone of his voice dropping but becoming, if anything, more heated. "That's par for the course for this self-styled 'resistance movement'—the murder of innocent civilians."

"And this De Valera . . . I have to say, I'm surprised you haven't caught him yet."

If anything, Shankar's scowl deepened further. A *tch* of disgust issued from his throat. "Not for lack of trying." A look of regret crossed his face. "Far be it from me to admit our own shortcomings, but his identity is the most well-kept of secrets. We've sent in a few operatives over the years, but each time they were lucky to make it out with their lives." He shook his head. "They are brutal people, Mr. Fielding—it would be better for the Caledonians themselves were the Black Watch gone, but they, of course, do not see it that way."

Kovalic tried to keep himself from snorting. Yes, the Illyricans would probably crack down less on Caledonia if they didn't have the threat of the Black Watch looming over them, but giving them up also meant ceding the last thing the Caledonians could call their own: hope. That was the path Earth had chosen. His lips compressed into a thin line. It hadn't been *his* choice—that was for sure.

"We've been working with the Caledonian Security Agency to keep tabs on the Watch," Shankar continued, "but . . ." He opened his hand, palm up, in a gesture of fruitlessness.

CalSec again. If they were investigating the Black Watch, keeping tabs on Wallace's apartment made more sense; they'd probably seen him with Eamon Brody. What else might they know? Kovalic scratched at his chin.

"So you wouldn't happen to know if there were, say, a warehouse in the port district with ties to the Black Watch?"

Shankar's eyes narrowed and stubby bronze fingers reached up to comb his white goatee. "Like the mythical djinni who grants but three wishes, I am afraid there are limits to my powers, Mr. Fielding. We have yet to discuss precisely what I—and through me, the Imperium, of course—stand to gain from this exchange."

Kovalic's eyes drifted over the rest of the café's patrons. It was a small place and even at this, its busiest hour of the morning, there were only a few other customers: an older gentleman enjoying a demitasse of coffee, and a young couple apparently in the morning-after phase, their drinks steaming away even as they refused to meet each other's eyes.

"Not that you have any reason to believe me," said Kovalic, "but we want the same thing here: security."

"Ah, but whose security?" asked Shankar, raising a finger. "Your citizens' or mine?"

"Can't it be both? Some things are larger than the petty issue of borders."

A snort issued from the bigger man at that suggestion. "Those words are dangerously close to treason, Mr. Fielding."

Kovalic's gaze didn't waver from the man across the table.

Shankar leaned forward, his elbows resting on either side of his coffee, chin atop his interlaced fingers. "You are a difficult man, Mr. Fielding. And an inscrutable one to boot."

"I'm told it makes me irresistible to women."

To that, the big man leaned back and roared his first genuine laugh of the encounter, causing the couple in the corner to start in surprise and rattle their coffee cups. "So it is with those in our profession," he said with an expression of mock suffering. "I'm afraid it is our burden to live with." After a lengthy sigh, he nodded. "Very well. I will offer you some information—but I require something from you; a *quid pro quo.*"

Kovalic spread his hands outward. "If it is within my power to give."

Shankar nodded. "Good. I will tell you what I require of you, and you may decide whether the price is acceptable. Fair?"

It was a generous proposition for Shankar to make. At the very least, Kovalic would not walk away empty-handed: whatever question the man asked would be revelatory in and of itself. Kovalic bowed his head in acquiescence.

Shankar drummed his fingers on the table as he weighed his decision. At last he spoke. "There is a man in whom the Imperial Intelligence Service has a particular interest. It is altogether possible that this man is currently in the Commonwealth." He raised his hands to forestall Kovalic's objections. "Of course, out of professional courtesy, I would not dream of asking you to confirm or deny that. All I want is that, should you come across him, you pass him a message from me."

"And that man is?"

Shankar looked around, his expression nervous for the first time, and lowered his voice even further. "Hasan al-Adaj."

Kovalic allowed his own eyebrows to arch. "The Marquis al-Adaj? The head of Illyrican intelligence?"

"The same. There's no need to dissemble, Mr. Fielding—I'm sure you're aware that he no longer holds that post, having defected from the Imperium several years ago. You probably even know that, despite their best efforts, our most elite agents have been unable to track him down."

"I see. Well, if he's such a hard man to find, I'm sure there's little chance I'll ever have the pleasure of meeting him, but I'll do what I can. What's the message?"

Shankar scraped the underside of his chin with his fingertips. "Tell the old bastard—not in so many words, of course—but tell him that he may have disappeared for now, but he cannot remain hidden forever. And should he ever set so much as a foot on Illyrican soil again, his incarceration and execution will swiftly follow."

Kovalic waited, but Shankar didn't continue, just once again leaned back in his chair. "Dramatic. I'm sure he'll take comfort in that. Is that all?"

"Also, please remind him that he still owes me three hundred marks for the scorch marks on a perfectly serviceable Bayern carpet."

"If I do see him, I'll be sure to pass it along."

"Thank you."

Kovalic shook his head, bemused, then resumed his original line of questioning. "So, the warehouse in the port district?"

"Ah, yes. The Black Watch have many fronts and, of course, a warehouse presents particular advantages and opportunities for an organization such as theirs to move goods without being detected. Alas, we have been unable to pin down precisely *which* of the many firms in the area belongs to them. Despicable though they may be, they are also—and I hate to admit this, as it is tantamount to admitting my own failure—extremely clever."

"No leads at all?" Kovalic pressed.

Shankar picked at an imaginary piece of lint on his lapel. "There were a couple of places that caught our attention, yes, but I hesitate to mention the most prominent of them."

"And why's that?"

Shankar gave a half-smile, but refused to meet Kovalic's eyes. "I suggest you talk to your good friend Walter Danzig about that."

Kovalic frowned. "Danzig?"

"Indeed."

"I don't understand."

"I'm reluctant to compromise an ongoing operation," said Shankar with an apologetic air. "But what I can tell you is that one of the warehouses we have under surveillance for Black Watch connections has been receiving regular shipments, signed for by our mutual friend, Mr. Danzig. Furthermore, those shipments have been marked with Commonwealth diplomatic seals." He made a hands-off motion, palms outward, as though the mere idea of violating that sacred trust had never even occurred to him.

Kovalic's eyes flicked rapidly back and forth, taking it in. "Very interesting," he murmured finally. Either Danzig had been holding out on him or something was going on right under the station chief's nose. He suppressed a grimace: that'd be his mission on Haran all over again.

Peering at the handheld comm on the table, Shankar looked back up at Kovalic. "And with that, I'm afraid our interview must come to an end. Even without your little distraction, it has gotten rather late and my workload is rather heavy these days: reports to collate, Emperor's Birthday security arrangements to review, other mysterious strangers to meet—you understand. So I'm afraid I'll be going—unless you wish to offer me another drink," he said, indicating the bottle on the table.

"Keep it," Kovalic suggested, getting to his feet. "A souvenir."

Shankar rose as well. "You'll forgive me if I decline. It would seem unwise to keep any, er, *mementos* of our encounter."

Kovalic grinned and reached over to grab the bottle. "Your loss. They make a great peach fizz."

The two stepped out of the café and into the bustling street. Shankar turned to face Kovalic, even as a compact, gray-haired man, staring intently at the handheld he carried, barreled down the sidewalk, oblivious to everything around him. Kovalic stepped out of his way, closing the distance between himself and Shankar to just a few inches.

Shankar sighed in exasperation, watching the man go. "People are always in a rush. No respect for other people's lives."

"Tell me about it." He felt a slight buzz from the inside pocket of his jacket. "Well, I'll not detain you any longer, major. Thank you for your assistance." He moved to raise his hand, but Shankar cut him off with a sharp jab of his chin.

"I have no wish to be seen shaking hands with a Commonwealth intelligence officer, Mr. Fielding. As it is, I fear that I've opened myself up to too much risk already. Good day." And with that, he turned and strode off.

Kovalic watched until Shankar disappeared around a corner, then turned and headed in the other direction. He rounded the corner of Muckross Place and walked down a few blocks, pausing to stare into a shop window. After a moment, a short man stopped next to him to eye the goods on sale.

"That close enough?" asked Tapper.

"Perfect, thanks." Kovalic pulled a device about the size of a deck of cards out of his front pocket. A light winked green on the front and he slid it back into his pocket. "I cloned his comm and his ID card; they've got to be encrypted to hell and back, but we'll set the computer to cracking them. If there *is* a secret Illyrican project on Caledonia, odds are Shankar's involved."

Tapper fell into step with him as they walked away from the shop. "Now what?"

"Well, it looks like Walter wasn't completely forthcoming with us," said Kovalic, ignoring a snort from the sergeant. "I think it's time we pay him another visit."

# CHAPTER FOURTEEN

To the scrawny blond man's credit, he did a reasonable job of trying to stop Kovalic from bulling his way into Danzig's office.

"Mr. Danzig is quite busy and I don't think he'd appreciate being disturbed!" the man protested, hands raised as if trying to shore up a collapsing wall. Kovalic pushed through him and slammed open the door.

The blond man surveyed his surroundings in surprise, as though not really sure how he'd ended up in the office, then squared his shoulders and cleared his throat. "Uh, Mr. Danzig? Mr. Fielding to see you."

Danzig had just been squaring away the last of his papers; pinching the bridge of his nose between thumb and forefinger, he waved his free hand. "Thank you, Lawson. I'll take it from here. And please, close the door on your way out."

The assistant scurried out, carefully and quietly closing the door behind him. Without a word, Danzig opened his top drawer and pulled out the small black ovoid in it, then placed the object on his desk. At the touch of its single button a light hidden below the surface began to pulse red.

Kovalic raised an eyebrow as he seated himself across from Danzig. "That's CID's top of the line baffle," he said, jutting his chin at the device. "You've upgraded since our last meeting."

"Nothing but the best for you, Mr. Fielding," Danzig replied, his voice bone dry. "I don't have to tell you its active anti-eavesdropping is virtually unbeatable."

Kovalic's lips shaped the word "virtually." In his experience dealing with engineers, that just meant nobody had cracked it *yet*. "It'll have to do."

"What can I do for you?"

"Straight to the point, Walter. I appreciate that. I'd like to see your ledger, please."

"I'm sorry?"

"Your ledger." Kovalic nodded at the cabinet that contained Danzig's secure safe. "The one where you record your meetings, comings and goings, other sensitive information."

The laugh that slipped out of Danzig was of the polite variety: a short, disbelieving chuckle. "I'm afraid that's quite out of the question. That ledger contains a wealth of sensitive material."

Kovalic smiled in apology. "Oh, sorry. I can see where you might be confused—poor choice of words." He leaned forward in the chair, letting the good-natured look slip off his face. "Give me the ledger, Walter."

The key to threats was always in the imagination of the person being threatened. Honestly, there was nothing Kovalic could invent that would be as terrifying as what the other person *thought* he might do.

But he had to admit that Danzig held up better than he'd predicted. The older man swallowed hard but didn't collapse into a mewling puddle. Somewhere in the man was a core of steel, even if it was surrounded by layers of bureaucratic bullshit.

Smiling tightly, the man came to his decision. "All right."

Internally, Kovalic heaved a sigh of relief. It wasn't as if he *wanted* to do anything to Danzig. The man had a ten-foot pole up his ass, but ultimately he was doing his job. Kovalic respected that.

Standing, Danzig walked over to the cabinet and opened the wooden doors, then scanned his retina and punched in his code on the keypad. With a heavy clank, the safe opened and he pulled out the familiar slim, leather-bound volume. He carried it back to the desk, clasped firmly to his chest like a protective mother.

"May I ask what you're looking for?"

"I'll know it when I see it." Kovalic reached out with an open palm, beckoning.

Teeth tightly clenched, Danzig put the ledger down and reluctantly slid it across the desk.

Kovalic flipped it open, thumbing through the pages. "Organized by date, I presume?"

Danzig gave a curt nod. "Most recent entries at the back."

"Are the entries encoded?"

"Of course," said Danzig stiffly. "I'll thank you not to question my competence."

Kovalic grinned and went back to flipping through the book. "Never, Walter."

Encoding the notebook was standard procedure—and for good reason. For one thing, it was easy to do. For another, it made it practically unbreakable. An entry that read "Delivered flowers to grocer" might mean that an assignment had been passed to a specific operative, but there was no way of knowing unless the person in possession of the book had another data point to correlate with: surveillance of the ledger's author, for example.

Unsurprisingly, Danzig had taken the time to put his records in a well-constructed code. There were repeated entries that might have signified regular assignments, contacts, or drops, but as far as Kovalic could tell they could just as easily have been records of Danzig's dry-cleaning. Even the dates had apparently been shifted by an arbitrary amount, giving the impression that Danzig was planning ahead for appointments he'd be having in the months to come.

After a minute of paging through the incomprehensible records, Kovalic sighed and tossed the book down on the table. "All right, Walter. I don't really have the time to deal with this shit. Let's say you and I work together on this one."

Danzig, who had remained calmly in his chair, hands folded, while Kovalic had perused the notes, now leaned back in his chair and eyed him with an appraising glance. "We might be able to come to some sort of arrangement—provided, of course, that I get something out of it."

"You've been spending too much time with politicians. What do you want?"

"Besides you never having darkened my door?" Danzig sighed. "Whatever operation you're on here, I want a share of the credit." Kovalic opened his mouth to say something but Danzig plowed on through. "*And* I want a formal apology from your commanding officer for the mess on Haran—on the record."

Kovalic waited, but the desk officer had run out of steam. "That all?"

"That would suffice."

"Done."

"Just like that?"

"You want to argue about it? I haven't got all day."

"What kind of guarantee do I have?"

"You have my *word*."

"Oh." Danzig cleared his throat awkwardly. "Very well, then."

"Now, if you don't mind, could we get on with the matter at hand?"

"Yes, yes. Give me that." He snatched the ledger from Kovalic's side of the desk, a child retrieving a favored toy. "What dates concern you?"

Kovalic rubbed his chin. "Bracket the dates that Andrews was active as an operative. I'm looking for regular diplomatic courier deliveries that you would have sent to a warehouse in Leith."

Licking a finger, Danzig paged gingerly through the ledger, tracing down the columns in the page, his lips moving silently as he translated his own code. "I sign off on a lot of diplomatic shipments," he said off-handedly as he scanned the entries. "Hold on." He paused, finger holding a place, then waved at Kovalic. "There's a Raleigh City map over there, on the end table. I encoded the shipping destinations by their map-grid coordinates."

Kovalic retrieved it and folded it open on his lap. It was an older map, made out of waterproof plastic sheets, with the city divided onto several different pages. "Try page 31," said Danzig. "Grid reference A4."

Turning to the appropriate page, Kovalic lined up A4. His finger ended up in an outlying area of Raleigh City, about as far from Leith as you could get. "Nope. Try again."

Danzig *hmmed* to himself, leafing forward a few more pages. "Page 17, reference F8."

That one was closer, yielding a side street off West Highland Avenue, but still a mile or so away from Leith. Kovalic shook his head.

"There's one more recurring set during that time period," said Danzig. "Several shipments via diplomatic courier to page 23, K12."

Kovalic turned to the appropriate page, his finger tracing down from the K column to the twelfth row, all the way down in the far corner of the page. That was more like it. He tapped at the page, then looked up at Danzig.

"Can you pull up a map on the terminal?"

"I think I can handle that."

Kovalic slapped the map on the table and turned it to face the other man, his finger pointing out the buildings in question. "I need the listings for these two structures."

Danzig keyed something in on his desk and a holographic screen appeared, facing them both. It zoomed in on the grid in question, overlaying street information on the satellite imagery. Reaching out, Kovalic tapped a finger on the first building and another overlay appeared, displaying the building's directory information. "Donan Import/Export," he said, shooting a questioning glance at Danzig.

"I believe that we've used that to stockpile certain humanitarian supplies. Medicine, food, and so on. We try to provide aid to a number of non-profit agencies operating on-world."

Kovalic raised his eyebrows, then touched the second building, highlighting it in yellow. The overlay read "MacDougal Shipping Incorporated."

"Son of a bitch." Kovalic exhaled, leaning back. "Good on you, Brody."

"What?"

"Nothing." He eyed Danzig. "Now you're going to tell me exactly what's in those shipments."

Danzig shook his head. "I have no idea."

"Oh, come now, Walter. I thought we were past this."

"They were sealed!" he protested. "I had my orders, and they did not include prying into the contents—just shipping them on to their final destination."

"Which, it might interest you to know, is a front for the Black Watch."

"The Black Watch?" Danzig echoed. The color had started seeping out of his face.

Kovalic smiled, leaning forward. "Yes, *that* Black Watch. The group the Illyricans consider terrorists, and would be very displeased to find out we'd been supplying with, well, pretty much anything."

Danzing shook his head. "I knew nothing about this! If that was part of Andrews's operation, I wasn't briefed on it."

"Goddamn it, Walter." Kovalic rubbed his forehead. "You're an *intelligence* officer. Would it kill you to show some fucking curiosity once in a while?"

Danzig shot him a sour look in return. "This is *protocol*, Mr. Fielding. And while you and your cavalier band of cloak-and-dagger . . . *cowboys* may have no respect for it, I assure you that CID takes it very seriously."

Kovalic raised his eyebrows, slowly mouthing "cloak-and-dagger cowboys" to himself, then shook his head. "Walter, we're on the same side here."

"If we're on the same side, why does your boss feel the need to dispatch one of his bloody black-baggers to *interrogate* me?"

Pressing a finger to his temple, Kovalic sighed. "Look, I know we haven't always seen eye-to-eye, but trust me on this. Something's rotten in the state of Caledonia, and I'm pretty sure it's as much in your interest as mine to clear the air. I'm not here to give you orders or boss you around." He took a deep breath and tried a different tack. "I'm here because I need your help. And I think you could use mine."

Danzig took off his glasses and rubbed at his eyes. "Very well."

"Okay. Good. First things first: I need more information about this Black Watch. Members, organization, known areas of operation. I take it we don't exactly have a full dossier on them?"

"No." Danzig grimaced. "We've remained uninvolved with them—well, up to now I suppose. Our intelligence isn't very developed."

"Great, just great." Of course Danzig wouldn't have gone an iota beyond his brief. Fine. The station head either hadn't had the resources or the interest to surveil the Black Watch.

But, as Shankar had mentioned, there was someone else who did.

"I don't suppose you know anyone at the Caledonian Security Agency?"

"Well," said Danzig, removing his glasses and buffing the lenses, "as it happens, I have a very good working relationship with CalSec's Deputy Commissioner."

"Why, Walter, I didn't realize you were part schmoozer."

Danzig flushed. "As far as I can tell, CalSec's always looking to cultivate new friendships. They're kind of the unfortunate stepchild here: the Illyricans left CalSec jurisdiction over planetwide law enforcement, but they barely trust the agency to run its own affairs—and despite the fact that they only employ native-born Caledonians, most people consider them little more than Imperial stooges."

"Stuck between a rock and an angry populace."

"Quite. That's made them eager to work with any third parties."

"All right then, reach out to your contact and get us everything they're willing to give—and I do mean *everything*." It was casting a wide net, to be sure, but right now they had little better than nothing.

Danzig tapped some notes into his tablet. "All right. Anything else?"

"I'll need a copy of the list of diplomatic shipments to that warehouse."

"Certainly. I can ask CID for a full list of shipments."

Kovalic shook his head sharply. "No."

"No?" Danzig peered over his glasses at Kovalic.

"You can't go to CID about this operation."

"Protocol strictly dicta—"

"Fuck protocol on this one, Walter." He sighed. "I realize I haven't exactly given you a good reason to trust me, but come on, you must be able to tell this whole thing smells." His eyes crinkled slightly, searching for something in the other man's expression. "Somewhere in there," he said, pointing at Danzig's chest, "is the Walter Danzig who signed on to be an intelligence officer—listen to him."

Danzig had straightened up, steeling for a rejoinder, and for a moment the entire room balanced on a knife's edge. But after a moment the bureaucrat's shoulders slumped and a long sigh escaped his lips. "We'll do this your way . . . for now. I'll have Lawson put the shipment info on a data card for you." He pressed a button on his desk, and then fixed a sharp glare back on Kovalic. "But if you don't get a handle on this situation in the next twelve hours—or if this gets any worse—then we're going to need to revisit this conversation."

Kovalic inclined his head. "That seems fair." He rose and touched two fingers to his brow, an informal salute. "You're a reasonable man, Walter—don't let anybody tell you different. Now, if you'll excuse me, I've got a warehouse to check out."

And with that, he strode out of the room, leaving Danzig alone with his thoughts.

# CHAPTER FIFTEEN

It was hard to look casual while casing a place, a problem faced by generations of criminals and undercover operatives alike. It was doubly hard when the place you were staking out gave very little in the way of excuses for idly hanging around. And though gentrification may have reached some of Raleigh City's rougher neighborhoods, there were no shops or cute little restaurants in the warehouse district among which to hide.

Kovalic drew deep on a cigarette and stifled the need to cough. It had been years since his last one; he'd never caught the habit, for which he was profoundly grateful. Nowadays most aficionados had moved on to stronger stuff—many considered cigarettes little more than an affectation, like wearing glasses instead of simply getting corrective surgery.

Still, it provided a useful excuse for loitering just about anywhere, which is exactly what Kovalic was doing now. He'd set up across the street from MacDougal Shipping Incorporated, which was about as nondescript as they came: a two-story concrete block lacking in windows, doors, and any and all personality. It was conveniently located near the waterfront, though fewer and fewer goods were traveling by sea these days. In Caledonia's nascent days, Raleigh City had relied heavily upon the sea trade to ship supplies to—and resources from—settlements on other continents, but as the colony's infrastructure had been built up, the spaceports and airports had started taking over the bulk of the traffic.

"Place looks clear," Tapper's voice said in his ear. The sergeant had volunteered for the slightly riskier job of checking the warehouse's perimeter. There was even less of an excuse for that undertaking, so if he got caught it was down to Tapper to do some fast-talking—not his strong suit, unless it was the kind of talking that involved punching.

"Got a door?" Kovalic took another drag.

"Yep. Checking for countermeasures now." Even if this hadn't been the storehouse of an illegal terrorist organization, there would still be security on the doors: businesspeople protected their interests. With an underground organization like the Black Watch, however, the likelihood of that security being disproportionately retributive was, as Page would say, of a higher order of magnitude.

"Ooh," said Tapper, his voice appreciative, "a contact spiker. Haven't seen one of these since my days in the Belt. Pirates used to put them on their weapon lockers—helped keep the crew in line. Enter the wrong code and *zap*. Crispy pirate."

Kovalic rolled his eyes and exhaled a cloud of smoke. He'd never found smoking that pleasurable *or* that calming, despite what its practitioners avowed. Most of all, he had a hard time understanding the appeal of inhaling hot smoke on a planet that routinely reached scorchingly oppressive temperatures during the day.

"Oi." It wasn't Tapper's voice, and that was enough to make Kovalic straighten up. A big fellow, about as broad across as one of the downtown transpo buses, was bearing down on him, with an expression that suggested he wasn't about to invite him to the neighborhood cookout.

"Uh oh," muttered Kovalic. "I've got company."

"You need backup?"

"Not yet, but you know the signa . . ." he trailed off as the man strode up to him. His stomach sank further as he recognized the guy: he'd been one of the two thugs that had been posted outside the Pig and Thistle last night. Assuming a surly expression, Kovalic hoped that this particular brute didn't happen to have a college degree to go with his impressive brawn.

"Whadya doin' here?" His voice was thick with what Kovalic had come to recognize as an Upham accent.

Kovalic arched an eyebrow, then mutely raised his right hand, cigarette pinched between thumb and forefinger, as if that were all the explanation he needed.

"I kin see that," said the man, his expression darkening. "Mind tellin' me why yer doin' it *here*?"

Craning his neck in an exaggerated show of looking around, Kovalic shrugged. "Didn't see any signs," he said reasonably.

"Really," said the bruiser. "Consider me a sign then. Pretend me face," and he circled a sausage-thick finger at his mug, which Kovalic had no desire to spend any more time looking at than necessary, "says 'No Trespassin'.'"

With a sigh, Kovalic raised his hands in defeat. "Look, I think we got off on the wrong foot. I don't want any trouble, I'm just waiting for my boss to come out of there." He nodded at the MacDougal warehouse. "Perhaps you'll tell me where I *can* stand."

The brute looked over his shoulder, presenting an all too tempting target in the form of an exposed neck. Need be, Kovalic could have taken him down, and it took a lot of willpower to resist the urge. But subtlety was the play here, and it *was* broad daylight—plus there was no way to get his cover back once he'd blown it in that spectacular a fashion.

The big man looked back at Kovalic, his suspicion tempered with cautiousness. "Who's yer boss, then, fella?"

"Name's Sterne. He's an independent businessman." He grinned as he dropped the cigarette to the cement and ground it out with his boot. "*Very* independent."

"Never heard of him."

"He wouldn't be very good at his job if you had."

"I need to check this out. Wait here." He started toward the warehouse.

"Oh, by all means," Kovalic called after him. "Interrupt my boss and—I presume—*your* boss while they're talking business, just to ask them if the guy standing outside is all right."

The big man slowed to a stop, turning to face him. "What're ye sayin'?"

Kovalic shrugged. "Oh, nothing. I'm sure you know your boss better than I do. It's just that in *my* line of work that'd be a quick road to unemployment . . . if he was in a good mood, that is."

Perhaps realizing he hadn't thought this plan all the way through, the big man faltered. Kovalic could see the mental effort on his face as he considered his options, then slowly shook his head. "I still can't have you hangin' around out here. I'll need to talk to my boss."

"Well, then, perhaps I should come in with you?"

"Fine. Hurry up, then."

Kovalic took his time strolling over to the man, who laid a heavy hand on his upper arm. They crossed the open expanse toward the warehouse, the big man chivvying him along, and had gotten within about ten feet of it when the metal front door of the building clanked open and a short, graying man stepped out. He took the situation in at a glance.

"What's going on?" he demanded, looking back and forth between Kovalic and his escort. "I leave you alone for five minutes and you've already got yourself in trouble?"

"Sorry, boss," said Kovalic as sheepishly as he could manage. "I guess this guy didn't like the look of me."

The short man fixed the bruiser with a nasty look. "I don't pay him for his looks, friend; I pay him for his skills. I don't know what *your* boss pays you for, but it clearly isn't either of those."

Opening his mouth to retort, the bruiser clearly thought better of it. "He looked suspicious," he said stolidly. "I was checkin' it out."

"Superb," said the short man, his voice steeped in sarcasm. "If everything is resolved to your satisfaction, I need my man in here to conduct some business. Unless you'd like me to call your boss and have him *confirm* that for you."

Clearing his throat, the bruiser released Kovalic's arm. "No, that won't be necessary. Sorry 'bout that."

Kovalic brushed at the wrinkles in his sleeve and straightened his jacket.

With a brusque nod, the man walked away before he got himself into the hot tub over his head. Kovalic watched him round the corner out of sight, then let out a breath and turned to Tapper. "Excellent timing as always, sergeant."

With a grin, Tapper tossed him a salute. "Smart of you to leave your comm open."

Kovalic gave a modest tilt of his head. "I've been known to have a good idea or two in my day. Shall we?" He gestured to the open warehouse door.

It was dark inside, especially after Tapper closed the door behind them. "While you two were having your little chat, I disabled the building security. Surprisingly top-of-the-line stuff, though at least the alarm wasn't tied into the local authorities."

"Well, they'd hardly want the constabulary poking around their shady warehouse, would they?"

"That they would not. Did find what looked like an attempted professional tap though. Eyes's work, unless I miss my guess."

"Attempted?"

"Ah." Tapper chuckled. "These folks are dead clever. They let the tap in, but then cross-wired it to the security cameras in the warehouse next door. So all IIS is getting is a feed of people unloading crates of smoked meats and cheeses." He shook his head in admiration.

The main floor of the warehouse was about the size of a light aircraft hangar, featuring floor-to-ceiling metal scaffoldings that were piled high with crates of all varieties: small, large, even groundcar-sized.

"There must be thousands of them," said Kovalic, sighing. "How the hell are we going to find the ones we're looking for?"

Tapper jerked his head up at what looked like a small trailer of corrugated iron hanging above the warehouse floor. "That's the shipping office. They must have some sort of inventory management system."

Kovalic tapped a finger against his lips. "Maybe we could cross-reference with the delivery dates from Danzig's ledger." He looked at Tapper, who raised his hands.

"Hey, I got you in. My work here is done." He lounged against a nearby support beam and twiddled his thumbs.

Kovalic snorted, then headed for the stairs. His feet clanged noisily off the steps, echoing in the vast emptiness of the warehouse. Stacks of boxes aside, the place was awfully empty. You didn't necessarily expect a warehouse to be a bustling hotbed of activity, even for an illicit organization like this one, but nobody at all? Well, not counting the bruiser outside. He'd bought that his boss was in here, which either meant that he wasn't very smart or he wasn't in the loop.

The office was a mess, just as Brody had described it. He saw the calendar on the wall with the name MacDougal Shipping Incorporated on it, and sent an appreciative thought in Brody's direction, wherever he was. Papers were strewn all over the desks in no apparent system, so he went straight for the terminal half-buried under stacks of notices.

It was an archaic computer system, even by Caledonian standards. With its two-dimensional flat-screen display and push-button keyboard, it wouldn't have been out of place in a museum back on Earth. Firing it up presented him with a prompt for username and password.

He triggered his comm. "Hey, you got Three's can opener on you?"

"Indeedy," came back the sergeant's voice. "I'll bring it up."

Leaning back in the desk chair, Kovalic stared at the glowing prompt on the screen. His mind spun, running over the situation to combat the vague feeling of unease that was perched on the back of his neck. An empty warehouse with archaic computer equipment in an office that was a little *too* strategically messy. He knew it was a front, but it was the artful detail with which that front had been constructed that set Kovalic on edge. Then again, the Black Watch had been doing this for twenty years now; surely they'd picked up a few tricks along the way. If De Valera had stayed ahead of IIS this long, he had to be smarter than your average criminal.

A sharp whistle broke his concentration and he saw Tapper at the doorway to the office, holding up a small data card. "Three's magical incantation, in concentrated form." He tossed it to Kovalic.

"Thanks. Let's hope it's an adequate substitute for the man himself."

"I believe he said it carries a money-back guarantee."

"I'll keep that in mind when his pay review comes up." Kovalic slid the card into the computer's data port. For a moment nothing happened, then the machine began to whir; the screen blinked, as if trying to right itself, then blinked again and displayed a load of garbage characters. A moment later it shut itself off, then cycled back on, showing scrolling lines of white text on a black background, finally coming to a stop at a command prompt.

"Quaint," said Kovalic. He flexed his fingers and typed in a few commands. The terminal spat the information back out at him, happy to help. "All right. Let's see what we can do about those dates."

The database itself wasn't password-protected, instead relying on the overall security lockdown for preventing access to the system in the first place. Page's ingenious data card had circumvented that by booting the terminal into its own custom operating system, putting all the information at Kovalic's fingertips.

Of course, the Black Watch were more than a little paranoid, so even once you were into their files, they'd designed it to look like nothing more than the shipping company it purported to be. Not unlike Danzig's ledger, the database employed its own sort of code for shippers, contents, and even the dates on which packages were received.

"Shit," Kovalic muttered as he scrolled through the data. "How the hell are we going to find a specific crate in a room full of crates? It's like trying to find a polar bear in a blizzard."

Something caught Kovalic's eye on the screen and he frowned. He stopped scrolling and reversed, trying to suss out whatever it was. There was so much data it was hard to tell exactly what had pinged his attention—but *something* in there had registered. Upon closer inspection, he noticed a string of characters that looked familiar.

"Huh."

"What's up?" said Tapper.

"They didn't encode the crate IDs."

Tapper peered over his shoulder. "How the hell can you tell that?"

"I may not have Three's eidetic memory, but I remember the format from Danzig's ledger." He pointed at an entry on the screen.

"If they changed the crate IDs, it would have been a lot harder to find the damn things on the floor," said Tapper slowly.

"So, all we have to do is cross-reference the list of crate IDs from Danzig's ledger and we're all set." Kovalic scratched his head. "Well, this is going to be a lot easier than I thought."

"I guess they didn't expect anybody to be crazy enough to come looking for a crate by ID number."

"Works for me." Rifling through his pockets, he pulled out the data chip with the entries from Danzig's ledger and plugged it into the terminal alongside Page's magic card. His fingers flew over the keyboard, running the intersection of the two data sets, and a list of a dozen crates popped up. Selecting out the location numbers, he grabbed a piece of scrap paper from the desk and jotted them down, then yanked both chips from the terminal and restarted it.

"And it's like we were never here."

●

Sorting through the crates on the warehouse floor wasn't difficult, but it was time-consuming. It took a solid ten minutes for them to locate the first one that Kovalic had found on the list; it had been tucked away behind a stack of larger containers that probably could have held small elephants.

There was an automated retrieval system for the crates, but they didn't want to risk turning it on in case it garnered unwanted attention. Instead, they had to crawl into the shelves themselves, crouching under the low overhangs and shining their pocket flashlights at the IDs on the boxes.

"Found it," Tapper crowed finally, waving Kovalic over toward him with his bobbing light. "Over here."

They brushed off the thin layer of dust on the crate and peered at the number which, sure enough, matched one on Kovalic's list. "All right, sergeant. Open it up."

There was a slight hiss as Tapper popped open the container, breaking the pressurized seal. "Um," said Tapper.

"Um?"

"Take a look, boss."

Kovalic joined Tapper at the crate, bending almost double to avoid whacking his head. Tapper held the top of the crate propped open with one hand while shining a torch into it with the other.

"Holy shit," said Kovalic, giving a low whistle. "That what I think it is?"

"HV-357 carbines," Tapper confirmed, reaching into the crate and pulling out one of the sleek, black killing machines. "Ooh, they opted for the retractable stock. Nice choice." He sighted down the barrel, then checked the magazine. Tilting the gun to one side, he ran the torch over it and shook his head. "But the ID barcode looks like it's been filed off—wait." He frowned. "That's weird."

"Weirder than a crate full of guns under Commonwealth diplomatic seal in a terrorist warehouse?"

Peering closer, Tapper ran a finger across a spot on the carbine's body, then rubbed his finger against his thumb. "The ID number wasn't just filed off—there were no scratch marks on the metal or rough edges. There was never an ID number here at all."

Galactic accords had long enforced the weapon ID program, even across enemy lines. The only way that a gun could avoid getting stamped was if it had just rolled off the assembly line.

Kovalic swallowed. "Hey, just to confirm: who makes the HV-357s?"

"That'd be Harlan Armaments."

"And they're based . . ."

"On Terra Nova." Which also happened to be the capital of the Commonwealth.

"Yeah, that's kind of what I was afraid of." He motioned at Tapper to return the gun to the crate and seal it up.

Twenty minutes later, they'd checked three further containers, which had respectively contained several thousand rounds of ammunition, a case of subsonic grenades, and a military-grade crowd dispersal device.

They hovered over a fifth crate as Tapper unsealed it and levered off the top. Casting the pale glow from his comm unit over the interior, his face hardened and he swore softly. Brow knit, Kovalic leaned over and peered inside. His own breath caught.

The fifth crate contained Jim Wallace.

"Damn it." Reaching in, Kovalic pressed two fingers to the man's neck, but it confirmed the obvious: Wallace's skin was ice cold.

Sighing, Kovalic pinched his nose between thumb and forefinger and slid down the crate to rest his back against it. "Shit."

"He was a good man," Tapper said, staring into the crate and shaking his head slowly. "Didn't deserve to go out like this."

Drawing a breath, Kovalic pulled himself up again and cast his eyes over Wallace's body. Ligature marks around his wrists suggested he'd been bound at some point before his death. Cause of death wasn't immediately apparent, but asphyxiation from lack of air in the container seemed likely. It also made it difficult to tell exactly when Wallace had died or how long he'd been in the crate.

Before he could utter a word, the sound of a door creaking echoed throughout the vast warehouse. Tapper and Kovalic exchanged a glance and Kovalic raised a finger to his lips. Footsteps rang in the silence—two pairs, by Kovalic's count—and as they grew nearer, he could hear the quiet murmur of conversation passing between them.

Motioning to Tapper, Kovalic crept toward the edge of the row they were in and pressed his back to one of the crates, trying to keep himself to the shadows. The voices became louder.

"To the ground?" said the first.

"That's what the boss said. Just move the boxes from this list first."

There was a snort from the first man. "I hope he knows what he's doing."

"He's the boss, Kingsley. You want to go up against De Valera, be my guest, but don't drag my name into it."

"Wouldn't want to tarnish your reputation, Shen."

"You're just sore he didn't pick you for this little jaunt of his."

"Hey, I'm happy to stay here where it's safe. Damn fool idea if you ask me."

"He *didn't* ask you."

"Whatever," grumbled the one who'd been addressed as Kingsley.

"Let's just do the job, okay? Don't want De Valera thinking we can't handle a simple task," replied the other one—Shen.

"Yeah, whatever. Maybe you're afraid of him—not me."

"Got the eye on the big chair yourself, do you? Good luck getting through Brody. Everybody knows he's next in line."

The two chose roughly that moment to walk past Kovalic's hiding spot, their backs to him. It wouldn't have been difficult for him to get the drop on them—they weren't armed as far as he could see and clearly weren't expecting any sort of trouble on their home turf. But it seemed like there might be more to gain from seeing what they were up to. He waved at Tapper, signaling that there were two men and pointing in the direction they were going. Tapper waved back and disappeared down the far end of the row.

Kovalic checked the knife in his boot top, making sure he could get to it in a hurry if need be, then skulked out to follow the two men's path.

They were still walking down the aisle, oblivious to his and Tapper's presence, making what looked to be a beeline for the office. Kovalic glanced up at the window overlooking the warehouse floor. They'd done a pretty good job cleaning up after themselves, but there was always the chance they'd missed something.

"Let me put it this way," he overheard Kingsley saying.

Kovalic's comm chose that extremely inopportune moment to buzz for his attention.

It wasn't a loud buzz, but it was loud enough—the warehouse wasn't particularly noisy and the man had taken a breath before launching into whatever he was going to say. Shen gave a brief glance over his shoulder, his eyes widening in shock as he looked right at Kovalic.

"What the fuck? Kingsley!"

Kingsley turned, even as Shen's hand went to the inside of his jacket. It could have been for a gun or a comm, but Kovalic wasn't about to wait and see. His instinct told him that the last thing they'd expect was for him to run *toward* them, and, to be honest, his instinct had a pretty good track record.

He charged.

The two men were probably about thirty feet away, a distance that Kovalic covered surprisingly quickly; Shen was still fumbling to extricate whatever was in his jacket when Kovalic's fist hit him in the upper abdomen. With a wheezing groan, he doubled over—but before Kovalic could take him down, a flicker in his peripheral vision told him that the second man, Kingsley, was already swinging at his head.

Normally he would have ducked, but there wasn't any time, so he put up an arm to block, wincing at the impact. Closing his hand around the other man's arm, he gripped it tightly and twisted it around and under, using it to pull himself closer and knee him in the groin. It may not have been the honorable thing to do, but it sure got the job done.

Kingsley crumpled to the floor, buying Kovalic enough time to check on the other man. He'd found what he was looking for, finally—a comm, as it turned out, not a gun—but he hadn't quite gotten his wind back. Kovalic reached down and clapped his hands on both sides of the man's head, hard, and his eyes rolled back. He hit the ground with slightly less force than his companion, the comm falling out of his hand and onto the concrete floor with a crack.

Straightening up, Kovalic surveyed his handiwork.

"Geez," said Tapper, coming up behind him. "You couldn't have saved me one?"

"Well, you can have them now if you like."

"You're all heart. Oh, and next time, consider turning your comm *off* when you're sneaking around."

"I'm not going to live that one down, am I?"

"Better not living it down than not living at all."

Kovalic grimaced, thinking of Wallace. Bending over, he scooped up the fallen comm unit. It was a shoddy one and the impact had shattered the screen. Slipping it into his pocket, he quickly frisked them; as he'd suspected, neither was carrying a weapon. Shen had a pack of cigarettes and a lighter, as well as an ID card that gave his name as Shenobi Dunne; the other, whose ID said Frank Kingsley, was carrying a comm locked with a passcode. Kovalic took that along with Shen's comm; Page might be able to do something with them if they had time, but it was starting to look like demand was outstripping their supply of that particular resource.

"What the hell do you want to do with them?" Tapper asked. "We can't leave 'em here and we're sure as hell not going to get 'em out with your new best friend outside."

"Yeah," said Kovalic slowly, looking around the warehouse. Sometimes—all too often, really—you had to make do with what you had.

In this case, that was a lot of crates. And sometimes one good turn deserved another.

He turned to Tapper. "Grab an arm."

They found a crate big enough to hold both men, and even left it cracked open so they wouldn't suffocate—a consideration that clearly hadn't been given to Wallace.

Over the body of the deceased operative, they took a quick moment of silence, and Tapper muttered a few words about the man. It wasn't much as memorial services went, but it was better than what a lot of folks in their line of work got.

With Wallace's soul hopefully laid to some sort of rest, Kovalic pulled out the data chip he'd recovered from the operative's apartment. If nothing else, he was going to make damn well sure that the man's death hadn't been in vain.

It took four tries to land on the finger Wallace had used to encrypt the data chip—fortunately this particular model didn't require that the finger's owner had a pulse—but when they did a wealth of information scrolled across the comm in Kovalic's hand. He'd have been lying to say it wasn't accompanied by a sense of relief: they were finally getting somewhere. Puzzles were fine by Kovalic, but he didn't much care for ones where you didn't have enough information to reason out a solution.

They sealed Wallace back up in the crate—it made as good a coffin as any—and wiped down their own prints. No sense in giving anyone a chance to pin the man's murder on them; not that the local constabulary would be likely to shake down this place.

Within ten minutes they had slipped out the back door and rearmed the security system.

"Well, at least we got the right place," said Tapper.

"They mentioned a trip of some sort." Kovalic frowned at his comm. It had been Page who had called while they were in the warehouse, but he hadn't left a message or called again. He debated calling him back, then hesitated; Page was smart enough to turn his own comm off in a sensitive situation, but Kovalic wasn't taking any more chances today.

"A nice pleasant beach vacation, maybe?"

"Right. But I think—" His sentence was interrupted by the comm unit vibrating in his hand. Page. He held up a hand at Tapper and answered it.

"You find him?"

"No, sir." There was a pause before Page continued, and when he did Kovalic had no trouble hearing the regret in the man's voice. "Target is in the wind."

Kovalic let out a long sigh and stared into the distance. There wasn't much more to be gained from Page staying down in Berwick. Brody wouldn't be holed up there, and if he was, it was getting to be a secondary concern at this point. "You're recalled," he said finally. "See you at the rendezvous."

"Roger that."

Flipping the comm closed, Kovalic lapsed into silence. They had some time before Page would make it back up here, but he couldn't shake the feeling that they were on someone else's clock. What exactly that clock was counting down to, now, that was the mystery. But he didn't fancy being stuck out in the cold while the main event was happening somewhere else.

"What're you thinking, boss?"

Kovalic frowned. "I'm thinking, sergeant, that it's about goddamned time we started putting some pieces together."

# CHAPTER SIXTEEN

The trip back to Raleigh City was so long that when Eamon opened the door to the flat, Eli plodded over to the bed and flung himself on it, boots and all. Eamon flipped on the light and Eli grumbled, squeezed his eyes shut, and burrowed deeper into the cool sheets.

"Juswanna *sleep*."

"So much for whatever basic training you ever had, huh?"

Eli rolled over, one arm flopping lazily across the bed like a dead fish. "*Basic* training? We just spent the better part of a day getting back here—what time is it, anyway?"

"Four."

"In the *morning*? Christ, Eamon, we could have been back in two hours if we'd just taken the train."

Eamon didn't deign to respond, just closed the door and locked it behind him. Of course, Eamon hadn't *wanted* to take the train, a fact he'd been only too happy to relay to Eli right after they'd slipped out of the back door of Ms. Munroe's house.

Only the "back door" was actually a cramped twenty-meter tunnel underneath the backyard that exited in a small garden shed on the adjacent property. Built during the initial occupation, Eamon had explained, much like the one that linked the Pig and Thistle to the Black Watch's warehouse. Apparently Sui Munroe and her husband—rest his soul—had been rather prominent freedom fighters during the first years of the resistance. Mr. Munroe had eventually been rounded up in a wave of Illyrican crackdowns and condemned to hard labor in the mines, a sentence from which he'd never returned. The authorities had attributed his death to a cave-in, but by that point the mining corporations had come under Illyrican control and the line between accident and assassination had to be navigated by tiptoe. Sui, meanwhile, had carried on her work for the cause in her own way. But she'd kept the tunnel well maintained, because you just never knew.

From the terminus of Ms. Munroe's tunnel, Eamon and Eli exited into the street behind the Munroes' house, where a groundcar was waiting for them.

Trains were out of the question, Eamon had explained. They were bottlenecks: once you got on one, you were trapped—not to mention they were closely watched by the authorities. Buses were a little better, but not enough that Eamon was willing to take one directly back to Raleigh City. That left the smaller conveyances.

The groundcar's driver was one of Eamon's associates—the unpleasant gentleman with the scar whom Eli had encountered in the warehouse. He was no more polite than he'd been during the interrogation, merely grunting assent when the two of them got in and then peeling off down the road toward the highway.

"Highway" was kind of a joke. The long ribbon of blacktop was interrupted all too frequently by sun-baked cracks from which weeds sprawled like grasping tentacles.

With high-speed rail lines linking the rapidly growing cities to the mining settlements where much of Caledonia's population worked, there was little need for personal ground transportation—and even fewer colonists who could actually afford such a thing. Plus, most groundcars ran on batteries these days, which were more suited for travel within a city than between them.

A fact that Eli brought up out of curiosity once they had cleared the city limits and were bumping along the road.

"This is a long-range model," Eamon explained. "We can get about a thousand miles out of it before recharging."

But the scar-faced man hadn't recharged the car in Berwick, apparently, because the estimated mileage on the dashboard only showed about half of that. Eli frowned, the vestigial pilot part of his brain automatically—if rustily—kicking into mental calculations of fuel to distance. "That still leaves us a couple hundred miles short of Raleigh City."

"I hope you brought your hiking boots," said the scar-faced man, who Eamon had addressed as "Kelly." Eli's initial impression had been one of dislike—the guy *had* threatened to kill him and dump his body. But, after spending more time with the man, his second and third impressions concurred completely: Kelly seemed like a nasty piece of work, and the fact that Eamon voluntarily associated with him left Eli with a distinct feeling of unease.

"Don't worry," said Eamon, with a tight smile, "I've got it all taken care of."

"Oh. Great."

As it turned out, "taken care of" meant that they were met by a heavy hauler en route from the MacAulay mine to Raleigh City. Eamon, Eli, and Kelly were unceremoniously bundled into the back of the truck, where they were given uncomfortable seats on a load of bauxite and iron ore which, Eamon assured him, would foil any conventional scanner. Just in case, though, they'd all been handed insulating wraps that would shield them from thermal detectors, on which they'd normally light up like fireworks on the Emperor's Birthday.

That ride was a lot shorter than the first leg in the groundcar, but infinitely more unpleasant. There was a very good reason that rock had never been the material of choice for furniture construction, and as the back of the truck had not been designed for passengers the three of them were jostled around like a makeshift baby rattle. Eli quickly discovered that the one thing worse than sitting on cold, hard, pointy rock was repeatedly finding yourself bounced into the air, only to land on cold, hard, pointy rock. Ten minutes into the trip, Eli had vowed he would never take sofas for granted ever again. *I wonder if De Valera gives his people hazard pay?*

Right before it entered the transport company's lot, the truck pulled over and the three of them slipped out. Eamon thanked the driver—a burly, bearded man whose red cheeks Eli queasily recognized as a clear sign of being at least one or two sheets to the wind—and shook his hand.

The lot was on the far southeastern outskirts of Raleigh City, as far as you could get from the northern reaches of Upham—a solid twenty-five kilometers. While Eli hobbled around, trying to work some feeling back into his now numb tailbone, he looked around for the next ingenious form of travel that Eamon had no doubt summoned. A motorbike with a sidecar? Had they rustled up a horse from one of the area's paltry farms and harnessed it to a buggy?

His heart sank when he saw Eamon zip up his jacket and begin trudging in the direction of the purple glow on the horizon that marked the nighttime aura of Raleigh City. It might have been pretty if it weren't so damn far away.

"We're *walking*?" he asked, his jaw dropping.

There was a rough shove from Kelly behind him and Eli stumbled to the ground. The dirt and gravel dug into his palms, scraping them raw. Getting to his feet, he brushed himself off and tamped down the anger and frustration that had been building since the morning.

Kelly was giving him an appraising stare, arms folded across his chest. He made a *tch* of disgust. "Say what you will about the crims, I never thought they made a soft soldier. What a fucking joke."

Eli's scraped hands balled into fists and he felt his temper rising. "Let's just get this out of the way then, shall we?"

Kelly shrugged off his jacket, revealing arms that were about as thick around as the hams that Eli's mother had cooked for holiday dinners. *Uh, shit.* He put up his hands anyway, wondering if maybe Kelly would at least respect him after turning his skin colorful shades of purple and black.

Fortunately, they didn't have to find out, as strong hands interceded, pushing them away from each other. Eamon Brody stood between them, his expression a familiar stony cold that Eli recognized all too well, though he'd never before seen it on his brother's face.

"Cut it the fuck out." He didn't yell or shout—his voice wasn't even all that loud—but something about it resonated on an almost molecular level.

Kelly's voice shifted into a sneer. "What, you want us to all just get along?"

"I could give a *shit* if you get along. This isn't about settling personal vendettas, Kelly." The edge on that statement was sharp enough that the scarred man's face contorted in fury and Eli could swear he saw the man's hand twitch, but no response came. "We've got work to do and I'll ask you to, at the bare minimum, keep things professional. Now shut the fuck up and let's move. We've got a lot of ground to cover before sunrise."

Kelly gave Eli a dark look and muttered something under his breath, but he snatched his jacket up from the ground and yanked it on as he walked toward the city lights.

"I could have handled him," said Eli.

"In a dogfight, sure," said Eamon. "Sadly, we don't have a starfighter to offer you. Down here, it's just fist versus fist—well, until Kelly pulls his knife anyway." He shrugged and started walking toward Raleigh City.

Eli shook his head. *Just another normal night with my self-righteous big brother and a violent psychopath. I never thought I'd miss the social scene at Davidson Base.*

With a sigh, he followed in his brother's footsteps. They threaded between the dark, looming giants of warehouses and industrial buildings that were the only things lining the roads in this part of town. There was no need to stick to the shadows—pretty much everything was shadow around here. Not to mention that, if there were any cameras, they could likely see in the dark better than any person could. But as long as Eamon wasn't planning to break into any of the buildings, they ought to be fine.

They made it back to the city proper about four hours later. About a half an hour after that, they reached Eamon's flat . . . well, Eli wasn't sure it actually belonged to his brother, but the accoutrements scattered around the room suggested that it was where he was currently staying. Kelly had peeled off before that point; he ignored Eli, but said something about meeting up with Eamon in the morning.

No sooner had Eli gotten comfortable on the bed than he heard the sound of a comm ringing. Forcing one eye open, he saw Eamon pull out the device and answer it.

Closing his eye again, he let himself start to drift off to sleep. There were pleasant things there—pleasant and warm, like a blanket wrapped around him on a cold night. He could just let himself go, like he was floating on a raft in the middle of the ocean, surrounded by nothing but—

"What?" Eamon's voice was quiet but sharp and it dragged Eli up and away from his peaceful almost-sleep. Without rolling over, he shifted slightly so that his head was facing his brother, who was talking intently into the comm while pacing up and down the room. The look on his face was anything but soporific.

"What do you mean he's 'gone?' I sent him and Kingsley to the ware-house this *afternoon*." He paused as he waited for the person on the other end of the line. "It's not done? Christ. I couldn't have made it any easier if I'd doused the whole place in kerosene." His cheeks puffed out as he released a long breath and leaned against the room's low desk.

Eli peered at him through one half-lidded eye, but Eamon's attention seemed more on the floor in front of him.

"Fine. No, it doesn't matter." He waved his free hand in disgust. "With-out Shen we've got nobody to fl—" His eyes drifted over Eli and stopped mid-sentence. "McKenna? Let me call you back." He paused. "Just a min-ute or two. Trust me." He flipped the comm off. Eli screwed his eyes shut but felt the pressure of Eamon sitting down on the bed.

"Lije."

He wasn't quite confident enough to risk a snore, but he kept his eyes closed and tried to keep the lids from fluttering. Maybe if he tried hard enough he could just fall asleep and Eamon would go away, and tomor-row this would all be over with.

"Lije, I know you're faking. We used to do the same thing to mom and dad all the time. Come on." He reached over and shook one of Eli's boots.

"Jesus, what?" said Eli. Opening his eyes, he glanced at Eamon who was regarding him thoughtfully.

"I've had a slight . . . bump . . . in my plans."

"Shame. Oh, wait, you basically kidnapped me. Never mind, I don't give a shit about your plans." He rolled over, away from his brother.

Eamon sighed. "Look, I'm sorry. You're my brother; I just wanted to keep you out of harm's way."

"Harm? From who?" he said, turning back toward his brother and wav-ing his hands at the otherwise empty room. "You're the one with the gun—who's keeping me out of *your* way?"

"Lije, look. I need your help. This is important."

"Important? Great. What is it?"

"I . . . well, I need a pilot."

Eli stared at him as though waiting for the punchline of a joke. "You need *a pilot*?"

"Yes."

Neither of them said anything for a moment, then Eli threw back his head and laughed. "Boy, did *you* ever kidnap the wrong person."

"Jesus, I'm asking you a favor," his brother said, heat creeping into his voice. "I'm sorry I forced you to come with me, and I'm sorry I threatened you. And really, if you want, you can leave right now. Just walk out that door." He gestured toward it. "I won't try to stop you, I promise."

Eli frowned, sitting up in the bed. "Eamon, really. What the hell is this all about?"

His brother looked away, staring at his knees. "I guess you could say that when it comes down to it, it's really all about Meghann."

A lump threatened to rise in Eli's throat. "Meghann?" *I think you should come home. Please. Come home.* "What do you mean?"

"What happened to her," said, Eamon, his eyes blurry and unfocused, "was all because the Illyricans felt like they could just walk all over us. Our entire planet. I know—" he held up a hand, palm out, "—I know you don't think this is your fight. But the whole reason I'm doing this is so that what happened to Meghann doesn't happen to anybody else. Not on Caledonia, not on any other planet."

Eli leaned forward. A face smiled at him in his mind—not even a face, just broad strokes: freckles, lively eyes, red hair. It looked nothing like the scared, helpless woman he'd seen rocking silently in her chair. It was everything that face wasn't.

It was alive.

"Eamon, what exactly are you going to do?"

A smile—a jagged one that Eli didn't entirely like—tugged at the corners of his brother's mouth. "The Illyricans have been working on something big."

Something immediately clicked in Eli's mind. *That superweapon project Fielding's boss was worried about. So it is true.*

"I—*we*," continued Eamon, "are going to take it away from them."

Eli swallowed. Even as teenagers, Eamon's schemes had tended to revolve around pretty much one thing: doing as much damage to the Illyricans as possible. And though there might not be much love lost between Eli and the Imperium, these days he felt less inclined to cause people harm, no matter who they were.

"I don't want to hurt anybody."

"I know. Look, if everything goes according to plan, nobody *should* get hurt." He smiled faintly, reaching out and grasping Eli's shoulder. "Trust me. We're going to do our sister proud."

Eli's throat had mysteriously seemed to close up, and he coughed into his hand. "Fine. For Meghann."

Eamon's expression turned surprised, as though he hadn't expected his brother to agree. "Are you sure?"

"Not even a little bit," said Eli honestly. "But like you said, we're flesh and blood. And that should mean something."

A smile—a real one—twitched at one corner of Eamon's mouth. "Thanks, Lije. You won't regret it. I'll fill you in in the morning. Just get some sleep." With that, his brother rose and disappeared into the bathroom.

Eli sighed and fell back onto the bed. Despite what Eamon said, he wagered there was a good chance he *would* regret this. He didn't know whether his brother had been bluffing about letting him walk out of there but he wasn't really sure he had anywhere else to go. The only other people he knew on Caledonia were Fielding and his crew, and he wasn't even sure how to find them.

But, more importantly, in his mind he could still see the look on Eamon's face when his brother had stepped in between him and Kelly—it was the same one Eli remembered seeing on their father's face right before he'd made his point with his fists or a belt. After all these years, and everything he'd been through, he'd only found two things that scared him so much that he couldn't think straight—one was getting back into a cockpit, an idea that always conjured images of ships exploding into fireballs, vaporized instantly amid truncated, static-mangled screams. The other was that look, which before today he hadn't seen in almost ten years.

And, of the two, that one scared him more.

●

Eli was shaken awake far too early in the morning. For a few minutes he held out hope that he'd slept through the entire day only to be woken up the morning after.

"Wahtimeizzit?"

"It's about 6:30," said Eamon.

Eli blinked. "6:30? That's not even a real thing."

"Time to go to work, Lije."

*Work?* Still sleep-addled, Eli wondered if he'd woken up in some alternate reality where he was holding down a steady job. He tried to push himself up, but pins and needles danced up and down his right arm; he'd fallen asleep on it. With effort, he tried to shake it awake. "Ow."

"Here," offered Eamon, tossing something at him. Eli didn't move quite fast enough; it hit him in the face, shrouding him in darkness. Slowly pulling it off his head, he stared at the item which appeared to be made out of dark blue cloth.

"You're dressing me, now?" he asked, sorting through the many sleeves that the garment seemed to possess. "I don't really *do* jumpsuits." He'd even managed to convince Colonel Antony to let him wear shirts and trousers on janitor duty, except for rare occasions.

"Clothes make the man," said Eamon, and as Eli's bleary vision cleared he realized that his brother was dressed in an identical get-up: a navy blue jumpsuit with an insignia sewn above the left breast in gold. He was clipping a plastic ID badge onto the right breast pocket.

Eli frowned. "Seriously? As I recall, the only job you held down for more than about three hours was working at the Raleigh City Country Club, and that was only because they let you drive that little cart around."

"Five wonderful days," said Eamon wistfully. "Now put it on."

Sighing, Eli ditched his jacket and shirt. "Jesus, not even mom tried to dress us alike. Though I do remember wearing an awful lot of your hand-me-downs."

Eamon grinned. "Even Meghann ended up with some of those, though *she* never complained."

Eli shook his head as he pulled off his trousers and struggled into the jumpsuit. "She was so excited when mom finally bought her a dress. Wore it so much it had holes inside a month." He zipped up the front. "There. How do I look?"

"Like a working stiff."

"I'm about five years out of date on fashion. Is that 'in' now?"

"Some things never go out of style." Eamon stepped forward and affixed to Eli's chest a white plastic ID card similar to the one on his own suit. Eli flipped it up when Eamon had finished and raised an eyebrow. "That's a picture of me."

"Pulled from your Illyrican Navy file, I'm afraid. I had Gwennie run it up as a rush job overnight. Your hair was shorter then, but I don't think anybody will care."

"Oookay. What, have you got a day job on a work crew now?"

"Today only. It's kind of a one-off."

Eli sat back down on the bed, its springs squeaking in protest. "I seem to recall something about you filling me in on a few details. So, uh, you can start whenever you're ready."

Eamon had pulled out a comm unit and was apparently composing a small book on it, tapping away with both thumbs at remarkable speed. He flipped it closed and stowed it in one of the jumpsuit pockets. "All in good time. But first we've got to meet the others in about ten minutes."

*Others?* Eli's train of thought was derailed by his stomach audibly rumbling; he winced. It was still roiling with acid from the previous twenty-four hours, during which he hadn't consumed anything more than a cup of bad coffee and whatever greasy, preservative-laden sandwich had been left in the one automatic food unit they'd found on their walk back.

"We can get some food along the way," said Eamon, raising an eyebrow.

Eli grimaced. "Yeah, I'm not sure that's necessary, to be honest. Last night's 'dinner' is still kind of using that space." He got to his feet. "If we're going, then let's go."

Light did little to increase the charm of their surroundings. The area looked grim in the early morning, full of dilapidated buildings, cavity-riddled concrete, and peeling paint. What windows there were had iron bars on them, and, at this time of morning, padlock-secured sliding aluminum shutters blocked off most of the storefronts.

"Nice neighborhood." Eli squinted against the morning light. "Did you have to specify 'sketchy' in the search criteria?"

Eamon shrugged. "The Illyricans want to gentrify the entire damn city. I don't mind a few eyesores in exchange for holding onto a genuine Caledonian neighborhood."

Looking around, Eli wasn't sure that a little bit of gentrification would be such a bad idea: a few flowers here, a nice tree or two there—what would be so wrong with that? But there seemed to be a peculiar sort of pride from the residents, a mix of "it was good enough for all the people before us" and "nobody spruces up my neighborhood but *me*."

Eamon bought two cups of coffee from a small convenience store and handed one to Eli, who stared at it and tried not to think about what it would likely do to his already rebellious insides. He contented himself by pretending to take a sip. Eamon also handed him a muffin which, if anything, was greasier than the sandwich he'd had last night. *What I wouldn't give for a piece of fruit or a bowl of cereal.*

Matters of sustenance addressed, the two made their way toward the city center. It was still early enough that the streets were only lightly trafficked; what few pedestrians there were looked to be on their way to work, and many of them carried identical coffee cups and muffins.

They turned a corner and found an entire squad of people dressed in the same navy blue jumpsuit, lined up on the side of the street like toy soldiers—if toy soldiers commuted by public transportation. But Eli started to feel antsy when he recognized a couple of them. One was Kelly, and even from a glance it was apparent that early rising had done nothing to improve his murderous disposition. His eyes went to Eli, narrowed, and then darted away; he made a poor show of covering his grimace with a sip of coffee.

The other was Gwen of the cheek-tingling backhand. She looked only marginally happier to see him than Kelly had. *And I had such high hopes for us.* The other faces didn't ring any bells, but by now his brain had warmed up enough to deduce that the rest of this work crew was made up of people Eamon knew, which meant that at least some of them had been at the warehouse to watch Eli's debut performance-art piece, "man tied to a chair."

He grabbed Eamon's arm while they were still approaching the bus stop, and his brother raised an eyebrow.

"What's up?"

"Okay, Eamon. Enough. I told you I'd help, but I'm not going any further until you tell me what exactly you're planning."

"We're just filling in for some friends." Despite the attempt at innocence, Eli knew all too well the glint in Eamon's eyes and the faint twitch of his lips that said his brother thought he was putting something over on the rest of the world.

"No offense, but altruism has never exactly been in your vocabulary. What's the scheme? You said you needed a pilot. What for?"

"Just a short trip—nothing that should be a challenge for you. Look, you'll be fine. Just relax and do what everyone else does."

"Like a mindless sheep?"

"Like a soldier," said Eamon, his expression hardening. "Which, as I recall, you were at some point." He looked down at Eli's grip on his arm.

*Yeah, it never really took.*

He released Eamon from his grasp and reluctantly trailed after his brother, who had joined the queue of the be-jumpsuited. All of them nodded at Eamon in turn, and Eli watched as they shook hands, exchanging pleasantries. Not much in the way of smiles, this crew. *De Valera needs to do something about morale.*

Eli fell in next to Gwen, who stood slightly off to one side. "And here I was going to offer to buy you breakfast," he said, trying to look suitably chagrined.

The redhead gave him a sidelong glance. "I don't think we're quite at that stage in our relationship."

"Well, I usually don't let women slap me around until at least the third date."

Her cheeks flushed and she at least had the decency to let a hint of shame creep into her face. "If it hadn't been me, Kelly would have been happy to find more convincing ways of making you talk."

"I can imagine. Still, you'll pardon me if I don't fall to my knees gushing with thanks."

"What do you want?" she said with an annoyed look.

"Oh, just making conversation. You come here often?"

The stare she gave him was out-and-out puzzlement, and her head shook slowly from side to side. "I don't get it," she muttered, almost to herself.

"What's that?"

Her eyes focused on something behind him and Eli glanced over his shoulder to see Eamon talking to one of the others, a severe-looking woman whose short, dark hair was arranged in a style that would probably have been called a "pixie cut" on somebody who looked less threatening.

"You just don't seem like brothers. He's always so serious."

"Well, he's the oldest, you know," said Eli, shrugging. "Always took the full weight of responsibility on his shoulders. So I had to be someone else." He eyed his brother. "I don't think he ever quite got over his disappointment."

She gave him an odd look and seemed about to say something, but before she could a transpo bus rounded the corner and pulled up in front of the jumpsuit crowd, slowing to a stop with a slight squeal. It wasn't a city bus, Eli noted with a frown, though it was close to the same size. The outside was black and unadorned with any sort of writing or logo and the windows were tinted.

A moment after it stopped, the door slid open and the group neatly lined up and filed on. Eli and Gwen were near the rear and followed suit, shuffling slowly as the crowd advanced.

*Last chance*, Eli thought to himself. Once he was on the bus, he was all in. He drew a deep breath and steeled himself, and when it came to his turn in line he climbed aboard.

Surprisingly, unlike most of the municipal transpo buses, this one wasn't unmanned; there was actually a driver at the front, an older man with wrinkled jowls and sparse wisps of white hair. He gave Eli a gruff nod as he stepped on and mumbled something, to which Eli responded with an automatic "You too."

It wasn't until he'd passed the driver and the bus had kicked into gear—he'd been the last person on—that he realized that the man had wished him a Happy Emperor's Birthday.

He swung into the seat next to Gwen. She looked a little exasperated that he'd done so, but didn't object. Eli was about to resume his line of conversation when the intercom clicked on.

"Next stop, Westenfeldt Base," the driver's voice crackled. "Travel time today is about thirty minutes."

*Westenfeldt?* Eli's head turned to look past Gwen at the tinted window, and he felt his stomach writhe and wriggle as though it were a slug on which some young kid had upended a salt shaker. Westenfeldt was the region's main Illyrican military base, just outside of Raleigh City; it also served as the departure point for all military space flight from the continent.

He wasn't doing this for Eamon, he reminded himself. *And it's not about me, either.* The idea of getting back in a cockpit was making his already-upset stomach do twirls.

It was for that little girl who'd never have a chance to grow up. Who might never have her own life, never be able to discover her own gifts, talents, and passions. He was doing this for her, even if she couldn't remember who he was. Yes, in part because he hadn't come home when she asked, because he hadn't replied to that last message. But really, when it came right down to it, it was much simpler. *It's because I'm her big brother. My job was to look out for her—and I screwed that up.* He sucked in another lungful of air and tried to calm his shaking hands.

*Time to make good.*

# CHAPTER SEVENTEEN

The Raleigh City Museum of Art was not as grand as its counterparts elsewhere in the galaxy, but most art enthusiasts would grudgingly admit it held a respectable collection.

More importantly, for Kovalic's purposes, the museum also made for an excellent rendezvous point. It was centrally located, easily accessible by public transport, housed in a large building with many exits, bustling without being crowded, and—best of all—offered free admission.

He was staring at a picture by Titian, on loan from Earth's National Gallery of Scotland, when he felt a presence beside him. A sidelong glance revealed Page, who, like him, was eyeing the painting with the detached interest of your average gallery-goer.

"You like art?" Kovalic nodded at the painting.

"Sometimes," replied Page, frowning at the picture which depicted a hunter stumbling upon a bevy of comely maidens, at least one of whom was an ancient goddess who would soon make him regret his transgression. "This isn't exactly my style but, objectively, I can appreciate its aesthetic qualities and see why some people would admire it."

"And here I thought they'd never perfected a human-looking AI."

"Sir?"

"Never mind. Let's go find Two."

Tracking down the sergeant wasn't difficult—Kovalic knew he had a proclivity for statuary and, sure enough, they found him in the museum's sculpture garden, which delivered significantly more on the promise of sculpture than on the promise of garden, given Raleigh City's general lack of greenery. It was also only sparsely occupied at this time in the evening, presenting an excellent opportunity to walk and talk with little chance of being overheard. The sun had just disappeared over the horizon and the lights interspersed among the sculptures were just coming up, casting long and, no doubt, artfully arranged shadows.

Tapper was admiring a particularly fine piece of marblework when they came upon him. By the looks of it, it was also on loan from Earth, a thought that caused Kovalic to grimace. Despite their pretensions of culture, the Illyricans were no better than the vandals of any previous era of Earth history; they'd still pillaged the planet and claimed its greatest works of art as their own. Robbery, plain and simple.

"Cap," said Tapper, as Page and Kovalic joined him. "I see we've found our errant schoolboy."

Page looked flustered, which was to say he looked vaguely uncomfortable, like he'd worn an overly itchy shirt. "My fault. I should have gone in with a closer cover, kept an eye on Brody."

Kovalic shook his head. "That was my call, lieutenant, not yours. The blame goes on me. Any luck tracing him?"

"I did uncover a few useful pieces of information," Page said, pulling out a notebook. Another of the man's anachronistic affectations—for some reason, he much preferred taking notes with pen and paper than on his comm.

"As we knew, the property in question is deeded to The Berwick Home for Wayward Girls, at which Meghann Brody has resided for five years." Page hesitated. "I did access their patient records—which really need better security, by the way—and she's been diagnosed with a form of catatonia, triggered by trauma." He gave a quick précis of her file and history: the affair with an Illyrican military officer, the pregnancy, the addiction and overdose.

"Jesus," said Tapper. "Poor kid."

Kovalic didn't say anything, but winced inwardly. Page's revelations were hardly news to him. Using Brody's sister as leverage hadn't been his choice—he'd been in favor of telling the kid everything from the start—but he'd gone along with the general's plan anyway. He'd intended to keep Page and Tapper out of the loop on her condition; they wouldn't like it any more than he did, but carrying that burden was his job, not theirs. Still, Kovalic sometimes worried that it was all too easy to forget that a name on a page was a person with a life and family. He cleared his throat. "What else have you got?"

"We only took a cursory look the first time around, so I dug a bit deeper into the organization's tax records. The chief employee—not that they have many—is a woman named Munroe. She checked out clean enough, but get this: her husband, who died about ten years ago, was Rafael Munroe. You don't have to go very far to find out about him." He flipped to another page in his notebook. "He was firmly in the middle of IIS's most wanted list for the ten years before his death—one of the prime movers and shakers in the early Caledonian resistance movement by the sound of things, and rumored to be a close confidant of De Valera himself."

Everything seemed to circle back to the Black Watch. Kovalic scratched at his chin. He hadn't shaved in two days and the stubble bristled under his touch. "You notice anything else while you were there?"

A frown appeared on Page's face. "I did a quick circle of the house when Brody first went in and noticed a man in a groundcar—I wouldn't have marked him except he had a rather distinctive appearance. A long scar, here." He traced a finger down the side of his jaw.

Kovalic looked up sharply.

"Well, what a coincidence," said Tapper, meeting his eyes. "If I recall correctly, a man matching that description gave Brody the old heave-ho from the pub last night."

"We could try to find the car," Page suggested.

"They'll have ditched it already," said Kovalic, shaking his head. "Either way it certainly seems to corroborate that the Black Watch is behind Brody's disappearance—but it doesn't explain *why*. Brody can't be a threat to them."

Tapper shrugged. "Maybe he went willingly?"

Kovalic hesitated. "I don't think so. From what Brody told us, there didn't seem to be much love lost between him and his brother."

"He could have been lying," Tapper pointed out. "Maybe this whole thing was a setup from the get-go."

"You're telling me that an *amateur* pulled one over on all three of us?" said Kovalic, eyebrow raised. It wasn't simply a matter of personal pride— if they'd gotten fooled by a kid who'd been stuck on an isolated backwater planet for the last five years then they might as well pack it in. "Let's not start in on the second-guessing just yet."

"Abashed" wasn't a look that showed up on Tapper's face very often; he shrugged awkwardly.

Kovalic glanced up at a statue of a beautiful woman whose arms flowed off into blank stumps; clearly the sculptor hadn't had the time or inclination to finish the piece. He found it disconcerting, not least of which because he'd seen the real thing in his time, and it was never that clean. In his head he started attaching white marble hands to her, just like putting together pieces of a puzzle.

"No, this is all about the Black Watch. They're cooking up something," he finally said. "They've got the weapons—hell, we *gave* them the weapons." CID, via Danzig and Wallace, had delivered the arms shipments right into the hands of the Black Watch, apparently in exchange for the information Eamon Brody had been providing about the supposed Illyrican weapons project. And while resistance movements always needed arms, the sheer quantity and quality suggested that these weren't simply for a rainy day.

"An attack, then," said Tapper, brow furrowed. "What's high on their target list?"

"Their profile says they tend to favor big, flashy demonstrations," Page put in. "The bombing of the ISC *Trident*, for example."

In Kovalic's head, a puzzle piece clicked into place. "Tomorrow's the Emperor's Birthday." His comrades exchanged a glance. "It'd be a hell of a splash."

Tapper exhaled. "That's a tall order. I mean, the locals are happy enough to riot when the Illyrican rugby team wins—or loses, for that matter. The Emperor's Birthday is the biggest Illyrican celebration of the year. Eyes is sure to take extra security precautions and Raleigh City will probably be crawling with uniforms. Why would the Black Watch make it hard on themselves?"

Tapper's point was good, and Shankar had told Kovalic as much over their breakfast date. Plus, given IIS's level of interest in and surveillance on the Black Watch, it seemed like they'd have their ear to the ground about any impending attack.

"But what if it's not *here*?" said Page suddenly.

"Then we are shit out of luck, because we might as well be playing pin-the-tail-on-the-who-the-fuck-knows," replied Tapper.

Something tugged at Kovalic's mind; there was a logic here that he just wasn't quite seeing. You didn't run a politically oriented terrorist group without having a clear goal. He flipped through the combinations, trying a slew of different puzzle pieces, rejecting the ones that made no sense until he landed upon one that seemed to nestle firmly in with what he knew.

"I don't know *where*," he said slowly, "but I think I know *what*."

Tapper raised an eyebrow. "Oh?"

"It's the same reason we came out here in the first place." He pulled his comm out of his pocket and dialed up the information from Wallace's data chip, then turned the screen toward his teammates.

Tapper and Page exchanged glances. "You're telling me that they're going to hit the Illyricans' secret weapons project?"

"It makes sense," Kovalic said. "Given the amount of firepower they have, what we know of the Black Watch's general means and motives, and the fact that Eamon Brody was the source of our information about the project."

"Due respect, cap," said Tapper, "Eamon Brody was also the *only* source of intel; Caledonia station didn't seem to catch wind of it. How do we know he didn't just invent the whole thing? Maybe the Illyricans are up to exactly nothing and this was just an excuse to get some Commonwealth-supplied weapons."

"Why kill Wallace then?" Kovalic argued, nodding at his comm. "They could have just left him dangling after they'd gotten their arms; he would have been recalled when the lead didn't pan out."

"They were worried he'd report back," Page suggested. "That the Commonwealth would find out what they were planning."

Tapper rubbed a hand against his forehead. "Which is what, exactly? Taking aim at the Illyricans? Last time I checked, we weren't exactly buddies with the Imperium—if there *is* a high-level weapons project, why wouldn't the Commonwealth want the Watch to blow it to high heaven?"

"The usual reason," said Kovalic. "Politics. CID might provide aid and arms to resistance groups, but it's all supposed to be under the table.

Something this high profile . . ." he shook his head. "It wasn't hard for *us* to deduce that the Commonwealth has been supplying those weapons; I don't imagine it'll be much of a problem for Eyes, either. And if they find out that Commonwealth-provided arms were used to destroy one of their top secret projects . . ."

". . . then this war goes hot," Tapper finished.

"I think someone at CID did the math when Wallace went missing," said Kovalic. "They realized their ass was hanging in the wind and decided to do some house-cleaning and turn the whole op deniable."

"Jesus," muttered Tapper. "Fucking bureaucrats."

Page crossed his arms. "So, where does that leave us?"

"Right in the middle of a gigantic mess," said Kovalic. There were too many balls in the air: Brody, his brother, the Black Watch, the Illyricans. He frowned. No, not juggling balls—spokes on a wheel. They just had to find the hub where everything intersected. He raised his comm and started sifting through Wallace's information; somewhere in here was the key to all of this and Wallace had known it. Not only had he encrypted the data, he'd hidden it in his apartment—and someone had gone through a lot of trouble to try and find it. Which meant there was something on here that they didn't want anybody to see.

He started digging through it from the top and let out a breath of relief he hadn't even realized he'd been holding. The chip contained Wallace's reports, in full. Dates, times, people, and—thank god—*places.*

Much of the material was standard: contact reports in which Eamon Brody was cagey and made allusions to needing "resources" from the Commonwealth in order to keep the Illyricans busy. True to his reputation, though, Wallace had been no dummy—he'd done his utmost to corroborate Eamon's story, and he'd had enough time on the ground to actually work the other angles. Consensus from those sources was that a hush-hush Illyrican project *did* exist and that the Imperium had spared no expense on the facility for housing and securing it. They'd done their best to keep the location secret, too, but Wallace had sniffed it out. And, fortunately, written it down for the record.

"Son of a *bitch*," he muttered.

Page and Tapper, who had been arguing some finer point of assault tactics against a fortified position, paused mid-bicker.

"Cap?"

Kovalic ignored Tapper, taking a few tentative steps to find a clear patch of sky. The gray smudges of clouds moved quickly in the brisk breeze, and as they broke he saw what he was looking for: the larger moon of Skye, low on the horizon, and bright with the reflected light of Caledonia's sun; and, higher in the sky, another disc—the smaller, more distant Aran.

His heart twinged—his earliest memories of home, of Earth, were the half-circle of the moon against a brilliant blue sky. Never mind that Luna Colony had been operating for more than two centuries and that the moon had been fully mapped decades before that—somehow it had still incited him to adventure, to the stars.

He pointed up at Aran. "It's on the goddamned *moon*."

The three of them stared silently at the satellite for a moment. *"A secret military base on one of Caledonia's moons."* Danzig had said something off-handed about it at their first meeting, but neither of them had taken it seriously.

Page broke the silence. "Makes sense. A lunar military installation would make it easy to control access. And Aran has an erratic orbit, which means it spends most of its cycle far away from the planet. That's pretty solid security."

"Yeah, I'm feeling less optimistic about this whole thing, boss," said Tapper.

Kovalic's eyes flicked rapidly as he factored in the new information. Getting to the moon would mean transport of some sort and, even as impressive as the Black Watch's resources had been to date, he couldn't imagine they had access to their own ship. Besides . . .

"Any ship that gets within a hundred thousand kilometers of that place without the proper authorization is going to get blown out of the sky," said Tapper, as if reading his mind.

"They'd need a legitimate launch point, then," said Kovalic. "And an aboveboard flight." That meant the local military base, Westenfeldt, and an Illyrican military flight.

Tapper shook his head. "I still think this is crazy. Not even these jokers are stupid enough to try and hit a highly-secured military installation. They'll get *wrecked*."

"They've done it before," Page noted. "The ISC *Trident* was under construction at the shipyards when they blew it up."

"Shipyards, sure," said Tapper, waving a hand. "But they're in orbit and there's civilian access to them—contractors come and go. A military installation on a remote moon is a *bit* different."

Looking back at the armless statue in front of him, Kovalic tapped his lips thoughtfully. "Not as crazy as it might seem at first glance. I've been thinking about this. The timing with the Emperor's Birthday is deliberate. Maybe it's just political but, from what I've seen of this De Valera guy's handiwork, I think there's a practical reason at work here, too."

Page cocked his head, brow creasing slightly. "Such as?"

"What if—and this is by no means a stretch of the imagination—the Black Watch knows something we don't? For example, that the Illyricans are pulling forces from their top-secret research facility to help beef up security at the Emperor's Birthday celebrations in Raleigh City."

Page's eyes flicked back and forth rapidly, as if computing the possibilities. "As conjectures go, that's not even that far-fetched. The Black Watch has a pretty high profile: a few well-placed threats at prominent targets in the capital or casual chatter on channels they know the Illyricans are monitoring and they could practically *ensure* an increased presence."

"A feint," said Tapper.

"Exactly." Hands behind his back, Kovalic started slowly wandering the sculpture gallery, taking in the assorted works of art from both Illyrican and Earth culture. The two mingled here, but Kovalic's seasoned eye picked out the subtle lines of force in the way they were arranged, the Illyrican works almost surrounding the Earth works—protecting them, you might be able to argue, but to Kovalic it looked more like surveillance.

The rest of his team had trailed after him; he stopped in front of a bronze sculpture of Atlas, the Earth hefted on his broad shoulders, and turned to face them. "All I know is that *we* could do it. And, no offense to our skills, but if we can do it, then someone else can do it too."

Page cocked an eyebrow. "I take it you have a plan, sir?"

"I've got the beginnings of one." His mind was already whirling away, trying to dovetail the resources they could draw upon with what they needed to accomplish. "The way I see it, we've got three priorities. First, strategic intelligence: we need to know *what* the Illyricans are working on."

Tapper nodded to Kovalic's comm. "Didn't Wallace know?"

Kovalic shook his head. He'd scrolled to the bottom of the data file but Wallace's reports ended without a definitive word on the nature of the project. "From what I can tell, he was killed before he could get the details." Probably deliberate timing on the Black Watch's part. Kovalic's lips thinned. A goddamned shame. Any death in the line of duty was a tragedy, but a needless death like Wallace's even more so. They'd find the bastard responsible, and when they did . . . "All he was able to ascertain was that it was some sort of weapon."

The sergeant snorted. "Shocker."

"Second priority," Kovalic continued, bracing himself for the inevitable objections, "is to stop the Black Watch from destroying the project."

Tapper and Page exchanged a glance and both seemed about to speak up; Kovalic raised his hand to ward them off. "Barring *that*, we at least need to conceal the Commonwealth's involvement."

"What's the third priority?" asked Page.

Kovalic took a deep breath. "Jim Wallace. He may have been CID, but he was still one of ours—and somebody sealed him in that container. That person needs to be held accountable." He could feel Page's eyes jump sharply to him and he knew the younger man was thinking of his own first mission, remembering—as was Kovalic—two dead intelligence officers lying in a sewer whom nobody would ever avenge. He couldn't bring himself to meet Page's gaze and almost heaved a sigh of relief when Tapper spoke.

"Too right. Nobody takes one of ours down and walks. So, those are our objectives—what's the plan, boss?"

Kovalic turned to Page. "Any more progress on decrypting that data we pulled off Shankar?"

Page hesitated. "I'm pretty sure I can break it but, given the limited power of the equipment we have, I'd estimate it'll take about twenty-four hours." Trace amounts of frustration colored his voice.

"Time we don't have if the Black Watch is already on the move," Tapper interjected.

"It's okay." Kovalic had been thinking about this. "We might not be able to break it, but what if we *clone* his ID?"

Page blinked. "Sure, we could do that. But if we just make a bit-for-bit copy, the encryption will still be intact." His eyes rolled up in thought. "Well, unless the Illyricans are using quantum crypt on their ID cards; then we're dead and just don't know it yet."

"That's a chance we'll have to take," said Kovalic.

"All right. What do you want me to copy it onto?"

Kovalic grinned. "Back onto an ID card. I just have to get an appropriate one." Which, in turn, was going to mean a little help from their good friend Walter Danzig. He was going to *love* this.

"One?" echoed Tapper. "You're going in alone?" The wrinkles on his face arranged themselves into a pattern of obstinacy. "On a goddamned *moon?*"

"Tap, getting one person in is going to be exponentially easier than three."

"If you get into trouble, we won't be able to help you." Tapper made no attempt to conceal the exasperation in his voice. "I like a good game of unstoppable-force-versus-immovable-object as much as the next guy, but getting in between the two of them seems like a good way to get crushed."

Kovalic smiled to himself as he eyed his subordinates. Not for the first time, he found himself struck by the stark contrasts between the two men. In the twenty years that Kovalic had known him, Tapper had never been one to hide his emotions—and right now he was annoyed, more than a little bit angry, and most of all worried. Page, on the other hand, was consistently composed, perpetual blackout curtains drawn across his soul. Every once in a while a hint of emotion would peek through a crack, but even then it didn't stick around.

"You know the deal. This is what we have to work with, so we roll with it." He crossed his arms and locked his gaze on Tapper. "I expect your cooperation, sergeant."

The sergeant bit his lip, but training won out over consternation. "Yes, sir." Above all else, Tapper was a soldier. There'd been a time when he'd been the one giving orders to a young, freshly enlisted private, but he'd taught that smooth-faced kid a thing or two about following—and giving—orders.

"Good. Let's get this done."

# CHAPTER EIGHTEEN

Given that it was about a thirty-minute trip from the embassy to the café he'd picked, Kovalic had been prepared to wait until about quarter after seven, so he was a little surprised when at five past a young black woman entered and calmly sat down across from him, as though she'd been explicitly invited to do so.

He chastised himself for not paying better attention, but his eyes had been on a wall-mounted vid-screen displaying one of the planetary news feeds. The top story this morning had been an early-hours fire at an awfully familiar warehouse in Leith; the video showed it burning merrily away in the darkness, another loose end tied up by the Black Watch. He tried not to think about Wallace and the two men that they'd left there. "Collateral damage," some would argue; not an ideal to aspire to in Kovalic's opinion. The fire would hardly ruin the Emperor's Birthday festivities, but it didn't exactly do much for his appetite. On the upside, concealing the Commonwealth's involvement in the Black Watch's plot had hopefully just gotten a lot easier.

Kovalic took a sip of the tea he'd ordered—coffee hadn't been agreeing with his stomach this morning—and inclined his head to the woman who'd taken the seat opposite him. "Hello."

"Hello," she said, returning the nod.

He took her in at a glance: dark skin, sharp features, carefully coiffed hair, and an air of unquestionable confidence.

"I got your message," she said. "Thought I'd bring the package to you."

"Thanks. How's Walter?"

"He's good. Told me to tell you he's still not happy about Haran."

Kovalic relaxed slightly. That sounded like Danzig. Then again, he was never happy about anything, was he? "And you are?"

"My name's Sarah. I work for Walter."

Station number two, likely. She'd have a certain level of clearance, then, even if it wasn't as high as Danzig's. "Nice to meet you, Sarah. You can call me Fiel—"

"Mr. Fielding, I know. Pleasure to meet you. I'd like to say I've heard a lot about you but, well, I don't have a high enough security clearance to even lie about that."

Kovalic grinned. "Fair enough. I presume you weren't followed."

"You can check behind my ears if you want."

"What?"

"They're dry, I meant. I know how to ditch a tail, Mr. Fielding. You might want to tell your backup to take a refresher though."

Kovalic raised an eyebrow. "What do you mean?"

"Either you didn't ditch *your* tail, or your backup is over by that lamp-post doing a rubbish job of reading that billboard."

"What makes you think he's mine?"

"Well, it takes most people about five seconds to read a billboard, but he's been standing there since I came in. Also, he keeps looking at me."

"You're an attractive woman; I'm sure lots of men look at you."

She gave him a skeptical look; she'd caught his deflection but didn't abandon course. "Please. I've been doing this job long enough to know the difference between someone checking me out and someone, well, checking me out, if you know what I mean."

He raised his hands. "All right, all right. Yes, that's my backup. He's a little—" he glanced over at Tapper, who was indeed standing outside, staring at an advertisement for some fizzy non-alcoholic beverage as though the secrets of the universe were contained therein, "—rusty."

"Uh huh."

"Now that we've made our small talk: You said you have my package?"

"Indeed," she said, removing a small yellow envelope from her jacket. "We weren't sure which side you were looking for, so I brought one of each. I can take back the other one if you'd like." She slid the envelope across the table.

Taking it, Kovalic cracked the seal and looked inside: two ID cards—one Commonwealth, one Illyrican. Staring back at him from both was the same picture that he'd used for his ID to get on planet. Danzig must have hacked into Illyrican Customs to snag it; then again, where else would he get a picture? The chance of even a station chief having access to Kovalic's personnel jacket was slimmer than the Illyricans waking up tomorrow and deciding to abandon Earth.

The Commonwealth card was, unsurprisingly, letter-perfect; the Illyrican was as close as it could reasonably be in such a short period of time. It might not stand up to an exhaustive investigation, but it didn't have to—in fact, he was kind of counting on it. His eyes drifted down to the names on the cards: the Illyrican one read "John Rousseau" and the Commonwealth's said "Michael Montaigne." His lip quirked.

"Why Walter," he muttered. "You *do* have a sense of humor—who knew?"

Sarah gave him a curious look, so Kovalic shook his head. "Nothing. Tell Walter thanks for these." He waved the papers. "And let him know I'm sorry."

"For what?"

"He'll know."

Kovalic drained the rest of his tea and stood, extending his hand. "I'm sorry to rush, but I really must be going. Nice meeting you, Sarah. I look forward to working with you again sometime."

She shook his hand, but her expression was dubious. "Whatever you've got planned, I sure hope for your sake that there *is* a next time."

●

Tapper joined him a block or two away from the café. "How'd I do?"

"You could teach a master class on sticking out like a football hooligan at a nun's funeral."

"So, according to plan, then?"

More than anything, covert work was all about misdirection. Even the best operatives got seen sometimes, so the trick was to give the other side something *to* see. If your backup was just obvious enough, then people patted themselves on the back for having spotted it—and, more importantly, *they stopped looking*.

"Far as I can tell. She didn't seem to make Three."

"Hell, I knew where he was supposed to be and even *I* didn't see him. Where'd you find that kid again? Raised by ninjas in some remote mountain fortress?"

"Genos Province, Terra Nova, actually," said a voice from behind them, so close that Tapper had already gone into a defensive posture and even Kovalic's heart rate did an evasive somersault.

It was impossible to tell exactly when Page had caught up with them, but Kovalic guessed he'd been waiting in the shadows for them to pass by, then calmly melted out and followed along, just as casually as if he'd happened to be a complete stranger heading in the same direction.

"Christ," said Tapper. "We're going to have to put a bell on you."

Kovalic ignored him. "Any unwanted company?"

Page shook his head. "She looked clean. I presume she checked out."

Kovalic raised the yellow envelope she'd given him. "Walter was uncommonly accommodating." He pulled the ID cards out and handed them to Page. "You know what to do."

About to fold up the envelope, he noticed something else at the bottom. Tipping the envelope over, a data chip slid into his hand. *Another present from Walter?* Frowning, he popped it into his comm and turned his attention to Tapper.

"You take care of our travel arrangements?"

"Course. Give me a little credit, boss. Not like you asked me to pilfer a luxury groundcar or anything actually *difficult*."

"Next time, maybe." He glanced back down at the reader again, flipping back through the information, which bore a header reading "Top Secret. Caledonian Security Agency." Right; he'd asked Walter for all of CalSec's information on the Black Watch. Well, better late than never.

A name in bolded type caught his eye as he scrolled past it, and he froze and paged back up to it: De Valera. The head of the Black Watch.

He sucked a breath in through his teeth; Tapper was the first to notice it, a frown creasing his already weathered face.

"What's wrong, boss?"

Kovalic shook his head as he reread the sentence again. "We've got another complication: It looks like Eli Brody is in way over his head."

●

Eli felt his stomach begin to turn well before they reached Westenfeldt Base. As much as he would have liked to blame it on the bumpy Caledonian roads, the transpo bus ride was surprisingly smooth. They skimmed through the barren scrublands, a virtual reverse of his trip from the spaceport just two days earlier. *Jesus, I can't believe that was just two days ago.*

After five years of keeping his boots on the ground, the past week had already seen him survive an interstellar trip involving multiple wormhole jumps. Still, he really didn't have a lot of enthusiasm for leaving solid earth again quite this soon. Not that he wanted to stay on this damn planet, either; after everything he'd been through with Fielding and Eamon, two days here had been just enough time for him to get, well, whatever the opposite of homesick was.

Eli had tried to strike up a conversation with Gwen a few times, but the redhead had kept to herself during the trip, staring out the window or nervously flipping her comm open and closed. He was a little worried that asking too many probing questions would make her suspicious or, more likely, irritated. Asking Eamon wasn't any better: he was sitting next to Kelly up front, and somehow Eli didn't think any questions raised in the scarred man's presence would be terribly productive.

So he'd had little more to do than think. Thinking had turned into dwelling, and dwelling had done nothing to help the condition of his stomach. It had started to feel a bit like he was treading ice-cold ocean water, but rapidly running out of the energy to do so. And there were sharks circling him. Hungry sharks.

What was worse was that the entire experience was overlaid with feelings from the *last* time he'd made this trip. It had been nine years, but retracing the same ground was like running a finger over an old scar. He remembered his parents and Meghann seeing him off at the transpo station as he'd boarded a bus not unlike this one, filled to the brim with other nervous, excited kids. And kids they had all been—eager to leave the old dirtball and change their lives forever. He wondered how many of them had died at Sabaea or in some other battle; hell, even training had taken its toll. How many were still alive? How many posted to some godforsaken outpost at the far edges of the Imperium?

Those that had graduated the academy with him would be just about at the end of their five-year tours by now. Some would stay on; others would leave active service with all the benefits offered to Illyrican veterans: moving on to new lives, new careers. Did any of them ever think about Elijah Brody and what had happened to him? Or did they all just assume he was dead, like everybody else involved in the Sabaean invasion?

And what about those that *had* survived? His breath caught; he hadn't thought about that. There had been others who had lived to tell the tale of the battle of Sabaea, though not many. Most of them wouldn't know Elijah Brody from a hole in the ground, but a few just might. Those were people he'd served with. Frankly, he'd rather they thought him dead than having betrayed them all.

Because that was exactly what he'd done.

The familiar sheen of cold sweat was filming over his brow as they drew closer to the Westenfeldt perimeter. He rubbed his palms against the rough fabric of the navy blue jumpsuit and wished that Eamon had given them something to wear that was even slightly more comfortable. He looked over at Gwen again; her mouth was set in a firm, thin line. She had to know what exactly they were doing, but he couldn't think of a way to ask her.

*What would Fielding do?*

The thought was just there; he didn't even remember thinking it. But once it stuck in a crevice of his mind, he found it a particularly difficult idea to excise. The man seemed to remain calm in any situation no matter how much the odds seemed to be stacked against him. Eli didn't know if it was luck or skill or divine fortune, but whatever it was he could use a little bit of it right now.

He leaned sideways as the transpo bus banked into a turn that would lead it up toward the military base's entrance. The bus slowed as it approached the perimeter guardhouse and Eli peered out the window, but there wasn't much to be seen from this angle.

"I love what they've done with the place," he said to Gwen. "Military-industrial chic is a bold choice."

Her sideways look was sour, but he thought he detected a touch of amusement. *If I do say so myself.*

"Tell me," she said, "do you find that making jokes actually makes you less nervous?"

"Let me think about that—nope, still pretty goddamn nervous."

Her head cocked to one side. "This doesn't really seem like your scene."

"Yours either. Unless there's a call for slapping people around."

"You're never going to let that one go, are you?"

"Not bloody likely."

She sighed. "Look, I just want the Illyricans out of Caledonia, okay?" But there was something unconvincing about her tone—there was more to it than that.

"Who doesn't? Heck, I'd like to see them off with a wave and a smile, but you don't see me joining up with—well, okay, I guess you *do* see me joining up." He trailed off, frowning blankly at the seat back in front of him. He'd agreed to help Eamon, but if he was going to be fair to himself he'd done so in a moment of weakness and without really asking what was involved. Then again, ignorance was no excuse, as his father had been so fond of saying. Usually at great volume.

"Yes, well, I'll get right on to standing for the Caledonian Parliament," said Gwen. "Then I can sit back and let the paychecks roll in while I do absolutely nothing."

"It's a sweet gig." That was pretty much all the Caledonian Parliament was good for: a punchline. The Illyricans allowed the body to continue operating to maintain the illusion of autonomy, and while it kept the trains running and the water flowing it had no real political power. That all belonged to the governor-general, who was appointed directly by the emperor. And though there may not have been a formal placard on the door, it was hard to miss the implicit sign that read "Caledonians need not apply."

"So, here I am," said Gwen, raising her hands.

"On an Illyrican military base," Eli said as the bus started up again; apparently they'd all passed muster, which did little to assuage his concern about what they were up to. If nothing else, it abolished any lingering, foolish hope that maybe Eamon had gotten a reputable job doing some sort of extraplanetary maintenance. He felt ridiculous even *thinking* that;

it was like suggesting that a regiment of Illyrican shock troopers had been deployed to rescue a kitten from a tree.

Small huts and low dwellings skimmed past their window, along with a number of people dressed in red uniforms going about their daily business. It made Eli's pulse do the fandango. He'd seen other soldiers since he'd been back; they'd been patrolling the spaceport as well as sprinkled throughout the streets of Raleigh City, but the concentration here was overwhelming. Surely, they'd know him for what he was just by looking at him: a traitor and deserter. Someone who'd taken the same oath they had and then done everything short of spit on it.

A light touch descended on his arm. "You okay?"

He glanced at Gwen and half-smiled. "I've been better, I'm not going to lie." He patted her hand. "You're too nice for this line of work; you should get out while you still can."

Her face fell and she withdrew her hand. "It's too late for that. *Alea iacta est*, as they say."

"What's that when it's at home?"

"'The die is cast.'"

Eli's eyes narrowed slightly, but he didn't say anything. His gaze drifted toward the front of the bus where he could only see the red top of Eamon's head. *Where'd you find this one, Eamon? Or was it the other way around?*

His attention wavered as they stopped in front of a low-slung gray concrete building; the rest of the bus's inhabitants had risen from their seats and were filing toward the front. There was little for Eli to do but follow along and try to blend in.

It was early enough that the weather was still cool, but the heat was coming—Eli could smell it in the air. The second he stepped out of the bus, his hearing was assailed by a loud rumbling blast that made him wince and cover his ears. He looked up in time to see a transport climbing rapidly skyward, a shimmering eddy of heat and exhaust trailing in its wake. Bile rose in his mouth, but he forced it back down.

The work crew filtered into the building where they were greeted by an Illyrican security checkpoint. The urge to run was filling Eli's chest, but he ignored the blood pounding in his ears and stepped forward when the officer in crimson gestured to him.

Eli was ushered into a small booth with glass doors on the front and back that slid closed when he stepped in. A current of warm, dry air blew down on him, matting his hair to his scalp, and red lights skimmed over his face and body, even as the booth started to whir like a microwave oven.

And then, as quickly as it had begun, it was over, and he was sent out of the booth to join the rest of the crew, including Eamon, who stood waiting with arms crossed. Gwen was right behind him, and Eli could see her closing her eyes as the air blew down on her. He gave Eamon a sidelong glance and saw him watching Gwen thoughtfully. It wasn't a particularly lascivious look, as Eli had half-expected—rather, something more calculating.

She'd been the last through the checkpoint so, once she cleared it, they set out down the corridor. It was at this point that Eli noticed they were being accompanied by two large containers on repulsor fields, pushed by burlier members of the work crew. They looked like standard cargo holders, probably filled with tools and supplies, but for some reason they only added to his uneasiness.

A left turn took them into a hub from which a jetway stretched down to the ground. They formed up in pairs of two, with the two cargo containers leading the way, just in case the notoriously unreliable micro-repulsor fields decided to collapse and send a couple tons of heavy equipment blazing a bowling ball's path right down the narrow corridor.

At the bottom of the jetway a pair of transparent doors slid open to dump them out onto the tarmac itself. It was hotter here, in part from all the ship exhaust as well as the black pavement, which had absorbed the heat of the morning sun.

On the blacktop sat a boxy transport, resting on four spindly landing struts. A large ramp, the breadth of two groundcars, gaped open like the maw of some hideous creature and the work crew made a beeline for it, pushing the cargo containers into the belly of the beast.

It was a gentle push to the small of his back that made him realize he'd stopped, frozen in the heat wash of the ship, on the middle of the tarmac. Gwen had come up behind him and was directing him toward the ramp. Every cell in his body was humming the same litany of resistance, bombarding his brain with a thunderstorm of electrical signals directing him to turn tail and run faster than he'd ever run before. And weighed against that, the feeling of a woman's hand on his back, telling him to move forward.

It was a no-brainer: he got on the goddamned ship.

# CHAPTER NINETEEN

Ilyrican transport ships were not designed for comfort, Eli decided once he could think again.

He'd started to shake the second he set foot on the ship's ramp, assuming that Eamon had meant for him to pilot the transport, but he was ushered into the rear passenger compartment like everybody else. The abject fear had given way to a slightly less nervous preoccupation as the crew began its pre-flight, readying the ship for takeoff.

His mind had quickly burned itself out with worry and stress, so he had settled for a sort of dreamy detachment in which he could observe without actually being present. Likewise, his stomach had been abstracted into something else entirely and even the shudders that had racked his body relaxed, like the respite of a fever.

Squirreled away in the back of the transport ship's spacious main cabin, Eli managed to conceal most of his plight from his fellow passengers—except for Gwen, who had taken up a buffer seat between him and the rest of the work crew. She held his hand as it went from sweaty to clammy and back again, squeezing it every time he started to convulse.

The benches were hard and the five-point restraints uncomfortable and chafing in all the wrong places, though they did have the notable upside of letting him slump over without making it obvious to the rest of the crew.

*It would be so much easier if I could just pass out.* The thought had occurred to him more than once, but every time he approached the black threshold his brain apparently decided that he could handle just a little bit more stress. Or Gwen's squeezing hand reminded him that he needed to stay upright. She was being awfully nice to him—perhaps it was just pity. Or maybe some sort of maternal instinct. Or maybe she actually liked him. It was possible, wasn't it? *I'm not such a bad guy—when I'm not about to throw up on your shoes.*

Besides the long benches that lined either side of the compartment, there wasn't much going on in the transport as far as decor was concerned. To call it spartan would have been potentially unkind to the ancient warriors, who at least knew a good piece of art when they saw one. The Illyricans were about bare-bones necessity; not that Eli was surprised—after all, he'd ridden Illyrican transports more than a few times. His bunks in the academy and aboard the *Venture* had been nothing to write home about, and they'd been dissuaded from personalizing them in any way. *Interchangeable cogs in a great clockwork war machine.*

Now, he somehow seemed to have become the wrench that got thrown into those cogs. The more he thought about that analogy, the less he liked it, since he was fairly sure that it was the wrench that got chewed up by the gears and then spat out again.

As his mind and eyes wandered, he thought he noticed Kelly's scarred face watching him from across the aisle. But then the thought would drip, treacle-slow, from his brain, and he'd be back to thinking about how much the benches hurt his ass.

Time went by in fits and spurts, like trying to get ketchup out of a bottle: sometimes it seemed like a minute stretched on for hours; other times he felt like he'd blinked and missed the better part of a day. The more cogent part of his mind, which had found a cozy place to hole up, knew that the entirety of the trip couldn't be more than a few hours—the ship was just a short-range transport not suited for wormhole travel—but he couldn't for the life of him tell how long had passed.

He guessed then that it was somewhere near the middle of the trip when he saw Eamon unbuckle and float his way over. The cargo bay was zero-gee; humanity had only recently achieved any success with what was turning out to be not the science but the fine art of producing artificial gravity. As such, they hadn't managed to make it cost-effective yet, especially on a ship this small. Larger capital ships—like Eli's old stomping ground, the *Venture*—could use their immense bulk to help bolster the gravity field, but on a small transport like this one it would have increased the cost of construction by an order of magnitude. *Not likely to win plaudits from the ever-efficient Illyrican military.*

Eamon pushed himself gracefully to the floor, hooking his feet under a bar provided for just such a purpose, and squatted down—as much was possible in the no-gravity environment—to rest at Eli's eye level. Gwen released his hand casually, crossing her arms over her chest and looking studiously away from the two brothers.

"What's the matter, Lije?" His tone was curious, if not particularly concerned. "Space-sick?"

Lots of people got space-sick, just as lots of people in the ages before them had gotten sea-sick, air-sick, car-sick, and probably even horseback-sick. Eli was about to muster a snort over the indignities of such a question—that a professional pilot like him would possibly be subject to the vagaries of a bout of space nausea—when he realized, somewhat to the dismay of the small fragment inside of him that still remembered what it was like to be a pilot, that he actually *was* space-sick.

"It's harder when I'm not flying," he mumbled, the half-truth coming easily. After all, he'd been sick on the way to Fielding's ship because the pilot had been greener than a crop of unripe space wheat. The transport ship pilot appeared to be competent enough, though, and it wasn't as though there was a lot of turbulence once they'd broken atmo.

"I'd have thought you'd all have armor-plated stomachs," said Eamon, scratching at his beard. "Specially formulated and injected by the Illyrican Medical Corps."

"I must have played hooky that day." Eli stared at his shoes and willed himself not to lose his cool. Eamon may have been a bastard, but he was still Eli's older brother, and he realized—to his surprise—that still appeared to count for something. "I'll be fine whenever we get where we're going."

Subtle shadows shifted over Eamon's face as his expression changed. He glanced over his shoulder and then back at Eli. "Listen," he said, his voice taking on an altogether more serious tone, "when we get there, stay back, all right? I know I dragged you into this and I appreciate you coming along, but it might get a little hairy."

Eli grunted, only partly from a wave of nausea that had rolled over him, and looked up at his brother. "I thought you said nobody would get hurt."

"I said nobody *should* get hurt. But there are a lot of variables where we're going, and some of them are outside my control."

*"Should." "Should" covers a lot. For example, I should have known better.* "I see. Speaking of which, where the hell *are* we going? This whole lot are like bloody gargoyles, just sitting and leering."

With a sigh, Eamon lowered his voice further, to the point that it was barely audible above the rhythmic thrumming of the ship's engines. "There's an Illyrican military installation on Aran, and they're building something—something big. Something we can't let them have."

The damn Illyrican project that had started this whole wild goose chase to find Eamon—it was on Aran. *Well, that makes sense. Nobody's likely to stumble across it there.*

"Why didn't you tell me?"

Eamon shrugged. "Obvious, isn't it? Just in case you did walk out that door last night, I didn't want you going and telling anybody where I was headed."

A knee-jerk reaction to protest bubbled to the surface, but he pushed it down. The thought had certainly crossed his mind; that was the reason Fielding had brought him along in the first place, wasn't it? Still, he couldn't ignore the twinge of unease in his gut that had nothing to do with being space-sick. It turned out that when everybody lied to you, it made it a lot harder to believe anybody. That was one thing he missed about the military proper: They didn't lie to you, they just didn't tell you everything. The blue-green world of Sabaea was permanently anchored to that thought.

"So this thing the Illyricans are building—what are you going to do about it?"

His brother's face went grim. "We're going to make sure that they never get a chance to use it."

Eli opened his mouth to ask the first in a torrent of questions—What was it? How were they going to stop it? Was this going to be the Bloody Hundred all over again?—but Eamon glanced at the timepiece on his wrist, rose, and slapped Eli on the shoulder.

"We'll be docking in half an hour. Try to hold your stomach in check for at least that long, hey?" He unhooked his feet from the rail and pushed off back toward the other side of the compartment, where he swam his way toward Kelly, who, Eli noticed, was eyeing him with the same fascination that a kid armed with a magnifying glass gave an ant on a sunny day.

Something warm and dry pressed into his left hand again, and he looked up to find Gwen's eyes on him.

"Everything all right?" she asked lightly, as though she hadn't been seated mere inches away from the entire exchange.

"Just rosy. Snug as a bug in a big old space-faring metal rug."

The cold metal of the bulkhead was the only thing behind him, but he rested his head on it anyway, feeling it leach away the heat at the point of contact. The designers hadn't been too concerned with creature comforts or perhaps even basic safety requirements like headrests.

Five minutes of distraction and mild daydreaming later, he suddenly felt the engine's pitch change as the thrumming diminished and was accompanied with a sensation of being pushed backwards. *They're firing reverse thrusters. Early.*

He was probably the first to notice, attuned as he still was to the language of spacecraft, but he wasn't the only one. Across the way, he saw Kelly and Eamon exchange a glance.

Gwen squeezed his hand again and whispered to him. "Just relax. Everything will be okay."

He frowned at her suddenly calm demeanor. There was a look in her eyes that was slightly out of place—expectation. But before he could say anything there was a blurt from the ship's intercom, followed by a static-tinged voice.

"This is the flight deck. Apologies, folks, but we've been put on a brief hold. Aran Control has informed us that there's a fast courier on the same vector and they've been given priority clearance. It'll tack another ten minutes or so onto our arrival time. Sorry again for the delay. Flight deck out."

Across the compartment, Kelly's face went set, as though he were gritting his teeth. Eamon, on the other hand, looked unnaturally relaxed, his long legs stretched out in front of him. But body language was one of those things that didn't really change over the years; Eli could see this wasn't part of the plan.

Fast couriers usually carried VIPs. Sometimes just messages, but for a trip like the one from Caledonia to Aran it would only be used for the most sensitive communications, since it was expensive and, of course, quite a bit slower than intrasystem comms.

Still, most fast couriers were small ships, and what there was of them was mostly engine. It probably wouldn't, for example, be carrying a company of Illryican marines to ambush them; though all it would really take was one person to tip off the base's existing complement of security.

Regardless, it appeared that they weren't about to be blown out of the blackness of space—after ten minutes of worrying, the ship's engines fired up again and they resumed their course. *Maybe the courier was just a routine thing.* He took a deep breath. They'd passed the point where his choice mattered, unless he was going to try and make a break for the ship's lifeboat—assuming it even had one. And that decision was only going to leave him worse off than he was now. Better to just stick it out and see what happened.

The ship's retro thrusters kicked on again and the engine sound went to a consistent rumble, the vibrations shuddering through the hull. Without armrests to grip, Eli's right hand clawed into the bench next to his thigh, while his left seized Gwen's in a vise.

Against all logic, Eli felt the pressure around him increase, as though he were submerged in some sort of deep-sea diving vessel instead of a space ship. His chest heaved with the attempt to drag out another breath and the unpleasant sensation of cold sweat dripped into his eyes. Just at the moment that he felt he couldn't take another second, that his chest was on the verge of caving in and his head exploding, there was a solid jounce from the ship as its landing struts hit rocky ground. The roar of the engines dropped into a low whine as the pilot powered them down, followed by the all-too-familiar noises of a ship making port: humming and buzzing as various systems were turned off or, in some cases, back on again. The lights in the cabin, dimmed for the duration of the journey, snapped back on full as the umbilical docking connection was made.

A symphony of clicks sounded as the rest of the work crew unbuckled their restraints. Eli glanced around, then fumbled at his own with shaky hands. The plastic fastener kept slipping through his grip, though, until finally Gwen took it from him and punched the red button, letting the belts zip back into the recesses from which they'd come.

With a grunt, Eli pulled himself to a standing position, waving away Gwen when she moved to help him. "I've got it." *Show her you can move on your own two feet,* he thought as he lurched astern toward the airlock. *Assuming, of course, that you* can *actually move on your own two feet.* He stumbled, but thanks to the moon's slightly lower gravity managed to grab hold of an overhead railing before toppling headfirst into one of the equipment crates, themselves being unfastened by a quartet of the work crew, including Kelly. The scarred man's face darkened as he looked up at Eli, then turned quickly back to the container's restraints.

"What's in those things?" he muttered to Gwen as they shuffled past.

The red-haired woman glanced at the crates, then back at Eli and shook her head. "If you don't already know, you probably don't want to."

A feeling that was decidedly unlike jelly was beginning to return to Eli's legs and he was moving more assuredly as they hung a left from the main cabin and into the short foyer that led to the airlock. The big round door there was still closed while the seal was established.

Aran did have a slight atmosphere, but its low concentration and high methane content meant that it wasn't fit for humans. During his training, Eli had briefly visited an outpost on a remote moon of Illyrica with an atmosphere of much the same composition. His overriding impression of that installation had been that, no matter how many scrubbers they ran the air through, it never quite managed to excise a faint tang of the pungent gas. It was kind of like working next door to a cattle farm while pretending it wasn't there.

The airlock door began to roll open, accompanied by the faint hiss of pressures equalizing and the high-pitched squeal of servomotors. The blue-suited work crew began to file into the small antechamber which terminated in another similar door on the opposite wall. This door too began to roll open as they approached, wafting in a gust of the base's air supply, which teased Eli's own nostrils with memories of his time on that Illyrican outpost. Several of the other crewmembers wrinkled their noses in disgust with a few waving hands under them. It would only be a matter of time though, Eli knew—the air filters might never manage to get rid of the smell, but the human nose was pretty good at adapting when necessary; inside fifteen minutes most wouldn't even notice it anymore.

The second airlock door let them into a bare compartment with the decided look of pre-fabrication couture. Most Illyrican bases were cut from roughly the same mold, Eli had quickly discovered in his brief tour of Imperial facilities. This particular module was large and square, probably model 8/A1179 (Airlock Compartment), assembled with an industrial welder and a screwdriver (included). There were a few stacks of cargo containers lining the walls, not unlike the ones that were now floating out of the airlock behind them.

A square pressure door on the other side of the compartment groaned open and three people strode purposefully to meet them. One was a tall, thin man, dressed in a jumpsuit like the one Eli and the work crew wore. Eli's heart jumped at the second man, who wore a crimson Illryican military uniform, a pistol on his belt, and frown creases on his forehead. The third was a woman in a white lab coat with frizzy brown hair that was pulled back in a loose ponytail.

Eamon threaded his way to the front of the work crew and advanced to meet the trio. Eli frowned—there was a tension in the air, as though someone was about to throw the first punch.

"It's about time," said the tall, thin man. "We were starting to think you wouldn't make it before the end of our shift."

Eamon shook his hand. "Sorry about the delay. Name's Mike Collins."

"Carl Tan. Glad to meet you. You filling in for Denison?"

"That's right. He's out with the flu, so I drew the short straw. Guess I'm lucky I got my antivirals this year, huh?"

Tan issued a short, bitter bark of a laugh. "Lucky, right. Shall we get this done?"

"By all means."

"This is our acting head of security, Lieutenant Gregorovich—"

"First Lieutenant," the uniformed man interrupted, drawing himself up.

Tan plastered a smile on his face and turned back to Eamon, rolling his eyes slightly. "*First* Lieutenant Gregorovich. And this is our head of research, Dr. Graham."

*Graham?* A faint memory surfaced somewhere in Eli's mind even as Eamon was shaking the woman's hand, a slight smile on his lips. "Nice to meet you, Dr. Graham."

The woman wasn't good enough to hide the glimmer of recognition in her eyes, which had lit up as soon as Eamon had taken her hand. Eli frowned, his brain rifling through a virtual database of faces and names, sure that he'd seen her before. During his time in the service, maybe?

"And you, Mr. Collins." The voice was light and girlish—*girlish?*—with a barely contained edge of flustered excitement under it.

*Graham. Graham, Graham, Graham—Graham?* A bell rang in Eli's head and he almost bit his tongue in surprise. In his mind's eye he saw a girl about ten years old, trailing behind him and Eamon as they played skip-the-stones in front of 17-North. Even seven-year-old Eli had been able to tell that the girl was smitten with his older brother; there was, after all, her constant—usually whining—insistence that they not leave her behind. Eli, for his part, had been annoyed by the competition for Eamon's attention, not to mention the persistent presence of a girl who, by definition, hampered the *clearly* guy things they were doing, like poking a dead bird with a stick or daring each other to sneak a drink from their father's bottle of whisky. Eamon had confessed to him one night as they'd been falling asleep in their bunk beds that he had no interest in the girl—his fancy had been struck by a rather older woman: his sixth-grade teacher Ms. D'Angelo. But Eamon, in his infinite twelve-year-old wisdom, had never been one to toss away something that he might need some day, and Lucy Graham—for that had been her name—had seen to it that he never lacked for answers to math or science homework, something at which she, unlike the brothers Brody, had excelled.

It wouldn't be fair to say she hadn't changed a bit; after all, it had been probably a decade since last he'd seen her. But it was unquestionably her. She'd grown a little taller and filled out some, though she still had the waifish figure she'd had as a kid, as though she might blow away on the next strong breeze. And now she just *happened* to be working on this station. *If that's a coincidence, I will buy a hat and then eat said hat.*

The welcome party had returned to the pressure door, where Gregorovich was thumbing the control pad. A light above the door blinked green and the hatch slid open, admitting the lieutenant, who apparently wasn't used to standing on chivalry. Tan, on the other hand, gestured at Dr. Graham, who smiled and inclined her head as she walked through, followed by him and Eamon, who glanced over his shoulder and nodded slightly to Kelly.

To Eli, who even after nine years away knew his brother better than almost anyone in the galaxy, the nod might as well have been a full-motion video message. In his mind, he found he could see exactly how this was about to go down. His pulse quickened as Kelly acknowledged the nod and proceeded to form up the work crew. Movement behind Eli caught his eye and he glanced over to see the severe-looking woman he'd noticed at the bus stop drifting slowly back toward the airlock door they'd come through.

Eli's muscles had gone tense, his hamstrings almost painful in their tautness. At Kelly's glare, he got in line with the rest of the crew and followed them through the pressure door into the station proper, giving one last lingering look over his shoulder at the woman, who slipped back through the open airlock door into the transport.

Being the last person in line, the pressure door slid closed after Eli and he joined the rest of the work crew in a nondescript gray corridor that could have been on any ship, base, or other installation he'd visited in the last decade. With no windows and only a few doors—all of them closed—the only things that caught Eli's eye were the half-dozen long colored lines on the floor.

Tan was apparently in the process of explaining this feature as Eli entered, waving a hand at the floor. ". . . for the different sections of the base, of course. Yellow takes you to the docking bay while blue takes you to the research section of the base, green leads to the commissary, purple to the infirmary, and red to the secured areas."

"What's at the end of the rainbow?" Eamon asked with a grin, nodding to the end of the hallway where most of the lines disappeared behind a heavy door.

Tan smiled wryly. "That's the main entrance to the base." As if alerted by the attention, the door whirred open and a dozen men and women, dressed in blue jumpsuits of a piece with Eamon's crew, trooped through. They looked tired and haggard, shuffling their booted feet against the floor and stooping under the weight of the heavy rucksacks they carried. Their expressions brightened somewhat as they beheld their replacements, and a ragged cheer issued from among their midst.

"Right on schedule," said Tan, waving his crew toward the pressure door. "Speed it up if you want to make it home in time for the fireworks, huh?" Even that encouragement didn't seem enough to overcome their obvious weariness. As they filtered by Eamon's crew, more than one of them could be heard offering good-natured jeers and advice.

"Hope you brought your thermals; heating's on the fritz."

"Stay away from the 'coffee' . . ."

". . . loose wiring in section eleven that should be looked at . . ."

". . . whole bottle in the supply cabinet in the infirmary . . ."

There were a few nods and smiles from Eamon's crew, but for the most part their expressions stayed grim and fixed as the current crew headed into the docking bay.

"Ooooh, well aren't you a serious lot?" said one, a heavyset dark-skinned man, in a mocking tone. "Probably why you don't mind working on the Emperor's Birthday, huh? Well, don't worry, we'll have a drink for you— maybe two or three."

"Hey," called Tan, "stow it, would you, Thompson?" He shook his head. "I'm going to have to listen to two hours of *that* on the way home." He extended his hand to Eamon. "Good luck to you, Mr. Collins. See you again sometime."

"Thanks," said Eamon, shaking his hand again. "Safe trip."

Tan tipped him a salute and followed his crew through the pressure door. Eamon's eyes darted to Kelly, who moved into a position next to the door's controls.

"All right," said Gregorovich, straightening up. "Now that the shift change's over with, let's get you guys to work. First thing's first, you'll need to log the—"

Had it not been for having fought next to him in dozens of scraps throughout their adolescence, Eli never would have seen the punch coming. But there was a telltale drop in Eamon's right shoulder as he brought his hand around and cold-cocked the lieutenant—*first* lieutenant—in the jaw. Gregorovich didn't get a chance to put up a fight, his eyes rolling back into his head and his body twisting with the momentum of the blow as he collapsed to the ground. Eamon reached down and unfastened the man's pistol from its holster, then stuck it in his own belt.

"Let's get to work," he said, turning to the crew, then looking back at Dr. Graham.

For her part, while the woman in the lab coat had looked startled at the sudden assault of an Illyrican officer, Eli noticed that she didn't look particularly surprised. As though the forecast had called for rain, but the first big fat drop had just landed on top of her head.

"Lucy, my dear," he said, taking her hand and kissing it theatrically. "You did perfectly."

Her eyelids fluttered at the compliment and she smiled hesitantly. "He'll be okay, right?" she said, tilting her head at the man on the floor. "I didn't want anyone getting hurt and, oh, I know he's a *nuisance*, but he's not a bad person."

"As long as everything goes according to plan, he'll be fine." Eamon patted her hand. "You have my word. Now: the rest of the security complement?"

"There's only six of them," she said, waving her free hand and clutching Eamon's with her other. "Two in the security office, two on patrol, and two off-shift, probably sleeping or eating. The rest of them got recalled planetside two days ago. Something about riot threats. But," her face creased with worry, "a courier arrived just before you did—an impromptu spot check by an IIS major."

It was going to take more than that to break Eamon's rhythm. "Alone?"

"Yes, alone."

"Did you catch the name?"

"Shankar—Major Jagat Shankar."

"Major Shankar," Eamon mused, his eyebrows raised. "Interesting." He turned to the crew. "It doesn't change our plans. Kaye, Lapan, take care of the patrol; Quinn and Tarik, the security office; Covell, Keisuke, find the off-duty pair and contain them. Radio in if you find our . . . unexpected guest. Eli, you're with—"

There was a sigh as the pressure door slid open and, in a flash, Gregorovich's pistol was in Eamon's hand and aimed at the door. But it was just the woman Eli had seen lurking in the docking bay. She held her hands out defensively and Eamon put his weapon up.

"Everything okay, McKenna?" he asked, an eyebrow raised.

"Airlock's hard-sealed from the outside and the docking clamps are locked in tight. They're not going anywhere until we release them or they cut their way out—and seeing as that's reinforced steel and titanium, that'll take a while."

"Excellent," said Eamon, grinning from ear to ear. "As I was saying: Eli, you're with me." He scratched at his beard, then turned to Lucy. "Now, I think it's time we said hello to Tarnhelm."

# CHAPTER TWENTY

As his time in the military had mainly been composed of the four years he'd spent at the Illyrican academy, Eli had been thoroughly drilled in command hierarchy, operation planning, and basic tactics. His older brother had clearly picked up something of those topics as well, though they weren't necessarily as formalized as what you might find among, say, an elite cadre of Illyrican shock troopers. Still, there were vestiges of military precision in many members of the team he'd assembled. Kelly, in particular, moved with an assurance and unconscious fluidity that reminded Eli of the Illyrican marines he'd encountered.

They'd passed through the main entryway into Aran Base, at which point the crew fanned out in different directions, teams of two splitting off as Eamon had instructed. Eight of the original work crew remained, including Eamon, Kelly, McKenna, Gwen, and Eli, plus three others—Ibanez, Clark, and Lyngaas.

The two cargo containers were brought into the base on their humming repulsor fields. Only the first one was opened, though; the second just hovered idly. The open container yielded a full complement of small arms for the work crew: pistols, rifles, and the occasional scattergun. Apparently they'd been divvied up ahead of time, for there was no bickering over who got what—just a mechanical process of the crew filing by and grabbing a weapon, checking it, and then moving on.

They were also one short, Eli realized as Gwen pulled the last weapon, a pistol, from the container. A mix of relief and regret washed over him: On the one hand, it stung, like being picked last in gym class, but at the same time he had little desire to shoot anybody. He looked up at

Eamon, who was conferring with Kelly. "So I'm supposed to what, throw a wrench?"

Eamon, for his part, didn't seem too apologetic about it. "Our bags were already packed. Just stay back and you'll be fine."

*Until the shooting starts, at which point I'll be a big fat bullseye.* His upset stomach had faded for the most part after he'd touched down on the base's solid ground, but it was in full force again at the prospect of armed confrontation. Sure, he'd had training, but there was a big difference between flying into combat with a safe, sound cocoon of steel and carbon fiber at your beck and call and running in with a gun and a prayer.

With Lucy Graham to lead them, Eamon's squad followed the red line painted on the floor, tracing it down a winding path of identical-looking corridors, punctuated only by anonymous metal doors. Eventually, all of the other colored ribbons peeled away down junctions or behind those faceless doors until the only thing that remained was the red path.

That eventually terminated at a heavy, reinforced blast door. Eamon put a hand on the small of Lucy's back, gently pressing her forward, and the worry on her face was wiped away with determination. She stepped up to the scanner attached to the door and placed a finger on it; soothing green light pulsed around the digit.

A harsh tone sounded and the doctor cleared her throat. "Graham, Lucy. Authorization epsilon-epsilon-phi, 3263827." It beeped again, and then the loud rumble of machinery came to life as the door split along its diagonal, with each side retracting into the wall.

Anti-climactically, the corridor onto which the door opened looked much the same as the one that had led to it, with the exception of large signs with bold text screaming AUTHORIZED ACCESS ONLY. Eli's natural inclination to obey such posted missives made his stomach lurch, but Eamon stepped forward without hesitation, squeezing Lucy's shoulder as he passed.

"Certainly got her under his thumb, hasn't he?" a voice murmured from next to Eli.

He raised an eyebrow at Gwen, who was watching the pair thoughtfully. "What, you jealous that he's already got a girlfriend?"

Gwen rolled her eyes. "Oh, your brother is charming enough in his own way, but he's not my type."

"I don't suppose you prefer scruffy, ne'er-do-well former janitors?"

"What?"

"Never mind."

"Consider it fully unminded," she said with a snort, walking after Eamon and Lucy before Eli could summon a reply.

*I tell you, if we make it out of whatever this is alive, I'm going to buy that woman dinner.*

Sighing, he followed after her, along with the rest of Eamon's squad; the heavy blast door slid closed behind them, clanking shut with a deep, funereal boom. Gwen's eyes were focused straight ahead, so Eli quickened his stride to fall into step with his brother. Eamon glanced sideways.

"Something I can do for you, Lije?"

"Who's Tarnhelm, exactly?"

Eamon gave a faint, cryptic smile. "*It's* a game-changer, that's what it is. The Illyricans are planning to fundamentally alter the nature of their war with the Commonwealth. They've been stuck in a stalemate for five years, ever since the decimation of the Imperial Navy—an event for which, if I recall, you had a front row seat."

The screams of his squadronmates, cut off by static, echoed in his head. "Yeah, I was there," said Eli tightly.

"Well, I'm trying to prevent the Illyricans from going back on the warpath."

"So this is about what? You saving the universe?" Eli tried unsuccessfully to keep the skepticism out of his voice.

Eamon shrugged. "Call it what you will."

"Well, I don't think philanthropy and heavily armed commandos *traditionally* go hand-in-hand. Come on, Eamon—what the hell are you trying to do here?"

"Same as always," he replied, his jaunty mood fading. "Keep the Illyricans on their toes, remind them that Caledonia is not and will never be theirs."

"You going to make a big sign that they can see all the way back home?"

Eamon jerked a thumb at the second cargo container, which was being pushed after them by the brawny man named Clark. It slid quite easily and noiselessly on the repulsor field, but there was something about it that made it seem heavy nonetheless. "Something like that. Let's just say that they're not going to be able to ignore this."

*Color me not reassured.*

They took a left at a T-junction where a pressurized door slid open to admit them into a room that looked a great deal like the docking bay in which they'd arrived. This one, however, was devoid of cargo containers; instead it was full of banks of displays and computing hardware, all of which were buzzing happily along, filling the room with a din of whirring machinery.

But that wasn't the room's most prominent feature: that was a large transparent viewport of reinforced glass that spanned the length of one wall. It looked out onto Aran's barren, rocky landscape of gray hills and craters. The base itself had apparently been laid out on the edge of a large chasm, which provided a spectacular view. But the window also provided a vantage on a somewhat less impressive man-made feature: a flat, gantry-garnished launch pad, at the center of which stood a very large, very boxy, astoundingly ugly ship. A lengthy white umbilical tube stretched out from the ship and apparently connected it to the base via a pressure door at the other end of the room.

Eli glanced at his brother, whose face had suddenly lit up.

"There we go," Eamon murmured. He slapped Eli on the shoulder. "Eli Brody, meet Project Tarnhelm."

"Project Tarnhelm? We came here for *that* hideous thing?"

"*That* hideous thing," said a sharp voice, "is the result of years of research and hard work." Lucy Graham had come up next to them, her face turned alien by the bluish light of the displays that hovered around the room. "Something I wouldn't expect you to know anything about, Elijah Brody."

"So glad you remember me," said Eli dryly. "And here I was worried that only one of the Brody boys had ever made an impression on you."

Lucy flounced to Eamon's side, taking his arm protectively and looking as though she were only a step away from sticking her tongue in Eli's direction. *She might be an adult, but it doesn't seem like she ever grew up.* "I remember a young boy with no interest in actually learning as long as he could get someone to do the work for him."

*Funny, I remember* two *young boys by that description, but I guess the past ain't what it used to be.* Eli flipped her a mock salute. "Well, I'm thrilled to see all your hard work paid off with a brilliant career that you've just flushed down the toilet." *And I know a thing or two about toilets.*

Clinging to Eamon's arm, Lucy's brow darkened. "There are some things more important than a life of science. This is a wake-up call!" Eli got the distinct impression she was quoting someone and, from the look of her death grip on Eamon's arm, he had a pretty good guess as to whom.

Eamon's comm chose that minute to chime and he lifted it with his free hand. "What's up?"

A woman's voice filtered out of the speaker, loud enough for Eli to hear. "It's Quinn. We've taken control of security; Keisuke's locked the off-duty officers in their bunk. According to the console, though, the last two officers are currently escorting the IIS major."

"Where?"

"Last security log shows them entering your present location."

Eamon glanced at Lucy. "They must be onboard." He nodded at the ship through the viewport.

"Station security doesn't have access to the ship's internal cameras," she said with a shake of her head. "Its feeds are only available from inside."

"Well, lucky for us, that just happens to be our next stop. Quinn, set the timelock on the transport ship's airlock for—" he looked at Lucy again.

She frowned and consulted one of the floating displays. "Call it a half hour to get onboard and prepped and maybe another fifteen minutes after that?"

Eamon spoke into the radio. "Forty-five minutes. Then regroup with the other teams and head this way. I'll have Dr. Graham make sure to release the security door for you." He released the transmit button and a faint acknowledgement crackled through.

"So, Major Shankar's onboard the ship," Eamon said, rubbing his chin. "This just gets more and more interesting."

"He *did* mention he'd heard a lot about it and wanted to take a look," said Lucy, looking worried. "Gregorovitch didn't seem to feel he could refuse the request, so he sent the security team along."

"Of course not. I'm sure he was most gracious." He slid the comm unit back into one of his jumpsuit pockets then snapped his fingers at Clark, who was still minding the second cargo container. The big man slid the container over to Eamon, where it coasted to a stop. Eamon touched some controls on the side and the lid popped opened.

Eli's technical expertise was limited mainly to the mechanics of ships and, even then, it was mostly about basic maintenance. If he'd ever had to replace a drive motivator or retune attitude thrusters he'd have quickly found himself at the mercy of an able technical crew. So, when the cargo container yielded a concoction of wires and metal boxes, it didn't mean anything to him. It wasn't until Eamon flipped a switch on the box in the center of the contraption, illuminating a countdown display that he realized precisely what he was looking at.

It was a bomb.

A very big bomb.

Gwen, who'd stepped up next to Eli, wore a wide-eyed expression that he could only assume was mirrored on his own face. "Did you know about this?"

She shook her head slowly, the red curls bouncing. "No."

*How the hell did he get* that *past the spaceport security?* Then again, the other container had been carrying more than a dozen small arms, so it probably wasn't just a matter of criminal incompetence on the part of Westenfeldt's security personnel. If Dr. Graham was any indication, Eli suspected the Black Watch had also had somebody inside the spaceport to get them through undetected.

In the end, it didn't really matter, because now there was a way bigger problem.

Eli sidled over to his brother. "Eamon, can I have a word?"

With a nod to his compatriots, Eamon waved Eli over into a corner of the room.

"What the hell do you think you're doing?" asked Eli, lowering his voice and glancing back at the rest of the crew.

Eamon blinked. "What do *I* think I'm doing? I told you: whatever's necessary to remind the Illyricans that they don't belong here."

"But a bomb that size will destroy the entire facility."

"So?"

"What about all the people working here? You're *murdering* them."

Eamon's mouth clamped shut and he pressed a finger firmly into Eli's chest. "I am *not* a murderer. The station was already on a skeleton crew because of the Emperor's Birthday, and Supervisor Tan and his crew are aboard the transport."

"Which you locked here."

"Time-locked," Eamon corrected. "I'm just delaying their trip a bit. In forty—" he glanced at a display, "—two minutes, the airlock will release and they'll be able to take off and wing their way back to Caledonia, unobstructed. The bomb won't go off for another fifteen minutes after that, giving them plenty of time to get clear of the blast."

"What if they don't leave? What if they decide to come back onto the station and try to stop it?"

"Not my problem. That's their choice."

Eli stared at him, then shook his head. "Same old Eamon. Maybe someday you'll grow up and take responsibility." He turned to storm off, only to be yanked back by the arm. Eamon wrenched him around, again bringing them face to face.

"Don't you *dare* judge me," he said, quiet ferocity infusing his voice. "You saw Meghann, what the crims did to her. Those people sided with the Illyricans just by being here; they haven't done a damn thing to stop the Imperium from running roughshod all over our world. They make a bad choice and get blown up as a result? Well, I won't shed a tear."

"Jesus, you're a cold bastard."

"They made their choice, I made mine. Time for you to make yours, Lije." His eyes went hard. "You with us or them?"

"Whatever," said Eli, pulling his arm loose then stalking over to rejoin Gwen. He didn't respond to either her questioning look or the light touch on his arm.

Eamon took a deep breath, smoothed his hands down the front of his jumpsuit and then, pulling the acting security head's pistol from his belt, turned to address his crew. "All right, everybody. Listen up. The ship is currently unmanned except for an IIS major and his security escort. Kelly, McKenna, Eli, and Gwennie, you're with Lucy and me. Ibanez, Clark, Lyngaas, you'll secure the ship's engine room. Neutralize any resistance as necessary."

The crew voiced their assent and proceeded to the ramp at the far end of the room. Once again, it was Lucy who stepped forward to enter a code on the keypad next to the pressure door. It whisked open; beyond it was a white, sterile-looking tent-like structure that led to the ship on the launchpad. They all traipsed through until they came to a round airlock door; Dr. Graham once again unlocked it and the work crew quickly spread into the ship proper, establishing their beachhead.

As ugly as Project Tarnhelm was on the outside, its interior looked more or less like any other Illyrican ship Eli had ever been aboard: the same gray metal bulkheads were riveted into place with, appropriately enough, military precision. The strip lighting overhead cast the same unforgiving blue-white glow. Even the exact same stencils declaimed this part as section B-13 and that as service junction L-27. There was little incentive for the Illyrican Navy to draw distinctions between its ships, especially since it made it that much easier to shift personnel wherever they were needed without significant retraining. From the layout alone, Eli thought he had a solid guess as to the location of the ship's recreational room (M-3) and the mess hall (M-7).

Even so, Eli followed the lead of Dr. Graham and Eamon, watching as the other three split off at an early junction and headed in the direction of precisely where he'd expected the engine room to be. Kelly and McKenna, the sharp-featured dark-haired woman, stayed on course toward the ship's bridge, as did Gwen. The latter's hand was resting on the pistol in her belt, and the lack of a sidearm once again made Eli's fingers twitch. He'd never exactly been a great shot, but he had to admit there was a certain reassurance in being able to shoot back.

After they'd spent five minutes tramping through the corridor, Eli was forced to concede that Project Tarnhelm was quite a bit larger than he'd gathered from the exterior view. Its utilitarian outer shell, all hard edges and gawky angles, combined with the decided lack of weapon emplacements, had led him to conclude that the ship was a converted bulk freighter: *Warhorse* class, unless he missed his guess. The *Warhorse* was the backbone of the Illyrican Navy, making up the better part of its shipping operations and was essential for logistical support: namely, moving supplies and munitions from place to place. They were a familiar sight in the fleet, as most carrier battle groups—including the *Venture*'s—sported at least a handful, usually for warehousing supplies and parts; in a pinch they could also be used to transport marines in space-to-ground missions. Frankly, you got so used to seeing the freighters that, after a while, you didn't notice them anymore.

*So why's this one so damn important?* The only theory he had was that the *Warhorse*'s size and large available internal volume made it an ideal testbed for developing technologies: a sort of spacefaring platform on which you could mount any sort of weapon.

But one that would change the balance of the war? He'd heard the rumors, of course, when he was in the academy. Whispers of the Imperium's weapons research division working on mass drivers that could propel an enormous metal rod into the crust of a planet—and perhaps even deeper. Narrow-spectrum cohesive lasers that could slice a ship from bow to stern in one sweep. Electromagnetic limpet mines that would glom onto a ship like a swarm of bees. Even, perhaps most terrifying of all, renewed development in planet-scathing nuclear weapons which had been outlawed on Earth centuries ago. (Really, that had been more an act of practicality than of taking the moral high ground—after all, when you began to talk planetary invasion and conquest, there was little point to irradiating the very land you were trying to occupy.)

Devastating as any of those weapons would be, Eli still had a hard time painting them as the kind of game-changer that Eamon had bragged of. *One thing's for sure*, he thought as they continued their way through seemingly endless corridors, *there's certainly enough space on this damn ship to build any number of nasty little surprises.*

Eli's party climbed a short staircase up onto the half-level that held the ship's command center. They paused outside the heavy blast door, above which the entry light showed green, meaning it was unsecured. Because who'd expect an armed incursion while still docked? The squad checked their weapons.

Eamon turned to address them. "Lucy, you'll open the door, then stand aside. Kelly and McKenna, you're first in. The security patrol will be uniformed. First priority is to neutralize them. I suspect the major will be in civilian dress—probably unarmed, as well. I want him *alive*; is that understood?" He held each of the others' gazes in turn, and they all nodded.

"All right, then. On my mark: three, two, one . . . *mark!*"

Lucy pressed the door control and then flattened herself against the bulkhead, leaving an unobstructed view into the bridge. Kelly and McKenna stepped through, followed by Eamon and Gwen, with the unarmed pair of Eli and Lucy trailing behind. Still, Eli had a perfect vantage point for the entire affair, which unfolded over the course of about three seconds.

The door opened onto a rounded compartment that looked like a smaller version of the bridge Eli remembered from the *Venture*. A tier of stations around the rim of the room hosted the ship's various command and control functions, while a raised platform in the center held holographic displays of the ship's status and consoles for the command officers. Directly in front of them sat the pilot's cockpit, sunken into the floor like an orchestra pit.

The bridge contained three people; as Eamon had predicted, two of them wore the crimson uniform of Illyrican military personnel while the third was dressed in civilian garb. The security officer closest to the door, a young woman with windswept sandy hair, looked up with a frown as Kelly and McKenna stepped through the door.

"Maintenance shift shouldn't start for another two hou—" But that was all she got out before a burst from Kelly's carbine took her in the chest, dropping her to the deck.

The second security guard, who had been leaning lazily against the other side of the compartment, watched this dumbfounded, his mouth dropping in shock. He was still fumbling for his pistol when McKenna shot him in the shoulder.

Through all of this, the third person stood on the command platform, facing away from the raiding party with his hands clasped behind his back. Something about his posture and the squareness of his shoulders suggested a readiness to spring into action, barely held back by something else: caution. With both of the security officers down, he put his hands in the air, turning slowly.

Eamon stepped forward, pistol held in one hand, though it was pointed at the floor. He smiled and inclined his head toward the man. "Ah, Major Shankar. A pleasure to meet you—except, of course, you're not Major Shankar, are you?"

The man's gaze swept across the fallen security guards: the one who McKenna had shot was groaning quietly on the floor, clutching his arm, white-faced; the other had not been so lucky—she'd been dead before she hit the ground. Shaking his head, the man sighed heavily and fixed Eamon with a reluctant look. Eli's breath caught as he saw the man's face straight-on for the first time.

"Was all this really necessary?" Fielding asked, his hands still in the air.

Eamon stepped up onto the dais, scrutinizing the man. They made an interesting contrast: Eamon's fiery red beard and hair against pale skin; Fielding almost monotone, from his dark brown hair to the rough stubble that was just shy of a beard at this point. His gray eyes swept the room, finally alighting on Eli with interest.

"Ah, Mr. Brody," he said, nodding his head. "I see you found your brother after all."

Eamon prodded him in the ribs with his pistol. "There's only one Brody you should be concerned with. And let me give you a hint—it's not that one." He pulled the gun back and cocked his head to one side. "So, you're the mysterious Fielding, I presume? I've heard a lot about you. How you duped that courier pilot into believing you were Shankar, I have no idea, but I'll admit I'm impressed."

"Having seen your own handiwork, I'll take that as a compliment."

"I'm only sorry we won't have a chance to compare notes further."

Fielding raised an eyebrow. "That is a shame. There are a few things I was hoping to pick your brain about—the murder of a Commonwealth intelligence officer, for one. Tell me, why *did* you kill Wallace? Especially after you passed him all that information about, well . . ." He waggled two fingers on one of his raised hands, taking in their surroundings. "If I had to guess, I'd wager he tried to put the kibosh on your little plan for the Illyricans' top-secret project. That's why you ransacked his apartment, right? To see what else he knew." His eyes narrowed. "Then again, maybe you just decided to try your hand at cold-blooded murder."

Eamon's face darkened. "Shut up."

"Ah," said Fielding, looking at the rest of Eamon's crew regretfully. "I never did know when to stop talking. Of course, you didn't bother to tell your comrades exactly where you got all those weapons they're holding."

Eamon didn't say anything, but the grip on his gun tightened and the barrel worked its way back up to Fielding's midsection.

"You seem to do best when you've given people just enough rope to tie themselves into knots," said Fielding.

The gun jabbed back into Fielding's ribs, but he regarded it with little more interest than he would have shown a fly.

"What is going on?" Gwen murmured to Eli. "Who the hell is this guy?"

"I'll tell you this much," Eli said under his breath, "if you've got money to place, I'm not sure I'd bet against him."

Eamon cast a glance over his shoulder at Kelly. "I want him secured. Now. This ship must have a brig somewhere." Kelly started forward, carbine raised. "Lije," said Eamon, still keeping his eye—and his gun—trained on Fielding, "I need you to prep the ship for takeoff."

Eli looked back and forth between his brother and Fielding. With all the adrenaline and excitement coursing through his veins, he'd almost forgotten the entire reason he'd been dragged along on this expedition. His knees wobbled slightly and he tasted acid in his mouth. "I—"

Fielding saved him the trouble. "For what it's worth, it was a good plan. Although I have to imagine that your brother wasn't your first choice of pilots. Given his condition."

It was Eamon's turn to look surprised; he turned on one heel to face his brother. "Condition?"

A bead of sweat rolled across Eli's brow and he avoided his brother's gaze.

"If you're relying on him, I sincerely doubt you're going to be able to so much as get off this rock," Fielding said. "Your brother is suffering from an acute form of post-traumatic stress disorder. Hell, I'm amazed you even got him into space at all."

"Lije?"

"Sorry," Eli muttered. He swore he saw his brother's shoulders droop slightly. *Just another disappointment.*

"Still," Fielding continued, "all told, you got pretty close. De Valera would be proud that you lived up to his name."

Eli's ears perked up at that and his forehead furrowed. "What the hell are you talking about?" said Eli, his head spinning. This time it was his brother who was unwilling to meet *his* eyes.

Fielding shook his head. "So many secrets in the Brody family. I suppose nine years will have that effect. Maybe you should consider family counseling."

"Shut your mouth," Eamon advised.

"Your brother's practically a one-man revolution," Fielding continued, undaunted. "He's not just part of the Black Watch—he *is* the Black Watch. De Valera himself, in the flesh. To be fair, I don't think even most of the rank and file know that."

Eli spun around to face his brother. "But . . . that's impossible. De Valera's been around since the occupation started—Eamon was just ten years old when the Illyricans invaded. Come on, Eamon. Tell him."

But even as the words came out of his mouth, he saw the look on his brother's face—that cold expression so reminiscent of their father. It was a look that would brook no argument, accept no backtalk. Not that that had ever stopped Eli.

*It's too much.* There was a voice in his mind—a dimly remembered one from another place, another time. Of a boy who'd followed his brother around, accepted his word as gospel, idolized him. Until one day, when it had just been too much. Looking back, Eli couldn't even remember what had made him realize it, but somehow he'd known his brother had changed, had turned single-minded in his ambition, had pushed away everything that could have possibly interfered.

And had never looked back.

"All this bullshit," said Eli slowly, shaking his head. "It's just business as usual for you. Manipulating people, getting them to do what you want. You'd like to be all noble, pretending this is about the Illyricans being on your planet or taking your brother away from you or leaving your sister for dead, but that's not it, is it? None of it. Those are just lies you tell yourself to justify your actions. It's only ever been about one thing, and that's Eamon Fucking Brody being the most important person in the entire galaxy, the man who single-handedly beat the Illyricans. Because, let's face it, you've never had much else going for you."

"You're one to talk," Eamon snapped. "I might have respected you if you'd joined the Illyricans because you believed in them, but no, it was all about what was best for *you*. Your commitment to the cause—any cause—has always been . . . *cavalier*, at best. You might be my brother by blood, but my brother in arms? Never." He stalked from Fielding over toward Eli, his eyes flashing. "You know why I agreed to take over for De Valera? We were kindred spirits, he and I—sons of Caledonia. It was our *duty*. Now he's dead and it's just me. I'm the last son of Caledonia and I'm going to do what he couldn't." Slowly, he swung his gun up to point at Eli's chest. "So prep the goddamn ship, if you know what's good for you." There was a click as he released the pistol's safety.

Eli crossed his arms over his chest; he didn't even have to think twice. "Screw you. Find someone else."

For a second he thought his brother might actually pull the trigger. Deadly serious, Eamon's eyes had locked on Eli's as unwaveringly as the aim of his gun. The sweat on his own brow was coming more consistently now. *Did someone turn off the air conditioning?* He tried not to blink as it dripped into his eyes.

"Goddamnit," Eamon growled, putting up his gun. "McKenna, Gwennie, I want you to go back to the transport ship, get the pilot, and drag him the hell over here. Kelly, take him," he indicated Fielding, "and my idiot brother down to the brig. If there isn't one, then lock them in a supply closet for all I care. Just get them out of my fucking sight. *Now.*"

# CHAPTER TWENTY-ONE

I t was far from the first time that Kovalic had found himself escorted at gunpoint. In fact, he realized as he totaled them up, it was far from the fifth or sixth, which suggested that perhaps it was devolving from occupational hazard to bad habit. Still, the scenario had lost most of its heart-pounding novelty.

Their boots clicked down the corridor, the scarred man called Kelly keeping the carbine trained on them from behind. Brody, for his part, appeared to still be in shock: the younger man was shaking his head to himself slowly, with eyes for nothing but the deck before him. As Kovalic had hoped, when the chips were down the kid had shown some spine in not blindly following his brother. Whether that ultimately proved to be the right choice, well, Kovalic hoped so, but without knowing exactly what Eamon was up to—what exactly this ship was—it was too early to say.

"Left." The curt commands were the only words Kelly had spoken to them since they'd been ushered from the bridge.

Kovalic glanced over at Brody again and found the man's gaze on him, though no less wide-eyed.

"How the hell *did* you get here, anyway?" Brody muttered.

"No talking," snapped Kelly.

Kovalic gave Brody a rueful smile and kept walking.

Getting onboard had actually been relatively simple. Relative, that was, to breaking into the governor's mansion on Sevastapol or the spacewalk he'd once taken to plant a listening device outside the quarters of the Illyrican ambassador to Jericho Station. And he did have Shankar to thank for it, though he supposed the good major would be less than gratified to discover that.

As Page had predicted, transferring the encrypted contents of Shankar's ID to the fake Illyrican identification that Danzig had provided was easy.

The hard part had been selling it: the fake information on Danzig's ID didn't match Shankar, of course, but Kovalic was counting on that. He'd shown up to Westenfeldt base and swiped the card for the guard at the gate, who had naturally been obligated to question the man with an ID claiming he was a high-ranking intelligence officer.

In ordinary circumstances, a quick comparison to the records would have sorted everything out, but here Kovalic had played a bit of a hunch, gambling that, like his own Commonwealth ID file, IIS officers' files didn't have pictures—it was significantly harder to be a covert operative when anyone could get a photo of you. Years of experience slipping in and out of secured facilities had also told Kovalic that junior officers, such as the gate guard, were readily susceptible to both intimation *and* intimidation, so he'd concocted a potent cocktail of the two—a tale of a secret mission that he was entrusting to the gate guard. The young corporal had drunk it right down, no questions asked.

With the corporal's implicit backing, Kovalic and his meager belongings had been ushered through the security process, a fast courier placed at his disposal, and he was off-world before anyone was the wiser. After ingratiating himself with the pilot, he'd impressed upon the young woman that his mission was, naturally, top secret and required radio silence. He only hoped that she would be spared serious punishment—after all, she'd just been following orders. The corporal at the gate would likely not be so lucky, but, well, omelets and eggs. At least the courier had set out back to Caledonia after depositing Kovalic; he'd assured his pilot that he would hitch a ride back on his own time.

Upon reaching the Aran base, the acting chief of security—for the usual occupant of that position had been summoned back to Caledonia for the Emperor's Birthday—had practically tripped over his own feet to show off his facility, all the while gushing about how it had been his lifelong dream to join the ranks of IIS.

Something told Kovalic that the poor fellow wasn't going to make the cut.

First Lieutenant Gregorovich had been only too happy to have his patrol show Kovalic the sights—of course, he'd added with false modesty that would have incurred the jealousy of many a professional politician, his own duties as acting head of security precluded him from escorting the major personally. After being whisked through the labs, Kovalic had confided to the patrol that his *real* mission lay in examining a certain top secret project, throwing in enough winks and nods to ensure that the two got the drift.

That had prompted the tour of the ship, though they had only just reached the bridge when Eamon and his team of commandos arrived. All before he'd had a chance to figure out exactly what Project Tarnhelm was.

The ship was, as far as he could tell, some sort of prototype. But, as a converted bulk freighter, it had nothing in the way of weapons to begin with and it didn't appear as though the Illyricans had added any. So it wasn't a warship. Some sort of flying bomb? A decoy? The only thing he'd been able to conclude was that the Illyrican Navy was using the ship as a platform for some new technology, but he was damned if he knew what . . . and he didn't plan on leaving until he found out.

Kelly didn't appear to be anybody's fool; he'd been trained somewhere, perhaps even the Illyrican military. The scarred man stayed a foot or two behind Kovalic and Brody the entire way, preventing Kovalic from easily wresting the weapon from him. And Kovalic suspected that he wasn't exactly the sentimental type—if push came to shove, he guessed Kelly would be just as happy to shoot them both and whistle his way right back to the bridge. Nor did talking him down seem like an option.

There are some people who like to plan things out every step of the way. To Kovalic, a plan was nothing more than a recipe for disappointment. There were only so many things you could account for, so many variables you could control. As a brilliant military tactician had once said, "No battle plan survives contact with the enemy." Kovalic preferred to think on his feet.

And his feet were at this moment taking a sharp right turn. For a split second he was out of Kelly's sightline. In that sliver of time, he flattened his back against the bulkhead. Kelly had been holding the carbine out ahead of him, just far enough that it was the first thing that rounded the corner. Kovalic grabbed the barrel of the weapon, shoving it up and away.

Startled, Kelly squeezed the trigger out of instinct, but the carbine was still set on burst fire. Three rounds punched a hole in the bulkhead, but Kelly didn't have time to both release the trigger and pull it a second time. The scarred man fought for control of the gun, lashing out at Kovalic with an off-handed blow that connected with his chin. His jaw blossomed in pain, but he blinked back the flashing lights and jabbed Kelly hard in the throat.

Hits to the throat cause instinctive panic, even for many of the most trained soldiers—there's a lot of vital stuff in there, and defending it is a basic human response. Kelly's hands flew to his windpipe, which Kovalic had at least bruised if not crushed. A knee to the gut made the scarred man double over, giving Kovalic a clear opening to slam his head into the wall with a sound like a church bell. He went down without a word.

It was over so fast that Brody hadn't finished exclaiming "Holy shit!" before Kelly hit the deck.

Brody stared at the downed man then looked to Kovalic, his voice taking on a hint of awe. "What the hell did you just do?"

Kovalic rubbed at his aching jaw, the stars fading from his vision. Good thing Tapper hadn't been here to see that; the old man would have given him a lecture about not protecting his face. Snorting to himself, Kovalic yanked the carbine from Kelly's possession, slung the strap over his own shoulder, and checked the magazine—still mostly full. At least he hadn't been one of those types who needed to put thirty rounds into every target. Efficiency was something Kovalic could admire, even if it was misdirected. He also found Kelly's radio, which he clipped onto his belt.

"What are you doing? What's going on?" Brody's voice had gone high-pitched, an all-too-familiar sign of panic.

Kovalic looked him square in the eyes and laid a hand on the man's shoulder. "First, take a deep breath."

Brody's eyes were fearful, but he nodded and followed Kovalic's instructions. While he was doing that, Kovalic slapped him in the face.

"Ow!"

"Now snap out of it."

"Was that really necessary?" Brody rubbed at his red cheek.

"Strictly speaking? No. But you're listening, aren't you?"

"I am *now*."

"Good. Your brother and his people want something with this ship."

"I still don't understand how Eamon could be De Valera. He's been running the Black Watch for two decades."

Kovalic sighed. "It's not a *person*, Brody; it's a title. Your brother inherited it from the last head of the Black Watch. A guy named Kitano." He'd had time to read through CalSec's extensive files on the Black Watch during his trip to the station and it had been a treasure trove of intel. Most of it was recent, too; assuming the information was reliable, CalSec had quite the inside source. It was a wonder they hadn't brought the organization down already. He was also a little amused to note that the Caledonians had, as predicted, been rather disinclined to share much of that information with IIS.

"Old man Kitano?" said Brody, his jaw dropping. "Christ. All those years, he just sat at the bar and didn't say a word. You're telling me that he was running the Watch the entire time?"

"So it would seem. Look, we don't have time to unravel all of life's little mysteries. Right now we need to figure out why they're taking this ship. I figured Eamon would just want to destroy it and rub the Illyricans' noses in the whole incident—"

"There's a bomb on the station with a timer. I saw them arm it."

"Makes sense." Kovalic rubbed the tender spot on his chin and tried not to wince. "They're covering their tracks. Whatever Project Tarnhelm is, all the data on it is probably in the facility, and that'll wipe the slate pretty damn clean."

Brody frowned, glancing around. "So you don't know what this is either?"

Kovalic shook his head. "Not a clue. But given all the trouble your brother's gone through to get here, it's clearly important."

"He called it a 'game-changer.' Pretty vague if you ask me."

The radio on Kovalic's belt crackled. "Kelly?" crackled Eamon's voice. "You take care of 'em?" Kovalic looked down at it.

"Give it here," Brody whispered, beckoning urgently. "I spent some time with Scarface there; I think I can pull it off."

Kovalic hesitated, then tossed the radio to Brody, who cleared his throat and clicked it on.

"Yep." Brody released the transmission button and raised a thumbs-up in Kovalic's direction.

With a sigh, Kovalic pinched the bridge of his nose and waited.

Eamon's voice came back. "Good. Come back up to the bridge when you're set. We'll take off as soon as McKenna gets the pilot aboard." There was a short squelch of static as he broke the connection.

With a click, Kovalic released the safety of the carbine and readied the weapon. "Personally, I'm all too happy to take your brother up on that offer. First, however, we're going to the cargo bay."

"The cargo bay?"

"I had to check some luggage." He turned in the direction they'd come from, but only made it a couple of steps before he felt Brody grab the back of his jacket.

"You don't want to go that way. It'll take you to the engine room, and smack into the rest of Eamon's team." He nodded to the way they'd been heading before Kelly had been dispatched. "This way's faster."

"I'll take your word for it. Lead on."

They trotted down the corridor. Kovalic checked every intersection, but Eamon's team seemed to have remained dispersed according to plan, for they encountered no resistance. Three minutes of twists and hairpin turns later they arrived at a heavy industrial-strength door.

Kovalic pointed toward the control panel, motioning for Brody to trigger it. They took up positions on either side of the doors, and Kovalic readied the carbine just in case. At his nod, Brody punched the control. Servos squealed and whined as the doors ground open slowly, revealing a vast, mostly empty compartment.

The *Warhorse* class were bulk freighters and, as such, were often used to transport equipment for ground-based operations, including tasks like deploying tanks, gun emplacements, pre-fabricated outposts, and the like. After a fleet's battle group cleared enemy defenses, the logistics unit would be brought in, either touching down on the ground itself or dropping the heavy equipment from low orbit.

Project Tarnhelm, however, had clearly never been used for such a purpose; its cargo bay remained vacant, an echoing cavern.

Traversing the room through the sights of the carbine, Kovalic didn't detect any sign of movement. He stepped inside and swept the catwalks that overlooked the bay, but they too seemed devoid of inhabitants. Not that he was complaining. He beckoned Brody in and the door groaned shut behind them.

Dim light pervaded the compartment, giving it an almost twilit appearance. Fortunately, they didn't have far to go—just inside the door sat a cargo container. Slinging the carbine over his shoulder, Kovalic stepped up next to it.

The container ran about six feet in length, four feet wide, and about as high. A glowing keypad stood on the top, and Kovalic checked it quickly for signs of tampering. It looked, however, like the weight of his assumed identity had held up and, as he'd hoped, even just the whisper of IIS had been enough to make sure the container was treated with nothing but the utmost reverence and respect.

He reached over and tapped a four-digit code on the keypad, then, holding his breath, hit the Enter button. There was a beep and the keypad blinked green, followed by a slight whoosh of escaping air as the pressurized seal broke.

"Brody, help me get this lid off."

They each took a side and together managed to maneuver the metal cover off the container.

"You don't pack light, do you?" grumbled Brody. "Did you really need this many pairs of shoes?"

Kovalic rolled his eyes. Some people dealt with stressful situations by internalizing everything, leaving nothing but a stony exterior. Brody was clearly not that kind of person.

The lid of the container clattered to the deck and Kovalic looked down at the contents.

"Uh," Brody said, peering inside, "when most folks pack a set of extra clothes, they usually take them *off* the people first."

Two familiar figures lay inside the container. Kovalic reached over, pressing his fingers against their necks in turn. Steady but slow pulses: they were still alive, though unconscious.

"Let's get them out," he said to Brody.

Brody nodded, apparently having run out of wise-ass quips for the moment, and between them they managed to hoist the two bodies out of the container and stretch them out onto the cargo bay's floor. The contrast between them was even more marked at that point: tall and short, thin and stocky, young and old. Breathing masks covered both of the men's faces, the canisters attached to them bearing lights that winked amber. As Kovalic watched, one of them turned red.

"Just in time," he said under his breath, peeling the masks off their faces. "Brody, there should be a medkit in the container. Find it."

Brody nodded and stood, digging around inside the container until he came out with a small black pouch, which he tossed to Kovalic. "Uh, you know there are guns in here too, right?"

"Really?" said Kovalic dryly. "I haven't the slightest idea how that might have happened."

Unzipping the medkit, Kovalic rooted through the contents until he found the vial he was looking for. This he screwed onto a subdermal injector; rolling up both men's sleeves, he pressed it to veins in each of their arms. Then, rocking back on his heels, he waited for it to take hold.

Brody was still poking around to see what else Kovalic had packed, so when Tapper came to with a shuddering gasp and sat bolt upright, he yelped and tumbled headfirst into the container. Page, for his part, awoke more peacefully, his eyelids calmly sliding open with a slow, indrawn breath, as though he were emerging from a pleasant dream.

"Welcome back to the land of the living, gentlemen."

Tapper rolled his neck and drew a couple deep breaths. "Let's not do that *ever again*," he growled.

"What's the problem? Didn't you have a nice trip?"

"The inflight service left something to be desired. Not to mention the legroom." He massaged his calves. "I've got cramps in muscles I probably haven't used since I was his age," he said, jerking his head at Brody, who was clambering, shame-faced, out of the cargo container.

"How the hell did you get all this onboard?" asked Brody. "Goddamnit, doesn't *anybody* check these containers? I'll tell you this: it doesn't exactly make me feel any better about flying."

A grin spread across Kovalic's face. "Well, I find that Eyes's reputation precedes itself. A lot of folks seem to think that the less they know about covert operations, the better. I find myself inclined to reinforce that—if not in so many words. First Lieutenant Gregorovich did an admirable job of making sure that Major Shankar's every need was met." He patted the container. "Especially bringing his top-secret cargo onboard."

The cargo container suddenly began to rattle against the floor as the entire ship started to shake. Brody grabbed onto the edge of the box and Kovalic spread his stance to steady himself.

"Guess they found their pilot," Brody said, swallowing. "I'd say we just lifted off." His complexion had gone decidedly pale.

A low thrum made its way from the deck plates through Kovalic's legs and all the way up to his teeth. Unfortunately, the fear inspired by the name of IIS had had an adverse impact on competence as well: whoever had loaded the container onto the ship had neglected to secure it for flight. Then again, they probably hadn't expected the ship to actually take off with the cargo still onboard.

The container began to slide. Brody was the first to notice, as he'd been bracing himself against the large metal box, which suddenly slid in the opposite direction. There was a grating sound as the container picked up speed, at which point all four men lost their own footing and succumbed to the sharply slanting deck.

Kovalic spotted a pop-out ring in the deck, the very thing which, in ideal circumstances, would have been used to lock down the container. As he dropped to the floor, he managed to grab hold of the ring. Tapper had the same thought and Page managed to wrap his hands around a girder supporting the catwalk that ran along the room's edge. Brody, however, wasn't so lucky—he'd been off balance when the container started to move and had toppled over backwards, sliding headfirst toward the back of the cargo bay.

The container flipped over before slamming into the rear bulkhead and scattering its contents. Brody somehow managed to right himself during the fall and hit the container's side with bent knees; he slid off to one side, where he also hit the bulkhead, though at a more controllable velocity.

The shaking diminished as they finished their ascent, and the ship began to level off. Kovalic climbed to his feet as soon as the deck steadied and picked his way to the back of the compartment. Tapper and Page had gotten up as well and were close behind.

Kovalic reached Brody first and helped him to his feet. "You all right?"

His face was, if anything, more drained of color than before, but he seemed to be moving his limbs without pain. "A few bumps and bruises, but I've had worse."

With a nod, Kovalic turned to Tapper, who was surveying the rest of their supplies with a somewhat more regretful air.

"The sidearms are shot," he said, lifting one pistol, whose barrel was bent at a ninety-degree angle. "Got caught between the container and the bulkhead."

"All of them?" asked Kovalic.

"We only had a couple to begin with. I've got one concussion grenade left. There was another, but," he waved his hand at the expanse of open compartment, "no idea where it's gone."

Kovalic unslung the carbine from his back. "Well, we've got one weapon. And a grenade. Anything else?"

A bang echoed through the compartment as Page righted the container and wiped his hands. The thin man leaned over and touched a control on the cargo's pad and its anti-gravity field sprang to life, gradually lifting the box until it floated half a foot above the deck plate.

"You guys want to take on a dozen men with just one gun and a grenade?" Brody stared at them. "You're nuts."

But Kovalic wasn't listening; he was staring at the cargo container. "Maybe not *just*," he said slowly. "Page, start disassembling the repulsor unit on that thing."

Page complied without question. Deactivating the field caused the container to sigh gently to the deck. He manhandled the box onto its side and pulled open an access panel on the bottom. Kovalic watched, nodding slowly to himself. It might just work. He rubbed the stubble on his chin, feeling it scrape along his hand.

"Come on," said Brody, looking around at them. "You really think the three of you can stop them?"

"Three? Probably not. *Four*, though, that's another matter."

"Four?" echoed Brody, then looked around. Tapper, Page, and Kovalic were all eyeing him thoughtfully. "Wait a minute. No way. This isn't my fight."

"Isn't it?" asked Kovalic, cocking his head. "I seem to recall a certain agreement we made back at Sabaea—it still stands, if you're interested."

"You know what?" Brody said, his voice stressed to the breaking point. "I'm sick and tired of feeling like a pawn in some intergalactic game of chess. Ever since I left Sabaea, everybody wants to tell me a different story. Help this guy, don't help that one, we need your help, nobody will get hurt, *I promise.* Why the bloody hell should I trust *you?*"

"Trust *us?*" Tapper scoffed. "That's rich. You're the one who did the double-crossing when you left us high and dry and ran off with your brother the terrorist. Which, don't get me wrong, worked out *great.*" He waved his hands at the compartment at large.

"He had a *gun.*"

"Ooooh," said Tapper, miming surrender. "Whatever can you do against a man with a gun? Oh, I know—don't run away from the people who were sent to help you."

"Yes, you mysterious fuckers just *exude* trustworthiness. At least you know who *I* am," he shot back. "How am I supposed to trust you when I don't even know your real names?"

Tapper's mouth opened for a retort, but Kovalic held up his hands. "Enough. He has a point—we owe him the truth about that, at least."

The sergeant looked back and forth between Kovalic and Brody, then stepped over to his boss and took him by the shoulder, leading him away from the others. "You can't be serious, cap. It breaks every regulation in the book."

Kovalic raised his eyebrows. "I didn't think there were any we hadn't broken yet. Besides, I don't see that we have much choice."

"Really? What do we need him that badly for? He's not trained for this sort of thing and he's already burned us once. You think we can trust him?"

"Sergeant, we're outnumbered, practically unarmed, and on enemy ground. We need all the help we can get. Brody knows his way around the ship and there's a chance—however small—that he can still talk his brother down. Or, at the least, provide a worthwhile distraction."

Tapper sighed. "I hope you know what you're doing."

Kovalic smiled and clapped him on the shoulder. "Have a little faith. After all, you're the one who taught me everything I know."

"Don't remind me," Tapper muttered. "It keeps me up at night."

They rejoined the others and Kovalic walked up to Brody. He extended his right hand toward the younger man, who eyed it warily. "Captain Simon Kovalic of the Commonwealth of Independent Systems, Special Projects Team. At your service."

Brody's eyes flicked upward to his own, as though he might find a flashing sign telling him if it were the truth or a lie. Kovalic held the gaze until Brody nodded and took the hand, shaking it. "Thank you."

"You're welcome." He nodded to Page.

"Page, Aaron," said the tall man, with a nod. "Lieutenant."

Brody inclined his head, then looked at Tapper, whose arms were crossed over his chest, his stance slightly less forbidding than the brick-wall expression on his face.

"Tapper."

"Just Tapper?"

"Don't-push-your-fucking-luck Tapper. It's a family name."

"Great," Kovalic interjected, stepping between the two. "Now that we're all friends, shall we do something about our little situation here?"

"Maybe it's just me, but I don't see why we have to do anything," said Brody. "He may have the ship, but if his plan isn't to blow it up, then what's he going to do with it? He can't take it out of the system. Gate control will shut down all traffic as soon as they get word of the security breach."

"He's already gained access to a highly-secured military installation and taken control of a classified research project," Page pointed out. "It's a reasonable hypothesis that he has some plan for accessing the gate as well."

Kovalic tapped a finger against his lips. "Why *not* just blow the ship up?" he muttered, more to himself than his comrades. "If all he wanted was to embarrass the Illyricans, then blowing up their facility and their top secret project would have probably done the trick."

"The Illyricans would have hushed it up," Brody pointed out.

"Maybe, but a concerted propaganda effort from the Black Watch would be hard to ignore. Aran's close enough in its orbit right now that the explosion would probably be visible. There'd be video footage on the nets and plenty of rumors—enough to do some damage to the Illyricans anyway. And, more to the point, regardless of public opinion, he *would* have dealt a significant blow to the Illyricans. So the only reason to take the ship is if there's more to be gained by possessing it than by destroying it. And in order to figure that out, we need to know exactly what makes it so valuable."

As if in answer to the question, a discernible silence suddenly flooded the compartment. All four men looked around for the source of the non-sound, but Brody was the first to get it.

"They've turned off the engines," he said, tilting his head to one side, as though listening.

An odd sensation overtook Kovalic, as though his stomach was starting to climb its way into his chest along with the rest of his internal organs. He moved to steady himself when he realized that his feet were no longer in contact with the deck, but instead floating a few inches above it. Around him, Brody, Tapper, and Page had all suffered the same fate, the lieutenant still fiddling with the repulsor equipment as he hovered in mid-air.

"The artificial gravity's down, too," said Page, raising an eyebrow.

"I hadn't noticed," said Tapper, who was waving his arms and legs as though treading water.

"What the hell is Eamon playing at—" Brody started to say when something hit all of them with a sharp jolt.

Kovalic's vision started to go black, his ears rang with the roar of the ocean, the air was pressed out of his lungs, and even his heart seemed to stop for a second. He was barely conscious of being slammed into the deck by what felt like a piledriver from a 250-pound wrestler. He'd never really wondered what toothpaste felt like when it was squeezed out of the tube, but he suddenly thought he had a pretty good idea.

And then it was over as quickly as it had begun, and he was lying on his back, wheezing. The pounding of his heart thumped against the floor and he could feel the blood rushing back to his head. With a groan, he levered himself upright, seeing the other three men in much the same condition. Page was massaging his temples and wincing, Brody was coughing from flat on his back, and even Tapper was looking shaken.

Kovalic caught the sergeant's gaze, and Tapper shook his head, wide-eyed. "What in the name of the nine fucking hells was *that*?"

"I don't know," said Kovalic as his heart rate started to return to a more reasonable tempo. "But if I had to guess, I'd say we've just been formally introduced to Project Tarnhelm."

# CHAPTER TWENTY-TWO

"The bridge," Fielding—*Kovalic,* Eli reminded himself—had said, once they'd all gotten back to their feet. Neither Tapper nor Page had seemed inclined to argue with their boss and, as far as Eli could tell, there was no reason to do so. If you were in a library and you had a question, you went to the reference desk. If you were on an enemy vessel and wanted to take control, you went to the bridge. No point in beating about the spaceship.

Eli had always considered himself quick on his feet, but when it came to Kovalic and his crew he might as well have been a seven-year-old dawdling along after his parents on a warm, sunny day. The team moved with the surety of a custom-built tool matched exactly to its purpose, jogging down the hallway in perfect timing, checking every possible cross corridor for hostiles. For Eli, sandwiched between Page and Tapper like a piece of limp lettuce, he couldn't help but feel as though he was being chivvied along, as useless as that little kid.

"Clear," came the whisper as Kovalic, in the lead, peeked around another corridor.

The rest of the team darted up the hallway to join him at the intersection.

"I hope you've thought through exactly what we're going to do when we get to the bridge," said Eli. "Because I suspect that politely asking Eamon to stand down isn't going to get you very far."

"Your brother doesn't exactly strike me as the diplomatic type, and I've got no desire to be shot in the head." He looked to Tapper, bringing up the rear. "We're going to have to storm it."

"With one gun and one grenade?" said Eli.

"Unless you've got a better idea, Brody. And if you do, please, by all means, speak up."

*How about we find the crew lounge, kick back, and have a drink?* That was what he wanted to suggest, but he had an inkling that his plan wouldn't exactly meet with Kovalic's approval.

"Page, we're going to need the schematics to the bridge if there's any chance of making this work. Find a terminal and see what you can dig up."

Page's return nod was crisp, and the man slipped off without a sound. Kovalic turned to Tapper. "Sergeant, what're the odds that concussion grenade will actually work as advertised?"

The stocky man pulled the smooth metal cylinder out of his pocket and turned it over in his hands. "No visible damage. It's not the most reputable of manufacturers, but I don't see any reason it shouldn't give us one hell of a song and dance."

"Good. Even better, you and Page still have surprise on your side. Brody and I will go in first and try to soften them up as much as possible."

"We'll *what?*"

Kovalic's grin was less than reassuring. "Don't sweat it, Brody. It'll be a piece of cake." He unslung the carbine and handed it to Tapper. "Just try not to shoot us."

Tapper shrugged. "In the heat of the moment, you never know."

Eli looked from Tapper to Kovalic. "You're kid—he's kidding, right?"

"Don't worry, kid," said Tapper. "We're professionals."

"How many times have you done this?" asked Eli, his voice shaky.

"Charge a heavily defended position with two friendlies in the mix, on a ship full of unknown, experimental technology?"

"Yeah."

Tapper's brown furrowed. "Once."

"Oh, okay."

"Including this."

Kovalic slapped Eli on the shoulder. "See? Nothing to worry about."

"Yeah, I feel like tap dancing."

"That's what I like to hear, because you and I are going to have to put on a show for our audience upstairs."

Page shimmered into existence next to them, his arrival unheralded by anything beyond a slight clearing of the throat. "The bridge schematics were under lock and key and I didn't have time to convince my way in. However, the maintenance plans show pretty clearly that there are a pair of service shafts that circle the bridge, which *should* provide a way in."

"Should?" asked Tapper.

"Well, assuming the bridge compartment isn't hermetically sealed."

"Would it be?"

Page shrugged. "On a standard *Warhorse,* I doubt it. But who knows what kind of modifications they've made."

"We're just going to have to take that chance. Page, Tapper, find the maintenance shafts. We'll give you a five-minute head start before we go in. Assuming they don't shoot us on sight, give us about two minutes to maneuver them into an advantageous position."

"And if we can't get access to the bridge from the service shafts?"

"Then we'll have to improvise."

"Good luck." Tapper jerked his head at Page and the two of them split off down a corridor, leaving Kovalic and Eli on their own. The captain was tugging at the sleeves of his jacket, making sure it sat right on his shoulders.

"So," said Kovalic. "Are you having fun yet?"

"Actually, I'm just trying to remember how I got into this mess."

"Well, I think that when you trace it all the way back, you'll see that it came down to one pretty simple misstep on your part."

"Yeah? What's that?"

"Not listening to me."

Eli snorted. "Well, can you blame me? You military guys are always talking about a need-to-know basis and operational security."

Kovalic eyed him for a moment, then shook his head. "I don't get it."

"What?"

"Well, as far as I can see, you don't have much use for authority or chain of command, you don't like being told what to do, and you're not trigger-happy, like most of the kids who join up. So what the hell were you doing in a uniform in the first place?"

"It was the fastest way off that planet. And, like I told you back on Sabaea, it let me fly."

The gray eyes narrowed. "I don't doubt that was part of it, but if that's all you really wanted, you could have joined a shipping company or the merchant service. I think there was more to it than that."

"Yeah?" Eli crossed his arms and leaned against the wall. "Well please enlighten me, O Source of All Wisdom."

"I think you knew it'd really piss off your brother."

Eli barked a laugh. "You think that's what it was all about? Sibling rivalry?"

Kovalic shrugged. "More or less. You don't strike me as the ideological type. You certainly didn't join up because you believed in the Imperium. And if you'd been half as ardent as your brother is about Caledonian independence, you'd never have been able to touch that uniform, let alone put it on every day."

"Stick to soldiering, Kovalic. Psychology doesn't suit you."

The man wasn't going to be deterred. "In that sense, this moment became inevitable. You and your brother were going to clash someday—it was just a matter of where, when, and how it was going to play out."

Eli gritted his teeth. *He thinks he can read my file and know me inside out.* "I think our five minutes are up, doc."

Kovalic acquiesced, but they hadn't gone more than a few steps toward the bridge when something in the air changed. Eli's sensitivity to shipboard life may have been rusty, but some things you never quite forgot.

"The engines are off again."

"Huh. But the gravity's still on this time." Kovalic reached out a hand to brace himself against the wall anyway. "Either they're getting the hang of working this thing or this is something else."

They waited, but there was no dramatic gravity spike or anything else that could be deemed out of the ordinary. Exchanging a glance, Kovalic and Eli continued down the corridor toward the short staircase that led to the bridge.

"So, you had a plan, right?" Eli asked as they reached the base of the steps.

"Just keep him talking long enough for Page and Tapper to get the drop on him from the maintenance shaft. Hopefully we can incapacitate him before he even knows they're there."

"What makes you think he's even interested in talking to me? The last time we were in there he didn't seem to care too much about what happened to me."

Kovalic rolled his eyes. "You're going to have to learn to read between the lines, Brody. If he didn't care what happened to you, he would have had Kelly knife you in the back and been done with it. But your brother sees himself as a freedom fighter, not a terrorist, and killing your own flesh and blood doesn't exactly mesh with that image."

Eli shook his head. "Again with the psychological profiling. You guys must have a hell of a job description."

Kovalic didn't reply, just smiled and started climbing up the stairs to the bridge's pressure door, leaving Eli no real choice but to follow.

The light above the door was still steady green. Kovalic glanced over his shoulder at Eli and tilted his head to one side. There was a familiar lurch in Eli's stomach that recalled the moment right before his fighter had dropped from the *Venture*'s fighter bay into the black tapestry of space around Sabaea—the realization of everything that was about to happen. As then, he shoved it into the back of his mind and just gave Kovalic a nod.

At the touch of the controls, the door slid open and the two of them stepped onto the bridge.

The people there didn't react immediately; that was the difference between them and an actual trained team of soldiers. Eamon's people had gotten complacent—and not without reason, since they'd been fairly secure in the knowledge that they were alone and in control of the ship.

It was Gwen, standing next to one of the engineering stations, who saw them first. Eli caught a slight widening of her eyes, followed, strangely, by hesitation. There was a pistol in her belt, but she made no move to draw it. The dark-haired woman, McKenna, had given an off-the-cuff glance at the door; she quickly did a double take and scrambled for the carbine she'd left lying on the console. With McKenna's gun trained on them, Gwen finally drew her own weapon and pointed it loosely in their direction. If Kovalic had been armed, Eli had little doubt he would have been able to take them both out without breaking a sweat.

Eamon was the last one to look up, and he looked no less surprised to see them. But he recovered quickly from that shock, a mask of control descending once again. He cleared his throat. "Should I ask what happened to Kelly?"

"He wasn't feeling well," said Kovalic.

"A mild case of blow-to-the-head," added Eli. "I'm sure he'll be fine."

Someone else might have missed the flicker of annoyance in his brother's eyes, but Eli knew him too well: Eamon Brody was well and royally ticked off, but he wasn't about to let anything interfere with his plan.

Eli's eyes darted around the bridge, taking everything in. Besides Eamon, McKenna, and Gwen, there was another man—the transport ship's pilot, he guessed—in the sunken cockpit on the deck; he was sweating profusely, his eyes locked on the console in front of him. Someone had apparently removed the corpse of the dead Illyrican security guard, though the one who'd been shot in the shoulder was propped up, white-faced, against one of the consoles, clearly unconscious. To Eli's surprise, his shoulder had been expertly bandaged. Of Lucy Graham there was no sign. *Maybe Eamon got all he needed from her and tossed her out an airlock.* Then again, that seemed a bit cynical, even for Eamon.

"Well," said Eamon, crossing his arms. "You're here. What can I do for you?"

"I think it's what *we* can do for you," said Kovalic.

"I don't follow."

"You must realize that this plan is a bit on the stupid side?"

If you'd have asked Eli how his brother would react to being called stupid, he'd have given you good money that the elder Brody would have gritted his teeth or flown into a rage. The very last thing he would have expected was for him to relax and crack a smile.

"Is it?" asked Eamon. "Do tell."

Eli could feel Kovalic's eyes boring into the back of his head. *As signals go, that's not exactly subtle.* He jumped in. "Well, for one, how much do you really know about running a starship?"

Eamon inclined his head to the man in the pilot's seat, who was craning his neck up to watch the conversation. Of the crew on the bridge, he was the only one that was unarmed. "Mr.—what was your name again?—Carroll here is a more than capable pilot. And I've picked my team carefully. I don't imagine that it will be quite as much of a problem as you might expect. But I appreciate your concern."

Eli caught a brief twitch of motion from behind one of the venting grates above. Lady luck was, for once, smiling upon Eli and Kovalic; Eamon's entire team had their backs to it. Eli plowed ahead, willing himself not to look directly at the vent.

"That's not your biggest problem," he continued. "Even if your pilot is competent, how the hell do you expect to get the ship through the gate without the Illyricans knowing? They'll have weapons lock on you before you can even see the wormhole."

Eamon's forehead creased in confusion and his eyes darted back and forth between Eli and Kovalic, looking for something. "You don't know," he said slowly. Delight seeped into his voice. "You have *no idea*, do you?" His face split into a broad grin. "Oh, this is *too* good." He threw back his head and laughed, wiping the tears from his eyes. "Honestly, the gate is the least of our worries."

A quiet rattle sounded from the bulkhead—Eli would likely not even have noticed it if his attention hadn't already been drawn there. Out of instinct, his eyes flicked to the vent. Cursing himself inwardly, he looked back to Eamon, but it was already too late. His brother's eyes had narrowed, and he was already turning his head when the vent was flung loose from the wall, accompanied by a booted foot. The small cylindrical grenade rolled out, hitting the deck with a heavy *clunk*. Eamon, to his credit, was already diving out of the way, even as the rest of his crew was still reacting.

Something heavy shoved Eli from behind—he realized later it was Kovalic—and they hit the deck so hard it knocked the wind out of him. The brilliant flash of white light seeped its way in through the cracks in Eli's eyelids, searing his eyes, and then a squadron of fighters broke the sound barrier directly over his head.

The next thing he knew he was being dragged to his feet, his head still throbbing like he'd pounded an entire bottle of whisky. He blinked several times, waiting for the stars to clear from his vision, and reeled over to the nearest console to prop himself up. When his eyesight returned, he saw that Kovalic had already taken advantage of the opportunity to scoop up both McKenna and Gwen's weapons. The dark-haired woman was glowering in their direction—at least as much as she was able to while her eyes still had trouble focusing—and Gwen was massaging her temples and working her jaw. Carroll, who had been the closest to the grenade, appeared to be senseless in the pilot's cockpit.

Frowning, Eli scanned the room. "Where's Eamon?" his voice sounding dull and thick in his own ears. There was no sign of his brother, who had last been standing at the front of the bridge. "Kovalic!" He looked toward the other man in alarm. *"Where's Eamon?"*

The soldier strode over and grabbed him by the shoulders. "*Stop shouting*," he mouthed.

The cotton-wool plugs in his ears were slowly replaced by the persistent whine of a referee blowing one long, continuous whistle. It was, if anything, less pleasant.

There wasn't anywhere in the compartment for Eamon to hide, leaving only the possibility that he'd somehow slipped out of the room in the confusion. Eli swore at himself again—he'd tipped him to the grenade. "He can't have gone far," he said, starting for the door.

"Wait," he heard Kovalic say through the fading ringing in his ears. "We may have bigger problems." He was crouching by the cockpit, his fingers on Carroll's throat. "He's out for the count."

"So wh—" Realization slammed home. "Who the hell is flying this thing?"

They both looked down at the cockpit

Kovalic scratched his head. "Right now I'd say no one."

"Well, *that's* not good."

"Nope," said Kovalic. He lugged Carroll's dead weight up and out of the pilot's couch, grunting as he managed to push him onto the deck. For a moment, he stared at the unconscious figure, then looked up and raised an eyebrow at Eli.

"What?"

"Wherever are we going to find a qualified pilot?" he said in mock dismay, throwing up his hands.

Eli took an involuntary step backwards. "Whoa. Wait a second."

"I would be happy to wait as long as you need, except for the minor fact that we're currently going *somewhere*."

"I don't fly. Not anymore."

"It's just like falling off a bike."

"Don't you mean—"

"*Get in the fucking cockpit, Brody.*"

Eli gulped, then dropped to the floor and slid his feet tentatively into the cockpit, wincing as if he were wading into a cold lake. The long padded couch was surrounded by panels of readouts and dials—it looked more complicated than the fighters he used to fly, but his pilot's training had already isolated the most important controls.

"You can do this," said Kovalic, crouching next to him. "I've been paying attention: you've hardly freaked out once since we've been onboard."

*Huh*, Eli thought. *He's right. Normally I would have been a gibbering idiot the moment the ship left the ground.* The adrenaline probably hadn't hurt, either: it was hard to freak out when you were hopped up on the fight-or-flight stimulants coursing through your brain. With a deep breath, he let himself slide the rest of the way into the cockpit, feeling the sensors readjust the controls to his height and size. The pedals shifted up to rest comfortably under his feet while the flight yoke moved to a more natural position. The readout panels by his right arm were showing solid greens.

"*Board is green.*" It had been five years, but the voice in his head was unmistakably familiar: the precise, scientific tones of Chris Larabie, his late wingman—who, along with the rest of his squadron, had been blown to bits at Sabaea. He felt the bile rising in his stomach all the way to the bottom of his throat, but he pushed it back down. Throwing up all over the controls wasn't going to help—they taught you that much on day one. Instead, he turned his attention to the navigation computer by his left arm.

"All right. Before we can go anywhere, I guess we need to know where the hell we are." He keyed the navigation display, which shimmered into view in miniature form before him, as well as onto a larger holographic tactical display at the front of the bridge.

Eli frowned. The display was showing five planetary orbits around a large class-G star, which was most certainly not the nine-planet layout of the Caledonian system. He must have called up the wrong display—maybe Eamon had been looking at something else. He double-checked the readouts, but they confirmed that it was the ship's current location.

"Must be a sensor misread," he muttered, scrutinizing the chart. There was something familiar about the diagram on the display, something that twigged his memory. There weren't that many inhabited systems in the galaxy and with all the drilling that pilots went through, most learned to recognize pretty much any known orbital layout by sight.

*Have we already gone through the gate somehow?* He wouldn't have said they'd been in flight long enough to even reach it. Not to mention that the only gate from Caledonia led to Earth, and this was most assuredly not Earth's solar system either. *In fact*, he thought, *it looks a whole lot like . . .*

"That's impossible," he said. Goosebumps pimpled his arms.

"What?" asked Kovalic, looking up from where he'd been securing McKenna and Gwen to the consoles. He'd jammed the redhead's pistol into his belt and slung McKenna's carbine over his shoulder.

But Eli didn't respond, instead staring up at the tactical display: five concentric rings, the fourth of which was highlighted in a deep green that marked it as a friendly inhabited planet. There was only one known system that matched that configuration, but it was two wormhole jumps away from Caledonia and no ship could have made the trip in the half-an-hour or so that they'd been onboard—not without breaking the laws of physics.

"That's Illyrica," said Eli slowly. He looked up at Kovalic. "The nav chart says we're in the Illyrican system."

Kovalic looked to the tactical display, and then back down at Eli. "It must be a mistake," he said. "Check again."

"I've *triple*-checked. I think I know how to read a nav chart."

Eli's head had started to spin, assembling all the information he'd absorbed during the last couple days. A superweapon being built on Aran. A secret Illyrican military facility. *"It's a game-changer."* Lucy Graham, genius scientist. *"The gate is really the least of our worries."*

"They did it," Eli said slowly. "Goddamnit, they *did* it. They built a working jump-ship."

Kovalic's jaw dropped. "What? I thought that was impossible."

"Me too." Eli rubbed at the goosebumps on his arms. "Then again, five hundred years ago, people would have said the same thing about traveling through wormholes."

Staring at the tactical display, Kovalic shook his head.

"A ship that can travel between systems without the need for gates," Eli murmured. Awe crept over his face. "All that talk of planet-destroying guns and population-scathing weapons, and it turns out that it's just a ship."

Kovalic's expression had turned grim. "No, Brody. It *is* a weapon."

"What?"

"In the wrong hands, this could be the most devastating weapon the war's ever seen. An invasion fleet could be on any world's doorstep without a single moment of warning. Or you could attach a bomb to it and fire it three systems away. This ship doesn't care what it's used for—it's people that make it into a weapon. A hammer can build houses or cave in a skull."

"But think of all the *good* it could do."

Kovalic grunted. "That's not my job. But let's leave the theoretical possibilities for later. We're in the Illyrican system. Your brother came here for a reason, and I think we both know it probably wasn't just to do a flyby of the Imperial Palace and flaunt his stolen prototype." He looked up at the system again. "Can you get us out of here?"

Eli considered the controls in front of him. "Given a couple hours and whatever technical documentation's on the computer? Sure."

Kovalic had walked over to the controls for the tactical display and keyed in a command. The display rotated and shifted, moving from a three-dimensional wireframe overview of the system to a flat "top-down" view of the system. A blinking green dot showed their position, and a hazy red-tinted circle surrounded the fourth planet.

"That's Illyrica's defensive perimeter," he said, pointing to the circle. "If we hit that then all hell's going to break loose."

"We're about two hundred thousand kilometers away and coasting right toward it, thanks to inertia," said Eli, consulting the readouts above the yoke.

"In that case, it looks like you have about twenty minutes to become intimately familiar with this ship."

Looking first at the pilot's screen, he glanced back at Kovalic. "No pressure, thanks. Anyway, all I have to do to buy us some time is hit the brakes." He reached for the throttle lever to the right of the yoke.

His fingers hadn't even closed around the control when every visible display in the cockpit flashed a bright red warning message and then went dark.

"Shit." Eli grabbed the throttle and yanked it down to the minimum, but it didn't seem to have any effect. The yoke was equally unresponsive, and all the readouts on his board were dark. He tapped a few of the keys on the console, but nothing happened. Only the tactical display was still online, showing the green dot getting ever closer toward the red perimeter.

"What happened?" asked Kovalic.

"It said 'access denied.'" Eli threw the yoke back in frustration. "I'm locked out."

"How is that possible? Aren't all executive functions controlled from the bridge?"

Eli racked his brain, trying to dredge up dusty Illyrican command-and-control protocols. "Usually, yes, but in extreme circumstances—hijacking, for example, or mutiny—it can be overridden from another location onboard." He looked up at Kovalic. "In most cases, the engine room. Eamon could have gotten down there and transferred command."

"Then we're going on a field trip. Come on." He extended a hand and helped Eli scramble out of the cockpit.

"We still have most of Eamon's crew unaccounted for," Eli pointed out. "There were about a dozen of them, all told, and you've only got two here. We're going to be outnumbered, even with the rest of our friends." He looked up toward the vents significantly.

"Well," said a voice from behind them, "if that's all that's holding you back, maybe I can help."

# CHAPTER TWENTY-THREE

t was the redhead who had spoken—Kovalic knew it before even turning around. But there was something about her voice; it wasn't that of a cowed and beaten foot soldier. Nor, when he faced her, did he see some girl dragged into affairs over her head. Instead, he saw a young woman who, despite being bound to a railing, looked completely and utterly at ease, as though this were just an ordinary day at the office.

Kovalic had noticed her hesitation when he and Brody had walked onto the bridge earlier. She'd had plenty of time to draw her pistol, probably even fire a shot, but she'd waited. Her eyes had gone to Brody, and he'd thought maybe she had a soft spot for the younger brother. But he'd felt her gaze on him, too, as if summing him up. Either way, she wasn't your ordinary run-of-the mill terrorist.

"*You* can help us?" Kovalic repeated, draping his hand over the pistol he'd taken from her.

"You bitch." The snarl came from the dark-haired woman tied up just a few feet away. "You little *bitch* traitor."

If the other woman's not particularly elegant words fazed the redhead, she didn't show it. "I'm pretty handy with a pistol."

"That may be," said Kovalic, "but at last recollection you were right by Eamon Brody's side when he hijacked this ship." He spread his hands. "So you'll forgive me for not immediately subscribing to your sudden change of allegiances."

"I have no love for Eamon Brody." Her brown eyes didn't blink. "Or the rest of his merry band of marauders." Her head tilted away from the other woman, who looked like she wished she could kill people just by staring at them.

"Again, I'd be happy to take your word for it, but circumstances being what they are."

She nodded. "Of course. I presume you've got a comm unit?"

Cocking his head to one side, Kovalic eyed her. "I do. But it's just a personal unit; not high-powered enough to let you call anyone from way the hell out here."

"Oh, you're not going to be calling anybody. I just want you to scan my arm."

Kovalic raised an eyebrow. Drawing the pistol from his belt, he slapped the butt into Brody's open hand and held the other man's gaze. "Remember—the only important thing is to stop Eamon. Shoot her, shoot me, I don't care. Got it?"

The kid looked stricken, and for once he didn't seem to have a witty retort already prepared. "Got it."

But the woman didn't try anything when Kovalic approached, nor when he pulled out his comm and held it up to her right arm, as instructed.

"It'll need to be a narrowband scan, 5023 megahertz."

Kovalic punched in the code and waved it over the arm. "Subdermal implant?"

"Right. It stays dormant unless triggered by a specific frequency."

After a moment it beeped, and he peered at the screen, his mouth curling immediately into a surprised smile. "Well I'll be damned."

He turned and tossed the comm to Brody, who fumbled it, thanks to the pistol in his other hand, but managed to read the text off the screen. His jaw fell about two stories and he snapped his head up to stare at the woman, then looked back down at the comm.

"You're CalSec?"

"Deep cover. Under for eighteen months. I've been after your brother for the last three years." She gritted her teeth. "And if you two have fouled up my collar, you're getting locked up right next to Eamon. Now." She tugged at her wrists and eyed them pointedly. "Do you mind?"

Kovalic pulled a folding knife from his boot and flipped the blade open. It was the work of a moment for him to cut her loose, and she massaged her wrists with vigor.

"Thanks."

"I swear to *god*," growled the dark-haired woman, straining at her bonds. "When I get out of here I'm going to fucking kill you. I'm going to rip you into little—" Whatever other awful fates she had planned were cut short as the redhead's fist made contact with her cheek, smacking her head back against the console and knocking her unconscious.

"Christ," she muttered, rubbing her knuckles, "I've wanted to do that for *months*."

Brody, for his part, didn't seem to have recovered from his shock. "*You* work for the Caledonian Security Agency," he repeated, his eyes glassy.

She inclined her head. "Special Agent Gwendolyn Rhys, Counterterrorism Division."

Retrieving the pistol from Brody's grip, Kovalic handed it back to her. That certainly explained all of CalSec's inside info, including De Valera's true identity. "I believe I've read some of your reports, Agent Rhys. Impressive work." Probably better to leave out that he'd also assaulted two of her colleagues outside of Jim Wallace's safe house.

"Wait a second," said Brody, his brow furrowed. "Why is CalSec investigating the Black Watch? Isn't that an Imperial matter?"

"It's part of a deal with the Illyricans," said Rhys. "A safe and secure Caledonia benefits us as much as it does the Illyricans. The Black Watch may say they have our planet's best interests at heart, but they also incite violence, run weapons, and even have connections to the drug trade. And because we're made up of native-born Caledonians, CalSec can get places the Illyricans can't."

"But don't you just end up working for the Imperium?"

"We work *with* the Imperium," Rhys corrected Brody stiffly. "Not *for* them. Or against them."

"Although that doesn't mean you have to share every single little detail with them either," said Kovalic, eyebrows arched. If they had, Eyes would have descended on Eamon Brody a long time ago.

Rhys flushed slightly, her lips quirking. "Let's just say it's a need-to-know basis."

Kovalic grinned.

Brody eyed the two of them. "Well, it would be lovely to stay here and chat all day, but as I recall, there are more pressing matters to attend to."

"Brody's right," said Kovalic. "Much as I hate to say it. Let's go."

They headed out of the bridge and down the corridor, rounding the first junction corridor only to find themselves looking down the barrel of a carbine.

The wielder snapped it up immediately upon recognizing Kovalic.

"Sorry, boss," said Tapper. "Thought it might be some more party crashers."

"Impeccable timing, as always. Where's Page?"

"He saw Eamon make a break for the exit and picked up his trail. Said he'd scout out the situation."

"Good. Let's give him some backup."

The four of them resumed course toward the engine room, winding their way through a maze of hallways and intersections, as Brody followed whatever latent instincts were guiding him. Kovalic eyed the party as they trotted: He and Tapper were both carrying carbines, while Rhys had her pistol—Brody was unarmed, though something told Kovalic that might be the wisest course of action. That would mean Page was unarmed as well, unless he'd managed to procure a weapon from somewhere else, which was hardly outside the realm of possibility.

Tapper had fallen into step with Kovalic as they made their way down the corridor. "What's the plan, boss?"

Kovalic tightened his grip on the carbine. "Priority number one is stopping Eamon Brody. By whatever means necessary."

"The hell you say," Rhys interrupted. "*I* want him alive."

The sergeant glanced over his shoulder. "Lady, if it's him or us, I'm going to choose us. If that's all right with you. Whoever the hell you are."

"Tapper, meet Special Agent Rhys of the Caledonian Security Agency."

"Well knock me over with a feather," said Tapper. "She's almost young enough to be my granddaughter."

Rhys snorted. "In that case, I hope you can keep up, old man."

"I *like* her."

"*Anyway*," said Kovalic. "Three guns among five of us. How many men would you say Eamon has left?" he asked Rhys.

"With McKenna—and, if you're right, Kelly—out of the equation, there are eight left, Eamon included. And Dr. Graham, though I'm not sure she knows which way to hold a gun, much less how to hit the broad side of a starship with one."

"Threat assessment?"

"McKenna and Kelly were the best trained. They were both ex-Caledonian militia. Eamon and Lyngaas both have formal training, but the rest of them are little more than thugs."

"Well, that might just give us a fighting chance."

●

They followed a twisting and turning set of similar-looking corridors until Eli slowed to a stop at a T-junction that led to the engine room. Page was, unsurprisingly, waiting for them. He nodded at Kovalic as the rest of the motley crew pressed itself against the walls.

"Good to see you, lieutenant. Where are we at?"

"Eamon disappeared in there somewhere. I figured you would be along shortly, so I decided to wait for backup."

"See?" said Kovalic, giving Tapper a look of mock suffering. "That's what *patience* looks like."

The older man gave a good-natured scowl, and Kovalic responded with a wide grin. "You're up, Tap. Check it out."

Without a word, Tapper slunk away from the wall, pressing himself to the opposite bulkhead, and slid out just far enough that he had an angle on the junction. The carbine was braced against his shoulder and he swept it back and forth, looking for threats.

"Clear."

Eli would have taken that as an opportunity to waltz straight ahead, but Kovalic was still leaning against the wall, eyes narrowed in the expression Eli had come to associate with him being deep in thought.

Kovalic's gaze caught Eli's, and the military man shook his head. "We can't just walk right in. Your brother will be expecting us now, and he's sure to have people watching the entrances. We might as well put our hands behind our heads and give up."

"So, what then?"

"We need to outthink him."

"Good luck with that."

The other man tapped a finger against his lips. "You know Eamon better than anyone—what's his blind spot?"

"Blind spot? I'm not sure he has one."

"Everyone has one. You were a fighter pilot. You should know that."

*Aft and just up*, thought Eli. On the R-78s that Eli had flown for most of his naval career, there was one prominent blind spot just behind and above. Engine wash obscured any trailing ship from your own sensors, and Eli had yet to meet the pilot who could swivel his head 180 degrees. If somebody sat in that spot and put one good burst into your engine, you were in the black.

But Kovalic was right: people were no different. And it didn't take much to figure out what Eamon's was. His brother had spent a long time with the Black Watch, and for him they'd become *almost* as good as family—but for someone who was fighting for his homeland, nothing would ever replace real honest-to-goodness blood. There was something too strong in the imagery, in the ties to patriotism. Come right down to it, little else divided the Caledonian natives from their Illyrican occupiers. Probably not even blood, if you wanted to get scientific, but some things went deeper than logic.

Eli's heart didn't just sink; it felt like it was burning up on re-entry. *He's your brother for chrissake.* Some things were just below the belt, emotionally speaking, and you didn't go around kneeing your brother in the groin, literally *or* figuratively.

"Yeah," he said, drawing a deep breath. "Meghann." *You're not betraying him. He's already broken your trust how many times?*

Eli might have been imagining things, but he thought the change in Kovalic's expression looked a bit like that glint of respect he'd first seen from him way back in Colonel Antony's office on Sabaea. But there was something else in there. Something buried beneath the respect.

*Guilt?*

"Your sister," said Kovalic.

"She's in—"

"I know." He avoided Eli's eyes. "Page pulled her file after you disappeared. I'm sorry, for what it's worth."

*Only that's not how you knew*, Eli realized slowly. Kovalic and his boss, they'd convinced him to go on this mission because of Meghann. So he'd already known when they sent him. But the anger that he'd expected to find surging within him just wasn't there. Instead, he just felt tired. *The military*, as he'd reminded himself earlier, *doesn't lie to you—they just don't tell you everything.*

Kovalic's mouth set into a grim line and Eli could see written on his face the same thought that was running through his own mind.

*Let's end this.*

"All right," said Kovalic with a nod. "Tapper and Page will circle around and try to take the high ground with the carbines." He unslung the weapon and handed it to Page, who quickly and automatically checked it over. "Deal with anybody you run into. Brody and I are going right up the middle—we have to get to that lockout console. Rhys, you're watching our back."

Drawing herself up, Gwen ducked her head in acknowledgment. Taking their back meant it would be only too easy for her to turn on them and box them in. There was a measure of trust inherent in this decision, and she wasn't dumb—she knew exactly what it meant.

"Brody," said Kovalic, turning to him. "You think you can get us to the console?"

Eli closed his eyes, picturing the layout of a standard naval engine room. Square in the middle would be the engine itself, a vast cocoon of carbon fiber and insulation foam. There would be plenty of room around it for all the cooling tubes and vents that kept it from overheating and blowing the ship into little pieces. To either side of the large compartment would be the interface consoles for the engineering crew, and, if what he remembered was still accurate, the primary console would be starboard in a cluster of three or four.

"Yeah," said Eli. "I'm pretty sure I can find it." *If they haven't changed anything in five years. And if this bloody ship conforms to the same layout as every other ship I've seen.* That was a metric ton of "ifs" that he wasn't about to share.

"All right. Let's do this."

Tapper grumbled something about being consigned to the service vents again, but he and Page dutifully disappeared down the corridor to look for an access shaft. Kovalic, now unarmed, massaged his right arm with his left, and flexed it a couple of times while Gwen checked her pistol again. They gave the others a two-minute count.

"Move fast," Kovalic said to Eli, "And for god's sake, keep your head down."

"Frankly, I was pretty good at that until I met you."

"Cute. Ready? One, two—*three.*"

Eli pushed off the wall and alongside Kovalic he sprinted the short corridor that led to the engine room, keeping his head tucked to his chest and his eyes just high enough to keep track of where he was going. His feet pounded off the deckplates; he tried to swallow the feeling that a shot might hit him at any moment, but it sat like a cold, gritty stone in his mouth.

About ten steps into the room he made the mistake of looking up and almost stopped dead in his tracks.

The room bore only the barest of resemblances to the engine compartments he'd seen on every other Illyrican ship, and the huge contraption that stood where the fusion core should have been looked utterly alien. Instead of a huge, insulation-swathed power plant, there stood a pair of enormous disks, easily a hundred feet in diameter each. They were each run through, off-center, with an enormous vertical pole and sat offset to each other, like a pair of poorly stacked plates. They were also revolving on the pole, each in opposite directions, in a kind of hypnotic undulation.

His sudden deceleration meant he wasn't the only one who was surprised. A shot ricocheted off the deck in front of him and he was suddenly yanked by the arm toward the starboard side of the room. Kovalic pulled him around a piece of heavy cooling machinery and they crouched behind it. A wide catwalk ran around the top of the room; Eamon had clearly positioned sharpshooters on it. Ducking behind the machinery meant the one on the opposite side couldn't hit them, and they were close enough to the catwalk that it was a tough shot for the person above. For now, anyway.

Kovalic was peering over their cover, looking for the gunman opposite them, but Eli's attention was on the console fifteen feet from where they sat. Fifteen unprotected feet. Eli could make it at a sprint, but he'd be a sitting duck once he got there, and Kovalic didn't have a weapon to cover him. They had to hope that Tapper and Page would be able to take out the sentries and give them some time to work. And even then, the size of Eamon's crew meant there were still around a half dozen left. He glanced back over toward the door they'd come in and froze as he saw two men detach themselves from the bulkheads on each side and start in their direction.

"Kovalic," he snapped, elbowing him sharply and pointing to the two men.

Kovalic looked back in their direction. "I guess now we find out if Rhys is on the up and up."

The lanky redheaded man advancing on them from the starboard side of the room—Eli pegged him as Lyngaas—had a nasty smirk on his face. He'd made it about two steps when there was a burst of shots and his chest went red. The smirk twisted into a grimace and he sank to the deck.

Kovalic craned his neck over their cover and Eli followed his sightline to catch sight of Tapper on the opposite side of the catwalk, bracing one foot on top of a slumped body and aiming down the barrel of a carbine at the man he'd just felled.

Kovalic nodded. "That's one of the sharpshooters down."

A scream that under other circumstances would have been comical suddenly echoed from above them—and it seemed to be getting louder. Kovalic grabbed Eli and pulled him back even as there was a sickening thud and crackle from a few feet away, like somebody had just dropped a watermelon from a great height.

"And that's two."

The man who had been on the port side of the doorway was suddenly looking more concerned, having seen one of his comrades shot in the chest and another tossed bodily off a catwalk. He was pulling back to cover in a position opposite Kovalic and Brody when Gwen stepped into the doorway, carefully lined up her pistol, and shot him in the back. His back arched and he tripped mid-run, skidding to the floor and leaving a smear of blood behind him.

Eli scanned the room, but there was no sign of anyone else watching. He had a clear run to the console.

"I'm going," he said, springing up and dashing for the bank of controls.

Nobody shot him, or even at him, on the fifteen-foot trip, but as he reached the computer display and was putting his hands down on the keyboard he heard the click of a safety being released. He froze, his hands hovering just mere millimeters off the controls, his eyes focused on the big red letters on the display before him: "Authorization Unlock."

"Keep your hands off the console, Lije. I really, *really* don't want to shoot you, but if you give me no other choice, I will."

His brother was standing against the bulkhead, about five feet down from the console, in a spot that had been obscured from Kovalic and Eli's hiding space by another piece of machinery. He held a pistol leveled at Eli, which was probably the single most salient detail of the moment, and certainly the first that jumped to Eli's mind.

"Step away," said Eamon, motioning with the gun.

Eli looked from the gun up to his brother's face, then shook his own head slowly. "I don't think you will."

"I never really took you for a gambling man, Lije."

"Eamon, what do you think you're going to accomplish? We're about ten minutes away from taking a flying leap into Illyrica's defensive perimeter, at which point this is all going to be academic because they're going to turn us into very small pieces of space dust."

Eamon sighed theatrically. "You know what your problem is, little brother? No faith. This," he gestured around him with his free hand, "is a top-secret experimental Illyrican military vessel. But I don't suppose you ever got far enough up the ladder to know how the defense control systems handle that. It's not as if they want to have just any traffic controller ogling it. The computer will identify the ship's transponder as having free transit authorization, and the traffic controller will pass it right through—no questions asked."

"But surely the Illyricans will have revoked the transponder code since the ship's been stolen."

Eamon laughed. "Right now, they're still wondering why the hell their moon blew up. They haven't even figured out the ship's missing yet."

That meant they'd jumped straight from Caledonia to Illyrica with no time loss. Even wormhole travel usually ate up a couple hours of transit time. The jump technology on the ship was instantaneous. *Holy shit. This* does *change everything.*

"You're starting to get it," said Eamon, watching his face. "It's a whole new ballgame, Lije."

Exploration to new systems without having to send colony ships on one-way trips; near instantaneous communication between systems; and no more blockades—you could just jump around them. *This must be what the first guy to build a bridge felt like.* The entire galaxy had just gone non-linear.

"They've been working on this tech for decades—*decades*, Lije." He tilted his head to one side, his eyes narrowing. "How long were you stuck on that planet?"

"Five years." *Five long years. And they had this? They left me to rot because of their failed invasion when they could have just popped over a ship and brought me home?* The anger flared in his stomach like a bad case of indigestion. Never mind that he hadn't even really *wanted* to go home at the time. He'd made the best of a bad situation, knowing there was no alternative. *Except there was.* "What are you going to do then, Mr. De Valera?"

"I'm going to deliver justice." He stepped to one of the consoles, keeping the gun loosely trained on Eli, and tapped something in with his free hand. A holographic display sprung to life, showing the same system outline that they'd seen on the bridge. Then the axis shifted and zoomed in, showing the course of the ship—it wasn't making for the large green dot that represented Illyrica, but for a smaller green dot that hung just off and away from the planet. It wasn't labeled, but it only took Eli a moment to figure out what it was.

His eyes snapped to Eamon. "You're going to blow their gate." Tickling fingers teased their way up his spine, lifting each and every hair.

Eamon lowered his gun slowly, and when he spoke again, there was an earnestness in his voice that Eli recognized from their childhood. "Let's give them a taste of their own medicine, Lije. Let's see how *they* like being stuck behind an impenetrable wall."

"Not to mention it'll isolate Illyrica from the worlds it occupies," broke in a third voice.

Eamon shifted the gun hastily toward Kovalic, who'd risen from his hiding place and walked over to stand behind Eli.

"Like Caledonia," Kovalic finished. "And Earth."

"Their transit routes to Sevastapol and Archangelsk will remain undisrupted, for what it's worth, but the worlds they forcibly occupied will rise up and free themselves. Cut off the head and the beast dies."

"You think, what, that the Illyrican military garrison on Caledonia will throw up their hands and let you guys go back to the way things were before they showed up? Not going to happen."

"Without orders from the homeworld and their precious emperor they'll be no match for the will of the people. And without reinforcements we can fight them off."

Now it was Kovalic's turn to laugh, a bitter edge creeping into his voice. "If anything, they'll push their thumb down even harder on your people, Brody."

"Christ, you should be *happy* about this plan, Fielding. You're from Earth, right? I can hear it in your voice. What wouldn't you give to free your homeworld? Here I'd taken you for one of those selfless patriots, fighting to avenge the occupation of Earth."

Kovalic's face set into a grim mask. "Not like this. All you're doing is seeding chaos and turmoil. And for what: a temporary victory? If Sabaea has shown us anything, the Illyricans will just rebuild their gate. And they're not the type to give up easy—they'll be dispatching more invasion fleets the second they re-establish contact."

A mischievous grin played over Eamon's face. "If they can."

Kovalic cocked his head to one side. "You know something."

Eamon shrugged. "I know a lot of things."

"Illyrica's not like Sabaea, Brody; it doesn't have an agricultural industry to fall back on when its supply lines are cut off. Without support from Earth and Centauri, there will be massive food shortages. Innocent civilians are going to die, all because of *your* political agenda."

"That's the Imperium's problem. Maybe the nobility will be forced to share with the common people. Anyway, I don't think your masters at the Commonwealth will bat an eye—I'm doing them a huge favor, shifting the balance of power. They might actually have a reasonable shot at winning this war."

Kovalic sighed and shook his head. "People always talk about winning the war. Honestly, there was a time when I could hardly think of anything else: had to win the war, had to drive the Illyricans out. But the older you get, the more you start thinking that you don't care *who* wins—you just want it over with. And this isn't going to end the war, Brody. If anything, it's going to make it worse."

"And what the fuck do you know?"

"I fought at Earthfall."

For a moment it seemed like complete stillness settled across the engine room, only broken by the incessant whirring of the strange engine. There wasn't an ounce of bragging or pride in Kovalic's statement; to Eli's ears, it sounded more like it had been pried from the man's mouth with tongs.

Eamon, for once, didn't have a quick retort ready. There weren't a lot of Earthfall veterans—mainly because very few of the Earth soldiers who had fought in the campaign against the initial Illyrican invasion had survived. If you'd fought *and* lived, then either you had the devil's own brand of luck on your side or you were quite the badass. In Kovalic's case, Eli had begun to suspect it was probably a bit of both.

"Righteous causes get you only so far, Brody," said Kovalic, shaking his head. "The victory doesn't always go to those who deserve it. Sorry, that's just the way it is." He turned to Eli. "Unlock the console."

"Don't," said Eamon, raising the gun to point at his brother. It wavered slightly.

"Do it, Eli." Kovalic's gaze didn't shift from Eli's eyes. "He won't shoot you."

Eamon's brow creased. "He's right," he said finally. "I can't shoot my own brother." He swung the gun barrel to point toward Kovalic. "But don't think I won't shoot your new best friend, Lije. And I *know* you don't want his death weighing on your conscience."

"Like what happened to your sister weighs on yours?" said Kovalic.

*The blind spot.*

Eamon's hand tightened on the grip of his gun and he closed the distance between him and Kovalic in a stride. "Shut your mouth, you son of a bitch." He was standing only about three feet away from Kovalic, and even though the gun was shaking in his hand there was no way he could miss.

"That's all this is, isn't it?" Kovalic continued, gray eyes hard. "*Guilt.* You weren't there to stop what happened to her, so you decided to take it out on an entire planet. De Valera—the old one, I mean—he knew it, too. That's why he picked you, shaped you, turned you into a tool that would do what he couldn't."

"Fuck you. I was *born* for this. I was even *named* for it, the old man said. This isn't about *me*." He closed the distance between them, jabbing the gun into Kovalic's chest.

The soldier winced when the muzzle hit his sternum, but he didn't give any ground. At Kovalic's sides, his fists clenched. A high-pitched whine had begun to build, like someone had overjuiced a capacitor. Eli looked back and forth between the two of them: his brother and the man he hardly knew. *Everybody's fighting for something.* His eyes went to the console just a foot away from where he stood. He could save Kovalic or he could stop Eamon's plan. But he couldn't do both.

"This," said Eamon, "is for my whole fucking *world.*"

"Then *do it already*," growled Kovalic.

Eamon's finger convulsed on the trigger. Eli dove for the console. A blinding flash of blue light filled the room.

# CHAPTER TWENTY-FOUR

Whatever modifications Page had made to the cargo container's repulsor coil had worked—if anything, a little too well. The fact that the jury-rigged apparatus strapped to Kovalic's right arm hadn't burned out was a good sign, but given the force produced by the device and the inescapable laws of physics the equal and opposite force had hit Kovalic with slightly less impact than a determined bulldozer.

Kovalic had unclenched his fist, palm out, causing the overloaded repulsor to trigger and emit a flash of blinding blue-tinged light. The blowback shoved him about ten feet, where he hit the deck and slid for another few feet until his movement was halted abruptly by a bulkhead slamming into his back.

There was a temptation to not get up at that point. To play dead or maybe even *be* dead. And he might have succumbed to that temptation had it not been for the growl in his head from a man he'd known a lifetime ago, who'd always smelled strangely of lavender.

*Get up, you lazy, no-good maggot. Marines don't die that easy.*

With a grunt, Kovalic rolled over and pushed himself up, grabbing a nearby pipe for support.

A hand took his elbow and he instinctively jerked away.

"Just trying to help," said a surprised voice, which turned out to be Rhys.

"Sorry. Thanks." He looked over toward where the brothers Brody had been standing. Relief flooded through him as he saw Eli standing at the authorization console, typing away. It hadn't all been in vain. "Where's Eamon?"

"Whatever the hell you just did sent him flying across the room like he was on a bungee cord. I didn't see him get up."

Kovalic rubbed at his neck. "I suppose we'd better go find out." He cast a look upward and saw both Page and Tapper standing on the topmost catwalks, carbines pointed downward. Between them, they covered most of the engine room. Tapper gave him a thumbs up while Page favored him with a curt nod.

"No sign of the rest of Eamon's men," Kovalic muttered. "Where the hell have they gotten to?"

"Let's hope that without his stellar leadership they'll scatter like rabbits."

Kovalic snorted at that as he came up behind Brody. "How's it going?"

The younger man frowned. "I'm trying to unlock the authorization, but it's going to take some time. It looks like Eamon just put it on autopilot and pointed it toward the gate. And I don't care *what* he says about top-secret authorization, if the gate defenses see a ship barreling toward them, there's a better than even chance that they'll shoot first and ask questions never."

"How far are we from the defensive perimeter?"

"About twenty-five thousand kilometers. Our speed's fairly steady at around five thousand kilometers per hour."

"Five minutes."

"We can't even make it to the bridge in five minutes."

"Then let's hope your brother was right about them not shooting us down immediately. Let me see if I can get you some help." He ducked out from under the catwalk and cupped his hands around his mouth. "Page, get down here, now!" The slim man withdrew and Kovalic went back to Brody. "Keep working."

"And here I was just going to lean back and have a drink."

"We get out of this alive, drinks are on me."

"We get out of this alive, a whole lot more than a drink is on you."

"Fair enough."

Kovalic made his way to Rhys, who was standing over Eamon. The elder Brody brother was unconscious on the deck; having taken the brunt of the repulsor blast, he'd hit a nearby conduit with considerably more force than Kovalic had hit the bulkhead. Rhys had produced a pair of restraints and was cuffing him to a pipe. She stood and brushed a lock of hair out of her eyes.

"Not bad for improvisation," she said, glancing at Kovalic.

"Let's hold off on judging that until we're out of Illyrican space."

Rhys shrugged. "That's a bigger problem for you than it is for me. Under our agreement with the Illyricans, CalSec's jurisdiction extends to hot pursuit. The method of our transit was, I'll admit, somewhat unorthodox, but I think the Illyricans will be able to overlook it in exchange for apprehending a wanted criminal."

"And me and my team?"

Her blue eyes widened, doe-like. "Why, I didn't even know you were here."

Kovalic returned a smile and extended a hand. "In that case, I'll just say 'good collar,' Agent Rhys."

Rhys shook his hand and they walked back to Brody, who had been joined by Page. The tall, slim man had taken over computer duties, his fingers tap-dancing over the keys.

"Anything?" Kovalic asked.

"There's an override sub-routine," answered Page, not lifting his eyes from the console. "But it's going to take me at least another three minutes to reroute. Of course, it would be faster if you could just get the code from whoever put it in."

Rhys shook her head. "Eamon's out cold. Short of pumping him full of stimulants—and let me say right now how bad of an idea that is—that's where he's staying."

"Well, in that case, I would appreciate uninterrupted quiet."

Brody raised his hands and sidled away from the keyboard. "Particular, isn't he?"

Kovalic shrugged. "He knows what he's doing." He turned and wandered over to look at the giant contraption that dominated the engine compartment; Brody followed after him. The two large discs were still rotating slowly, but nothing else seemed to be happening. "Kind of dull looking, isn't it?" Kovalic crossed his arms over his chest. "I always thought spaceship engines should be more impressive. Flashing lights, glowing tubes, that sort of thing."

"You can blame all those science-fiction vids for that," replied Brody. "Real engineering is rarely as impressive as it looks in other people's imaginations."

Kovalic snorted. "Yeah, I've seen what passes for a war story."

They lapsed into silence, but the younger man was unable to keep himself from fidgeting.

"What's on your mind, Brody?"

He hesitated. "What's going to happen to my brother?"

"Well, assuming we *do* in fact manage to get out of here without the Illyrican home fleet turning us into a giant ball of dust, I imagine that Agent Rhys will deliver him back to Caledonia, where he'll be tried in a court of law and convicted—the Illyricans will see to that."

Brody ran one hand through his hair; the other covered his mouth, through which he exhaled slowly. "Treason's a capital crime in Illyrican law."

"Yes."

Brody's eyes slid to Kovalic, his hand still over his mouth. He spread his fingers slightly to speak through them. "Kovalic, he's my brother. He's done terrible things, I know, but he's still my brother. I don't want him dead."

"You'd better hope he gets a hell of a lawyer, then."

Brody opened his mouth to say something, but was interrupted by a ping from the console. Kovalic glanced over his shoulder at the display. The green dot that represented the ship had intersected with the glowing red circle and, even as they watched, it moved deeper into the shaded area surrounding Illyrica.

"We've hit the outer defensive perimeter," said Kovalic. "Keep your fingers crossed. Page?"

"I'm going as fast as I can." Tension was bleeding through his usually stoic demeanor. "If you've got another idea, I'm all ears."

Kovalic frowned, then looked back toward the engine. "Wait a second. We're in a jump-ship. Why don't we just jump the hell out of here?"

"Not that easy," said Page absently. "We're too far into Illyrica's gravity well, and wormholes are gravimetric phenomena. It's like trying to dig a hole on the beach when you're below tide—the waves will keep filling it up."

Brody and Kovalic stared at him and the silence was enough that Page paused to look up.

"What? I studied theoretical physics at school. Here."

Page looked back down at the console and touched a few keys. A new overlay faded into view on the system chart. It was considerably larger than the defensive perimeter, which was outlined in red. The green dot that represented the gate was just outside of it, on the far side of the planet.

"Shit," said Kovalic, looking at the display. "In that case, keep working, lieutenant." He stepped out from under the catwalk and looked up at Tapper, who was leaning on the railing, carbine in hand. "How we doing, sergeant?"

"Still clear, cap."

Rhys had stepped over to join them again, her mouth set in a firm line. "There are still five unaccounted for, including Dr. Graham."

"Maybe they circled back to the bridge?" Brody suggested. "To try and take control?"

"Not the most reassuring idea I've heard all day," said Kovalic, eyes flicking in that direction. "I'd say we should try and track them down, but they've got the advantage in numbers, and we need Page here to get the console unlocked, Tapper to cover us, and Brody to fly this thing if we ever get it working. That leaves you and me, Rhys, and while I'm in no way questioning your competency, I see no reason to stack the deck against us."

"Agreed." Rhys pulled her hair back and fastened it with a tie. "We've got Eamon. We get control of the ship and the advantage is ours. I'd recommend we fortify this position."

Kovalic nodded to the doorway they'd come in from. "That's the biggest vulnerability right there. It must have some sort of security door for situations like this. Or in case of a reactor meltdown. If we can lock this room down, then we won't have to spread ourselves as thin."

"You think they'll try to attack us here?" Brody asked, glancing around as though a sniper might take a shot at any moment.

"It's what I would do."

"It's what you *did*," Brody pointed out.

"There you go."

"I'll look for the security door controls," Rhys volunteered.

Kovalic nodded. "I'll check the perimeter for any other entrances."

"What the hell am I supposed to do?" asked Brody.

"Sit tight and get ready to fly."

●

*Easy for you to say*, thought Eli as Kovalic slipped away. Just sit down and fly a totally unfamiliar ship after five years during which he could count on one hand the number of times he'd even been *aboard* a spacecraft. Not that Kovalic seemed like the kind of guy to accept excuses, even if they were reasonable. He looked over at Page, his lanky form hunkered over the authorization terminal, and then at the tactical display. They'd hit the gate in about fifteen minutes. His eyes shifted back and forth between Page and the display, his stomach sinking with a lead weight of realization.

"There's no time," he said slowly. "I'll never make it back to the bridge before we reach the gate. Especially not with another half dozen commandos running around."

Page didn't look up from the terminal. "That's going to be a problem, yes."

Eli took a deep breath. *Wait, this may be an experimental prototype, but it's still an* Illyrican *ship. Interchangeable little cogs.* The Illyrican Navy put an emphasis on modular control functions, so there were few tasks that were really tied to a single place on the ship. That way, if a certain location—the bridge, for example—was compromised, whether by hostile forces or by some sort of physical damage, command-and-control could be rerouted elsewhere. To almost any other console, in fact. Such was the glory of software.

"I *think* I can transfer the pilot controls down here."

Page raised an eyebrow, his gaze still firmly on his console. "I'd suggest you not waste time talking about it, then."

*Thanks for the encouragement.* Now he just had to remember how to do it. He turned to the console next to Page's and, flexing his fingers, dove in.

Fortunately, the Illyrican software hadn't changed much in five years. This ship was running a modified version of the Mark IV operating system that had been standard when he'd still been in the service. *Typical military, resistant to upgrades.* At first the memories came slowly, but once his fingers started moving over the keys they flooded back.

*Send helm controls to console*—he glanced at the small ID plate on the machine in front of him—*E/178C. Yes, I am bloody sure*, he grumbled to himself as it asked for confirmation. An authorization dialog box popped up, requesting an administrator code.

"Uh," he said, looking sidelong at the man next to him. "Don't suppose you've got an authorization code I could borrow?"

Page tapped in a few more commands and Eli's screen suddenly went from the red "access denied" graphic to a green "access granted." "Helm controls unlocked," said Page, drawing himself up to full height and stretching his back. He glanced at Eli's screen, then reached over with one hand and keyed something in.

The engineering readouts winked out of existence, replaced by an extremely condensed version of the helm controls. Pitch, yaw, roll, and throttle readouts took up the majority of the top display, while the lower console's touch-sensitive surface had been reconfigured for flying. *That's going to be interesting.* Placing his hands on the virtual controls, Eli gently tweaked the ship's roll. The ship's inertial dampeners compensated for the motion, but Eli could feel the ever-so-slight adjustment through his legs. *All right, I've definitely got control.*

"Page," he said in an aside to the man next to him, "can you lock out everybody else? I'd hate to have to go through that whole rigmarole again."

The tall lieutenant gave him a curt nod and turned back to his own console while Eli considered his situation. They were still on course for the gate, and, just as Eamon had predicted, nobody had moved to stop them. *But as soon as we change course, they're probably going to be on us like vultures . . . unless it's an extremely gradual course change.* Even a change of a few degrees on the current heading should end up taking them wide of the gate, but there was no way of knowing how much deviation Illyrica's traffic controllers would accept.

*Just one small decision*, he thought. *That's all it takes to change everything.*

He reached for the controls and, for the first time, noticed that his hands were shaking. Gripping the edge of the console, he willed them to stop. *Easy. It's just flying. It's not like last time. It won't be like last—*

●

The bridge of the Sabaean warship hung right in the middle of Eli's cross-hairs. "You can all *go to hell*, you sons of bitches." But he didn't fire.

"Illyrican fighter, repeat: this is the Sabaean cruiser *Dogs of War*. We have you in our sights—stand down."

The targeting reticle blinked red—there was no viewport looking into the bridge, but he could picture the hushed silence that had probably fallen over the crew there, waiting to see whether or not he'd pull the trigger.

"Green Seven, this is Green Two—" the voice of Kantor, the squadron's second-in-command, sounded scraped raw, "—take the shot and move to point three five; I'll cover for you." Eli glanced at his HUD; Kantor was hanging aft and to his starboard, just inside the cruiser's firing range.

The Sabaeans had dropped their jamming, so other voices filtered through Eli's headset, interspersed with static. Yelling, pleading for help, even the occasional truncated scream accompanied by a stomach-wrenching shriek of metal and followed by an even more sickening silence.

The targeting computer's audio cue was a solid tone in his ears—there was no way the shot could miss.

"Illyrican fighter," said the Sabaean communications officer, "repeat, stand down."

"Take the *shot*, Green Seven," yelled Kantor.

Eli's finger hovered over the trigger, but his mind felt like it had been dipped in liquid nitrogen. Frozen into a blank, like the outside voices didn't exist. And suddenly, into that empty canvas, came a single thought.

*I don't want to be here.*

It hit him with the force of a body slam, nearly knocking the breath out of him. What the hell was he doing here? How had he found himself with the power of life and death over hundreds of people he'd never met nor, really, had anything against? *Except that they just killed your friends.*

*Of course, they'd have never had that opportunity if we hadn't tried to invade.*

His brain was thawing from its freeze and he didn't like the way it felt: it ached terribly.

"Brody," Kantor's sharp voice broke into his thoughts. "*Take the fucking shot. That's an order.*"

Training told Eli's finger to squeeze the trigger, but something deeper than that held him back. There was no turning back; if he fired, he would kill people. This wasn't the heat of the battle anymore, this was cold-blooded murder. And he'd be a murderer, despite whatever the medals pinned to his chest might say.

*What medals? The Sabaeans blew their gate, remember? Nobody's going to give you a medal, because you're stuck here. One carrier and its fighters against an entire fleet. You can't win.*

The thought filled him with relief. They couldn't win. It was impossible, no matter what had been drilled into them about being the best military ever trained. They weren't Earth's legendary three hundred Spartans holding off the Persian hordes—and besides, hadn't they all died? Eli didn't want to die. And he didn't want to kill anyone else. And in that moment, his choice was made.

"Sabaean cruiser," he said, his voice cracking, "this is Illyrican fighter, designation Green Seven. Standing down." He punched the button that powered off the targeting computer and then throttled back on his engines to match the cruiser's speed. His fighter hung above its hull like a baby fish floating next to its mother.

"That's fucking *treason*, Brody," shouted Kantor. "I'll have your commission for this. I'll see you court-martialed and *execu—*"

Eli flipped off the radio.

●

"Brody. *Brody.*" Someone shook him hard enough that he started and struggled away from them.

It was Kovalic. "You still with us?"

"What?" He looked around, but his head was still spinning. For some reason he was sitting on the deck, slumped against the console with both Page and Kovalic peering down at him. "Yeah. Yeah. Sorry."

"What the hell happened there?" There might have been an edge of concern to Kovalic's voice, but Eli assumed he was imagining it. *Or he's just worried about who's going to fly this thing.*

"I just—I—bad memories."

Kovalic's lips tightened into a grimace. "We don't have time for this."

A burning sensation spread through Eli's chest, up from his stomach to his throat, until it poured out of his mouth as pure vitriol. He was on his feet before he realized it, shouting in Kovalic's face. "I saw my entire squadron blown to *fucking bits*, Kovalic. Right in front of my eyes. And you know what I did? I *surrendered*. So fuck *you*. I'm a coward and a traitor, and I should be *dead*. So excuse me if I have a little trouble putting myself in that kind of situation again." He ran out of steam and the anger was gone as quickly as it had come, leaving him shaking like a junkie coming down off a high.

Kovalic stood with crossed arms, taking the tirade in stride. "Got that out of your system?"

"I—yes."

"I read your file, Brody. I know all about Sabaea."

"Is this the part where you tell me it's not my fault?"

"Oh, it's absolutely your fault. You made a choice to stand down. That cruiser was a sitting duck—you could have taken it out with one shot. And, by the way, the flying needed to get into that position was not inconsiderable. I'm not going to tell you that your choice was right or wrong; that's not for me to say. But in choosing not to fire that shot, you chose not to take lives. I can respect that."

"People still died. People I knew. People I cared about."

"They made their own choices, as we all have to."

Eli didn't say anything. He found himself staring at his hands—to his surprise, they weren't shaking anymore. With a frown, he clenched and unclenched his fingers, as if seeing them for the first time, and found himself marveling that they responded to his thoughts. It was like he was floating outside himself.

A hand descended on his shoulder and he looked up to find Kovalic's gray eyes upon him.

"Now you have to make another choice. What happened at Sabaea, it's never going to go away. Trust me. But you can't let it rule you. If you do, you'll be more of a coward than Sabaea ever made you." Kovalic nodded at the console behind Eli. "You can do this—I know it."

"How?" Eli said miserably. "How could you possibly know that?"

Surprisingly enough, Kovalic smiled. "I saw the look on your face when we took that transport up from Sabaea. It wasn't just space sickness, there was something else. Something deeper." His eyes locked onto Eli's. "Envy. Like somebody was dancing with your girl. You can't give up flying—it's part of who you are."

Eli took a deep breath.

Kovalic squeezed his shoulder. "Now, get us the hell out of here."

He straightened and gave Kovalic a nod in return. He could do this. After all, flying was what he'd been born to do. It was the reason he'd left Caledonia, joined the Illyrican Navy, gotten stationed aboard the *Venture*. He was good at it. He could fly *anything*. It would take more than some hunk of junk bulk freighter to prove otherwise.

"All right," said Eli. "Let's do th—holy *shit*." A shot ricocheted off the bulkhead just a couple of feet to his right.

"Oi!" shouted Gwen. She had her back pressed against the wall next to the door, pistol clasped tightly in both hands. "They're coming!"

Eli looked around wildly but he couldn't see who had taken the shot. Kovalic's hand grabbed his upper arm firmly and the man locked his gaze on Eli's once again. "Listen to me, Brody. You focus on flying this thing— we'll watch your back. You need to trust us."

There was little option but to nod in understanding. *No pressure.* Kovalic's eyes had gone to Page, and he pointed to Eli. "Nothing happens to him, got it?"

"Yes, sir."

And with another clap on the shoulder, Kovalic sprinted off to join Gwen. Eli turned his attention back to the piloting console. They'd lost even more time; avoiding the gate but still getting out of Illyrica's gravity well was going to take a sharp course adjustment, and it wasn't going to go unnoticed.

Eli nudged the slider for their heading, putting the ship on a new course that would take it toward one of the system's other four planets, all of which were uninhabited. Fortunately, there ought to be enough of a gap between the two gravity wells to make the jump . . . if he could just figure out how.

"Hey, uh, Page," he said, not lifting his eyes from the console. "So, you studied physics. Any idea how to create a self-sustaining singularity that lets us connect two disparate points in space-time?"

"We never got that far in the textbook."

"Well, you'd better figure it out real fast. And find us some place safe to go when we do manage to get out of here."

*So far, so good*, thought Eli, looking at the system overview. Their new heading was outlined as a solid green line, diverging from the dashed path that showed their previous course. At this heading and speed, they'd clear the gravity well in under ten minutes. And from there, home free. The sound of gunfire being exchanged echoed in the large space. *Let's just hope that they don't hit anything vital.*

There was a chime from the console, followed by a new voice blaring out of the speakers. "Unidentified vessel, you have deviated from your course heading. Please advise."

Eli shot a glance at Page, who shrugged. "We could answer them, but I haven't got any traffic authorization codes, so we're going to get in over our heads pretty fast."

"Fake a communications outage?" said Eli.

"If we don't say anything, it at least fits with the profile of a hush-hush mission."

"Let's hope they buy that. But just in case they don't." Eli slid the throttle up and watched their speed increase. Unfortunately, the *Warhorse*-class vessel had been built for cargo capacity, not performance, so that only cut their time in half. Five minutes. They weren't going to do much better than that.

A scream pierced the air and Eli glanced over his shoulder in time to see a figure dressed in a blue maintenance jumpsuit fall to the floor. It also gave him an eye on another one of Eamon's crew creeping up behind a conduit, in Kovalic's blind spot. *And Tapper can't see him either.*

"Page," he said urgently. When the lieutenant looked up, Eli jutted his chin toward the man.

Calmly, Page unshipped the carbine he was holding and lined up the shot. When the other man peeked out to aim at Kovalic, Page neatly shot him in the head, then went back to the console without another word. Eli felt like he was going to be sick, but he forced himself to turn back to the helm.

"Unidentified vessel," came the traffic controller's voice again. "Come to a full stop and await our escorts. That is a priority one order."

"Sounds like they didn't buy it," noted Page, arching an eyebrow.

"Yeah, didn't really think they would."

A handful of small green blips appeared on the tac display, radiating out of Illyrica. They moved swiftly in formation toward the dot that represented their position, and even from the display it was easy to tell they meant business.

"Illyrica's scrambled fighters from an orbital defense platform," said Page. "Assuming standard defensive interceptor load-out, they'll be in firing range in around two minutes."

"We'll be clear of the gravity well in about three. How's that jump solution coming?"

"I'm working as fast as I can." From out of the corner of Eli's view he could see Page's eyes rapidly moving back and forth over what looked like a page of text. "User friendliness was clearly not at the top of the engineers' priority list."

There was a barrage of shots from the door, followed by another abbreviated scream and the thump of bodies hitting the deck, but this time Eli didn't risk a glance. His entire world was comprised of the tactical display and the helm controls. "Hey, can you divert power from non-essential systems to the engine?"

"Probably, if I weren't trying to figure out a system that half a dozen people in the galaxy have ever used. And if I don't get this just right, I could very well put us inside a star, on the event horizon of a black hole, or on the other side of the galaxy."

"Thanks for that. I feel much better."

"Happy to help. Fighters closing, one minute to range."

"*Shit*," muttered Eli. The tac display said the freighter was still two minutes out from the gate and there was no way of closing that distance without more engine power. "We're going to have to go evasive."

"Evasive?" repeated Page, looking up with an expression that was as close to alarm as Eli suspected the man got. "You do realize this is a bulk freighter, right? Not a starfighter?"

"We don't know if this boat has any weapons and, even if it did, we certainly don't have the time or manpower to figure out how to use them. There's nothing to hide behind out here, we're flying a straight line course and we can't outrun them. Besides," he grinned at Page, "they'll never see it coming." *And we only need to keep them off of us for a minute.* Though that was saying a lot. In a dogfight, a minute was an eternity.

"Clear!" came Gwen's voice.

*Thank god. One less thing to worry about.*

"I count five bodies down," he heard Kovalic say.

"Then what the hell happened to Dr. Graham?" asked Gwen.

That brought Eli's head up, and he whipped around to look at the pipe Eamon had been cuffed to—the cuff was still there, locked securely to the metal, but the other end dangled loose. Notably absent was any trace of Eamon Brody.

"Kovalic! Gwen!" he shouted over his shoulder, trying to keep one eye on the pilot controls. *Thirty seconds until they're in firing range.*

The pair arrived at a dead run, and he wordlessly jerked his head at the loose cuff. The red-haired CalSec officer let out a string of curses that would have made a Caledonian dockworker's ears curl. "That bloody blonde doctor got him out somehow. He's got her wrapped around his little finger."

"Well, there's nowhere for them to go," said Kovalic, looking around. "So they're somewhere on the ship."

A klaxon shrieked overhead, stopping the conversation in its tracks. "Fighters are in range!" said Page.

"I suggest everybody find something to hold on to," Eli suggested.

Kovalic, Page, and Gwen looked at each other and then scattered to the nearest stanchions, consoles, and conduits, each wrapping their arms around whatever stable object they could find.

Eli sucked in a deep breath and fixed his eyes on the console. *This is it, Brody. One shaky hand and we're all nothing more than a cloud of space dust.* His palms were sweaty on the glass of the touchscreen in front of him; he would have traded his trousers and shirt for a pilot's yoke over these goddamned infernal, intangible controls.

The ship shook underneath him, another alarm sounding loud in his ears. His eyes darted to the sensor readout in one corner of the display, the blip of a fighter strafing across the ship's port flank. Another was coming up on the starboard side, all too fast.

"Oh well, why *not*," he muttered to himself, dialing the starboard thrusters down and doubling power to the port, which sent the ship into a spin. "Deal with that, flyboy."

The fighter to port had been approaching at attack speed, and the sudden shifting of the bulk freighter meant that they were now spinning directly across the fighter's course. In his head, Eli could hear the pilot's startled shriek and he watched with a grim smile as the blip on his display pulled up to compensate. The ship's inertial dampers meant that the spin didn't feel as severe to those onboard, but it was still making them an all too easy target.

His left hand realigned thruster control, bringing them back onto a straight bearing and he watched as the fighter squadron looped around for another pass. They were keeping their distance this time, so the same trick was definitely not going to work again. One of the fighters had dropped below the freighter and was coming up on its presumably undefended underside.

*There's got to be something else on this boat I can use.* He scanned the consoles, his eyes running across each of the additional systems. Besides the thrusters and main engines, he only had access to the built-in sensors, limited power diversion options, and controls for the landing repulsors.

*Repulsors!* He blinked, remembering Kovalic's trick from earlier, then glanced around at his compatriots, each holding on for dear life. Page was hugging a nearby support for the catwalk while Tapper, up above him, was starting to look a bit green. "Nobody let go!"

"Don't have to tell me twice," he heard someone mutter.

He brought up a visual camera of their underbelly, resting his hand near the repulsor controls. A small gray dot against the black background of space slowly resolved into the shape of a fighter, which began spewing high-velocity slugs. As the ship started firing, Eli smacked the repulsor control.

Fast as those slugs were, the anti-gravitational power of the repulsors were responsible for lifting a ship that weighed hundreds of thousands of tons. The rounds rebounded off the antigrav field—some deflected out to the side, but more than a few reversed course toward the fighter, which promptly took evasive maneuvers to avoid being the victim of its own fire.

Eli's enthusiasm was quashed mid-grin as an impact knocked him to his knees; he narrowly avoided smacking his head on the console. Pulling himself back up, he caught sight of the red-tinted warning on his display, which suggested that he seal off part of the top decks since they were now venting atmosphere into the void of space.

"Page! I need some help!"

The lanky lieutenant somewhat reluctantly released his death grip and staggered over to the console next to Eli's. He took in the damage report at a glance and immediately set about making the necessary adjustments.

The deck stabilized under Eli's feet.

"Twenty seconds until we're clear of the gravity well," said Page. "Just keep them off of us a little bit longer."

*Easier said than done.* Eli diverted the power they'd spared from sealing off those top decks straight to the engines, boosting their speed ever so slightly. *Great, probably nineteen seconds now. Would it be unseemly to start praying?*

Keeping one eye on the radar, he sent the ship into a zig-zagging course, trying to keep the maneuvers as unpredictable as possible. Despite that, the bulk freighter could hardly turn on an industrial-sized manhole, much less a dime. More impacts registered from slug rounds, but to Eli's relief nothing seemed to come close to the engines or the jump drive.

The edge of the gravity well inched closer; there were snails that were probably outrunning them. They needed something, some sort of distraction to keep the fighters off for just a few more seconds. He swallowed.

"I'm shutting down the engines," he announced.

Four pairs of eyes burned holes into his head.

"You're *what?*" Tapper exclaimed.

"Trust me!" His fingers danced over the controls, bringing up the emergency engine shutoff.

"Isn't that, you know, the *opposite* of what we're trying to accomplish?"

"The inertia will keep us moving," said Eli, eyes flicking rapidly back and forth to the relevant pressure gauges. "And that means that I can use the engine to do *this.*" He slapped the venting controls, sending the engine's exhaust emissions pluming behind them in an expanding cloud of vapor.

Flying through that much radiation wasn't too bad for a ship like the bulk freighter, which was heavily shielded to protect its cargo and crew, but the Illyricans built their fighters to, well, fight, and not necessarily to survive giant radiation clouds. It was just one of the many ways the military saved on its expenses.

Eli held his breath, watching the blips; of course, if these guys were suicidal, or were really into following orders to the disregard of their own safety, they might just fly through the thing anyway. But if it were him, he knew what he would have done. *Break. Break. Break!*

The blips hesitated for a second then split apart to each side of the cloud. They'd come around wide for another pass in a moment, which, if they were hunting any other ship, would have only lost them a few seconds.

*But this isn't any other ship.*

He let out the breath as they cleared the line that marked Illyrica's gravity well. Looking over at Page, his mouth started to form the word "Go!" even as the lieutenant touched a control on his console.

The ship went quiet and Eli looked over in alarm, only to realize that the gravity had cut out as well, and they had all started to float a few inches above the deck. *Oh shit, I remember what comes next.*

"Hold on," he started to say, even as gravity kicked in at what felt like twice the standard strength. He heard an exclamation from Gwen and a grunt that sounded suspiciously like a curse from Tapper as they all slammed flat to the deck. Eli had managed to grab hold of a support strut next to the console, but it felt like his arms were about to be torn off.

And then, with an ear-popping pressure, the gravity was back to normal. Breathing heavily, Eli let himself drop back to the deck where he windmilled his sore arms and hoped he hadn't torn any crucial—or hell, non-crucial—ligaments, tendons, or muscles. The rest of the team were picking themselves up off the deck, rubbing sore necks, legs, and arms.

"Let's not do that again, real soon," said Kovalic, grimacing.

Eli looked around. "We need to find Eamon." Ignoring Kovalic's insistent call to wait, he started off toward the last place he'd seen his brother.

●

It was the sound of sobbing that eventually led them to the missing pair. They rounded one of the collections of machinery that dotted the engine room and found Dr. Graham kneeling on the deck, Eamon's head on her lap. Her normally white lab coat was soaked pink with blood.

She looked up at them, tears streaked over her pale cheeks. "It was the gravimetric field," she said, in a detached voice, not really focusing on any of them. "The wormhole creates an immense amount of gravity, offset only barely by the ship's artificial gravity generators running in reverse. It doesn't cancel out the effect entirely." She laughed bitterly to herself. "We were working on making the transition more gradual, but it can take you by surprise if you're not ready for it." She looked down at Eamon's face and stroked a hand over his brow. It came away coated in his blood. "I don't think he even saw the railing."

*Oh no.*

They were all staring at Eamon, so even Kovalic and Page's trained reflexes weren't fast enough to catch the gun in the woman's free hand as it came up and jammed into the fleshy spot under her own chin. The shot was quieter than Eli thought it would be, but the image was burned into his brain as he spun around and threw up all over the deck.

# CHAPTER TWENTY-FIVE

The general's office on Terra Nova was more ornate than the spare room he'd commandeered on the *Indefatigable*, but it still couldn't be called anything more than stark. A marble bust of the first Emperor of Illyrica—real marble, Kovalic had discovered on one visit—stood on a pedestal in one corner, and paintings—those were reproductions—hung on the walls. The view was also better than the blank wall of the *Indefatigable*'s cabin: a window looked out onto a thick, leafy rainforest that was no less real than the sculpture.

"So, then," said the old man, leaning on the carved black walnut of his cane as he limped over to the bar against one wall. "Drink?"

"Anything but Caledonian whisky," said Kovalic, making a face.

The old man gave a low chuckle. "Didn't grow on you?"

"Foul stuff. Give me a beer or a cocktail with a little umbrella any day."

"I'm afraid I'm all out of beer," said the old man, pulling out the stopper in a crystal decanter. "Bourbon?"

Kovalic nodded. Any port in a storm, as the old saying went. The general poured two tumblers of amber and lifted them in his free hand, then ambled over to Kovalic with his usual stiff-legged gait, placing the two glasses on the desk. He settled himself behind the desk with a sound that was part natural creaking of a man in his advanced years and part whine of servos.

"So," he said, raising the glass. "To a job well done."

Reaching out, Kovalic took the glass from the desk, but he didn't drink, just stared at the honey-colored waves sloshing against the side of the glass. "A success maybe," he said after a moment, "but I'm not sure about well done."

The general raised an eyebrow, then started to tick off items on his fingers. "You located Eamon Brody, severely disrupted a major Illyrican military research project, and did so without harm to your own personnel. Most importantly, the Special Projects Team maintains its flawless record, which will look nice the next time our budget comes up for review by the Commonwealth Executive." The old man tilted his head to one side, his eyes narrowing thoughtfully. "It would have been nice to take Eamon Brody alive, I agree, but that was outside of your control."

Kovalic grimaced and took a swig. It burned its way down his throat, sending smoke signals back up after it. "Agent Rhys wasn't very happy about it, either." That was an understatement of galactic proportions. She'd tried everything short of giving the man CPR and even then had insisted upon getting Eamon to the ship's medical bay and putting him in an emergency cryogenic tank. It wouldn't matter—they had both known that—but this was Rhys's collar of a lifetime and privately Kovalic thought she'd actually liked the man. He understood that: undercover work often came with its fair share of internal struggle.

"Yet she didn't try to take you in or recover the prototype?"

One corner of Kovalic's mouth twisted in a wry smile. *"I told you, I don't work for the Illyricans, and I could care less about their toys,"* she'd said. *"Hell, one less weapon for their arsenal is fine by me."*

*"What about you?"* Kovalic had asked. *"How are you going to explain your part in this?"*

*She'd smiled ruefully and shrugged. "I'll come up with something."*

Not to mention, she'd had little chance of insisting upon anything, outnumbered three-to-one as she was. "She . . . made do with the hand she was dealt." At least she'd gotten Kelly, McKenna, and most of Eamon's team. "Meanwhile, the Illyricans have attributed the explosion on Aran to a rogue comet impact. Not the most believable story, but anybody who'd say different is locked up or dead."

"And the Black Watch?" asked the old man. "How do you think they'll take their leader's death?"

"They've been fighting the Illyricans for twenty years," said Kovalic. "Brody isn't the first De Valera they've lost. They may go underground for a while as they rebuild, but their roots run deep into Caledonian culture by now. The Imperium hasn't heard the last of them."

He took another sip of the bourbon, wincing as it caught a not-yet-healed cut on his lip. He had a few bruises and lacerations from various fights, though he privately suspected that most of them had resulted from being repeatedly slammed against the deck by artificial gravity.

"Simon."

Kovalic looked up to meet the ice blue eyes, the skin around them crinkling in an imitation of a kindly grandfather.

"Something's on your mind. I've known you long enough to see that much. Is it Brody's brother?"

After the kid had been sick all over the engine room, Kovalic had escorted him—well, dragged him—out into the corridor and then to the nearest head where he'd promptly been sick all over again. Kovalic hadn't said anything, just handed him some paper towels when he was finished and waited while he cleaned himself up.

*"I've been there when people died," Eli had said, his tone almost combative. Then it faltered. "But not like that."*

It was a fact of life—everybody encountered death sooner or later—but Kovalic wasn't unsympathetic. He wouldn't have wished that particular experience on anybody. Still, if the kid hadn't exactly bounced back by the time they'd gotten back to Commonwealth space, he at least didn't seem to be succumbing to shock. He'd make it.

"He did a good job," said the general. "Better than we expected by far. Quite a resourceful young man." He eyed Kovalic significantly.

Kovalic raised his eyebrows. "Indeed," he said neutrally.

"So, if it's not Brody's brother or the mission, what's bothering you?"

The leather of the chair creaked as he leaned forward and put the glass down on the general's desk. "Eamon Brody or one of his men may have pulled the trigger on Jim Wallace, but the people at CID who buried the op—they *let* him die. I want to know what we're going to do about them."

"Immediately? Nothing."

"That's not—"

The general held up his hand. "I said 'immediately.' We're in this for the long game, Simon. Thanks to the reports on Wallace's data chip we know that the entire mission was personally overseen by Aidan Kester, CID's

Deputy Director of Operations. And," he said, with a faint smile, "we have proof just in case it ever becomes necessary."

Kovalic grimaced. "Small comfort for Jim Wallace."

"Agreed. But it will have to do for now. Anything else to report?"

Reclaiming his glass, Kovalic turned it around in his hand. "There's one more thing—but it's probably nothing."

"As I recall, that was what you said before I sent you to Haran," said the general dryly. "Where you managed to uncover that not only had the Illyricans compromised the Commonwealth's entire planetary intelligence network, but they'd also quite neatly suborned CID's own station chief. So you'll pardon me if I don't easily dismiss your hunches." He raised his glass in an ironic salute.

"It's something that Brody said—Eamon Brody, I mean. When I asked him why the Illyricans wouldn't just rebuild their gate, he said 'if they can.'" Kovalic shook his head, feeling the slight buzz of the bourbon warming his brain. "Maybe it was just an idle remark," he hesitated, "but I don't think so. I think he knew something. He wouldn't have gone to those lengths to just inflict a temporary setback on the Illyricans. I read his profile and I met the man; he had a cause and he's—he *was*—ready to die for it."

The old man frowned, then drummed his fingers on the desk. "Pretty thin," he said at last. "But I'll talk to some of my sources and see if they have anything." He touched a pad on the desktop, rapidly keyed in a note on the holographic screen that appeared, and then dismissed it with a flick. "Anything else, captain?"

Kovalic picked the bourbon back up off the desk, downed the rest of it, and got to his feet. "No, sir."

"Then you and your team have earned yourselves some well-deserved rest, Captain Kovalic. The SPT can stand down."

"Thank you," Kovalic said with a nod. He turned and made for the door, but as he reached for the handle he realized he *had* forgotten something. He looked back at the general. "Actually, there was one more thing."

The old man was cupping his tumbler in both hands and staring at one of the paintings on the wall, an abstract piece with splotches of color against a pure white background, but he looked up and smiled when Kovalic addressed him. "Yes?"

"I was asked to give you a message."

"Oh?"

"From Major Shankar."

"Dear old Jagat," murmured the old man. "How is he?"

"Well enough, but he had some strong words for you. The Illyricans don't know exactly where you are, but they clearly know you're somewhere in the Commonwealth, and he didn't really beat around the bush in terms of what happens if they *do* find you."

"An IIS Special Operations Executive team, I should think," said the general, with a rueful smile. "I should know—I sent any number of them on similar assignments in my day."

"He also wanted me to give you a bill for some property damage."

The general snorted. "Still harping on about the burns on his carpet?"

"Yes, sir."

"It wasn't even that nice a carpet!" Hasan al-Adaj shrugged and raised his glass again. "Thank you for the message, captain. Always nice to hear from old friends." His eyes went this time to the white marble bust in the corner, and Kovalic saw an expression on his boss's face that he had only seen there a handful of times. It was one he preferred not to remember, all the more so because he'd seen it in the mirror more than once.

It was the look of a man who could never go home again.

"Sir." Kovalic opened the door and stepped out into the hallway.

●

Eli didn't like his new shirt. For one thing it was itchy, despite assurances to the contrary by the salesman who'd sold it to him. It was also too heavy for the current season on Terra Nova; the collar was already sticking to the back of his neck in the humid air. *Hopefully I won't be staying long enough for it to be a problem.*

His legs dangled off the edge of the outdoor patio, his arms and chin resting on the lower rung of the railing. Below his boots lay thirty feet of empty air, which gave him a nice view of the mountain jungle growing below. And that's all there was: jungle. As far as he could tell, there wasn't another living soul within miles of this little retreat. They'd had to take a sub-orbital flyer here from the Terra Nova spaceport—he'd survived the trip with only a modicum of wracked nerves—and past a certain point, the signs of civilization had vanished beneath the dense canopy of foliage. He'd asked Kovalic about it, but the soldier had just said that the old man liked his privacy.

The tall leafy trees buzzed with life, everything from the hum of insects to the squawks of what Eli hoped were birds. There hadn't been a lot of indigenous wildlife on Caledonia or in the arctic regions of Sabaea, and that about summed up Eli's experience with non-shipboard life. One time he'd seen a mouse aboard the *Venture*—the maintenance crewman he'd reported it to had just chuckled and said that somehow they always managed to find their way into the stores.

He was so deep in thought, trying to remember the last time he'd encountered a truly wild animal, that he didn't notice the footsteps behind him until Kovalic was right at his shoulder.

"Brody."

He looked up at the soldier towering over him. The heat didn't seem to bother the man at all, though perhaps that jacket was more breathable than it looked. Eli moved to get up but Kovalic motioned him to stay where he was, then took a seat next to him, threading his own legs through the railing.

"Everything go all right?" asked Eli, more for sake of conversation than anything else.

"Just a formality. I already filed my report, but there were a few things I deemed wiser not to commit to the permanent record."

"Your boss . . ." Eli said slowly. "He's Illyrican, isn't he? High class, too—I recognized the accent the first time we met, though it took me a while to place it. I knew a guy in the academy who sounded like that. Plus," he added, jerking a thumb back toward the office, "that sculpture in there. It's not just decorative, is it?"

The look on Kovalic's face was half impressed, half trying to conceal the fact he was impressed. "You're right—he is Illyrican. But he left the Imperium a while back and has the full backing of the Commonwealth Executive."

Eli grunted, giving him a sidelong look. "I'm still not sure I entirely understand what you do."

"Do you want to?"

"What?"

Kovalic smiled ruefully. "You held up your end of our deal, and we'll honor ours. You can, I don't know, go sit on a beach for a few years, all on the Commonwealth's dime." The implicit alternative hung in the humid air.

"Or?" said Eli finally.

"Or you can do something with the rest of your life."

"Doesn't sitting on a beach drinking count as 'something?'"

Kovalic hesitated, looking out over the treetops. "Look, I know it couldn't have been easy to see your brother like that."

The smile evaporated from Eli's face. *Her white lab coat was soaked through. And I stood their slack-jawed as she blew her brains out.* "From what I've seen, I'm not sure I *like* what you do, Kovalic."

"I'd be worried if you did."

Eli rubbed at his eyes, trying to scrub away the image in his head and replace it with one of waves lapping gently at his feet. It just didn't seem *real*, though. Sometimes you could just picture your future, what it would be like, but this time Eli just felt like he was watching a vid of somebody else's life. Not that he could imagine how Kovalic's life went, for that matter, but something about that reassured him. *At least I know it probably wouldn't be anything like I expected.*

"Let me get this straight," said Eli slowly. "You want me to give up a free ride for some undefined promise of 'doing something?'"

"If you can just walk away now, well, more power to you. But I've been where you are now, and if you think all that idleness is going to be anything other than replaying that moment in your mind, well . . ." he trailed off.

Eli stared at his feet over the edge. There was a brief sensation of vertigo, of falling down into the greenery that lay below, and he sucked in a lungful of air and grabbed the railing until it bit into his hands. He screwed his eyes shut. "I'm not much good to anybody right now," he said through clenched teeth.

"There's help for that, if you're willing. I saw what you did on that ship and I'm convinced that you *can* get over it. More than that, I think you need to."

His eyes still closed, Eli remembered what it had felt like to lose himself in flying. Not just on the jump-ship, but every time he'd slid into a cockpit over the past fifteen years. It was like putting on your favorite outfit and feeling like you were unstoppable. It made you grin uncontrollably, like you'd just kissed the girl of your dreams. It made your breath catch, like you were riding the galaxy's best roller coaster. And more than all of that, it was an undeniable part of what made up Eli Brody. He couldn't give it up any more than he could have parted with an arm, or a leg, or a witty comeback. *That's why you can't see yourself on that beach.*

He sighed and opened his eyes again. "All right. But I need something from you."

Kovalic raised an eyebrow and waited.

"You promised I'd be able to look after my sister." He shook his head. "But I can't go back to Caledonia, not after all this." Practicalities aside, there was just too much tied up with the whole place. Even the thought of it made his stomach ache—he'd had enough of bloody Caledonia. But Meghann . . . the ache traveled up from his stomach until it wrapped around his heart. He couldn't abandon her, not again.

"Eamon's gone," said Eli, and he mostly managed to not twitch at the words. "I'm all the family she has left, and I need to make sure she's okay."

"I understand. I'll make sure everything is taken care of." He hesitated. "It won't be easy, but I think we could probably even arrange an opportunity to go see her. If you wanted."

Eli faltered, remembering the way she'd shrunk away from him. *She doesn't know me anymore.* "Maybe." *I'm not sure I could take that again.* But even as he thought about it, there was a pang in his chest. It wasn't all about him. Anyway, somebody had to tell her Eamon wasn't coming back. "Eventually."

"Agent Rhys probably wouldn't mind seeing you either," said Kovalic, grinning.

He couldn't escape a faint smile. There hadn't been a lot of time for goodbyes, and Eamon's death had cast a pall over everything, but they'd still had a moment together before going their separate ways. *"Come and see me sometime,"* she'd said. *"I'll buy you dinner."* She'd poised on tiptoes, brushing a kiss on his cheek; a less shell-shocked Eli probably would have had a sharp response, but all he'd managed was a smile and a nod. And then she'd been gone, and only the whisper of the kiss had remained.

"Anyway," Kovalic continued. "Like I said, we can figure something out. If you want to stay."

A bitter laugh escaped Eli's throat. "I must be crazy." He turned to Kovalic. "You really believe it? You, Tapper, Page—you really think three people can make a difference?"

"Three people? Not a chance. *Four*, though . . ."

# ACKNOWLEDGMENTS

Somewhere there are probably monks who toil away in solitary cells to single-handedly bring their life's work to fruition. But for those of us out here in the wider world, producing a book is a team effort—and this one is no exception.

First and foremost, my thanks to my tireless agents, Joshua Bilmes at JABberwocky and Sam Morgan, now at Foundry, without whose constant guidance and encouragement this book would have languished on a hard drive somewhere, collecting digital dust.

Thanks, too, to my editor Jason Katzman and the rest of the team at Talos Press, for making sure that the final product lived up to the highest of standards, from stem to stern. Sebastien Hue's gorgeous cover art seems to be plucked directly from the world of the book, and Rain Saukas did a wonderful job laying it out to great effect.

I started writing this book more than eight years ago, and it's gone through many a revision along the way. Jason Snell, Brian Lyngaas, Glenn Fleishman, Anne-Marie Gordon, and Keith Bourgoin all read early versions and offered invaluable insights. Special thanks to Serenity Caldwell, who spent more time with this manuscript than any reasonable person should have to. Gene Gordon contributed his physics and science prowess where my own knowledge fell short, and Iain MacKinnon generously provided his Gaelic expertise. Any errors in the final work are mine and mine alone.

A big thanks to all my friends at The Incomparable, Relay FM, and the Fancy Cats for their unflagging support. Much-needed writerly solidarity came from Myke Cole, Antony Johnston, Helene Wecker, David J. Loehr, John Moltz, Jeff Carlson, and Adam Rakunas.

To Kat, who probably didn't realize what she was signing up for when she started dating a writer, but who has handled everything from the lowest of lows to the highest of highs with grace and good humor, mere words hardly seem sufficient—but they'll have to do. Thank you so much, love.

Finally, I would not be anywhere without the love and support of my entire family, who imparted their collective passion for books, language, and learning to me from the very beginning. I'm unbelievably lucky to have them, and I've always counted them as one of the best parts of my life. I could not have done this without them.